I0674213

Jack Vance

Sail 25
and Other Stories

Jack Vance

Sail 25
AND OTHER STORIES

Jack Vance (signature)

Spatterlight Press Signature Series, Volume 6

Planet of the Black Dust © 1946, 2005
Dead Ahead © 1950, 2005
The Enchanted Princess © 1954, 2005
The Potters of Firsk © 1950, 2005
The Visitors © 1951, 2005
The Uninhibited Robot © 1951, 2005
Dover Spargill's Ghastly Floater © 1951, 2005
Sabotage on Sulfer Planet © 1952, 2005
Three-legged Joe © 1953, 2005
Four Hundred Blackbirds © 1953, 2005
Sjambak © 1953, 2005
Parapsyche © 1958, 2005
Sail 25 © 1962, 2005
by Jack Vance

All rights reserved. This book or any portion thereof
may not be reproduced or used in any manner whatsoever
without the express written permission of the publisher
except for the use of brief quotations in a book review.

Published by Spatterlight Press

Cover art by Howard Kistler

ISBN 978-1-61947-149-8

Spatterlight Press LLC

Spatterlight
P R E S S

340 S. Lemon Ave #1916
Walnut, CA 91789
www.jackvance.com

CONTENTS

Planet of the Black Dust

About the middle of the dog watch Captain Creed came up on the bridge of the space-freighter *Perseus*. He walked to the forward port and stood gazing at the blood-red star which lay ahead and slightly to the left.

It was a nameless little sun in the tail of the Serpens group, isolated from the usual space routes. The Earth–Rasalague route ran far to one side, the Delta Aquila ran far to the other and the Delta Aquila–Sabik inter-sector service was yet a half light-year further out.

Captain Creed stood watching the small red star, deep in thought — a large man, with a paunch, a bland white face, a careful coal-black beard. His heavy black eyes, underhung with dark circles, were without expression or life. He wore a neat black suit, his boots shone with a high polish, his hands were white and immaculately kept.

Captain Creed was more than mere master of the *Perseus*. In partnership with his brother he owned the European-Arcturus Line — a syndicate impressive to the ear.

The home office, however, was one dingy room in the old Co-Martian Tower in Tran, and the firm's sole assets consisted, first, of the *Perseus* itself, and second, of the profit anticipated from a cargo of aromatic oils which Captain Creed had taken on consignment from McVann's Star in Ophiuchus.

The *Perseus* could not be considered the more valuable of the two items. It was an old ship, slow, pitted by meteorites, of little more than 600 tons capacity.

The cargo was another matter — flask upon flask of rare aromatics, essence of syrang blooms, oil of star-poppies, attar of green orchids, musk of crushed mian flies, distillation of McVann's blue bush — exotic liquids brought in by the bulb-men of McVann's Star a half ounce at a time. And Captain Creed was highly annoyed when the insurance evaluator permitted but an eighty-million-dollar policy and had argued vehemently to have the figure moved closer to the cargo's true value.

Now, as he stood on the bridge smoking his cigar, he was joined by the first mate, Blaine, who was tall and thin and, except for a scrub of black hair, egg-bald. Blaine had a long knife-nose, a mouth twisted to a perpetual snarl. He had a quick reckless way of talking that sometimes disconcerted careful Captain Creed.

"They're all fixed," he announced. "They'll go in about ten minutes —" Captain Creed quelled him with a frown and a quick motion of the head, and Blaine saw that they were not alone. Holderlin, second mate and quartermaster, a young man of hard face and cruel blue eyes, stood forward at the helm.

He wore only loose tattered trousers, and the scarlet glare from the star ahead gave a devilish red glow to his body, put a lurid cast on his face. Like two hawks they watched him, and his expression did not entirely reassure them. After a moment Captain Creed spoke smoothly.

"I doubt if you are right, Mr. Blaine. The period of that type of variable star is slower and more even, as I think you'll find if you check your observations."

Blaine shot another quick look at Holderlin, then, mumbling indistinguishably, left for the engine room.

Creed presently stepped across the bridge.

"Take her five degrees closer to the star, Mr. Holderlin. We're somewhat off course, and the gravity will swing us back around."

Holderlin gave him one look of surprise, then silently obeyed. What nonsense was this? Already the ship was gripped hard by gravity. Did they still hope to beguile him with such slim pretexts? If so they must think him stupid indeed.

Even a child would by now have been warned by the happenings aboard the *Perseus*. First at Porphyry, the space-port on McVann's Star, Captain Creed had discharged the radioman and the two ship's mechanics for reasons unexplained.

Not an unusual circumstance, but Captain Creed had neglected to hire replacements. Thus, the only other man aboard beside Captain Creed, Blaine and Holderlin, was Farjoram, the half-mad Callistonian cook.

On several occasions, after Porphyry had been cleared, Holderlin had surprised Blaine and Creed intent at the radio. Later, when he inspected the automatic frequency record, he found no trace of calls.

And four or five days ago, while off watch below and supposedly asleep, he had noticed while leaving his tiny compartment that the entrance port to the starboard lifeboat was ajar. He had said nothing, but later, when Blaine and Captain Creed were both asleep, he inspected the lifeboats, port and starboard, to find that the fuel in the starboard lifeboat had been drained except for the slightest trickle and that the radio transmitter had been tampered with.

The port boat was well fueled and provisioned. So Holderlin quietly refueled the starboard boat and thoughtfully stowed away spare fuel.

Now came Blaine's unwary statement to Captain Creed, and Creed's peculiar orders to steer toward the star. Holderlin's tough brown face was unexpressive as he watched Creed's great bulk by the port, blotting out the sun ahead. But his brain searched through all angles of the situation. For fourteen years of his thirty-three he had roved space and of necessity had learned how to care for Robert Holderlin.

A slight shock shook the hull. Captain Creed turned his head negligently, then once again looked out on space. Holderlin said nothing, but his eyes were very alert.

A few minutes passed, and Blaine came back to the bridge. Holderlin sensed, but did not see the look which passed between Creed and the gaunt mate.

"Ah," said Captain Creed. "We seem to be close enough. Starboard ten degrees and set her on the gyroscope."

Holderlin turned the wheel. He could feel the surge of power into the jets, but the ship did not respond.

"She doesn't answer, sir," he said.

"What's this!" cried Captain Creed. "Mr. Blaine! Check the steering jets! The ship does not answer the wheel!"

Creed must dislike too blunt action, thought Holderlin, to insist on such elaborate circumstances — or perhaps they suspected the gun in his pocket. Blaine ran off, and returned in a very short time, a wolfish grin lifting his already contorted lip.

"Steering jets fused, Captain. That cheap lining they put in at Aureolis has given out."

Captain Creed looked from the furious little sun ahead to Blaine and Holderlin. With his entire fortune at stake, he seemed strangely unperturbed by the prospect of disaster. But then Captain Creed's white face was always controlled. He gave the order that Holderlin had been expecting.

"Abandon ship!" he said. "Mr. Blaine, despatch the distress signal! Mr. Holderlin, find Farjoram and stand by the starboard lifeboat!"

Holderlin left to find the cook. But he noted as he passed that Blaine, at the transmitter, had not yet flipped down the big red 'Emergency' relay.

Presently Captain Creed and Blaine joined Holderlin and the cook on the boat walk.

"Shall I accompany your boat, Captain, or Mr. Blaine's?" asked Holderlin, as if he had not understood Captain Creed's previous order, or was challenging it. Blaine looked in sudden alarm at the captain.

"You will take charge of the starboard boat, Mr. Holderlin," replied the Captain silkily. "I wish Mr. Blaine to accompany me." He turned to enter the port boat. But Holderlin stepped forward and produced a sheet of paper he had been carrying for several days.

"A moment, if you please, sir. If I am to be in charge of the boat, for the protection of myself and the cook — in the event your boat is lost — will you sign this certification of shipwreck?"

"Neither of us will be lost, Mr. Holderlin," replied Captain Creed, smoothing his black beard. "Mr. Blaine contacted a patrol cruiser only a hundred million miles away."

"Nevertheless, sir, I believe the Astronautic Code requires such a document."

Blaine nudged the captain slyly.

"Well certainly, Mr. Holderlin, we must observe the law," said Captain Creed, and so signed the certification. Without more ado, he and Blaine entered their lifeboat.

"Take off, Mr. Holderlin!" Captain Creed ordered through the port. "We will wait till you clear."

Holderlin turned. The cook had disappeared.

"Farjoram!" he cried. *"Farjoram!"*

Holderlin ran to find him and at last discovered the fuzzy-skinned little Callistonian huddled in his cabin, red eyes bulging in great terror. There was foam at his mouth.

"Come," said Holderlin gruffly.

The Callistonian babbled in frenzy.

"No, no — I not go in lifeboat. Get away, you go! I stay!"

Then Holderlin remembered a tale which had gone the rounds of how this Farjoram and eight others had drifted in a lifeboat for four months through the Phenesian Blackness. When at last they had been picked up, there was only Farjoram among the picked bones of his fellows. So now even Holderlin shuddered.

"Hurry!" came Captain Creed's call. "We are almost into the sun!"

"Come!" said Holderlin roughly. "They'll kill you if you don't."

For answer the Callistonian whipped out a long knife and spasmodically stabbed himself in the throat. He fell at Holderlin's feet. Holderlin returned alone.

"Where's Farjoram?" queried Creed sharply.

"He killed himself, sir. With a knife."

"Humph," murmured Creed. "Well, take off alone then. The rendezvous is at a hundred million miles on the line between this star and Delta Aquila."

"Right, sir," said Holderlin. Without further words he sealed himself in the boat and took off.

The sun was close, but not too close. It would have pulled an unfueled lifeboat to doom, but it was not so near as to prevent another ship from approaching the *Perseus*, shackling into the fore and aft chocks and towing it off to safety.

Holderlin used his blasts for a few seconds, then cut them, as if his fuel were exhausted. Presently, as he drifted away from the *Perseus*, apparently helpless in the red star's gravity, he saw the port boat break clear and speed, not out toward Delta Aquila, but back along the blast-track.

Holderlin drifted quietly a few minutes, in the event that Captain Creed or Blaine were watching him through glasses. But there was little time to waste. The ship lying astern would presently draw alongside and, after transferring the precious cargo, would let the *Perseus* hurtle into the scarlet sun.

Holderlin had different plans. He assured himself that the certificate signed by Captain Creed was safe — then, judging the interval to be adequate, started his blasts and whisked himself back to the *Perseus*.

He brought the bow of the lifeboat against the *Perseus'* forward tow ring, then slipped into his air-suit, clambered out into space and shackled the two together. Then, back in the lifeboat, he eased open the throttle and nudged the bow of the *Perseus* to a safe position of space.

He pushed himself across the emptiness, this time to the *Perseus'* entrance port and, shedding his space-suit, ran up to the bridge. He sent out a detector wave, and the almost instant contact bell told him the other ship stood close — too close for flight to the only refuge he could think of — the lone planet of the red star.

He picked up this ship in the teleview. It was a long black vessel with high-straked bow, great thick-ribbed tubes and a bridge built smooth into the hull. Holderlin instantly recognized the type — a class of fast heavily-armed ships designed for the Scorpio–Sagittarius frontier run, built by the Belisarius Corporation of Earth.

Two years before he had shipped aboard one of the same class, and he recollected an incident of that voyage. Out past Fomalhaut, they were engaged in a running battle with a war-sphere of the Clantlalan system, and there had been a lucky shot into the main generator which had put them out of action.

Only the arrival of three Earth cruisers had staved off capture and slavery. Holderlin recollected the exact details of that lucky shot. The bolt had struck amidships, just forward of the lower drive-jet. It had broken into the hull through a small drain, the Achilles' heel of the heavy armor.

So Holderlin watched and waited as the sleek black vessel cruised close. The shuttle dangling against the *Perseus'* bow was turned partly away in the shadow, and was, he hoped, not too conspicuous.

But the ship came easing up with an insolent leisure, and there seemed to be no suspicion aboard. Holderlin's hard face creased in a grin as he sighted along the *Perseus'* ancient needle beam.

The encounter was of dream-like simplicity. Like a tremendous black shark, the ship drifted over him, her little black drain drawing the sights of his needle-beam like a magnet.

He pulled the trigger and laughed aloud as a great hole opened where the drain had once been. As before, the lights died, the driving beams cut off, all evidence of life vanished, and the black ship rolled sluggishly in recoil from the blast, a great helpless hulk.

Holderlin ran to the bank of jet controls. He could consider himself safe now, for at least a few hours, when, with luck, he would be so well concealed that the black ship could seek in vain. And if those aboard were not able to rig up an auxiliary generator quickly, they themselves might be forced to take to their lifeboats — for the red star glowed close ahead.

He threw on acceleration and, with the lifeboat dragging crazily from the bow, blasted away toward the lone planet of the scarlet sun.

An hour later the planet loomed large, and he entered the green-tinted atmosphere. In order to escape the teleview plates of the raider, he circled to the far side, nudging the *Perseus'* bow around with the lifeboat.

Through his own teleview, the planet showed as a world of about half Earth's size, scarred with gorges and precipitous crags, interspersed with plains. These plains brimmed with a black froth, which the teleview presently revealed to be thick fronded vegetation.

The atmosphere, of a marked green tint, supported great fleecy clouds, glowing in the lurid sunlight in all shades of orange, gold, red and yellow.

Holderlin let the *Perseus* fall toward the base of a great black peak where dense forest indicated good concealment. Single-handed he landed the ship with its steering jets fused, an epic in itself.

For two tense hours he crouched in the lifeboat, jockeying the nose of the *Perseus* back and forth as it settled on its landing blasts through a green murk past the hot-colored clouds.

He had led two cords into the lifeboat with him — one made fast to the throttle that he might blast the ship to safety if the terrain were too soft or too rough, the other to kill the tubes when the ship finally settled solidly.

The *Perseus* teetered low through the green air and crashed down through the black forests onto solid soil. Holderlin yanked his cut-off cord, and the roaring blasts died. He fell limply back in his bucket seat.

He stirred himself. The green of the atmosphere hinted unhealthiness — and once more climbing into his air-suit he returned to the *Perseus*.

He twisted the dial at the radio. There was only silence. Through the skyport, he saw that the soft black fronds had closed over the ship. The *Perseus* was well concealed. Holderlin slept.

When he awoke all was as before, the radio still silent. He tested the atmosphere with the Bramley Airolyzer, and as he suspected the dials showed poison. But apparently there were no tissue-irritant gasses, and there was a sufficiency of oxygen.

So he charged a respirator with appropriate filters and jumped out on the planet to inspect the steering jets. He sank to his ankles in an impalpable black dust like soot, which every passing puff of air blew into whirls of black smoke.

As he walked, he stirred up clouds of this dust, which settled in his clothes and into his boots. Holderlin cursed. He could see that a grimy period lay before him. He plodded around to the steering jets.

They were both better and worse than he had expected. The linings were split and broken, and fragments had wedged across the throat of the tube. The electron filaments were destroyed but the backplates of telex crystal were still whole.

The tubes themselves were sound, neither belled, warped nor cracked, and apparently the field coils were not burnt out. Holderlin surmised that a small charge of vanzitrol had been exploded in each.

He could not recall seeing any spare linings aboard, but to make sure he ransacked the ship — to no avail. However, the Naval Regulation Lining Oven and a supply of flux was in its place as provided by Article 80 of the Astronautic Code, a law from the early days of space-flight, when durable linings were unknown.

Then every ship carried dozens of spares — yet often as not these would burn out or split in the heat and pressure, and the ship would be forced to land on a convenient planet and mold another supply. Now Holderlin's concern was to find a bed of clean clay.

The ground at his feet was covered by the black dust. Perhaps, if he dug, he might find clay.

As he stood by the jets, Holderlin heard a heavy shuffling tread through the forest. He ran back to the entrance port, knowing that on strange planets prudence and agility are better safeguards than a needle-beam and steel armor.

The creature of the footsteps passed close beside the ship, a thin shambling being fifteen feet high, vaguely manlike, with a spider's gaunt construction. The arms and legs were skin and bone, the skin was greenish-black, the face peculiarly long and vacant.

It had a fierce shock of reddish hair at the back of its head, the eyes were bulging milky orbs, the ears were wide and extended. It passed the *Perseus* with hardly a glance and showed neither awe nor interest.

"Hey!" cried Holderlin, jumping to the ground. *"Come here!"*

The thing paused a moment to regard him dully through the red light, then slowly shambled off in its original direction, stirring up black clouds of dust. It disappeared through the feathery black jungle.

Holderlin returned to the problem of repairing the tubes. He must find clay enough to mold four new linings — three or four hundred pounds. He brought a spade from the ship and dug into the surface.

He worked half an hour and turned up nothing but hot black humus. And the deeper he dug, the thicker and tougher grew the roots of the fungus trees. He gave up in disgust.

As he climbed, sweating and dusty, from his hole, a little breeze raced along the top of the jungle stirring the fronds, and in the black fog which floated down, Holderlin discovered the origin of the black powder at his feet — spawn.

He must find clay, clean yellow clay, the nearer the better. He did not fancy carrying this clay on his shoulder any great distance. He looked to where the lifeboat dangled by its nose from the bow of the *Perseus*.

He saw that the shackle, with the entire weight of the lifeboat hanging on it, was locked. Holderlin scratched his head. He would have to balance the boat on the gravity units, releasing the shackle from all strain, to remove it.

But when he finally poised the boat in mid-air and climbed out on the nose, he discovered that his shift of position had weighted the bow and that if he unscrewed the shackle, the boat very likely would nose down and throw him to the ground.

Cursing both shackle and lifeboat, Holderlin let the boat hang against the hull as before and made his way to the ground. He entered the ship and outfitted himself with a sack, a light spade, a canteen of water and spare charges for his respirator.

"Aboard the *Perseus*! Aboard the *Perseus*! Respond, *Perseus*!"

Holderlin chuckled grimly and sat down beside the speaker.

"Aboard the *Perseus*!" came the call again. "This is Captain Creed speaking. If you are alive and listening, respond immediately. You have bested us fair and square, and we hold no grudge. But no matter how you reached this planet you cannot go farther.

"A detector screen surrounds you, and we will heterodyne any distress call you broadcast."

Evidently Captain Creed had not yet surmised who had run off with his ship, or how it had been accomplished. Another voice broke in, harder and sharper.

"Respond immediately," said the new voice, "giving your position, and you will receive a share in the venture. If you do not, we shall know how to act when we find you, and we will find you if it means searching the planet foot by foot!"

All during this pronouncement, the strength of the radio carrier wave had increased rapidly, and now Holderlin heard a low mutter, rapidly waxing to a roar. Running to the port, he spied the black pirate ship sweeping toward him across the green sky, just under the canopy of many-colored clouds.

Almost overhead the brake blasts spewed forward, and the ship slowed in its majestic course. Trapped — thought Holderlin. With racing pulse he leapt for the lifeboat. The shackle he'd blast away with his needle-beam!

But the black ship passed across the mountain, where it slowly sank from sight, sunlight glinting from its sides. Holderlin breathed easily again. This world was small, and the mountain made a prominent landmark. Probably the same reasons that had brought him here to hide, led them here to seek him.

At least he knew where his enemies were stationed, a matter of some advantage. How to escape them, he as yet had no notion. They seemed invulnerable with a fast well-armed ship against his wrecked hulk, and certainly no less than thirty or forty in the crew.

Holderlin shrugged. First he must repair the tubes. Then he would try his luck at winning clear. And if he could bring that scented cargo only as far as Laroknik on Gavnad, the sixth of Delta Aquila, the universe lay open to him.

He'd buy a space-yacht, a villa on Fan, the Pleasure Planet. He'd buy an asteroid and create a world to his whim, as did the Empire's millionaires. Holderlin put aside his dreaming. He took his sack and plodded off through the black dust in the direction of the mountain, seeking clay. A half mile from the ship, the feathery black canopy overhead thinned, and he entered a clearing.

Within the clearing moved a score of the tall manlike creatures. But their hair was not reddish like that of the creature that had passed him in the wood. It was a greenish-black. They stood busy with an enormous beast, evidently domesticated.

This had a great round body, as big as a house, supported on a circle of wide arching legs. With two long tentacles it stuffed the black tree-fronds into a maw on top of its hulk. Below hung a number of teats at which the black things worked, squirting a thin green liquid into pots.

Holderlin passed through the clearing, full in the red sunglow, but beyond a few dull glances, they took no heed of him. Continuing a mile or so, he came to the edge of the forest and the steep rises of the mountains.

Almost at his feet he found what he sought. In the diminished gravity he loaded into his sack a great deal more than he might have carried on Earth — perhaps a half of his needs — and set out in return.

But as he waded through the black dust the sack grew heavy, and by the time he reached the clearing where the natives tended their beast, his arms and his back ached.

He stood resting, watching the placid natives at their work. It occurred that possibly one of them might be induced to serve him.

"Hey — *you*!" he called to the nearest, as best he could through the respirator. "Come here!"

This one looked at Holderlin without interest.

"Come here!" he called again, although plainly the creature could not understand him. "I need some help. I'll give you —" he fumbled in his pockets and pulled out a small signal mirror "— this."

He displayed it, and presently the native shambled across the glade to him. It stooped to take the mirror, and a hint of interest came over the long doleful face.

"Now take this," said Holderlin, giving over the sack of clay, "and follow me."

At last the creature understood what was required of him, and with no show of either zeal or reluctance, took the bag in its rickety arms and shuffled along behind Holderlin to the ship. When they arrived, Holderlin went within and brought out a length of shiny chain, and showed it to his helper.

"One more trip, understand? One more trip. Let's go." The creature obediently followed him.

Holderlin dug the clay, loaded the bag into the native's arms.

Above them came the sound of voices, footsteps, scuffling and grating on the rock. Holderlin crept for cover. The native stood stupidly, holding the sack of clay.

Three figures came into sight, two of them panting through respirators — Blaine and a tall man whose pointed ears and high-arched eyebrows proclaimed Trankli blood. The third was a native with a red mop of hair.

"What's this?" cried the Trankli half-breed, spying Holderlin's helper. "That sack is —"

They were the last words he spoke. A needle-beam chattered and cut him down. Blaine whirled about, grabbing for his own weapon. A voice brought him up short.

"Drop it, Blaine! You're as good as dead!"

Blaine slowly dropped his hands to his sides, glaring madly in the direction of the voice, his malformed lip twitching. Holderlin stepped from the shadow into the scarlet sunlight, and his face was as ruthless as death itself.

"Looking for me?"

He walked over and took Blaine's needle-beam. He noted the

native's reddish mop of hair. This was the one that had passed him in the woods, who was evidently in league with his enemies.

The needle-beam spoke once more, and the tall black body crumpled like broken jack-straws. Holderlin's worker watched impassively.

"Can't have any tale-bearers," said Holderlin, turning his ice-blue eyes on Blaine.

"Why don't you give it up, Holderlin?" snarled Blaine. "You can't get away alive."

"Do you think you'll outlive me?" mocked Holderlin. "What's that you've got? A radio, hey? I'll take that." He did so. "The native was taking you to the *Perseus*, and you were going to flash back the position. Right?"

"That's right," admitted Blaine sourly, wondering at what moment he was to be killed.

Holderlin mused.

"What ship are you in?"

"The *Maetho* — Killer Donahue's. You can't get away, Holderlin. Not with Donahue after you."

"We'll see," said Holderlin shortly.

So it was Killer Donahue's *Maetho*! Holderlin had heard tales of Donahue — a slight man of forty years, with dark hair and a pair of black eyes which saw around corners and into men's minds. He had a droll clown's face, but past deeds of blood and loot did not echo the humor of his countenance.

Holderlin thought a moment, staring at the flaccid Blaine. The surviving native stood disinterestedly holding the clay.

"Well, you wanted to see the *Perseus*," Holderlin said at last. "Start moving." He gestured with the needle-beam.

Blaine went slowly, sullenly.

"Do you want to die now," inquired Holderlin, "or are you going to do as I say?"

"You got the gun," growled Blaine. "I got no say at all."

"Good," said Holderlin. "Then move faster. And tonight we'll cook linings for the steering jets." He motioned to the waiting native. With Blaine ahead, they plodded off toward the ship.

"What's over the mountain? Donahue's hideout?" Holderlin asked.

Blaine nodded dourly, then decided he had nothing to lose by truckling to Holderlin.

"He gets thame-dust here, sells it on Fan."

Thame was an aphrodisiac powder.

"The natives collect it, bring it in little pots. He gives them salt for it. They love salt."

Holderlin was silent, saving his energy for plowing the black dust.

"Suppose you did get away," Blaine presently put forward, "you never could sell those oils anywhere. One whiff of syrang and you'd have the Tellurian Corps of Investigation on your neck."

"I'm not selling them," said Holderlin. "Think I'm a fool? What do you think I got that certification of shipwreck for? I'm going to claim salvage. That's ninety percent of the value of ship and cargo, by law."

Blaine was silent.

When at last they arrived, weary and begrimed with black dust, the native dropped the sack and held out a gangling arm.

"*Fawp, fawp*," it said.

Holderlin looked at him in puzzlement.

"It wants salt," said Blaine, still intent on ingratiating Holderlin. "They do anything for salt."

"Is that so?" said Holderlin. "Well, we'll go in the galley and find some salt."

So Holderlin gave the native the bit of chain and a handful of salt and dismissed it. He turned back to Blaine and gave him the radio.

"Call up Creed or Donahue and tell them that the native says you won't reach the ship till tomorrow night — it's that far off."

Blaine hesitated only an instant, long enough for Holderlin to lay a significant hand on his needle-beam. He did as he was told. He called Creed, and Creed seemed satisfied with the information.

"Tell him you won't call again till tomorrow night," said Holderlin. "Say that's because Holderlin might catch an echo of the beam from the mountain."

Blaine did so.

"Good," said Holderlin. "Blaine, we're going to get along very well. Maybe I won't even kill you when I'm done with you."

Blaine swallowed nervously. He disliked this kind of talk. Holderlin stretched his arms.

"Now we'll make tube linings. And because you ruined the last set, you'll do most of the work."

All night they baked linings in the atomic furnaces, Blaine, as Holderlin had promised, working the hardest. His bald head glistened in the glow from the furnace.

As soon as the linings were finished — no longer clay, but heavy metallic tubes — Holderlin clamped them in place. And when the angry little sun came over the horizon, the *Perseus* was once more in condition to navigate.

With Blaine's help, Holderlin unshackled the lifeboat from the hull and brought it to the ground beside the *Perseus*. Then Holderlin locked Blaine in a storage locker.

"You're lucky," he observed. "You can sleep. I have to work." Holderlin had seen a ten-pound can of vanzitrol in the *Perseus* armory — a compound stable chemically, but uncertain atomically. Holderlin ladled about a pound into a paper sack, enough to blast the *Perseus* clear through the planet.

He found a detonator, and entering the lifeboat took off. Feeling safe from observation after Blaine's information, he skimmed low over the black jungle until, about thirty miles from the *Perseus*, he found a clearing which suited him, not too large, not too small.

He landed and buried the vanzitrol and the detonator in the center. Then he returned to the *Perseus* and slept for four or five hours.

When he awoke, he aroused Blaine. They got in the lifeboat, flew to the mined clearing. Holderlin set the lifeboat down two hundred yards out in the jungle.

"Now Blaine," he said, "you're to call Creed and tell him you've found the *Perseus*. Tell him to take a bearing on the radio beam and come at once. Tell him there's a clearing handy for him to land in."

"Then what?" asked Blaine doubtfully.

"Then you'll wait in the clearing until the *Maetho* is about to land. After that I'll give you a choice. If you want to return aboard the *Maetho*, you can stay where you are. If you want to stay with me, you'll run like mad for the lifeboat. Suit yourself."

Blaine did not answer, but a suspicious look crept into his eyes, and his lips curled craftily.

"Send the message," said Holderlin.

Blaine did so, and Holderlin was satisfied. They had cornered Holderlin in the *Perseus*, said Blaine, and Mordang, the Trankli half-breed, was holding him while Blaine radioed.

"Very good, Blaine!" came back Creed's voice. Then Donahue asked a few sharp questions. Had the *Perseus* crashed? No, replied Blaine, she was sound. Could the *Perseus* bring her needle-beam to bear on the clearing? No, the clearing was quite safe, a half mile astern of the *Perseus*. Donahue ordered Blaine to wait in the clearing for the ship.

Twenty minutes later Holderlin, hidden in the jungle, and Blaine standing nervously in the clearing, saw the hulk of the *Maetho* come drifting overhead.

It hovered about five hundred yards above. Blaine, nakedly caught in the red sunlight, waved an arm to the ship at Holderlin's brittle command.

There was a pause. The cautious Donahue apparently was inspecting the situation.

Presently Holderlin, waiting tensely at the edge of the forest, saw a small scout boat leave the *Maetho*, drift down toward the clearing. His mouth tightened. He cursed once, bitterly.

This meant Creed or Donahue had smelled a rat. His plan could not succeed — he'd have to move fast to escape with his skin! Blaine also knew the jig was up, was uncertain which way to jump.

He decided that under the circumstances Holderlin offered the least immediate danger, and casually began to leave the clearing. At once Donahue's voice crackled from a loud speaker.

"Blaine! Stay where you are!"

Blaine broke into a frightened run, but the black dust hampered him. From the *Maetho* a needle-beam spoke, and amid a great puff of black dust, Blaine exploded to his component atoms.

Holderlin was already to the lifeboat. A slim chance remained that the scout boat on landing would miss the mine, and the *Maetho* would land and be blown to scrap. But this he doubted, as the detonator was sensitive, the clearing small.

An air-rending blast as he entered his boat assured him he was right. The ground swayed like jelly, and a hail of earth, rocks, bits of trees spattered far over the jungle. The *Maetho* was tossed upward like a toy balloon. A tremendous choking pall of black dust thickened the sky.

Holderlin jerked his lifeboat into the air and dashed away, low to the ground, through the trees. He flew for his life, threading the trees as best he might, crashing through those he could not dodge.

Nor was he too early, for the *Maetho*'s armament had opened a savage fire on the jungle, blasting at each square yard. Twice million-watt bolts missed him by feet.

After rocking minutes he gained clear of the area, and slowing his mad flight, wove a more careful course through the trees.

When the *Maetho* was finally finished, the jungle lay torn into craters and tangled rubbish for miles around. Holderlin, gingerly raising the boat so he could peer through the tree tops, saw the great sullen shape of the war-ship winging back across the mountain to its base. Over the clearing towered a black sky-filling cloud.

He returned to the *Perseus,* and sat brooding in his quarters. His bolt seemed to be shot, and it would only be a matter of hours before Creed and Donahue found another native to guide them to his ship.

He sprawled on his bunk, hands behind his head. A nucleus of information Blaine had given him suddenly blossomed to a plan of action. He got up, spooned some more vanzitrol from the can, gathered up a few sacks of salt from the galley, took off in the lifeboat.

Three or four hours later, with night fast falling across the black forest he returned, and there was a spring in his walk, a triumphant set to his jaw.

Holderlin went to the teleview and boldly sent forth a call. "Aboard the *Maetho*! Creed or Donahue, come in! *Maetho*, come in!" The screen flickered to life at once. There was Donahue, and behind him the black-bearded face of Captain Creed.

"Well," said Donahue crisply. "What do you want?"

Holderlin grinned. "Nothing. In about two minutes I'm blasting your ship to bits. If you enjoy life, you'll get clear."

"What's this?" Donahue's voice snapped like breaking wood. "Are you trying to bluff me?"

"You'll know in two minutes," responded Holderlin. "Three of the pots of thame-dust you took aboard today are loaded with vanzitrol. I've got a gamma-ray detonator you can't jam. Now! You've got two minutes to get clear."

Donahue whirled, cut in the ship's loud speaker. "Abandon ship! All hands!" he shouted. "*Get clear!*"

Then like a cat he whirled about. Holderlin watched in interest. Captain Creed was striding for the door. He met Donahue's eyes, and saw murder. He stopped in his tracks and slowly turned to face Donahue.

Donahue began talking, and Holderlin saw he was not sane. Obscenities poured from his lips.

"You white-faced dog, you've ruined me!" screamed Donahue in a high-pitched crazy voice, and his thin body was as tense as an epileptic's.

"Let's leave this ship and argue later," Creed suggested coolly.

"You'll stay here, you fat filth!" cried Donahue, and whipped out his needle-beam.

Creed fired his sleeve gun, and Donahue fell to the ground, screaming, his shoulder mangled.

He picked up the needle-beam with his left hand and began throwing wild shots at Creed. Creed crouched behind the radio locker, unable to gain the door. A bolt smashed the teleview feeder lines. The screen went dark.

Holderlin sat looking at his watch. He held one hand poised over a little black key.

Twenty seconds, ten seconds, eight seconds, seven, six, five, four, three, two — "I'll give them five seconds more," he told himself. One — two — three — four — five! He snapped closed the key, and sat like a statue, waiting for the shock from across the mountain.

Whoom!

Holderlin stood up, a grin on his face. He sealed all the ports and sat himself at the controls. Ahead of him lay a busy week, wherein he must do the work of four men. He cracked back the throttle, and took off for Laroknik on Gavnad.

Dead Ahead

CHIRAM CAME INTO THE ROOM, walked with short, firm steps to the desk, sat down. Only then did he appear to notice the two dozen men and women seated on neat rows of folding chairs.

"I can give you about twenty minutes," said Chiram. "Exactly what do you want?"

"How about a short statement?" suggested Ed Jeff, of *All-Planet News-Fax.* "Then perhaps you'd answer a few questions."

Chiram leaned back, a stocky middle-aged man with an air of decision. He had a leonine ruff of hair the color and texture of steel wool, eyes sharp and monitory, a heavy well-shaped mouth. His clothes were gray and dark blue — conservative but informal, as if Chiram dressed by habit, uninfluenced by either vanity or ostentation.

"My associates and I," he said, "financed by Jay Banners, have embarked on a program of research which will ultimately lead to an attempted circumnavigation of the universe." He stopped; the reporters waited. Chiram said drily, "That is the statement."

Voices collided and tumbled getting to Chiram's ears. He held up his hand. "One at a time…You, sir — what was your question?"

"You said circumnavigation of the universe? Not merely the galaxy?"

Chiram nodded. "The universe."

"How do you know it's round?"

"We don't," said Chiram, smiling grimly. "There is no first-hand evidence, very little mathematical indication, one way or another. It's an assumption on which we're staking our lives."

The reporters made respectful sounds. Chiram relaxed a trifle. "Estimates of the circumference run in the neighborhood of ten to a hundred billion light years. We plan to set out from Earth, assume a course — almost any course. After a sufficient period of flying, at a sufficiently high speed, we hope to return from the opposite direction."

"What're the chances of hitting Earth on the way back?"

Chiram compressed his lips; the question had been put in what he considered a light tone.

"In theory," he replied stiffly, "if we steer a sufficiently exact course we will return automatically. Our research program is concentrating on the mechanics of straight flight. A hundredth of a second error at a hundred billion light years means three hundred thousand light years. If we missed the home galaxy by that margin we'd be lost forever. Our first problem is to guarantee ourselves a mathematically straight course."

"Can't you line up on stars ahead or behind?"

Chiram shook his head. "The light from behind can't catch up with us; in fact, we'll overtake it and add the images of the stars behind to those of the stars ahead." He clasped his blunt hands on the desk. "That is our second problem: seeing. Our speed will approximate instantaneity. Assuming ninety per cent efficiency in our destriation field, an average speed of six or seven thousand light years a second will take us a hundred billion light years in six months. The impact of radiation on an unshielded object at this speed would be cataclysmic. The weakest infra-red light would be compacted by a kind of Doppler effect to cosmic rays; ordinary visible light would become a thousand times harder, more energetic, and cosmic rays would strike at a frequency of ten to the thirty-first or thirty-second power. I can't imagine the effect of radiation like that, but I know it would hurt. We are trying to develop a system of vision that can function under this tremendous impact. Longitudinal sight will be normal, of course, with light striking the side of our ship at normal frequencies."

"How long will it take to lick these problems?"

Chiram said in a measured voice, "We are making satisfactory progress."

"How will you know for sure when you've returned? One galaxy must look a lot like another…"

Chiram drummed his fingers on the table. "That's a good question. I'm sorry to say I have no precise answer. We will trust to alertness, and careful examination of any galaxy in our path which shows the proper size and configuration. The fact that our galaxy is roughly double the average size will help us. We shall have to trust a good deal to luck."

"Suppose the universe isn't spherical, but infinite?"

Chiram fixed the man with a contemptuous stare. "You're talking foolishness. How can I answer that question?"

The reporter hurriedly corrected himself. "What I meant, will you set a limit to the time before you turn around and come back?"

"We believe the universe is spherical," said Chiram coolly. "In a fourth-dimensional sense, of course. We will remain under constant acceleration and our speed will increase constantly. If the universe is spherical, we will return; if it is infinite, we will fly on forever."

Two ships landed, a slender cylinder and a peculiar impractical-looking hull the shape of a doughnut. Chiram stepped out of the cylinder, marched up the concrete ramp to the glass-walled office.

Jay Banners, who was putting up the money, and a lank young man were waiting for him. Banners resembled Chiram in outward proportion, but his hair was sparse, the lines of his face were softer. He looked easy, amiable; there was nothing of the spartan or the ascetic in Jay Banners.

Chiram was associated with the discovery of striatics, the gravitron and the subsequent inertia-negative destriation fields; he had been a member of the original Centauri expedition. Banners had never been into space, but he held majority stock in Star Island Development, and he was director of half a dozen other corporations.

He waved a pudgy hand at Chiram. "Herb, meet my son, Jay Junior. And now I'll give you a surprise. Hold your hat. Jay wants to go along on the trip. So I told him we'd see what we could do." He glanced at Chiram expectantly.

Chiram pulled up the corners of his mouth, squinted as if he were eating an unexpectedly sour pickle. "Well, now, Banners...I don't know if it's advisable...Inexperienced member," he muttered. "Got a crew pretty well lined out..."

"Oh come now," said Banners bluffly. "It isn't as if Jay was a rank amateur. He's just out of engineering school; he knows space inside out; studied astrogation and all that stuff, hey, Jay?"

"That's right," said Jay languidly.

Chiram turned chilly eyes up and down Jay Banners Jr. — a loose-limbed young man with oily black hair worn over-long for Chiram's taste. He said, "It's a pretty tough grind, young fellow. Strict discipline. We're cooped up in a little cabin with no amusements, a very serious proposition. And about one chance in ten of getting back... An old man like me can afford to throw his life away. A lad like you has that all before him."

Jay carelessly shrugged, and the older Banners said, "I've told him all this, Herb, and he insists that he wants to go. And then I figured that maybe it would be a good thing to have a Banners aboard. Make it the Chiram–Banners Expedition for a fact, eh, Herb?"

Chiram drummed his fingers savagely on the desk, at a loss for words.

Jay said, "We've learned a lot of new methods at school. Might help you out once in a while if you get stumped."

Chiram became red in the face, turned away.

"Now, Jay," said Banners, "take it easy on an old man. I know you're up to snuff on all the latest ideas, but don't forget that men like Herb Chiram pioneered the whole business."

Jay shrugged, moodily puffed a cigarette.

"It's settled, then," said Banners jovially. "And look here, Herb, don't hold back on him on my account. Treat him like a hired hand. He's tough — just like his old man. He can stand it. If he gets out of line, give it to him good."

Chiram walked to a window, stood looking out.

Banners said, "We saw you bringing down the ships. How did the test turn out?"

"Very well," said Chiram. "From Earth to Pluto we deviated nineteen inches off the true line. That's on the order of ten to the minus eighth or ninth part of a second. Maybe closer. I haven't figured it out yet. It's close enough."

Jay flicked ashes to the floor with his little finger. "Probably be best to install gyro-compasses just to be on the safe side."

Chiram said in a keen, cold voice, "Gyro-compasses are grossly inaccurate compared to the sleeve and piston principle."

"Explain to Jay how it works," said Banners. "I never could quite get the hang of it. I know that Nip and Tuck alternate the lead —"

Chiram spoke in a heavy impatient voice. "An object in free flight moves in a true course, when it's insulated from gravity — as inside a destriation shell. Our problem was to combine free-flight accuracy with acceleration. We decided to use two ships, alternately accelerating and flying free — the ship in free flight correcting the course of the ship under acceleration.

"Assume one component flying free — say Nip, the cylinder. Tuck, the tube, is ten thousand miles astern. Tuck accelerates; the application of power may or may not cause a slight deviation. As soon as the destriation shells meet, radar beams make contact and any slight deviation in course is corrected. Tuck slides over Nip, the power is shut off, it flies free on ahead. When it has taken a ten-thousand-mile lead, Nip accelerates, plunges through the hole in Tuck. The process is automatic, very rapid, very accurate."

Banners said seriously, "Doesn't that constant start and stop jar you, Herb?"

Jay looped a leg over the desk. "Nope. Don't forget, pop, we've integrated inertia completely with the ship since your day. Don't feel a thing any more, except the normal built-in gravity."

Banners laughed indulgently, clapped Chiram's stiff shoulder. "Don't say I didn't warn you, Herb. This lad here is pretty far ahead of us old-timers... That's how it goes — out with the old, in with the new."

Jay blew a complacent gust of smoke across the room. Chiram stared at him for several seconds, took two short paces up the room, two back.

"Banners," he said crisply, "everything considered, I don't think it wise for your son to make the trip."

Jay raised his eyebrows; his mouth sagged. Banners stared; then his face relaxed. "Now Herb, I know it's dangerous, I know you don't like the responsibility. But Jay's got his mind made up. Some girl's been after him, I expect. And I'd like to see the lad make the trip. In fact, I've been thinking I might even go myself..."

Chiram said hastily, "Very well, very well... I warn you, young fellow, it's a tough grind. It's snap to orders and no back-talk. If that's understood — I guess I have nothing further to say."

"You'll get along, you'll get along," exclaimed Banners. "With your experience, Herb, and your training, Jay — I can't see how the trip won't be a great success. Think of it, Herb! The Chiram–Banners Expedition — Commander, Herb Chiram; Navigator, Jay Banners Junior! Doesn't that sound good, now?"

"It makes my head swim," said Chiram.

Jay dropped his cigarette butt to the floor, said thoughtfully, "You know, that Nip and Tuck idea may be sound — but I'd trust more to a good gyroscope… At least we ought to ship a couple for the corroboratic index."

Chiram frowned. "'Corroboratic index'? What's that?" he asked contemptuously.

Jay said, "A rather new concept. One of these days I'll explain it to you. In rough terms, it's the average area of the integral under a series of probability curves, each given the proper weighting."

Banners nodded heavily. "Young fellow's got a sound head on him, Herb. Maybe we'd better install a couple gyroscopes. No harm playing safe."

Chiram bowed slightly to Jay. "The gyroscopes are in your charge. See that they do not exceed two cubic feet in volume."

Jay nodded. "Fine. I can cut it smaller than that. Machinery has become more precise since your time, Mr. Chiram." He rubbed his upper lip. "In fact — if you like — I'll take the navigation clean off your hands. I'm pretty good at it — made an A in navigation all during school."

Chiram snorted. "You'll do no such thing, young fellow. And you'll understand right now, before the day's a minute older, you'll do what you're told, you'll obey orders, and you'll keep your school-book ideas to yourself unless they're asked for!"

Jay stared in astonishment; he turned and looked at his father, who wagged his head solemnly. "That's the way it goes, Jay. Old Herb here is a tough one. You've picked a tartar when you try to put it over Herb. What he says, goes; remember it."

Chiram, Jay Banners Jr., a taciturn technician named Bob Galt, and Julius Johnson, the cook, a taffy-colored smiling man with a flat face and flat head, made up the crew of Nip the cylinder. Two old-time spacemen, Art Henry and Joe Lavindar, were stationed aboard Tuck the tube.

The takeoff was recorded by cameras, television, and witnessed by a crowd of four million. The two ships rose separately and left for a rendezvous a million miles past the Moon. Here they would join, orient themselves, and set out toward Deneb in Cygnus, slightly up from the prime plane of the Milky Way.

Chiram called his crew together in the small saloon below the bridge deck, which would serve as mess hall and recreation room. Bob Galt sat at one end of the bench, a stooped, small-boned man, completely self-possessed and self-sufficient, with a face like an angry parrot's. Beside him sat Julius, the cook, his wide mouth curved in a perpetual grin. Jay slouched back at the end of the bench with legs crossed, eyes half-closed.

Chiram faced them, stocky, erect, his ruff of iron-gray hair freshly trimmed.

"Now, men, as you know, we have a stiff grind ahead of us. If we return, we're heroes. The chances are we'll never get back. If space is infinite we'll fly forever. If our course deviates from a straight line, we're just as bad off. Then of course you've all read the fantastic speculations on the possibility of attack by alien space-vessels or creatures inhabiting space. I do not need to label this as nonsense.

"Our greatest danger is ourselves. Boredom, petty irritations — these are our worst enemies. We're crowded together, tangled in each other's arms and legs. I can think of no situation so calculated to bring out the best or worst in a man. Now you, Bob, and you, Julius, I've shipped with you many a time; I know you well. You, Jay, you represent your father, and I'm sure that, like the rest of us, you're determined to make the trip as easy on all our nerves as possible.

"There's not much work to do. I wish there were more. Julius, of course, is in charge of cooking and the galley." His voice took on a sardonic edge. "Jay has his gyroscopes to attend to, and I understand he's keeping a detailed record...Well, every man to his own poison.

"I'll take the first watch, Jay the second, Bob the third. Our main duties will be to lubricate the machinery, to chart what we can see in the vision panels, and keep the destriation field at normal percentage.

Each of us will be responsible for the cleanliness of himself, his clothes, his bunk. Everyone must be neat. Nothing is as demoralizing as slovenliness. Shaving and clean clothes are mandatory…That's all for now."

He turned, swung himself up on the bridge deck.

The moon was a tremendous silver melon spattered with black frost; it hulked below and off to the left. Directly ahead floated Tuck, the tube, with a cluster of stars shining through the hole.

Chiram nosed the cylinder into the opening, thrust home a switch; the cylinder shivered, jerked as the guide beams excited relays, pulled the ships into rigid alignment.

Dead ahead was Deneb — the line of their way around the universe.

Chiram called by radio to Tuck. "Everything all right in there?"

"Ready to go," came back Henry's voice.

Chiram said, "Throw in your field." He yanked another switch; the gravity unit buzzed, rattled, settled into a drone; the crew was tied to the ship, and, like the ship, free of inertia.

Chiram spun a polished wheel, and the voyage had begun.

An instant passed. Then a flicker at the side port was Tuck, racing ahead. Another flicker was Nip threading Tuck. The flickers became swifter, became a continuous quiver, vanished.

Stars began to move, slide past each other, like shining motes in a drift of sunlit air. They streamed past — now bunched, now sparse, clusters, swarms, flaring clouds of gas, and as they passed aft of amidships they vanished, their light lagging behind the thistledown rush of Nip and Tuck.

Flame, dazzle, flicker — stars in pairs, trios, quartets, stars in hurrying multitudinous companies. Stars in rivers and stars like isolated beacons. Stars approached from far ahead, passing over, around, under, like wind-blown sparks. And presently the stars vanished in front and to the side, and Nip and Tuck were in intergalactic space.

Speed added to speed, built up in constant increments. Ship threaded ship like a needle in a shuttle, each guiding the other down a geometrically straight line. So straight that in a thousand light years the error might be a hundred miles — an error which might or might not average out over longer distances.

Jay checked the course on his gyro-compass. He looked a minute, tapped the case with his finger. "Right on," he announced. "We're right on course."

"Glad to hear it," said Chiram sardonically. "Watch it close now."

The great nebula in Andromeda passed under them, a whirling pancake of cold fire. It passed behind, out of sight.

Speed, speed, speed. Acceleration as fast as the relays could shuttle ship back and forth through ship. Speed building up toward instantaneity.

Watches passed, days passed. The galaxies flitted by like luminous bats — straggling watch-springs, hot puddles of gas. At the start and close of every watch Jay checked his gyroscope, then spent two or three hours writing in his journal — minutiae of the voyage, vignettes of personal philosophy, observations on the personalities of his shipmates.

Julius and Bob played cards and chess; occasionally Chiram joined them. Jay played a few games of chess — long enough to find that Julius could beat him as often as he set his mind to it — then gave up. Julius grinned his grin, spoke little; Bob wore his angry parrot's face, spoke not at all. Chiram kept himself aloof, watched every detail of the voyage with a careful humorless eye, gave what orders were necessary in a carefully modulated voice. And Jay, after a few futile attempts to argue navigational techniques with Chiram, became as taciturn as the others.

The galaxies slid backward. After every watch Jay peered intently at his gyroscope. One day he called Chiram over.

"We're off course. Look — there's no doubt about it. A whole degree. I've been watching it for several days."

Chiram looked down a moment, shook his head, half-turned away. "You've got a precession somewhere."

Jay sniffed. "More likely that those spacer beams between the hulls are out of focus."

Chiram glanced down his nose at the gyroscopes, said stonily, "Hardly possible. They're automatically compensated, double-checked. Two separate sets of spacers are involved, don't forget — one correcting on a basis of wave interference, the other by correlation of angle and beam strength. They're perfectly synchronized; if they weren't the alarm would go off... Your gyro is out somewhere."

Grumbling, Jay turned to look at the dial. "One degree," he mumbled. "That's a million light years — a hundred million light years —" But Chiram had walked away.

Jay seated himself beside the gyro, watched the face like a cat at a tank of goldfish. If it told the truth they were irretrievably lost. He dropped to his hands and knees, checked every part of the gyro as well as he could; it seemed in perfect order.

Jay slouched to the table, where Bob and Julius played chess, stood looking down with hands clasped behind his back. They took no heed of his presence.

"Well," said Jay, looking across the room toward the gyro, "we're goners. We're done for."

"Yeah? How's that?" asked Julius, moving a pawn.

"The gyro doesn't lie," said Jay. "We're a degree off course, according to the gyro."

Bob Galt darted an unemotional glance up at Jay, returned to the board.

"I told the old man," Jay said bitterly. "I told him before we took off that his rig was too damn complicated to work."

"We all got to die sometime, kid," said Julius. "It might as well be out here…I'm not worryin'. We're eatin' good; I got old Galt here on the run…" The grin widened.

Bob sneered. "The hell you say." He moved a knight to threaten the pawn. "Try that on."

Julius bent his heavy head over the board. "Relax, kid, watch the scenery…"

Jay hesitated, then turned away, crossed the room, flung himself on his bunk, moving his lips in silent curses. He lay quiet twenty minutes, staring up at the hull. A degree off course…

He rose on his elbow, watched the galaxies flitting past in the vision panels. Stars — millions, billions of stars, curdled into luminous whorls. These out here were nameless, unknown to the astronomers on that far atom, Earth…He considered Earth, so far distant as to be unknowable. How could they ever again locate that precious fleck? Presumably if they returned to the home galaxy Earth could be found. But now — a degree off course! And no one aboard cared a fig either way...Well, by God, thought Jay furiously, these dull animals might not care a nickel for their lives, but he was Jay Banners Junior and he had his whole life to live!...Now then, if he returned the ship to its course, there would still be a chance of hitting the galaxy on the way back. They would thank him for it, Chiram and Bob Galt and Julius, when he finally told them; there would be jocular comment, chaffing — and, of course, that bull-headed Chiram would walk around with his neck stiff. Nevertheless he'd have Jay to thank for bringing them home; he'd have to back down, admit himself wrong...And if the story happened to leak out — Jay's vision soared. Newspapers, television, cheers from crowded streets...

Jay rose to his feet. Chiram lay in his bunk asleep, his feet in white socks neatly placed one on the other.

Jay glanced across the cabin. It was nominally Galt's watch; he sat absorbed in his game, with one hand crooked over his queen. Julius, his brow furrowed, was wiping at his mouth with a big yellow hand.

Jay sauntered across the room, climbed the three steps to the bridge deck, nonchalantly leaned across the chart table, watching the view on the forward screen. Black space, the galaxies like luminous jellyfish in a midnight ocean. They floated in from far ahead, drifted effortlessly past, the near ones sliding over the far ones in an implausible shift of perspective.

The sight was soothing, hypnotic, dreamlike in its silent majesty... Behind him Julius laughed. Jay blinked, straightened, came back to himself. He looked cautiously toward the controls, in a railed box to his right. Only Chiram was supposed to enter the box. He peered out the side vision panel. Tuck, the partner ship, was naturally invisible, flitting back and forth across Nip in the constant acceleration. Jay glanced at the computer dial for their speed: already 6,200 l.y.p.s. and steadily mounting. He turned his attention back to the controls. There it was — a bright knurled knob. A mere touch, and the spacer beams would weaken infinitesimally on one side, to twist the axis on which the two ships rode.

He took a casual step toward the control box, darted out his arm, touched the knob...A great blow fell on his shoulder. He reeled back, sank to the deck. He became aware of three pairs of legs, heard a harsh unsympathetic voice: "I've been waiting for a trick like this ever since he showed me that fool machine of his."

"He's just an addled kid," came Julius' voice, light, careless.

Bob Galt's feet moved abruptly, turned half away.

Chiram said in the same harsh voice, "Pick him up, take him to his bunk, chain his ankle to the stanchion...Julius, you throw a plaster on the bullet-hole. Can't trust a lunatic like that at large."

Jay had nothing to complain of. Julius was careful with his wound; his big, taffy-colored hands moved quickly, gently; his grin never vanished.

He was fed from a tray, and released to use the latrine. These were the only attentions he received. What sluggish life there was in the ship flowed on and past him. His presence was ignored, no one spoke, he spoke to no one.

From his bunk he could see the length of the ship and all that happened aboard: Julius and Bob Galt at their interminable chess; Julius facing him, rubbing his big flat face with a hand when puzzled or preoccupied, Galt sitting crouched over the board with only the hard angles of his profile showing. Chiram played no more cards or chess; his sole diversion was a slow pacing up and down the cabin with half an hour's work at an exerciser morning and night.

The picture became utterly familiar to Jay. It was changeless, uniform. The same colors, the same pattern of shadows, the same pragmatic thud to Chiram's tread, the same grin on Julius' face, the same slope to Galt's shoulders.

The ship had plunged into darkness. There were no more galaxies, no more nebulae. "We've evidently passed the outer fringe of the exploding universe," Jay heard Chiram say ruefully. Jay asked himself, what will it be now? Infinity? He had understood that the exploding universe was like a balloon being inflated, time and space and all — not just the blast of a trillion stars into nothingness...

Was space infinite? Were they flitting like dreams into blackness? To go on and on and on — and then on some more.

The ports showed dead black outside, without spark or flash. They were still accelerating. What was it now? 8,000, 10,000 l.y.p.s.?

Jay turned his back to the cabin, wrote in his journal. He wrote copiously — pages of introspection, fragments of quick-scribbled poetry, which he often returned to, copied, revised. He kept statistical charts: the detailed study of Chiram's pacing, his average number of steps per square foot of deck, the pattern behind Julius' menus. He carefully noted his dreams and spent hours trying to trace their genesis from his past. He wrote careful and elaborate excoriations of Chiram — "for the record" he told himself — and equally cogent self-justifications. He made interminable lists — places he had visited, girl-friends, books, colors, songs. He sketched Chiram, Julius, Bob Galt time and time again.

Hours, days, weeks. Conversation dwindled, died. Julius and Bob played chess, and when Bob was at his watch duties Julius played solitaire — unhurriedly, carefully, glancing at each card as if it might be a surprise.

Chess — pacing — food — sleep — the trips to the latrine, with Julius marching placidly at his back. And occasionally Jay considered an attempt to overpower Julius, kill all on the ship. But Julius was stocky and tough. And what good would result in any event?

Darkness outside the port…Were they actually moving? Or was motion a peculiarity of the home space, where there were objects to measure it? Was infinity merely a soft dark trap where no effort could produce meaningful progress? Eternal darkness outside the port. Suppose one were on foot, walking out there…

Jay put down his journal, stared. His eyes bulged. A sound scraped up his throat. Chiram paused in his pacing, turned his head. Jay pointed a long trembling arm toward the port.

"It was a face! I saw it looking in the port!"

Chiram turned startled eyes to the vision panel. Galt, asleep, grumbled, grunted. Julius, playing solitaire, shuffled the cards with imperturbable movements of smooth yellow arms. Chiram looked skeptically back at Jay.

Jay cried, "I saw it plain as day, I tell you! I'm not crazy! It was a whitish figure, and it came flitting up and then the face looked in through the port…"

Julius stopped shuffling, Galt was leaning out of his bunk. Chiram strode across the floor, peered out briefly. He turned back to Jay, said in a brusque voice, "You've had a bad dream."

Jay laid his head on his arm, blinked at tears. So far, far from home…
Ghosts peering in from space…Was this where souls came when
they died? Out here to wander the void, so completely forlorn and
lonesome…

"I saw it," he said. "I saw it, I tell you. I saw it."

"Relax, kid, relax," said Julius. "You'll give us all the willies."

Jay lay on his side, staring at the port. He gave a great gasp. "I saw it
again! It's a face, I tell you!" He rose up from his bunk, his lank black
hair, very long now, dangling past his forehead. His mouth wobbled,
glistened wetly.

Chiram went to the medicine chest, loaded a hypospray. He motioned; Galt and Julius held Jay's arms and legs; Chiram pressed the
trigger, and the opiate seeped through Jay's pale skin, into his blood,
into his brain…

When he awoke, Galt and Julius were playing chess, and Chiram
was asleep. He looked fearfully to the port. Darkness. Blackness.
Lightlessness.

He sighed, moaned. Julius flashed him a glance, returned to the
chess-board. Jay sighed, reached for his journal.

Weeks, months. Fantastic speed toward — what? One day Jay called
Chiram from his pacing.

"Well?" asked Chiram crisply.

"If you'll let me loose," muttered Jay, "I'd like to take up my duties
again."

Chiram said in a carefully passionless voice, "I'm sorry that you've
had to be confined. It was necessary, not for punishment, but for the
safety of the expedition. Because you are irresponsible. Because I can't
trust you."

Jay said, "I promise you that I'll act — well — responsibly. I've learned
my lesson…Suppose we go on forever like this? Into nothing? Do you
intend to keep me chained the rest of my life?"

Chiram stared at him thoughtfully, trying to fathom the ultimate
justice of the situation.

Galt called down from the bridge deck, "Hey, Cap! There's a glow
ahead! *Light!*"

Three bounds took Chiram to the port. Jay rose on his elbow, craned his neck.

Far ahead hung a ball of glowing fog.

Chiram said in a hushed voice, "That's what a universe of billions of galaxies would look like — from a great distance."

"Have we made it around, Cap?" Galt asked, his voice sharp.

Chiram said slowly, "I don't know, Bob...We've come so far — so much farther than anyone had predicted...It might be our universe, or it might be another. I'm as much in the dark as you are."

"If it is our universe, Cap, what are the chances of hitting home?"

There was a pause. Chiram said, "Darned if I know, Bob. I'm hoping."

"Think we better slow down? We're hitting an awful clip."

"Twenty-two thousand light years a second. We can slow down a lot faster than we pick up, just by slacking off the field."

There was silence. Then Galt said, "She's expanding mighty fast..."

Chiram said in an even voice, "It's no universe. It's a cloud of gas. I'm going to get a spectral reading on it."

The glowing fog grew large, flooded under the ship, was gone. Ahead was blackness. Chiram came down from the bridge-deck, took up his pacing, head bent.

He looked up and his eyes met Jay's. Jay was still propped up on his arms, still looking out ahead into the void.

Chiram said, "Very well. I'll take a chance on you."

Jay slowly sank back on the bunk, lay lax and loose. Chiram said, "These are your orders. You are forbidden to set foot on the bridge deck. Next time I'll shoot to kill."

Jay nodded wordlessly. His eyes glistened under the long lank hair. Chiram pulled a key from his pocket, unlocked the shackles, and without a word resumed his pacing.

For five minutes Jay lay unmoving on his bunk. Julius said from the galley, "Come and get it."

Jay saw he had set four places at the table.

Jay washed, shaved. Freedom was a luxury. This was living again — if it were nothing but eat, sleep, look out into darkness. This was life: it would be like this the rest of his life...Curious existence. It seemed natural, sensible. Earth was a trifling recollection, a scene remembered from childhood.

The gyroscopes...Yes, what would they tell him now? They had been far from his mind; perhaps he had banned them from his consciousness as being a symbol of his disgrace... Still, what did they say?

He went to the corner of the workbench where they lay, raised the dust-lid. He stared for a minute.

"Well, kid, how's it look?" Julius asked him lightly. "Are we on course?"

Jay slowly replaced the lid. He said, "The last time I looked we were one degree off to the right. Now we're seventy-five degrees off — to the left!"

Julius shook his head in genial perplexity, grinning. "Looks mighty bad from here."

Jay chewed at his lip. "Something damn strange is working around the ship..."

Galt yelled loudly. "Hey, Cap! There's more light ahead — and this time it's stars for sure!"

They came on the universe like a ship raising an island from the sea — first a blur without detail, then larger, clearer, and finally the great masses dwarfed the ship. Galaxies pelted at them, flats of wild light rushing past.

Chiram stood like a man of marble on the bridge deck, one hand on the control of the destriation field. Galt stood beside him, head hunched down into his shoulders.

They passed flat over a great whirlpool galaxy, and the individual stars glinted and glanced and told of wonderful bright planets.

Galt said, "That sort of looks like her, Cap."

Chiram shook his head. "Not large enough. Don't forget we've got a markedly large galaxy — several times average size. That's what I'm watching for. Of course," and his voice blurred, "this may not even be our home universe. It might be a different set of galaxies entirely. There's no way of knowing... If we run directly into an exceptionally large galaxy, with approximately the right configuration — we'll turn off the power."

"Look," said Bob, "there's a big one out there, see it? That looks about like ours, too." His voice rose. "That's it, Cap!"

Chiram said irresolutely, "Well, Bob, I don't know. She's a long way to the side...Of course, we've come a long way, but if we once turn off our course, and we've made a mistake — then we're goners for sure."

"We're goners if we drive past," said Galt.

Chiram wavered in a hell of indecision. Jay saw his mouth twitch. He reached, took a firm grip on the field control.

Jay said suddenly, "That's not it: this isn't even the right universe."

Galt turned an angry red face down. "Shut up!"

Chiram paid no heed. His hand tightened on the field cut-off.

Jay said, "Captain, I can prove it. Listen!"

Chiram turned his head. "How can you prove it?"

"By the gyroscope." He spoke hurriedly, over Galt's contemptuous snort, trying to wash down Chiram's wall of hostility with words.

"The gyroscope holds a steady axis. It points in a constant direction. When we were a few weeks out I saw a degree of deflection. I misinterpreted the reading. I thought it indicated an error in course. I was wrong; it was showing how far around we had traveled. One three hundred and sixtieth. I just looked at it again. It read seventy-five degrees to the other side — or two eighty-five degrees around. In other words, we've come more than three-quarters of the way. And when the gyro is back at zero again we'll know we're home."

Chiram narrowed his eyes, surveyed Jay — looked at him, through him, beyond. Galt's angry mouth pushed out doubtfully, his color faded. He glanced to the big galaxy, now passing close by amidships.

Chiram asked, "What does the gyro read now?"

Jay ran, raised the dust lid. "Two eighty-six."

Chiram said, "We'll go on. Dead ahead."

"Dead ahead," said Galt.

Chiram smiled grimly. "I hope not."

They passed the universe, and off into a new ocean of blackness. It was the old routine — except now there was a restless watchfulness aboard. Chiram watched the gyro as carefully as Jay; steadily the lubber-line ticked around, day after day after day. 290 — 300 — 310 — 320.

Galt spent his time on the bridge deck, watching ahead, hardly coming down to eat. No more chess—Julius played solitaire, slowly, with careful attention to each card.

330, and Chiram joined Galt's restless watch.

340. "We should be getting close," said Galt, staring into the bottomless blackness.

Chiram said, "We'll be there when we get there."

350. Galt bent forward, hands pressed to the chart table, head on a level with his elbows.

"It's light! Light!"

Chiram came to stare at the pale glow dead ahead.

"There it is." He cut off the acceleration; they plunged free at constant speed. For the first time since the start of the voyage the partner-ship Tuck appeared; they had almost forgotten its existence.

At 355 galaxies swept past like the first suburbs of a city.

At 357 they felt as if they were riding down familiar streets.

358. They looked here and there expectantly. There was quick movement of feet on the deck, the restless movement of heads. Chiram kept saying, "Too soon, too soon...There's a long way to go yet..."

359. Chiram had tacitly relaxed his orders to Jay, and all four stood on the bridge deck together pointing, looking, muttering.

360. "There! The big one! Golly, it looks almost like the face of someone you know!"

Dead ahead lay the great wheeling galaxy. It grew huge, its arms of glowing stars spread open to embrace the ship. Chiram relaxed the field. The striations of space gripped at their atoms, the ship slowed like a bullet shot into water.

They coasted into the outer lanes of stars, across the far-flung tendrils, past the globular clusters, across the central knot.

Ahead, like magic, the sky suddenly showed full of familiar patterns.

"Dead ahead!" cried Chiram. "See—that's the constellation Cygnus; that's where we started for...And there—dead ahead—that yellow star..."

The Enchanted Princess

James Aiken recognized the man at the reception desk as Victor Martinon, former producer at Pageant. Martinon had been fired during the recent retrenchment, and the headlines in *Variety* sent gooseflesh along every back in the industry. If flamboyant, money-making Martinon went, who was safe?

Aiken approached the desk, puzzled by Martinon's presence at the Krebius Children's Clinic. A versatile lover, Martinon never stayed married long enough to breed children. If Martinon were here on the same errand as his own — well, that was a different matter. Aiken felt a sharpening of interest.

"Hello, Martinon."

"Hi," said Martinon, neither knowing Aiken's identity nor caring.

"I worked on *Clair de Lune* with you — built the Dreamboat sequence."

Clair de Lune was Martinon's next to last picture.

"Oh, yes. Quite an effort. Still with Pageant?"

"I'm in my own lab now. Doing special effects for TV."

"A man's got to eat," said Martinon, implying that Aiken now could sink no further.

Aiken's mouth quivered, reflecting mingled emotions. "Keep me in mind, if you ever get back in pictures."

"Yeah. Sure will."

Aiken had never liked Martinon anyway. Martinon was big and broad, about forty, with silver hair pomaded and brushed till it glittered. His eyes were vaguely owlish — large, dark, surrounded by fine wrinkles; his mustache was cat-like; he wore excellent clothes. Aiken had no mustache; he was wiry and dark. He walked with a slight limp because of a Korean bullet, and so looked older than his twenty-five years. Martinon was suave and smelled of heather; Aiken was abrupt, angular and smelled of nothing much in particular.

Aiken spoke to the nurse behind the desk. "My sister has a little boy here. Bunny Tedrow."

"Oh, yes, Bunny. Nice little boy."

"She came to visit him yesterday, and told me about the film you were showing. I'd like to see it. If I may, of course."

The nurse looked sidewise at Martinon. "I don't really see any objection. I suppose you'd better speak to Dr. Krebius. Or if Mr. Martinon says it's all right —"

"Oh." Aiken looked at Martinon. "Some of your stuff?"

Martinon nodded. "In a way. The films are, well, experimental. I'm not sure we want anyone checking them just yet."

"Here's Dr. Krebius," said the nurse placidly, and Martinon frowned.

Dr. Krebius was stocky, red-faced, forthright. His hair was whiter than Martinon's and rose from his scalp like a whisk-broom. He wore a white smock, and gave off a faint odor of clean laundry and iodoform.

The nurse said, "This gentleman heard about the films; he wants to see them."

"Ah." Dr. Krebius looked at Aiken with eyes like little blue ball-bearings. "The little stories." He spoke in a heavy accent, gruff and deep in his throat. "You are who?"

"My name is James Aiken. My sister saw the films yesterday and told me about them."

"Ah ha," growled Krebius, turning to Martinon as if he would clap him on the back. "Maybe we charge admission, hey? Make money for the hospital!"

Martinon said in a measured voice, "Aiken here works in a film laboratory. His interest is professional."

"Sure! What of it? Let him look! He does no harm!"

Martinon shrugged, moved off down the hall.

Krebius turned back to Aiken. "We show not much. Just a few little stories to please the children." He glanced at his wristwatch. "In six minutes, at two o'clock precisely. That is the way we work here, precise on the second. That way we cure the sick little legs, the blind eyes."

"Oh," said Aiken. "Blind children too?"

"My specialty! You know of the Krebius Klinik in Leipzig?"

Aiken shook his head. "Sorry."

"For ten years we do tremendous work. Far ahead of what you do here. Why? There is more to do, we must be bold!" He tapped Aiken on the chest with a hard forefinger. "Two years ago I give up my wonderful hospital. There is no living with the Communists. They order me to make lenses, soldiers to see better down the guns. My work is to heal the eyes, not putting them out. I come here."

"I see your point," said Aiken. He hesitated. Martinon's attitude had given him the uncomfortable sense of interloping.

Krebius looked at him under bristly eyebrows.

"Incidentally," said Aiken, "as Martinon says, I'm in the special effects business. Part of my work is keeping up with what's going on."

"Of course. Why not? I have no interest in the film; it is not mine. Look as you please. Martinon is the cautious one. Fear is caution. I have no fear. I am cautious only with the tools of my work. Then!" He held up his blunt hands. "I am like a vise. The eye is a delicate organ!"

He bowed, walked off down the corridor. Aiken and the nurse watched him go. Aiken, grinning a little, looked at the nurse, who was grinning too.

"You should see him when he's excited. And then — well! I was raised on a farm. The old kitchen range used to get red hot. When water spilled on it..."

"I'm a farm boy myself," said Aiken.

"That's Dr. Krebius. You'd better go. He wasn't fooling. We work by the split-second around here. Right down the end of the hall, that's the ward for today's films."

Aiken walked down the corridor, pushed through the swinging door into a large room with curtained windows. Crippled children occupied beds along the walls, wheel-chairs down the center of the room. Aiken looked around for Bunny, but saw him nowhere. A table near the door supported a sixteen millimeter projector; on the far wall a screen hung. Martinon stood by the projector threading in the film. He nodded curtly at Aiken.

The clock on the wall read half a minute to two. Martinon flicked on the projector's lamp and motor, focussed the image. A nurse went to sit under the screen with a big red book.

The minute hand touched twelve.

Two P.M.

"Today," said the nurse, "we watch another chapter from the life of Ulysses. Last time, you'll remember, they were trapped by a terrible one-eyed giant called Polyphemus, on the island that we call Sicily today. Polyphemus is a horrible creature that's been eating up the Greeks." A delighted shudder and buzz ran around the room. "Today we find Ulysses and his men plotting an escape." She nodded. The lights went out. Martinon started the projector.

There was a chattering sound. The white rectangle on the screen quivered, shook. Martinon switched off the projector. The lights went on. Martinon bent over the projector with a worried frown. He banged it with his knuckles, shook it, tried the switch again. The same chatter. He looked up, shook his head despondently. "Don't think we're going to make it today."

"Aw," sighed the children.

Aiken went over to the projector. "What's the trouble?"

"It's been coming on a long time," said Martinon. "Something in the sprockets. I'll have to take it to the repairman."

"Let me take a look. I've got the same model; I know it inside out."

"Oh, don't bother," said Martinon, but Aiken was already investigating the mechanism. He opened a blade of his pocket knife, worked ten seconds. "She'll go now. The screw holding the sprocket to the drive gear was loose."

"Much obliged," muttered Martinon.

Aiken took his seat. Martinon caught the nurse's eye. She bent over the book, began to read aloud. The lights went out.

The Odyssey! Aiken was looking into a vast cave, dim-lit by firelight. Hoary walls rose to fade into high murk. Off to one side lay a great manlike hulk. At his back a dozen men worked feverishly, and in the vast smoky volume of the cavern they were miniatures, manikins. They held a great pointed pole into the flames, and the red firelight played and danced on their sweating bodies.

The camera drew closer. The features of the men became visible —

young, clean-limbed warriors moving with passionate determination, heroic despair. Ulysses stood forth, a man with a face of the Sistine Jehovah. He signalled. The warriors heaved the spear to their shoulders. Crouching under the weight, they ran forward against the face half-seen in the dimness.

It was a lax, idiotic face, with one eye in the middle of the forehead. The camera drew away showing the length of Polyphemus' body. The Greeks came running with the flaming pike; the eye snapped open, stared in wonder, and the pike bored into the center — deep, deep, deep.

Polyphemus jerked his head, the spear flung up, the Greeks scuttled into the shadows, disappeared. Polyphemus tore in agony at his face, wrenched loose the spear. He lunged around the cave, groping with one hand, clasping his bloody face with the other.

The camera went to the Greeks pressing back against the walls. The squat, bulging legs tramped past them. A great hand swept close, scraped, grabbed. The Greeks held their breaths, and the sweat gleamed on their chests.

Polyphemus stumbled away, into the fire; the logs scattered, embers flew. Polyphemus bellowed in frustration.

The camera shifted to the Greeks, tying themselves under monster sheep.

Polyphemus stood at the mouth of the cave. He pushed the great barrier rock aside and, straddling the opening, felt of the back of each sheep as it passed between his legs.

The Greeks ran down to the golden beach, launched their galley over the wine-dark sea. They hoisted the sail and the wind drove them off-shore.

Polyphemus came down to the beach. He picked up a boulder, flung it. Slow through the air it flew, slanting down toward the Greeks. It crashed into the sea, and the galley was tossed high on a fountain of water and bright white foam. Polyphemus stooped for another boulder. The scene faded.

"And that's all for today," said the nurse.

The children sighed in disappointment, began to chatter.

Martinon looked at Aiken with a peculiar sidelong grin. "What do you think?"

"Not bad," said Aiken. "Not bad at all. A little rough in spots. You could use better research. That wasn't any Greek galley — more like a Viking longboat."

Martinon nodded carelessly. "It's not my film; I'm on the outside looking in. But I agree with you. All brains and no technique, like a lot of this avant garde stuff."

"I don't recognize any of the actors. Who made it?"

"Merlin Studios."

"Never heard of them."

"They've just organized. One of my friends is involved. He asked me to show the film to some kids, get the reaction."

"They like it," said Aiken.

Martinon shrugged. "Kids are easy to please."

Aiken turned to go. "So long, and thanks."

"Don't mention it."

In the hall, Aiken met Dr. Krebius, standing with a pretty blonde girl of sixteen or seventeen. Krebius gave him a genial salute. "And the film, you liked it?"

"Very much," said Aiken. "But I'm puzzled."

"Ah ha," said Krebius with a foxy wink at the girl. "The little secrets that we must keep."

"Secrets?" she murmured. "What secrets?"

"I forget," said Krebius. "You know none of the secrets."

Aiken looked intently at the girl, glanced quickly at the doctor, and Krebius nodded. "This is little Carol Bannister. She's blind."

"That's too bad," said Aiken. Her eyes turned in his direction. They were a wide, deep Dutch blue, mild and tranquil. He saw that she might be a year or two older than he had first imagined.

Krebius stroked her silken-blonde head as he might pat a spaniel. "It's a pity when lovely young girls can't see to look and flirt and watch the boys' hearts go bumping. But with Carol — well, we work and we hope, and who knows? Someday she may see as well as you or I."

"I sure hope so," said Aiken.

"Thank you," the girl said softly, and Aiken took his leave.

In an unaccountably gloomy mood, he returned to his lab and found himself unable to work. For an hour he sat musing and smoking, then, on a sudden inspiration, called a friend, who was legman for a famous Hollywood columnist.

"Hello, Larry. This is Aiken."

"What's on the fire?"

"I want some dope on Merlin Studios. Got any?"

"Nothing. Never heard of 'em. What do they do?"

Aiken felt like dropping the whole thing. "Oh, they've made a few snatches of film. Fairy tales, things like that."

"Any good?"

Aiken thought back over the film, and his wonder revived. "Yeah," he said. "Very good. In fact — magnificent."

"You don't say. Merlin Studios?"

"Right. And I think — just think, mind you — that Victor Martinon is in on it."

"Martinon, eh? I'll ask Fidelia." Fidelia was Larry's boss. "She might know. If it's a tip, thanks."

"Not at all."

An hour later Larry called back. "I've learned three things. First, nobody in the trade knows anything about Merlin Studios. It's a vacuum. Second, Vic Martinon's been doing some fancy finagling, and he has been heard to use the words 'Merlin Studios'. Third, they're arranging a sneak preview tonight."

"Tonight? Where?"

"Garden City Theater, Pomona."

"Okay, Larry. Thanks."

Aiken watched five minutes of feature film, which was immediately followed by a slide reading:

Please do not leave the theater.
You are about to witness a
SNEAK PREVIEW
Your comments will be appreciated.

The slide dissolved into a title: a montage of colored letters on a silver-green background:

VASILLISSA
THE ENCHANTED PRINCESS.

*A fantasy based on an ancient
Russian fairy tale.*

THE MERLIN STUDIOS.

The silver-green background dissolved into orange; bold gray letters read: *Produced by Victor Martinon.*

There were no further credits. The orange dissolved into a blur of gray mist, with wandering hints of pink and green.

A voice spoke. "We go far away and long ago — to old Russia where once upon a time a young woodcutter named Ivan, returning from the woods, found a dove lying under a tree. The dove had a broken wing, and looked at Ivan so sorrowfully that he took pity on it..."

The mist broke open, into the world of fairyland, a landscape swimming in radiance, richness, color. It was real and it was unreal, a land everyone hoped for but knew never could be. There was a forest of antique trees, banks of ferns with the sun shining through the leaves, moist white flowers, beds of violets. The foliage was brown, gold, rust, lime and dark green, and down through the leaves came shafts of sunshine. Beyond the forest was a green meadow sprinkled with daisies, buttercups, cowslips, cornflowers, and far away down the valley the dark wooden gables of a village, the onion dome of a church could be seen.

The story proceeded, narrated by the voice. "Ivan nursed the dove back to health, and received a malachite casket for a reward. When he opened the casket a magnificent palace appeared on the meadow, surrounded by beautiful gardens, terraces of ivory, statues of jade and jet and cinnabar.

"The Czar of the Sea, riding past, saw the palace. Angry at Ivan's presumption he set Ivan impossible tasks — cutting down a forest overnight, building a flying ship, breaking an iron stallion to the saddle.

"The dove came to aid Ivan. She was Vasillissa, a beautiful maiden with long honey-blonde hair..."

The fable vaulted from miracle to miracle, through battles, sorcery, quests to the end of the earth, the final defeat of the Czar.

There was no sound from the audience. Every eye stared as if seeing the most precious part of their lives. The landscapes glowed with marvelous light: pink, blue, black, gold. The scenes were rich with imagery; real with the truth of poetry. The Czar, a great swarthy man, wore a scarlet robe and over this a black iron corselet embossed with jade. Chumichka, his steward, hopped around on malformed legs, glaring wildly from a pallid sidelong face.

The story swarmed with monsters and creatures of fable: griffins, hedge-hounds, fish with legs, fiery birds.

And Vasillissa! When Aiken saw Vasillissa, he muttered and stirred in his seat. Vasillissa was a beautiful golden-haired girl, swift as dandelion fluff, gay as any of the flowers. Vasillissa was as much a thing of magic as Ivan's wonderful palace. Like the fairy landscapes, she awakened a yearning that could never be satisfied. In one scene she came down to the river to catch a witch who had taken the form of a carp. The pool was like bottle-glass, shadowed by black-green poplars. Vasillissa stood silent, looking over the water. The carp jumped up in a flurry of silver spray; she turned her head so suddenly that the blonde hair swung out to the side.

"I must be completely mad," said Aiken to himself.

Vasillissa and Ivan finally escaped the raging Czar. "And they lived happily ever after, in the palace by the Dorogheny Woods," said the voice. And the picture ended.

Aiken drew a great breath. He joined the applause of the audience, rose to his feet, drove back to his apartment at breakneck pace.

For several hours he lay awake thinking. Magic Vasillissa! Today he had seen her as a blind girl, with silky blonde hair; slight, thoughtful, rather shy. Carol Bannister — Vasillissa. She was and she wasn't. Carol was blind. Vasillissa had bright blue eyes and could see very well indeed. What a strange situation, thought Aiken, and lay tossing and dozing and dreaming and thinking.

James Aiken was hardly a handsome man, although he had an indefinable flair, the concentration of character that equals color. His mouth drooped at a harsh saturnine angle; he was thin and angular; he walked with a limp. He smoked and drank a good deal; he had few friends, and made no great play for women. He was clever, imaginative, quick with his hands, and the Aiken Special Effects Laboratory was doing good business. He aroused no great loyalty from his employees. They thought him cynical and morose. But a cynic is a disappointed idealist; and James Aiken was as tender, wistful an idealist as could be found in all Los Angeles.

Vasillissa the Enchanted Princess!

He brooded about Carol Bannister. She had not acted Vasillissa, she *was* Vasillissa! And the magic longing rose in his throat like a sour taste, and he knew nothing else in life was as important.

At quarter of ten next morning he drove north on Arroyo Seco Boulevard, up winding Lomita Way to the Krebius Children's Clinic.

At the desk he gave his name, asked to speak to Dr. Krebius, and after a ten minute wait was ushered into an austere office.

Krebius rose to his feet, bowed stiffly. "Yes, Mr. Aiken." No longer the bluff and genial doctor of yesterday, he seemed stubborn and suspicious.

Aiken asked, "May I sit down?"

"Certainly." Krebius lowered himself into his own chair, erect as a post. "What do you wish?"

"I'd like to talk to you about Carol Bannister."

Krebius raised his eyebrows inquiringly, as if the choice of topic had surprised him. "Very well."

"Has she ever done any acting? In the movies?"

"Carol?" Krebius looked puzzled. "No. Never. I have known her many years. My sister is married to the cousin of her father. She has done no acting. Perhaps you are thinking of her mother. Marya Leone."

"Marya Leone? Carol's mother?"

Krebius indulged himself in a wintry smile. "Yes."

"I feel even sorrier for Carol." Marya Leone, a long-faded soubrette, was known along Sunset Strip as a confirmed and unregenerate alcoholic. A fragment of long-dead gossip rose into his mind. "One of her husbands killed himself."

"That was Carol's father. Four years ago. That very night Carol lost her vision. Her life has been clouded by great tragedy."

Krebius pushed himself back in his chair, his white eyebrows came lower down over his hard blue eyes.

Aiken said in a conciliatory voice, "Do you think there's a connection? Between the blindness and the suicide? Shock perhaps? Somewhere I've heard of things like that."

Krebius spread his hands in a non-committal gesture. "Who knows? They were high in the mountains, in a lodge that Marya Leone at that time still owned. Carol was fourteen. A thunderstorm came at night, bringing evil emotions. There was quarrelling. Howard Bannister shot himself, and in the next room a bolt of lightning struck through the window at little Carol. She has seen nothing since."

"Hysterical blindness. That's the word I was thinking of. Could she be suffering from that?"

Krebius made the same non-committal gesture. Aiken felt in him a lessening of suspicion and hostility. "Perhaps. But I think not. The optic nerve no longer functions correctly, although in many ways it reacts like perfectly healthy tissue. Carol is victim to a unique disability. The cause, who knows? Glare? Electricity? Shock? Terror? In the absence of precedent, I must strike out for myself. I attempt to stimulate the nerve; I have devised special equipment. I love her as my own child." Krebius leaned forward, pounded the desk for emphasis.

"What are her chances of seeing again?"

Krebius leaned back in his chair, looked away. "I do not know. I think she will see — sometime."

"Your treatments are helping her?"

"I believe and trust so."

"One more question, Doctor. How does Victor Martinon fit into the picture?"

Krebius became subtly uncomfortable. "He is her mother's friend. In fact —" His voice trailed off. "In fact it is said at one time —"

Aiken nodded. "I see. But why —"

Krebius interrupted him. "Victor is helping me. He is interested in therapy."

"Victor Martinon?" Aiken laughed in such sardonic disbelief that Krebius flushed. "I can easily see Martinon playing in a Salvation Army Band."

"Nevertheless," said Krebius, "he assists me in giving treatments."

"To Carol?"

"Yes. To Carol." Krebius was once again stubborn and hostile. His eyes glared, his white eyebrows bristled, his chin thrust out. In an icy voice he asked, "May I ask your interest in Carol?"

Aiken had been expecting the question, but had no easy answer ready. He fidgeted uncomfortably. "I'd rather not answer that question...You can think of it as a romantic interest."

Krebius' busy eyebrows rose in surprise. "Romance? Little Carol? A child yet!"

"Perhaps you don't know her as well as you think you do."

"Perhaps not," muttered Krebius deep in thought. "Perhaps not. The little ones grow up so fast."

"Incidentally," Aiken asked, "does Carol have any sisters? Or a cousin who looks like her?"

"No. Nothing. No one."

Aiken said no more. He rose to his feet. "I won't take up your time, Doctor. But I'd like to talk to Carol, if I may."

Krebius stared up truculently as if he might refuse, then shrugged and grunted. "I have no objections. She must not leave the hospital. She is in my care."

"Thank you." Aiken left the office, went to the reception desk. Martinon was just coming in through the main entrance. At the sight of Aiken his pace slackened.

"Hello, Aiken. What are you doing here?"

"I might ask the same of you."

"I have business here."

"So have I." Aiken turned to the nurse. "I'd like to speak to Carol Bannister. Dr. Krebius gave me permission."

"I'll ring for her. You can wait in the reception room."

"Thanks." Aiken nodded to Martinon, went into the reception room which opened off the lobby, across from Krebius' office.

Martinon looked after him, turned, walked into Krebius' office without knocking.

Time passed. Aiken sat on the edge of his chair, his hands moist. He was extremely nervous, and correspondingly annoyed at himself. Who would come through the door? Carol Bannister? Vasillissa? Was he confused, mistaken, making a fool of himself? The minutes passed, and Aiken could no longer sit still. He rose to his feet, moved around the room. Through the open door he saw Martinon come into the lobby followed by Dr. Krebius. Martinon was pale and glittering-eyed. Krebius looked surly. They marched up the corridor, neither speaking to the other, and disappeared into a room next to Krebius' office, with *Laboratory* painted on the door.

The corridor was now empty. Aiken went back to the couch, forced himself to sit quietly.

A nurse appeared in the doorway. "Mr. Aiken?" she asked briskly.

"Yes." He rose to his feet.

Carol came into the doorway, felt her way past the jamb. In her white blouse and gray flannel skirt she looked like a college freshman; her honey-colored hair was brushed till it shone. She seemed slighter and more fragile than Aiken had remembered, but of course his recollection was colored by the image of Vasillissa, agile, vital, reckless.

She looked uncertainly in Aiken's direction, with wide, blank, Delft-blue eyes.

"Hello," said Aiken in a voice that was not quite his own.

"Hello." She was puzzled.

Aiken took her arm, led her to the couch. The nurse nodded briefly at Aiken, disappeared. "My name is James Aiken. I spoke to you in the hall yesterday."

"Oh, yes. I remember now."

Aiken was studying her face. Was this Carol? Or Vasillissa? And if she were Vasillissa, how did Carol see? He made up his mind. It was definite. There was something in the poise of the head, the slant of the jaw that was unmistakable. This was Vasillissa. But she lived in a new country, in a new time, unable to use her magic. The dove with the broken wing.

She moved restlessly. Aiken hastily said, "I suppose you're wondering what I want."

She laughed. "I'm glad you came. I get lonesome."

"Dr. Krebius tells me you lost your sight in a lightning storm —"

Her face went instantly blank and cold. He had said the wrong thing.

"He says that it's very likely you'll see again."

"Yes."

"These treatments — do they do you any good?"

"You mean, the Opticon?"

"If that's what they call it."

"Well, up to three or four months ago I thought I saw the colors. You know, little flashes. But I don't see them any more."

"How long has Martinon been working with you?"

"Oh, about that long. He works differently from Doctor Krebius."

"How?"

"Oh," she shrugged. "He doesn't do very much. Except read to me."

Aiken was puzzled. "What good does that do?"

"I don't know. I guess it keeps me amused while the machine is turned on."

"Do you know that Martinon used to be a motion picture producer?"

"I know he used to work in the movies. He's never told me exactly what he did."

"How long have you known him?"

"Not very long. He says he used to know Mother. Mother was in the movies."

"Yes, I know. Marya Leone."

"She's quite a drunk now," Carol said in an even voice which might or might not conceal deep feeling. She turned her blank eyes toward him. "May I feel your face?"

"Certainly."

Her fingertips felt his hair, forehead, brushed over his eye sockets, nose, mouth, chin. She made no comment.

"Well?" said Aiken.

"Are you a detective or something like that?"

"I'm a frustrated artist."

"Oh. You're asking so many questions."

"Do you mind? I've got a lot more."

"No. If you'll answer some for me first."

"Go ahead. Ask."

She hesitated. "Well, why did you come to see me?"

Aiken smiled faintly. "I saw a movie last night, called *Vasillissa the Enchanted Princess.*"

"Oh? The fairy tale? I know that one very well. About Ivan and the wicked Czar of the Sea."

"In this movie Vasillissa was a very beautiful girl. She had long silken hair like yours. She had blue eyes like yours. In fact —" Aiken hesitated over the fateful phrase "— in fact, she was you."

"Me?"

"Yes. You. Carol Bannister."

Carol laughed. "You flatter me very much. I've never acted, not even in grammar school. Watching Mother emote killed any urge I had."

"But it *was* you."

"It couldn't be!" She was smiling, half-worried, half-amused.

"The film was produced by Victor Martinon; Martinon's been hanging around here. You live here. The coincidence is too great. There's something fishy going on."

Carol was silent. She was thinking. A queer look came over her face.

"Yesterday I saw another film," said Aiken. "Part of *The Odyssey*."

"*The Odyssey*...Victor read *The Odyssey* to me. Also *The Enchanted Princess*."

"This is very strange," said Aiken.

"Yes. And these last few days..." She was blushing, blushing pink scarlet.

"What's the matter?"

"He's been saying some rather awful things. Asking questions."

Aiken felt the skin at the back of his neck slowly going taut. Carol turned her head, as if she could actually see him, swiftly put her hand up, touched his face. "Why, you're angry!"

"Yes, I'm angry."

"But why?" She was puzzled.

The words spilled out of Aiken's mouth. "You may or may not understand. I saw this picture last night. I saw Vasillissa — this may seem very strange to you — but everything she did, every angle of her head, every motion of her head — they meant something to me. I sound like a high school boy, but I fell in love with Vasillissa. And I come here and see you."

"But I'm not Vasillissa," she said.

"Yes, you are. You're Vasillissa under a spell. Vasillissa frozen in a block of ice. I want to help you, to make you the free Vasillissa again."

Carol laughed. "You're Ivan."

"At heart," said Aiken, "I'm Ivan."

She reached up again, touched his face, and the touch had a different texture. It was less impersonal. "You don't feel like Ivan."

"I don't look like Ivan."

A figure loomed in the door. Carol dropped her hand, turned her head.

"Mr. Aiken," said Krebius, "I would much appreciate a word with you in my office."

Aiken slowly rose. "Just one minute, Doctor."

"Now, if you don't mind."

"Very well." Aiken turned to Carol, but she had stood up. She was holding his arm.

"Doctor," she said, "does what you want to talk about concern me?"

"Yes, my child."

"I'm not a child, Dr. Krebius. If it concerns me, I want to be with you."

He looked at her in bewilderment. "But Carol, this will be men's talk."

"If it concerns me, I want to know."

Aiken asked, "Are you planning to warn me off? If you are, you can save your breath."

"Come with me!" barked Krebius. He turned, stamped across the lobby to his office, flung the door open.

Aiken, with Carol holding to his arm, started to walk through; Krebius put out his arm to bar Carol. "To your room, child!"

"You'll talk to us both, Doctor," Aiken said in a low voice. "And you'll tell us both the truth, or I'll go to the Board of Health and demand an investigation! I'll charge you with malpractice."

Krebius' arm dropped like a wet sack. "You threaten me! I have nothing to hide! My reputation is of the utmost value!"

"Then why do you allow Martinon to use Carol as he has?"

Krebius became stern and stiff. "You speak of matters you know nothing of."

Carol said, "I know nothing about them either."

"Come in, then," said Krebius. "Both of you." He turned, stopped short, staring at his desk. Four glossy 8 × 10 photographs were lying face up. Krebius stumped hastily across the room, snatched the photographs, tried to stuff them under the blotter. His hands were shaking; one photograph fell to the floor. Aiken inspected it quizzically, lit a cigarette. Krebius grabbed up the photograph, furiously pushed it under the blotter with the others.

"It's not true," he said hoarsely. "It's a fraud! A fake!" He jumped to his feet, banged his fist on the desk. "It's nonsense of the worst sort!"

"Okay," said Aiken. "I believe you."

Krebius sat down, breathing heavily.

"Tell me," said Aiken, "is Martinon blackmailing you with these pictures?"

Krebius looked at him dully.

"They're nothing to worry about. If he showed them to anybody, he'd get in worse trouble than you would."

Krebius shook his head. "I want you to leave this hospital, Mr. Aiken," he croaked. "Never come back."

"Doctor, tell us the truth. How did Martinon make those pictures? Somehow, he's been photographing Carol's thoughts."

"My thoughts?" Carol drew a deep breath. *"Photographing my thoughts?"* She considered a minute or two. "Oh, golly!" She hid her face in her hands.

Krebius was leaning forward on his desk, hands clenched in his hair. "Yes," he muttered. "May God forgive me."

"But, Doctor!" cried Carol.

Krebius waved his hand. "I found it out when I first tried the Opticon. I noticed images, very faint. I was amazed."

" 'Amazed' is no word for the way I feel," said Carol.

"I built this machine for you alone. You had a unique handicap — all the equipment for sight, but no vision. The Opticon was to stimulate the optic nerve. I could fire bursts of colored light into your retina, observe results through a microscope. I was astonished to find images on your retina."

"But why didn't you tell me?" Carol demanded.

"You would become self-conscious. Your thoughts would not flow freely. And it was only in you, one person in all the world, in whom I could see these marvels." Dr. Krebius sat back in his chair. "We knew vision always as going one way. Light strikes the retina, the rods and cones send little electric messages to the visual center. In Carol the one way is cut off. But in her there is this reversible process. The energy comes down the optic nerve from the brain, it forms an image on the retina.

"I took some photographs. They were scientific curiosities. I went to your mother's house to ask for money. She pays me nothing. I am not wealthy. I met Victor, and we drank whiskey." Krebius narrowed his eyes. "I showed him the photographs. He wanted to experiment. I saw no great harm. There might be money for all of us. For you, Carol, for you most of all. I said yes, but the treatments must continue; no compromise with the cure!"

"But actually you don't know what Victor's been doing?"

"No. I thought there was no need."

"He hasn't been giving any treatments."

Krebius sat silently.

"He doesn't want Carol to see," said Aiken. "She's a gold mine for Victor."

"Yes, yes. I see this now."

"Also, she gave him a club over you." Aiken turned to Carol. "Did Victor ever ask you about Doctor Krebius?"

Carol's face was pink with embarrassment. "He asked some awful questions. I couldn't help but think about what he was saying."

"Carol has a strong visual imagination," said Krebius mournfully. "It's not her fault. But these pictures…"

"They'd never stand up in court."

"No, but my reputation!"

Aiken said nothing.

Krebius muttered, "I've been a fool, a wicked fool. How may I expiate my weakness?" He rose, lurched over to Carol. "My dear girl," he faltered. "I will cure you. You will see again. You have a good retina, you have a healthy optic nerve. Stimulation! We will make you see!" And he said humbly, "If only you will forgive me!"

Carol said something in a muffled voice. Her face was pinched, constricted. She seemed dazed.

Aiken said, "I'd like to call in somebody else for consultation. Doctor Barnett."

"No," said Krebius. "I have forgotten more about eyes than any man in California knows."

"But do you know anything about the brain?"

Krebius was silent for a moment. Then, "You are obsessed with psychology. Today all is psychology — miracles. And good old-fashioned surgery goes out the window."

"But certainly you've seen cases of hysterical blindness," Aiken protested.

Carol said faintly, "I'm not hysterical. I'm just mad."

"In the front lines," said Aiken, "when something terrible happens, sometimes men can't walk, or hear, or see. I've seen it happen."

"I know all this," said Krebius. "In Leipzig I have treated several such cases. Well, we will try." He took a deep breath, took Carol's hands. "My dear, do you agree to an experiment? It might be unpleasant."

"What for?" she asked in a low voice.

"To help you to see!"

"What will you do?"

"First, a little injection to quiet the brain. To make it easy for you to talk."

"But I don't want to talk," she said in a stony voice.

"Even if it will help you see?"

For a moment a refusal seemed to be on her lips, but she bit it back and said, "Very well. If you think it will help me."

"Hello!" said Victor Martinon from the doorway. He looked from Krebius to Aiken to Carol, and back to Aiken. "You still here, Aiken? Must be wonderful to have time to waste. Let's go, Carol. Time for exercises."

"Not today, Victor," said Krebius.

Martinon raised his handsome eyebrows. "Why not?"

"Today," said Krebius, "we try something different."

"Oh, so?" said Martinon in a tone of mild wonder.

"Come, Carol," said Krebius. "To the Opticon. We will try to photograph the beast that rides your brain."

Carol rose stiffly, walked through the door. Aiken followed. Out in the hall Martinon said, "I'm sorry, Aiken, but I don't think Doctor Krebius wants strangers watching his treatments. Do you, Doctor?"

Krebius said stiffly, "Aiken comes if he likes."

Martinon shrugged. "Just as you like. I won't answer to Carol's mother for the consequences."

Carol said, "Since when has Mother cared two cents one way or the other?"

"She's very fond of you, Carol," Martinon said patiently. "And she's a sick woman."

Carol's face took on a bleak look. "Probably only a hangover."

Aiken said conversationally, "I didn't know you were still thick with Marya Leone."

"I've known her for years," Martinon said with simple dignity. "I gave her her last part — in *They Didn't Know Beans*."

Krebius pushed open the laboratory door. Carol went in, walked directly to a heavy black ophthalmologist's chair, seated herself. Krebius unlocked a cabinet, rolled out a heavy device with two long binocular eye-pieces. "Just one moment," said Krebius, and left the room.

Martinon seated himself in a chair at the far wall, crossed his legs with an expression of patient boredom. "Everybody figures me for a cad, I see."

Aiken said, "I can't speak for anybody else. As for myself —"

Martinon made a careless gesture with his cigarette. "Don't bother. The trouble is, you don't see what I'm trying to accomplish."

"Money?"

Martinon nodded slowly. "Money, of course. But also a new way of making pictures. Somebody's got to start. There's a whole new industry ready to spring to life."

Martinon fell silent.

Aiken patted Carol's hand. "You look scared."

"I am scared. What's going to happen?"

"Nothing very much."

"Do you think I'm crazy? And that's why I can't see?"

"No. But there may be something in your mind that doesn't want to see."

"But I do want to see! If I want to see, why can't I? It doesn't make sense!"

"Theories come and theories go," said Martinon in a tired voice.

After a moment Carol said, "I'm afraid of that Opticon. I'm afraid to think."

Aiken glanced at Martinon, who met his eyes blandly. "I imagine you would be."

"You lack the scientific outlook," said Martinon.

"You lack something too," said Aiken.

Krebius came in with a loaded hypodermic.

"What's that?" Aiken asked.

"Scopolamine."

"The truth drug," said Martinon.

Krebius ignored him. He swabbed Carol's arm with alcohol. "Now, Carol. A little prick. And pretty soon you'll relax."

Half an hour passed in dead silence. Carol lay with her head back, a small pulse showing in her throat.

Krebius leaned forward. "How do you feel, Carol?"

"Fine," she said in a leaden voice.

"Good," said Krebius briskly. "Now, we make our arrangements." He laid her arms in her lap, clamped her head gently between two foam-rubber blocks, wheeled the Opticon close, adjusted it so that the binoculars pressed against her eyes. "There. How does that feel?"

"All right."

"Can you see anything?"

"No."

"Do you want to see?"

There was a pause, as if Carol were groping for several different answers. "Yes. I want to see."

"Is there any reason why you can't see?"

Another pause, longer. "I think there's a face I don't want to see."

"Whose face?"

"I don't know his name."

"Now, Carol," said Dr. Krebius, "let's go back five years. Where were you?"

"I was living in Beverly Hills with Mother. I was going to junior high school."

"You could see?"

"Oh yes."

Krebius pressed a switch; the Opticon began to hum and click. Aiken recognized the sound of film winding past a shutter. Krebius reached to the wall, turned out the lights. A faint neon night-light glowed ruby-red beside Martinon. The room was nearly pitch dark.

Krebius said gently, "Do you remember when you went to the lodge by Holly Lake, up in the Sierras?"

Carol hesitated. "Yes. I remember." She seemed to go gradually rigid. Even in the dark Aiken could sense her hands tightening on the arms.

"Don't be frightened, Carol," said Krebius. "No one will hurt you. Tell us what happened?"

"I don't remember very well."

"What happened, Carol?"

Tension began to build up. Everyone in the room felt it. Krebius' voice was sharper; Martinon had stopped smiling.

Carol spoke in a low voice. "Mother was desperate. Her last picture was a flop. The studios wouldn't take up her option... She was drinking."

"What happened the night of the thunderstorm?"

A pause of five seconds. The chair creaked where Martinon leaned forward.

Carol's voice was a husky whisper. "Mother had a friend visiting her. Her lover. I never knew his name. They were in the kitchen mixing drinks and laughing... My father drove up... I loved my father; I wanted to stay with him, but the court gave me to Mother... Outside it was thundering. The wind howled — first loud, then it died altogether. And the clouds came in very low, thick and wet. You could feel them pressing down."

Martinon said, "You're scaring the poor kid to death!"

"Shut up!" Aiken said softly.

"Go on," said Krebius. "Go on, Carol. Tell us. Get it off your chest. Then you can see. Once you look the truth in the face."

Carol's voice began to rise. "Daddy walked in. I talked with him, told him what I had seen. He was very angry. Mother came out laughing, staggering. Daddy said he was going to take me away, that Mother wasn't fit to keep me. Then he saw Mother's lover." Carol was wailing now, in grief and terror. "Outside was lightning. And the lights went out." She screamed. "He shot Daddy. I saw him during the lightning flashes. And then — there was the most terrible sound. The whole world exploded…" Her voice rasped, she panted. "And the flash of lightning — right in my eyes…"

Was it Aiken's imagination? Or did he see white light flicker from Carol's eyes? Carol had sagged. She was inert.

Krebius rose to his feet. "Phew!" he muttered, "that is awful. All this time she carries knowledge deep in her little head — her father murdered before her eyes!"

"And goes blind, so she won't have to look at her mother's face," said Aiken.

Martinon said, "Aren't you jumping to conclusions? Maybe the lightning made her blind. Maybe she'll always be blind."

"We'll soon find out," said Aiken. He felt Carol's forehead; it was hot and damp with sweat; the hair clung to his fingers.

Krebius turned the lights on dim.

Martinon went over to the Opticon. "In any event, it's an interesting session. I'll develop this film; I'd like to see what's on it."

"No," said Aiken suddenly. "You keep away from those films."

"Why should I?" Martinon asked. "They're films which I've provided for this machine. My films!"

"They're evidence," said Aiken. "Bannister never killed himself. You heard what Carol said. He was murdered. The man's face is on that film."

"Yes," said Krebius, "I'd better take charge of the film, Victor."

"I hate to insist," said Martinon. "But they're my films. You can see them whenever they're developed." He busied himself at the Opticon.

Aiken came forward. "I also hate to insist, Martinon. But I want these films. I'm anxious to see who that lover was."

"Keep your distance," said Martinon levelly.

Aiken pushed him away from the Opticon. The film came with Martinon; the roll clattered to the floor, unwound in lazy coils.

Martinon said, "Now you'll never see the man's face!"

Aiken could no longer bear Martinon's look of complacent self-possession. He aimed a punch at the neat gray mustache. Martinon blocked it expertly, struck back, set Aiken sprawling among the coils of film.

"Gentlemen, gentlemen!" cried Krebius. "We must act like gentlemen!"

Aiken rose to his knees, crouched, butted Martinon, who staggered across the room, flung his arms out against the wall to catch himself. At this moment Carol's eyes opened, and Victor was right in front of her.

She stared into Martinon's face and screamed, a hoarse, cracked cry of fear. She struggled to escape from the chair, but the rubber blocks held her head in place. She was pointing at Martinon.

"I know you. I know your face! You shot my father!"

"Well," said Martinon, "this is a pretty pickle. I've got a nasty job here." He reached into his pocket and came out with a pocket-knife. He gave it a switch, the blade snapped out. He strode toward Carol.

"Martinon!" cried Aiken. "You're crazy!" He pushed the Opticon; it toppled into Martinon, crashed over on top of him. Aiken stepped on his wrist; the knife clattered over the floor. Aiken grabbed the knot of Martinon's tie, twisted, ground his knuckles into the jugular, banged Martinon's head on the floor.

Presently Martinon lay still. Aiken released him. "Call the cops." He got to his feet. Martinon rolled over, groaned, lay limp.

Krebius ran out into the hall. Aiken turned, looked at Carol. She was crouched, her legs drawn up on the chair, her eyes wide.

Aiken said, "Hello, Carol. You can see, can't you?"

"Yes. I can see."

"Do you know me?"

"Of course, you're James Aiken."

"Lots of excitement for a while."

"Who's that?" she whispered, looking at the man on the floor. "Is it — Victor?"

"Yes."

"All this time he's worked on me…" Her lids fell shut. "I'm so sleepy and tired…"

"Don't go to sleep yet."

"I won't…"

A squad car squealed to a stop outside the door, and Victor Martinon was taken away.

In Krebius' office Carol drank black coffee. "Now I don't want to go to sleep. I'm afraid I might wake up blind."

"No," said Aiken. "You never will again. Because the spell is broken. Vasillissa is free again."

"Magic!" said Carol. She looked at him smiling. And she was the real Vasillissa, as gay and clever and daring as ever had been the enchanted princess. She reached out, took his hand.

"Magic," said Aiken. "Magic."

THE POTTERS OF FIRSK

THE YELLOW BOWL on Thomm's desk stood about a foot high, flaring out from a width of eight inches at the base to a foot across the rim. The profile showed a simple curve, clean and sharp, with a full sense of completion; the body was thin without fragility; the whole piece gave an impression of ringing well-arched strength.

The craftsmanship of the body was matched by the beauty of the glaze — a glorious transparent yellow, luminescent like a hot summer afterglow. It was the essence of marigolds, a watery wavering saffron, a yellow as of transparent gold, a yellow glass that seemed to fabricate curtains of light within itself and fling them off, a yellow brilliant but mild, tart as lemon, sweet as quince jelly, soothing as sunlight.

Keselsky had been furtively eying the bowl during his interview with Thomm, personnel chief for the Department of Planetary Affairs. Now, with the interview over, he could not help but bend forward to examine the bowl more closely. He said with obvious sincerity: "This is the most beautiful piece I've ever seen."

Thomm, a man of early middle-age with a brisk gray mustache, a sharp but tolerant eye, leaned back in his chair. "It's a souvenir. Souvenir's as good a name for it as anything else. I got it many years ago, when I was your age." He glanced at his desk clock. "Lunch-time."

Keselsky looked up, hastily reached for his brief case. "Excuse me, I had no idea —"

Thomm raised his hand. "Not so fast. I'd like you to have lunch with me."

Keselsky muttered embarrassed excuses, but Thomm insisted.

"Sit down, by all means." A menu appeared on the screen. "Now — look that over."

Without further urging Keselsky made a selection, and Thomm spoke into the mesh. The wall opened, a table slid out with their lunch.

Even while eating Keselsky fondled the bowl with his eyes. Over coffee, Thomm handed it across the table. Keselsky hefted it, stroked the surface, looked deep into the glaze.

"Where on earth did you find such a marvelous piece?" He examined the bottom, frowned at the marks scratched in the clay.

"Not on Earth," said Thomm. "On the planet Firsk." He sat back. "There's a story connected with that bowl." He paused inquiringly.

Keselsky hurriedly swore that nothing could please him more than to listen while Thomm spoke of all things under the sun. Thomm smiled faintly. After all, this was Keselsky's first job.

"As I've mentioned, I was about your age," said Thomm. "Perhaps a year or two older, but then I'd been out on the Channel Planet for nineteen months. When my transfer to Firsk came I was naturally very pleased, because Channel, as perhaps you know, is a bleak planet, full of ice and frost-fleas and the dullest aborigines in space —"

Thomm was entranced with Firsk. It was everything the Channel Planet had not been: warm, fragrant, the home of the Mi-Tuun, a graceful people of a rich, quaint and ancient culture. Firsk was by no means a large planet, though its gravity approached that of Earth. The land surface was small — a single equatorial continent in the shape of a dumbbell.

The Planetary Affairs Bureau was located at Penolpan, a few miles in from the South Sea, a city of fable and charm. The tinkle of music was always to be heard somewhere in the distance; the air was mellow with incense and a thousand flower scents. The low houses of reed, parchment and dark wood were arranged negligently, three-quarters hidden under the foliage of trees and vines. Canals of green water laced the city, arched over by wooden bridges trailing ivy and orange flowers, and here swam boats each decorated in an intricate many-colored pattern.

The inhabitants of Penolpan, the amber-skinned Mi-Tuun, were a mild people devoted to the pleasures of life, sensuous without excess, relaxed and gay, guiding their lives by ritual. They fished in the South Sea, cultivated cereals and fruit, manufactured articles of wood, resin and paper. Metal was scarce on Firsk, and was replaced in many instances by tools and utensils of earthenware, fabricated so cleverly that the lack was never felt.

Thomm found his work at the Penolpan Bureau pleasant in the extreme, marred only by the personality of his superior. This was George Covill, a short ruddy man with prominent blue eyes, heavy wrinkled eyelids, sparse sandy hair. He had a habit, when he was displeased — which was often — of cocking his head sidewise and staring for a brittle five seconds. Then, if the offense was great, he exploded in wrath; if not, he stalked away.

On Penolpan Covill's duties were more of a technical than sociological nature, and even so, in line with the Bureau's policy of leaving well-balanced cultures undisturbed, there was little to occupy him. He imported silica yarn to replace the root fiber from which the Mi-Tuun wove their nets; he built a small cracking plant and converted the fish oil they burned in their lamps into a lighter cleaner fluid. The varnished paper of Penolpan's houses had a tendency to absorb moisture and split after a few months of service. Covill brought in a plastic varnish which protected them indefinitely. Aside from these minor innovations Covill did little. The Bureau's policy was to improve the native standard of living within the framework of its own culture, introducing Earth methods, ideas, philosophy very gradually and only when the natives themselves felt the need.

Before long, however, Thomm came to feel that Covill paid only lip-service to the Bureau philosophy. Some of his actions seemed dense and arbitrary to the well-indoctrinated Thomm. He built an Earth-style office on Penolpan's main canal, and the concrete and glass made an inexcusable jar against Penolpan's mellow ivories and browns. He kept strict office hours and on a dozen occasions a delegation of Mi-Tuun, arriving in ceremonial regalia, had to be turned away with stammered excuses by Thomm, when in truth Covill, disliking the crispness of his linen suit, had stripped to the waist and was slumped in a wicker chair with a cigar, a quart of beer, watching girl-shows on his telescreen.

✳

Thomm was assigned to Pest Control, a duty Covill considered beneath his dignity. On one of his rounds Thomm first heard mentioned the Potters of Firsk.

Laden with insect spray, with rat-poison cartridges dangling from his belt, he had wandered into the poorest outskirts of Penolpan, where the trees ended and the dry plain stretched out to the Kukmank Mountains. In this relatively drab location he came upon a long open shed, a pottery bazaar. Shelves and tables held ware of every description, from stoneware crocks for pickling fish to tiny vases thin as paper, lucent as milk. Here were plates large and small, bowls of every size and shape, no two alike, ewers, tureens, demijohns, tankards. One rack held earthenware knives, the clay vitrified till it rang like iron, the cutting edge chipped cleanly, sharper than any razor, from a thick dripping of glaze.

Thomm was astounded by the colors. Rare rich ruby, the green of flowing river water, turquoise ten times deeper than the sky. He saw metallic purples, browns shot with blond light, pinks, violets, grays, dappled russets, blues of copper and cobalt, the odd streaks and flows of rutilated glass. Certain glazes bloomed with crystals like snowflakes, others held floating within them tiny spangles of metal.

Thomm was delighted with his find. Here was beauty of form, of material, of craftsmanship. The sound body, sturdy with natural earthy strength given to wood and clay, the melts of colored glass, the quick restless curves of the vases, the capacity of the bowls, the expanse of the plates — they produced a tremendous enthusiasm in Thomm. And yet — there were puzzling aspects to the bazaar. First — he looked up and down the shelves — something was lacking. In the many-colored display he missed — yellow. There were no yellow glazes of any sort. A cream, a straw, an amber — but no full-bodied glowing yellow.

Perhaps the potters avoided the color through superstition, Thomm speculated, or perhaps because of identification with royalty, like the ancient Chinese of Earth, or perhaps because of association with death or disease — The train of thought led to the second puzzle: Who were the potters? There were no kilns in Penolpan to fire ware such as this.

He approached the clerk, a girl just short of maturity, who had been given an exquisite loveliness. She wore the *pareu* of the Mi-Tuun, a flowered sash about the waist, and reed sandals. Her skin glowed like one of the amber glazes at her back; she was slender, quiet, friendly.

"This is all very beautiful," said Thomm. "For instance, what is the price of this?" He touched a tall flagon glazed a light green, streaked and shot with silver threads.

The price she mentioned, in spite of the beauty of the piece, was higher than what he had expected. Observing his surprise, the girl said, "They are our ancestors, and to sell them as cheaply as wood or glass would be irreverent."

Thomm raised his eyebrows, and decided to ignore what he considered a ceremonial personification.

"Where's the pottery made?" he asked. "In Penolpan?"

The girl hesitated and Thomm felt a sudden shade of restraint. She turned her head, looked out toward the Kukmank Range. "Back in the hills are the kilns; out there our ancestors go, and the pots are brought back. Aside from this I know nothing."

Thomm said carefully, "Do you prefer not to talk of it?"

She shrugged. "Indeed, there's no reason why I should. Except that we Mi-Tuun fear the Potters, and the thought of them oppresses us."

"But why is that?"

She grimaced. "No one knows what lies beyond the first hill. Sometimes we see the glow of furnaces, and then sometimes when there are no dead for the Potters they take the living."

Thomm thought that if so, here was a case for the interference of the Bureau, even to the extent of armed force.

"Who are these Potters?"

"There," she said, and pointed. "There is a Potter."

Following her finger, he saw a man riding out along the plain. He was taller, heavier than the Mi-Tuun. Thomm could not see him distinctly, wrapped as he was in a long gray burnoose, but he appeared to have a pale skin and reddish-brown hair. He noted the bulging panniers on the pack-beast. "What's he taking with him now?"

"Fish, paper, cloth, oil — goods he traded his pottery for."

Thomm picked up his pest-killing equipment. "I think I'll visit the Potters one of these days."

"No —" said the girl.

"Why not?"

"It's very dangerous. They're fierce, secretive —"

Thomm smiled. "I'll be careful."

Back at the Bureau he found Covill stretched out on a wicker chaise lounge, half-asleep. At the sight of Thomm he roused himself, sat up.

"Where the devil have you been? I told you to get the estimates on that power plant ready today."

"I put them on your desk," replied Thomm politely. "If you've been out front at all, you couldn't have missed them."

Covill eyed him belligerently, but for once found himself at a loss for words. He subsided in his chair with a grunt. As a general rule Thomm paid little heed to Covill's sharpness, recognizing it as resentment against the main office. Covill felt his abilities deserved greater scope, a more important post.

Thomm sat down, helped himself to a glass of Covill's beer. "Do you know anything about the potteries back in the mountains?"

Covill grunted: "A tribe of bandits, something of the sort." He hunched forward, reached for the beer.

"I looked into the pottery bazaar today," said Thomm. "A clerk called the pots 'ancestors'. Seemed rather strange."

"The longer you knock around the planets," Covill stated, "the stranger things you see. Nothing could surprise me any more — except maybe a transfer to the Main Office." He snorted bitterly, gulped at his beer. Refreshed, he went on in a less truculent voice, "I've heard odds and ends about these Potters, nothing definite, and I've never had time to look into 'em. I suppose it's religious ceremonial, rites of death. They take away the dead bodies, bury 'em for a fee or trade goods."

"The clerk said that when they don't get the dead, sometimes they take the living."

"Eh? What's that?" Covill's hard blue eyes stared bright from his red face. Thomm repeated his statement.

Covill scratched his chin, presently hoisted himself to his feet. "Let's fly out, just for the devilment of it, and see what these Potters are up to. Been wanting to go out a long time."

Thomm brought the copter out of the hangar, set down in front of the office, and Covill gingerly climbed in. Covill's sudden energy mystified Thomm, especially since it included a ride in the copter. Covill had an intense dislike of flying, and usually refused to set foot in an aircraft.

The blades sang, grabbed the air, the copter wafted high. Penolpan became a checkerboard of brown roofs and foliage. Thirty miles distant, across a dry sandy plain, rose the Kukmank Range — barren shoulders and thrusts of gray rock. At first sight locating a settlement among the tumble appeared a task of futility.

Covill peering down into the wastes grumbled something to this effect; Thomm, however, pointed toward a column of smoke. "Potters need kilns. Kilns need heat —"

As they approached the smoke, they saw that it issued not from brick stacks but from a fissure at the peak of a conical dome.

"Volcano," said Covill, with an air of vindication. "Let's try out there along that ridge — then if there's nothing we'll go back."

Thomm had been peering intently below. "I think we've found them right here. Look close, you can see buildings."

He dropped the copter, and the rows of stone houses became plain.

"Should we land?" Thomm asked dubiously. "They're supposed to be fairly rough."

"Certainly, set down," snapped Covill. "We're official representatives of the System."

The fact might mean little to a tribe of mountaineers, reflected Thomm; nevertheless he let the copter drop onto a stony flat place in the center of the village.

The copter, if it had not alarmed the Potters, at least had made them cautious. For several minutes there was no sign of life. The stone cabins stood bleak and vacant as cairns.

Covill alighted, and Thomm, assuring himself that his gamma-gun was in easy reach, followed. Covill stood by the copter, looking up and down the line of houses. "Cagey set of beggars," he growled. "Well… we better stay here till someone makes a move."

To this plan Thomm agreed heartily, so they waited in the shadow of the copter. It was clearly the village of the Potters. Shards lay everywhere — brilliant bits of glazed ware glinting like lost jewels.

Down the slope rose a heap of broken bisque, evidently meant for later use, and beyond was a long tile-roofed shed. Thomm sought in vain for a kiln. A fissure into the side of the mountain caught his eye, a fissure with a well-worn path leading into it. An intriguing hypothesis formed in his mind — but now three men had appeared, tall and erect in gray burnooses. The hoods were flung back, and they looked like monks of medieval Earth, except that instead of monkish tonsure, fuzzy red hair rose in a peaked mound above their heads.

The leader approached with a determined step, and Thomm stiffened, prepared for anything. Not so Covill; he appeared contemptuously at ease, a lord among serfs.

Ten feet away the leader halted — a man taller than Thomm with a hook nose, hard intelligent eyes like gray pebbles. He waited an instant but Covill only watched him. At last the Potter spoke in a courteous tone.

"What brings strangers to the village of the Potters?"

"I'm Covill, of the Planetary Affairs Bureau in Penolpan, official representative of the System. This is merely a routine visit, to see how things are going with you."

"We make no complaints," replied the chief.

"I've heard reports of you Potters kidnaping Mi-Tuun," said Covill. "Is there any truth in that?"

"Kidnaping?" mused the chief. "What is that?"

Covill explained. The chief rubbed his chin, staring at Covill with eyes black as water.

"There is an ancient agreement," said the chief at last. "The Potters are granted the bodies of the dead; and occasionally when the need is great, we do anticipate nature by a year or two. But what matter? The soul lives forever in the pot it beautifies."

Covill brought out his pipe, and Thomm held his breath. Loading the pipe was sometimes a preliminary to the cold sidelong stares which occasionally ended in an explosion of wrath. For the moment however Covill held himself in check.

"Just what do you do with the corpses?"

The leader raised his eyebrows in surprise. "Is it not obvious? No? But then you are no potter — Our glazes require lead, sand, clay, alkali, spar and lime. All but the lime is at our hand, and this we extract from the bones of the dead."

Covill lit his pipe, puffed. Thomm relaxed. For the moment the danger was past.

"I see," said Covill. "Well, we don't want to interfere in any native customs, rites or practices, so long as the peace isn't disturbed. You'll have to understand there can't be any more kidnaping. The corpses — that's between you and whoever's responsible for the body, but lives are more important than pots. If you need lime, I can get you tons of it. There must be limestone beds somewhere on the planet. One of these days I'll send Thomm out prospecting and you'll have more lime than you'll know what to do with."

The chief shook his head, half amused. "Natural lime is a poor substitute for the fresh live lime of bones. There are certain other salts which act as fluxes, and then, of course, the spirit of the person is in the bones and this passes into the glaze and gives it an inner fire otherwise unobtainable."

Covill puffed, puffed, puffed, watching the chief with his hard blue eyes. "I don't care what you use," he said, "as long as there's no kidnaping, no murder. If you need lime, I'll help you find it; that's what I'm here for, to help you, and raise your standard of living; but I'm also here to protect the Mi-Tuun from raiding. I can do both — one about as good as the other."

The corners of the chief's mouth drew back. Thomm interposed a question before he spat out an angry reply. "Tell me, where are your kilns?"

The chief turned him a cool glance. "Our firing is done by the Great Monthly Burn. We stack our ware in the caves, and then, on the twenty-second day, the scorch rises from below. One entire day the heat roars up white and glowing, and two weeks later the caves have cooled for us to go after our ware."

"That sounds interesting," said Covill. "I'd like to look around your works. Where's your pottery, down there in that shed?"

The chief moved not a muscle. "No man may look inside that shed," he said slowly, "unless he is a Potter — and then only after he has proved his mastery of the clay."

"How does he go about that?" Covill asked lightly.

"At the age of fourteen he goes forth from his home with a hammer, a mortar, a pound of bone lime. He must mine clay, lead, sand, spar. He must find iron for brown, malachite for green, cobalt earth for blue, and he must grind a glaze in his mortar, shape and decorate a tile, and set it in the Mouth of the Great Burn. If the tile is successful, the body whole, the glaze good, then he is permitted to enter the long pottery and know the secrets of the craft."

Covill pulled the pipe from his mouth, asked quizzically, "And if the tile's no good?"

"We need no poor Potters," said the chief. "We always need bone-lime."

Thomm had been glancing along the shards of colored pottery. "Why don't you use yellow glaze?"

The chief flung out his arms. "Yellow glaze? It is unknown, a secret no Potter has penetrated. Iron gives a dingy tan, silver a gray-yellow, and antimony burns out in the heat of the Great Burn. The pure rich yellow, the color of the sun…ah, that is a dream."

Covill was uninterested. "Well, we'll be flying back, since you don't care to show us around. Remember, if there's any technical help you want, I can get it for you. I might even find how to make you your precious yellow —"

"Impossible," said the chief. "Have not we, the Potters of the Universe, sought for thousands of years?"

"…But there must be no more taking of lives. If necessary, I'll put a stop to the potting altogether."

The chief's eyes blazed. "Your words are not friendly!"

"If you don't think I can do it, you're mistaken," said Covill. "I'll drop a bomb down the throat of your volcano and cave in the entire mountain. The System protects every man-jack everywhere, and that means the Mi-Tuun from a tribe of Potters who wants their bones."

Thomm plucked him nervously by the sleeve. "Get back in the copter," he whispered. "They're getting ugly. In another minute they'll jump us."

Covill turned his back on the lowering chief, deliberately climbed into the copter. Thomm followed more warily. In his eyes the chief was teetering on the verge of attack, and Thomm had no inclination for fighting.

He flung in the clutch; the blades chewed at the air; the copter rose, leaving a knot of gray-burnoosed Potters silent below.

Covill settled back with an air of satisfaction. "There's only one way to handle people like that, and that is, get the upper hand on 'em; that's the only way they'll respect you. You act just a little uncertain, they sense it, sure as fate, and then you're a goner."

Thomm said nothing. Covill's methods might produce immediate results, but in the long run they seemed short-sighted, intolerant, unsympathetic. In Covill's place he would have stressed the Bureau's ability to provide substitutes for the bone-lime, and possibly assist with any technical difficulties — though indeed, they seemed to be masters of their craft, completely sure of their ability. Yellow glaze, of course, still was lacking them. That evening he inserted a strip from the Bureau library into his portable viewer. The subject was pottery, and Thomm absorbed as much of the lore as he was able.

Covill's pet project — a small atomic power plant to electrify Penolpan — kept him busy the next few days, even though he worked reluctantly. Penolpan, with its canals softly lit by yellow lanterns, the gardens glowing to candles and rich with the fragrance of night-blossoms, was a city from fairyland; electricity, motors, fluorescents, water pumps would surely dim the charm — Covill, however, was insistent that the world would benefit by a gradual integration into the tremendous industrial complex of the System.

Twice Thomm passed by the pottery bazaar and twice he turned in, both to marvel at the glistening ware and to speak with the girl who tended the shelves. She had a fascinating beauty, grace and charm, breathed into her soul by a lifetime in Penolpan; she was interested in everything Thomm had to tell her of the outside universe, and Thomm, young, softhearted and lonely, looked forward to his visits with increasing anticipation.

For a period Covill kept him furiously busy. Reports were due at the home office, and Covill assigned the task to Thomm, while he either dozed in his wicker chair or rode the canals of Penolpan in his special red and black boat.

At last, late one afternoon, Thomm threw aside his journals and set off down the street, under the shade of great kaotang trees. He crossed through the central market, where the shopkeepers were busy with late trade, turned down a path beside a turf-banked canal and presently came to the pottery bazaar.

But he looked in vain for the girl. A thin man in a black jacket stood quietly to the side, waiting his pleasure. At last Thomm turned to him. "Where's Su-then?"

The man hesitated, Thomm grew impatient.

"Well, where is she? Sick? Has she given up working here?"

"She has gone."

"Gone where?"

"Gone to her ancestors."

Thomm's skin froze to stiffness. *"What?"*

The clerk lowered his head.

"Is she dead?"

"Yes, she is dead."

"But — how? She was healthy a day or so ago."

The man of the Mi-Tuun hesitated once more. "There are many ways of dying, Earthman."

Thomm became angry. "Tell me now — what happened to her?"

Rather startled by Thomm's vehemence the man blurted, "The Potters have called her to the hills; she is gone, but soon she will live forever, her spirit wrapped in glorious glass —"

"Let me get this straight," said Thomm. "The Potters took her — alive?"

"Yes — alive."

"And any others?"

"Three others."

"All alive?"

"All alive."

Thomm ran back to the Bureau. Covill, by chance, was in the front office, checking Thomm's work. Thomm blurted, "The Potters have been raiding again — they took four Mi-Tuun in the last day or so."

Covill thrust his chin forward, cursed fluently. Thomm understood that his anger was not so much for the act itself, but for the fact that the Potters had defied him, disobeyed his orders. Covill personally had been insulted; now there would be action.

"Get the copter out," said Covill shortly. "Bring it around in front."

When Thomm set the copter down Covill was waiting with one of the three atom bombs in the Bureau armory — a long cylinder attached to a parachute. Covill snapped it in place on the copter, then stood back. "Take this over that blasted volcano," he said harshly. "Drop it down the crater. I'll teach those murdering devils a lesson they won't forget. Next time it'll be on their village."

Thomm, aware of Covill's dislike of flying, was not surprised by the assignment. Without further words he took off, rose above Penolpan, flew out toward the Kukmank Range.

His anger cooled. The Potters, caught in the rut of their customs, were unaware of evil. Covill's orders seemed ill-advised — headstrong, vindictive, over-hasty. Suppose the Mi-Tuun were yet alive? Would it not be better to negotiate for their release? Instead of hovering over the volcano, he dropped his copter into the gray village, and assuring himself of his gamma-gun, he jumped out onto the dismal stony square.

This time he had only a moment to wait. The chief came striding up from the village, burnoose flapping back from powerful limbs, a grim smile on his face.

"So — it is the insolent lordling again. Good — we are in need of bone-lime, and yours will suit us admirably. Prepare your soul for the Great Burn, and your next life will be the eternal glory of a perfect glaze."

Thomm felt fear, but he also felt a kind of desperate recklessness. He touched his gun. "I'll kill a lot of Potters, and you'll be the first," he said in a voice that sounded strange to him. "I've come for the four Mi-Tuun that you took from Penolpan. These raids have got to stop. You don't seem to understand that we can punish you."

The chief put his hands behind his back, apparently unimpressed. "You may fly like the birds, but birds can do no more than defile those below."

Thomm pulled out his gamma-gun, pointed to a boulder a quarter-mile away. "Watch that rock." And he blasted the granite to gravel with an explosive pellet.

The chief drew back, eyebrows raised. "In truth, you wield more sting than I believed. But—" he gestured to the ring of burnoosed Potters around Thomm "—we can kill you before you can do much damage. We Potters do not fear death, which is merely eternal meditation from the glass."

"Listen to me," said Thomm earnestly. "I came not to threaten, but to bargain. My superior, Covill, gave me orders to destroy the mountain, blast away your caves—and I can do it as easily as I blasted that rock."

A mutter arose from the Potters.

"If I'm harmed, be sure that you'll suffer. But, as I say, I've come down here, against my superior's orders, to make a bargain with you."

"What sort of bargain can interest us?" said the Chief Potter disdainfully. "We care for nothing but our craft." He gave a sign and, before Thomm could twitch, two burly Potters had gripped him, wrested the gun from his hand.

"I can give you the secret of the true yellow glaze," shouted Thomm desperately. "The royal fluorescent yellow that will stand the fire of your kiln!"

"Empty words," said the chief. Mockingly he asked: "And what do you want for your secret?"

"The return of the four Mi-Tuun you've just stolen from Penolpan, and your word never to raid again."

The chief listened intently, pondered a moment. "How then would we formulate our glaze?" He spoke with a patient air, like a man explaining a practical truth to a child. "Bone-lime is one of our most necessary fluxes."

"As Covill told you, we can give you unlimited quantities of lime, with any properties you ask for. On Earth we have made pottery for thousands of years and we know a great deal of such things."

The Chief Potter tossed his head. "That is evidently untrue. Look—" he kicked Thomm's gamma-gun "—the substance of this is dull opaque metal. A people knowing clay and transparent glass would never use material of that sort."

"Perhaps it would be wise to let me demonstrate," suggested Thomm. "If I show you the yellow glaze, then will you bargain with me?"

The Chief Potter scrutinized Thomm almost a full minute. Grudgingly: "What sort of yellow can you make?"

Thomm said wryly: "I'm not a potter, and I can't predict exactly — but the formula I have in mind can produce any shade from light luminous yellow to vivid orange."

The chief made a signal. "Release him. We will make him eat his words."

Thomm stretched his muscles, cramped under the grip of the Potters. He reached to the ground, picked up his gamma-gun, holstered it, under the sardonic eyes of the Chief Potter.

"Our bargain is this," said Thomm, "I show you how to make yellow glaze, and guarantee you a plentiful supply of lime. You will release the Mi-Tuun to me and undertake never to raid Penolpan for live men and women."

"The bargain is conditional on the yellow glaze," said the Chief Potter. "We ourselves can produce dingy yellows as often as we wish. If your yellow comes clear and true from the fire, I agree to your bargain. If not, we potters hold you a charlatan and your spirit will be lodged forever in the basest sort of utensil."

Thomm went to the copter, unsnapped the atom bomb from the frame, discarded the parachute. Shouldering the long cylinder, he said: "Take me to your pottery. I'll see what I can do."

Without a word the Chief Potter took him down the slope to the long shed, and they entered through an arched stone doorway. To the right stood bins of clay, a row of wheels, twenty or thirty lined against one wall, and in the center a rack crowded with drying ware. To the left stood vats, further shelves and tables. From a doorway came a harsh grinding sound, evidently a mill of some sort. The Chief Potter led Thomm to the left, past the glazing tables and to the end of the shed. Here were shelves lined with various crocks, tubs and sacks, these marked in symbols strange to Thomm. And through a doorway nearby, apparently unguarded, Thomm glimpsed the Mi-Tuun, seated despondently, passively, on benches. The girl Su-then looked up, saw him, and her mouth fell open. She jumped to her feet, hesitated in the doorway, deterred by the stern form of the Chief Potter.

Thomm said to her: "You're a free woman — with a little luck." Then turning to the Chief Potter: "What kind of acid do you have?"

The chief pointed to a row of stoneware flagons. "The acid of salt, the acid of vinegar, the acid of fluor spar, the acid of saltpeter, the acid of sulphur."

Thomm nodded, and laying the bomb on a table, opened the hinged door, withdrew one of the uranium slugs. Into five porcelain bowls he carved slivers of uranium with his pocket knife, and into each bowl he poured a quantity of acid, a different acid into each. Bubbles of gas fumed up from the metal.

The Chief Potter watched with folded arms. "What are you trying to do?"

Thomm stood back, studied his fuming beakers. "I want to precipitate a uranium salt. Get me soda and lye."

Finally a yellow powder settled in one of his beakers; this he seized upon and washed triumphantly.

"Now," he told the Chief Potter, "bring me clear glaze."

He poured out six trays of glaze and mixed into each a varying amount of his yellow salt. With tired and slumped shoulders he stood back, gestured. "There's your glaze. Test it."

The chief gave an order; a Potter came up with a trayful of tiles. The chief strode to the table, scrawled a number on the first bowl, dipped a tile into the glaze, numbered the tile correspondingly. This he did for each of the batches.

He stood back, and one of the Potters loaded the tiles in a small brick oven, closed the door, kindled a fire below.

"Now," said the Chief Potter, "you have twenty hours to question whether the burn will bring you life or death. You may as well spend the time in the company of your friends. You cannot leave, you will be well guarded." He turned abruptly, strode off down the central aisle.

Thomm turned to the nearby room, where Su-then stood in the doorway. She fell into his arms naturally, gladly.

The hours passed. Flame roared up past the oven and the bricks glowed red-hot — yellow-hot — yellow-white, and the fire was gradually drawn. Now the tiles lay cooling and behind the bricked-up door the colors were already set, and Thomm fought the impulse to tear open the brick. Darkness came; he fell into a fitful doze with Su-then's head resting on his shoulder.

Heavy footsteps aroused him; he went to the doorway. The Chief Potter was drawing aside the bricked-up door. Thomm approached, stood staring. It was dark inside; only the white gleam of the tiles could be seen, the sheen of colored glass on top. The Chief Potter reached into the kiln, pulled out the first tile. A muddy mustard-colored blotch encrusted the top. Thomm swallowed hard. The chief smiled at him sardonically. He reached for another. This was a mass of brownish blisters. The chief smiled again, reached in once more. A pad of mud.

The chief's smile was broad. "Lordling, your glazes are worse than the feeblest attempts of our children."

He reached in again. A burst of brilliant yellow, and it seemed the whole room shone.

The Chief Potter gasped, the other Potters leaned forward, and Thomm sank back against the wall. "Yellow —"

When Thomm at last returned to the Bureau he found Covill in a fury. "Where in thunder have you been? I sent you out on business which should take you two hours and you stay two days."

Thomm said: "I got the four Mi-Tuun back and made a contract with the Potters. No more raiding."

Covill's mouth slackened. "You *what?*"

Thomm repeated his information.

"You didn't follow my instructions?"

"No," said Thomm. "I thought I had a better idea, and the way it turned out, I had."

Covill's eyes were hard blue fires. "Thomm, you're through here, through with Planetary Affairs. If a man can't be trusted to carry out his superior's orders, he's not worth a cent to the Bureau. Get your gear together, and leave on the next packet out."

"Just as you wish," said Thomm, turning away.

"You're on company time till four o'clock tonight," said Covill coldly. "Until then you'll obey my orders. Take the copter to the hangar, and bring the bomb back to the armory."

"You haven't any more bomb," said Thomm. "I gave the uranium to the Potters. That was one of the prices of the contract."

"*What?*" bellowed Covill, pop-eyed. "*What?*"

"You heard me," said Thomm. "And if you think you could have used it better by blasting away their livelihood, you're crazy."

"Thomm, you get in that copter, you go out and get that uranium. Don't come back without it. Why, you abysmal blasted imbecile, with that uranium, those Potters could tear Penolpan clear off the face of the planet."

"If you want that uranium," said Thomm, "you go out and get it. I'm fired. I'm through."

Covill stared, swelling like a toad in his rage. Words came thickly from his mouth.

Thomm said: "If I were you, I'd let sleeping dogs lie. I think it would be dangerous business trying to get that uranium back."

Covill turned, buckled a pair of gamma-guns about his waist, stalked out the door. Thomm heard the whirr of copter blades.

"There goes a brave man," Thomm said to himself. "And there goes a fool."

Three weeks later Su-then excitedly announced visitors, and Thomm, looking up, was astounded to see the Chief Potter, with two other Potters behind — stern, forbidding in their gray burnooses.

Thomm greeted them with courtesy, offered them seats, but they remained standing.

"I came down to the city," said the Chief Potter, "to inquire if the contract we made was still bound and good."

"So far as I am concerned," said Thomm.

"A madman came to the village of the Potters," said the Chief Potter. "He said that you had no authority, that our agreement was good enough, but he couldn't allow the Potters to keep the heavy metal that makes glass like the sunset."

Thomm said: "Then what happened?"

"There was violence," said the Chief Potter without accent. "He killed six good wheel-men. But that is no matter. I come to find whether our contract is good."

"Yes," said Thomm. "It is bound by my word and by the word of my great chief back on Earth. I have spoken to him and he says the contract is good."

The Chief Potter nodded. "In that case, I bring you a present." He gestured, and one of his men laid a large bowl on Thomm's desk, a bowl of marvelous yellow radiance.

"The madman is a lucky man indeed," said the Chief Potter, "for his spirit dwells in the brightest glass ever to come from the Great Burn."

Thomm's eyebrows shot up. "You mean that Covill's bones —"

"The fiery soul of the madman has given luster to an already glorious glaze," said the Chief Potter. "He lives forever in the entrancing shimmer —"

The Visitors

CHIEF OFFICER AVERY came up the tube into the bridge sucking a bulb of coffee. Second Mate Dart rose stiffly from the seat where he had spent his watch. "She's all yours."

Avery was thin, hawk-nosed. His complexion was sallow leather color, his hair lank and sparse. He had black eyes between narrow lids and the angle at which they crossed his cheeks gave his face a look of clownish melancholy. Dart was stocky, stub-featured. His hair was Airedale-red; he was abrupt and positive in his movements. Stretching with a quick wide sweep of short arms, he joined Avery by the forward cupola.

Avery leaned forward, looked up, down, right, left, tracing the veins of rose and electric blue across the black of macroid space. He said over his shoulder, "She's dim. Turn her up. Can't see twenty feet at this level."

Dart, blinking, half-asleep, adjusted a rheostat, increasing the flood of polarized light from the bow projectors, and the gristle-like lines of force out in macroid space shone with greater brilliance and detail.

Avery grunted, "That's a lot different. And there's a focus coming up, where those two stringers dent in toward each other."

Dart came to watch as the lines trembled, bulged toward each other. Films of color began to flow from the area: wan yellow, pink, green. Suddenly a hot spark of red appeared.

"There's the focus," said Avery sourly. "Three feet from your nose, the center of a sun."

Dart ruefully rubbed his chin, thankful that Avery rather than Captain Badt had caught him dozing.

"Yeah, I guess so."

"Small to medium, from the kink to that inner blue line," said Avery. "Well, let's check for planets; that's what we're out here for."

Inch by inch they searched the cupola, up, down, right, left. Dart said, "By golly, here it is. Just like the illustration in the text. Maybe we'll slice that bonus yet."

The hot red spark faded to yellow; the twist of colored veins which signified a planet started to uncoil. Avery sprang back, snapped the drift switch, and the lines became static.

For a moment he studied the pattern in the hemispherical cupola. "The sun's right about here." He indicated a point between himself and Dart. "The planet's just inside the cupola."

"We're big men," said Dart.

Avery twisted his mouth in a saturnine grimace. "Either big, or a long way off in a freak direction."

"With all these guys running loose claiming to be geniuses," said Dart, "it's funny one of them hasn't figured it out."

Avery had been searching the cupola for further kinks. "Figure what out?"

"What happens when we go into macroid space."

"You're a dreamer," said Avery. "The universe shrinks, or we and the ship get cosmically big. The main thing is, we get there. Talk to Bascomb, he'll give you ten answers, all different. That's genius for you." Bascomb was the ship's biologist, who had gained himself the reputation of a tireless polemist and theoretician.

Avery took one more look at the kink. "Call the captain, ring general quarters. We're going into normal space."

The unigen was an intelligent organism, though its characteristics included neither form nor structure. Its components were mobile nodes of a luminous substance which was neither matter nor yet energy. There were millions of nodes and each was connected with every other node by tendrils similar to the lines of force in macroid space.

The unigen might be compared to a great brain, the nodes corresponding to the gray cells, the lines of force to the nerve tissue. It might appear as a bright sphere, or it might disperse its nodes at light speed to all corners of the universe.

Like every other aspect of reality, the unigen was a victim of entropy; to survive, it processed energy down the scale of availability, acquiring the energy from radioactive matter. The unigen's business of living included a constant search for energy.

There were periods of plenitude when the unigen would wax heavy with energy and might expand the number of its nodes by a kind of parthenogenetic fission. Other times the nodes would wane, glowing only feebly, and the unigen would seek energy stuff like a wolf, stalking the planets, satellites, meteors and dark stars for crumbs of even low-grade energy material. During a lean time, one of the nodes, approaching the planet of a small sun, became aware of quanta suggesting the presence of radioactivity: a spangle of distinctive color against a mottled background.

Hope, an emotion compounded of desire and imagination, was not alien to the unigen. It speeded the node forward and the radiation came hard and sharp. The node flitted down through a high scud of cloud. The glow of colored light stretched, elongated, and near its middle shone a markedly bright spot, like a diamond on a band of silver, evidently where the radioactive material broke surface. Toward this spot the unigen directed the node.

As it dropped, the unigen sought evidences of danger: the spoor of energy-eaters, sources of static electricity, such as clouds, which might disrupt the tight coils of a node with a spark.

The air was clear and the planet seemed free of dangerous life-forms. The node fell like a bright snowflake toward the central concentration of radioactivity.

The ship circled the planet in a reconnaissance orbit. Captain Badt, taciturn and something of a martinet, stood by the bridge telescreen, receiving reports from the technicians and keeping his opinions to himself.

Dart muttered to Avery in a disgruntled voice, "I'd hardly call the place a tourist planet."

"Looks pretty grim in spots, but it looks like a bonus."

Dart sighed, shook his round red head. "There never yet was a world so tough that colonists wouldn't flock out to it. If it's not cold enough to freeze air and not hot enough to boil water, and if you can breathe without popping your eyes, then it's land, and men seem to want it."

"I was born on a planet a hell of a lot worse than this," said Avery shortly.

Dart was silent a moment; then, with the air of a man who refuses to admit discouragement, went on. "Well, it's livable. Breathable atmosphere, temperature and gravity inside the critical area, and — so far — no signs of life." He went to the cupola, which now overlooked the world below. "At home the ocean's blue. It's yellow on Alexander, red on Coralasan. Here it's green. Grass by-Jesus green."

"Different proposition altogether," said Avery. "The red and yellow come from plankton. This green is algae or moss or seaweed. No telling how thick it is. Might be a man could walk out on it and pasture his cows."

"Lots of good grazing," admitted Dart. "About four million square miles in sight from here. Probably the source of the planet's oxygen. According to Bascomb, there's no surface vegetation. Maybe lichens, a few shrubs and such…That sea-bed must be thick with humus…"

The speaker from the laboratory click-clicked. On the other wing of the bridge Captain Badt snapped, "Report!"

The code-sono opened the circuit; the voice of Jason the geologist said, "Here's a full report on the atmosphere. Thirty-one per cent oxygen, eleven per cent helium, forty per cent nitrogen, ten per cent argon, four per cent CO_2, the other four per cent inert. Substantially an Earth-type atmosphere."

"Thank you," said Captain Badt formally. "Off."

He paced up and down the bridge frowning, his hands clasped behind his back.

"The old man's in a hurry," Avery said quietly to Dart. "I can read his mind. He doesn't like survey duty, and he's figuring that if he finds a good Class A planet, he can use it as an excuse to take off for Earth."

Captain Badt marched stiffly back and forth, paused, went to the speaker. "Jason."

"Yes, sir?"

"What's the story on the geology so far?"

"I can't tell much from this high, but the relief seems generally a product of igneous action rather than erosion. Naturally, that's a guess."

"A good ore planet, possibly?"

"At a guess, yes. There's plenty of folding, lots of faults, not too much sediment. Where those mountains break up through the coastal strip, I'd expect schists, gneiss, broken rocks cemented with quartz and calcite."

"Thank you." Captain Badt went to the magniscreen, watched the landscape drift past. He turned to Avery. "I think we'll dispense with further investigation and set down."

The speaker click-clicked. "Report!" said Captain Badt.

It was Jason again. "I've located an extensive outcrop of radioactive ore, probably pitchblende or possibly carnotite. It shines like a search-light when I drop the X-screen across the scope. It runs along the shore just south of the long inlet."

"Thank you." To Avery: "We'll set down there."

The reconnaissance party, consisting of Avery and Jason, walked along the black gravel pebbles of the shore. To their left, the ocean spread out to the horizon, a green velvety flat like a tremendous billiard table. To the right, black-shadowed gullies led back into the mountains — crag-crested barrens of rock. The sun was smaller and yellower than Sol; the light was wan, like Earth sunlight through a pall of smoke. Although the air had been certified breathable, the men wore head-domes, precautions against possibly dangerous bacteria or spores.

Through a pick-up TV eye mounted above Avery's dome, Captain Badt watched from the ship. "Any insects, animal life of any sort?" he asked.

"Haven't noticed any so far…That upholstered ocean should make a good home for bugs. Jason threw a stone out and it's still sitting high and dry. I believe a man could walk out there with a pair of snowshoes."

"What is that vegetation to your right?"

Avery paused, inspected the shrub. "Nothing very different from those around the ship. Just one of those paint-brush plants a little larger than the others. Country seems rather arid, in spite of this ocean. Takes rain to make good soil. Right, Jason?"

"Right."

Captain Badt said, "After a while, we'll check into the ocean. Right now I'm interested in that uranium reef. You should be almost on top of it."

"I think it's about a hundred yards ahead, a ledge of black rock. Yep, Jason's detector is buzzing like mad...Jason says it's pitchblende — uranium oxide." He stopped short in his tracks.

"What's the trouble?"

"There's a swarm of lights over it. Flickering up and down like mosquitoes."

Captain Badt focused the image on the screen. "Yes, I see them."

"Might be some sort of fireflies," hazarded Jason.

Avery took a few cautious steps forward, halted. One of the luminous spots darted up, sped toward him, swung around his head, circled Jason, returned to the uranium ledge.

Avery said uncertainly, "I guess they're not dangerous. Some kind of bug, apparently."

Captain Badt said, "Peculiar how they're concentrated along that ledge. As if they're feeding on the uranium, or like the feel of the radiation."

"There's nothing else nearby. No vegetation of any sort, so it must be the uranium."

"I'll send Bascomb out," said Captain Badt. "He can investigate more closely."

The node which originally discovered the planet settled on an outcrop of the uranium oxide and was presently joined by other nodes, fleeting in from less rewarding areas. The absorption of energy began; pressing against the massive blue-black rock, a node would generate sufficient heat to vaporize a quantity of the ore. Enveloping the gas, the node worked a complicated alchemy which released the latent energy. The node absorbed this energy, compacting and augmenting its structure, kinking its whorls of force into harder knots. At the same time it discharged a flood of energy into the lines to the rest of the unigen, and everywhere in the universe nodes shone with a new golden-green luster.

Insofar as surprise may be equated to witnessing events which have previously been dismissed as improbable, the unigen felt surprise when it sensed the approach of two creatures along the shore.

The unigen had observed living creatures on other worlds. Some of these were dangerous, like the mirror-metal energy-eaters swimming in the thick atmosphere of another uranium-rich planet. Others were unimportant as competition for food. These particular slow-moving creatures appeared harmless.

To investigate at close hand, the unigen sent out a node, and received a report of infra-red radiation, fluctuating electromagnetic fields.

"Harmless autochthones," was the unigen's summation. "Creatures living by chemical reaction at a low energy level, like the land-worms of Planet 11432. Useless as energy sources, incapable of damage to the hard energy of a node."

Dismissing further consideration of the two creatures, the unigen absorbed itself with the uranium bank...Odd. On the surface of the ore had appeared what seemed to be a vegetable growth, a peppering of tiny spines rising from little flat collars. They had not been evident previously.

And here came another of the slow-moving creatures. This one, like the others, emitted infra-red radiation, several different weaker waves.

The creature halted, then slowly approached the ledge.

The unigen watched with mild curiosity. Precise visual definition was beyond its powers, so the land-worm's movements came as blurs of shifting radiation.

It seemed to manipulate a metal object which glinted and reflected sunlight — evidently a bit of pitchblende which had attracted its attention.

The land-worm moved closer. It made a few blurred motions, and suddenly appeared to have extended one of its members. It moved once more, and a mesh of carbonaceous material fell around one of the nodes.

Interesting, thought the unigen. The land-worm evidently had been attracted by the glitter and motion. The action implied curiosity; was the creature more highly evolved than its structure indicated? Or possibly it sustained life by trapping small bright animals, such as phosphorescent jellyfish from the sea.

The land-worm drew the net close. To resolve the problem, the unigen permitted the node to be carried along.

A brittle shell of another carbon compound was cupped over the node and an enclosure effected.

Was this perhaps the land-worm's organ of digestion? There appeared to be no digestive juice, no grinding or crushing action.

The land-worm moved slightly away from the ledge and performed a series of mysterious gyrations. The unigen was puzzled.

Two metal needles entered the brittle cage. In sudden consternation the unigen sought to snap the node free.

Avery and Jason continued along the pitchblende ledge. Presently it dipped from sight, and the shore of black-gray pebbles slanted up from the green velvet ocean to the heavy shoulder of the mountain.

"Nothing out here, Captain," said Avery. "Just looks like more shore and more mountains for ten or twenty miles."

"Very well, you can return." He added in a grumbling voice, "Bascomb's on his way out to check on those flickering lights. He thinks they're emanations, like will o' the wisps."

Avery winked at Jason, and cutting off the band to the ship said, "Bascomb won't be satisfied till he has one of 'em pinned to a board like a butterfly."

Jason held up a hand, signed Avery to listen. Avery switched back on the communication band, heard Bascomb's precise voice.

"— from a distance of thirty feet, the spectroscope shows a uniform band, radiating at apparently equal intensity in all frequencies. This is curious. Normal phosphors emit in discrete bands. Perhaps some such occurrence like St. Elmo's Fire is involved, though I confess I don't quite understand —"

Captain Badt growled impatiently, "Are they alive or aren't they?"

Bascomb's voice was petulant. "I've no idea, I'm sure. After all, this is a strange planet. The word 'life' has a thousand interpretations. Incidentally, I note a very odd type of vegetation growing on the pitchblende itself."

"Avery mentioned no vegetation," said Captain Badt. "I questioned him specifically."

Bascomb sniffed. "He could hardly have missed it. It's a line of shoots about six inches tall. They're like spikes, apparently stiff and crisp, rising from suckers clamped to the surface. Very similar to something I saw once on Martius Juvenal where a pitchblende vein breaks surface... It's very peculiar. The roots seem to have drilled into the solid rock."

"You're the biologist," said Captain Badt. "You ought to know."

Bascomb's voice took on a note of cheery assurance. "Well, we'll see. I've read of emanations being observed near pitchblende deposits, but I have never observed them. Possibly the concentrated radioactivity might be acting on minute condensations of moisture..."

Captain Badt cleared his throat. "Very well, handle it your own way. Be careful and don't stir them up; they might be dangerous in some way."

Bascomb said, "I've brought along a net and specimen bottle. I planned to capture one of the motes and examine it under the microscope."

"I suppose you know what you're doing," said Captain Badt in a tired voice.

"I've devoted my life to the study of extraterrestrial life," replied Bascomb stiffly. "I rather imagine that these motes are analogous to the sparkle-ticks of Procyon B... Now, if I just adjust my net. There! I've got one. Into the specimen jar. My, how it shines! Can you see it, Captain?"

"Yes, I can see it. What's it like under the microscope?"

"Hm..." Bascomb brought his pocket magnifier to bear. "There's no resolution. I see a central concentration of fire; undoubtedly that's where the insect is. I think I'll pass an electric spark through the creature and kill it, and perhaps I can examine it under higher power."

"Don't stir 'em up —" began Captain Badt. The screen flared white in his face, went dark. "Bascomb! Bascomb!"

Captain Badt received no reply.

Destruction of a node sent a restless shiver through the unigen. A node represented an integral fraction of the unigen's brain; it had been conditioned to modify a definite class of thoughts. When the node was destroyed, the thinking in the class was curtailed until another node could be produced and endowed with the same precise channels.

The implications of the event were further cause for anxiety. The metal energy-eaters on another planet used the same technique — a stream of electrons smashing across the center of the node, to upset the equilibrium. The result was a flash of released energy, which the metal ovoids were able to absorb. Apparently the land-worm had been surprised by the explosion and destroyed — possibly mistaking the node for some less energetic type of creature.

It might be wise, thought the unigen, to destroy the land-worms as soon as they appeared, and thus prevent further accidents.

Still another vexation: the spike-vegetation was spreading its collars across the surface of the ledge, sinking deep roots into the energy-stuff. Apparently it built the displaced material into the spike. When the unigen sent a node to absorb the leached uranium, it found a hard shell of inert substance, proof against the node's kernel of heat.

Nodes flickered and quivered all over the universe as the unigen marshaled its computative abilities. Rigorous steps would have to be taken.

Far down the beach, Avery and Jason saw the white flash of the explosion, saw the black gullies light up in a ghastly swift glare. Then came a rolling sound and a jar of concussion.

Avery cut anxiously into the communication band. "Captain Badt, Avery calling. What's happened?"

Captain Badt said harshly, "That fool Bascomb's just blown himself up."

"We're up the beach about a mile, I think, from where the explosion came," said Avery hurriedly. "Should we —"

Captain Badt interrupted. "Don't do anything. Don't touch anything. This is a strange planet, and it's dangerous. Bascomb's just proved that."

"What did he do?"

"He apparently ran an electric current through one of those bright spots of light, and it went off in his face."

Avery stopped short, looked warily up the shore. "We went past pretty closely and they didn't bother us. It must be the electricity."

"You be careful on your way back. I can't afford to lose any more men. Keep out of the way of those lights."

"Yes, sir," said Avery. He motioned to Jason. "Let's go. We'd better skirt the water as close as possible."

Crowding the soggy verge of the ocean, they rounded the bend in the shoreline, approached the scene of the explosion.

"Doesn't seem to be much left of Bascomb," said Jason in a hushed voice.

"Not much crater either," said Avery. "It's a funny deal."

"Look, now there's thousands of those light-bugs. Like bees around a hive. And look at that stuff growing out of the ledge! That wasn't there when we went past! Talk about mushrooms…"

Avery turned his binoculars along the ledge. "Probably it's got something to do with the light-flecks. The lights could be spores or pollen or something of the sort."

"Anything's possible," said Jason. "I've seen vines thirty miles long, as thick around as a house, and if you jab them with a stick they quiver their whole length. They're on Antaeus. The kids in the Earth colony tap out Morse code back and forth to each other. The vine doesn't like it, but there's nothing it can do."

Avery had been watching the dancing lights over his shoulder. "They're like eyes watching us…Before a colony's sent out here, these damn things will have to be destroyed. They'd be dangerous flying loose around electricity."

Jason said, "Duck! Here comes a couple of them after us!"

Avery said in a nervous voice, "Don't get excited, kid. They're just drifting on the breeze."

"Drifting, hell," said Jason, and started to run for the ship.

The unigen observed the land-worms returning along the shore, evidently seeking the sea-matter on which they fed. To guard against the accidental destruction of any more nodes, it would be wise to destroy the creatures as they appeared, and clean them from this particular section of the planet.

It dispatched two nodes toward the land-worms. They seemed to sense danger and broke into lumbering motion. The unigen accelerated the nodes; they darted forward at half-light speed, punctured the land-worms, reversed, shuttled back and forth a score of times, each time leaving a small steaming hole. The land-worms collapsed to the black pebbles, lay limp.

The unigen brought the nodes back to the uranium bank. Now to a more serious matter: the vegetation which was choking off the face of the uranium with its collars and roots.

The unigen concentrated the heat of twenty nodes on one of the spikes. A hole appeared, weakening the entire shoot. It sagged and shriveled, collapsed.

Pleasure was a quality which the structure of the unigen was incapable of expressing, the nearest approach being a calm coasting sense, an awareness of control and mastery of movement. In this state the unigen began a systematic attack on the spikes.

A second member fell over, became pale brown and a third...

Overhead appeared a flying object, similar to a land-worm except that it radiated more strongly in the infra-red.

Were the creatures everywhere?

Second Officer Dart had made the original suggestion, diffidently at first, half-expecting Captain Badt to freeze him with a stare the color of zinc. But Captain Badt stood like a statue looking into the blank magniscreen, still tuned to Avery's band.

Dart said with somewhat more boldness, "So far we have no conclusive report to make. Is the planet habitable or not? If we leave now we haven't proved anything."

Captain Badt answered in a voice without resonance, "I can't risk any more men."

Dart rubbed at his bristling red hair. It occurred to him that Captain Badt was getting old.

"Those little lights are vicious," Dart said emphatically. "We know that. They've killed three of our men. But we can handle them. An electric current blows 'em apart. Another thing, they're like bees around a hive; they mind their own business unless they're bothered. Bascomb, Avery, Jason — they got it because they approached that pitchblende ledge too closely. Here's my idea, and I'll take the risk of carrying it through. We knock together a light frame, string it with wire, and charge the strands alternately positive and negative. Then

I'll go up in the service 'copter and drift it across the ledge. They're so thick now that we can't help but knock out two-three hundred at a swipe."

Captain Badt clenched and unclenched his hands. "Very well. Go ahead." He turned his back, stared into the blank magniscreen. This would be his last voyage.

With the help of Henry, the ship's electrician, Dart built the frame, strung it with wire, equipped it with a high-potential battery. Strapping himself into the 'copter harness, he rose straight up, dangling a mile of light cable. He became a speck on the gray-blue sky.

"That's it," said Henry into the communication mike. "Now I'll make fast this fly trap affair, and then — I've got another idea. We want the thing to move flat-side forward, so I'll tie on a bridle with a bit of drag at the end."

He arranged the drag, snapped the switch on the battery. "She's ready to go."

A mile above, Dart moved across the sky toward the ledge of pitch-blende.

Captain Badt maintained an iron grip on the hand rail in the bridge, watching Dart's progress on the magniscreen.

"Up, Dart," he said. "Up four feet…There…Steady. That's about right. Take it slow…"

The unigen's range of perception included the lowest radio waves as well as the hottest ultra-cosmics, a spectrum of a million colors. Stereoscopic vision was implicit in the fact that each node served as an organ of sight. Resolution of images was achieved by accepting only radiation normal to the surface of the node. In this manner a coarse spherical picture was received by each node, although detail as fine as the frame strung with wire was nearly invisible.

The unigen's first warning was a pressure from the approaching electrostatic fields; then the frame swept across the ledge, full through the heaviest concentration of nodes.

The blast seared the ground, melted it into a flaming molten basin for a radius of fifty feet. The nodes which escaped the screen were flung pell-mell by the explosion out across the ocean.

Directly under the explosion, the spike-vegetation was scorched; elsewhere, little affected.

The structure of the unigen was no more capable of anger than pleasure; however, its will to survive was intense. Overhead flew the land-worm. One like it had destroyed a node through electricity; perhaps this one was somehow associated with the last catastrophic explosion. Four nodes slanted up at light speed, snapped back and forth through the land-worm like sewing-machine needles hemming a sheet. The creature fell to the ground.

The unigen assembled its nodes a hundred feet over the bank of uranium. Ninety-six nodes destroyed.

The unigen weighed the situation. The planet was rich with uranium, but it was also the home of lethal land-worms.

The unigen decided. There was uranium elsewhere in the universe, on thousands of worlds that were silent and dark and free of any kind of life. A lesson had been learned: avoid worlds inhabited by life-forms, no matter how primitive.

The nodes flashed off into the sky, dispersed into space.

Captain Badt relaxed his grip on the table. "That's it," he said in a flat voice. "Any world where we lose four good men in four hours — any world inhabited by swarms of crazy atomic bees — that's no world for human beings. Four good men..."

He stood silent a moment, limp and dejected.

The cadet wandered into the bridge, stared wide-eyed. Life-long habit reasserted itself. Captain Badt filled out, became erect, rigid. His tunic and trousers hung crisp, his eyes once more shone with authority.

"Ensign, you will act as chief officer until further notice. We're leaving the planet, returning to Earth. Please attend to all exterior ports."

"Yes, sir," said the new Chief Mate.

The planet was quiet. The ocean spread bright and green, the mountains rolled back into the badlands: crags, ravines, plateaus — black rock, gray rock, pockets of drifted ash.

On the pitchblende ledge the vegetation waxed tall, five, ten, twenty feet, gray spines mottled with white, ivory, silver. In each a central vein opened; the spike became a tube straight and stiff as a cannon barrel.

At the bottom of the tube, the fruit of the plant began to develop. There was a spore-case, enclosed by a jacket into which water percolated. Below the spore-case opened another compartment, globe-shaped, communicating with the base of the spike by four splayed channels.

A nub of uranium 235 accumulated in this chamber — one ounce, two ounces, three ounces, more and more diffused through the membranes of the plant by some evolutionary freak of a metabolism.

The fruit was ripe. One by one, the spikes reached a culmination. A tension within the water-jacket increased past the breaking strain. The jacket split, flooded the compartment below the spore-case, surrounded the knob of uranium.

Explosion. Steam bursting through the stern-pointing channels, back into the tube. Thrust, straight up. Sharp whipping blasts as the cases left the spikes. Up, up, up, at furious acceleration, into space…

The water dissipated, the last puff of steam left the tubes. The spore-cases floated free on momentum. The gravitational field of the planet faded to a wisp, a film. The spore-cases drifted on. Now they cooled, cracked wide. From each a thousand capsules spilled into space, and the tiny jerk of the splitting case sent them in courses slightly divergent, enough to scatter them off toward different stars.

Endless seeping of life across space.

Smite into planet, the sift of spores, the search for the hot element, the growth, the culmination, the blast, the impulse.

Then space, years of drift. Out beyond, and past beyond…

THE UNINHIBITED ROBOT

I

THE BARTENDER WAS THE BIGGEST MAN at the Hub. He had a red slab-sided face, chest and belly like a barrel of meat and bone. He bounced his drunks by butting them to the door with this same belly, dancing close, thrusting forward like an uncouth and elephantine cooch-dancer. Reliable information compared the blow to the kick of a mule. Marvin Allixter, nervously lean and on his way to forty, wanted to call him a blackguard, a double-dealing pinch-penny, but cautiously restrained his tongue.

The bartender twisted the bubble back and forth, inspecting the enclosed little creature from all sides. It glowed and glinted like a prism — sun yellow, emerald, melting mauve, bright pink — the purest of colors. "Twenty franks," he said without enthusiasm.

"Twenty franks?" Allixter dramatically beat both fists against the bar. "Now *you're* joking."

"No joke," rumbled the bartender.

Allixter leaned forward earnestly, thinking to appeal to the man's reason. "Now, Buck, look here. The bubble is pure rock crystal, maybe a million years old. And mind you the Kickerjees dig a year and think themselves lucky to find one or two, and then only in a great chunk of quartz. They grind and polish and twist and turn and then one slip — *smash!* — the bubble breaks, the mite oozes out and dies."

The bartender turned away to pour straight shots for a pair of grinning warehousemen. "Too fragile. If I bought it and one of these drunks busted it I'd be out of twenty franks."

"Twenty franks?" Allixter asked in astonishment. "That's no figure to mention in the same breath with this little jewel. Why, I'd sell my ear for twenty franks first."

"Suits me." Buck the bartender jocularly flourished a knife.

Allixter now thought to arouse the man's cupidity. "This item cost me five hundred franks at the source."

The bartender laughed in his face. "You guys on the tube gang all sing the same song. You pick up a trinket somewhere off in the stations, you smuggle it back through the tube, you spin a fancy yarn about how much it cost you and hustle the item to the first sucker who listens to you." He drew himself a small glass of water, drank it with a wink to the warehousemen.

"Sure, I got stuck once. I bought a little varmint from Hank Evans, said it could dance, said it knew all the native dances of Kalong, and the thing looked like it could dance. I put down forty-two franks for the animal. Come to find it had sore feet in the new gravity and was just hopping from one to the other to ease the pain. That was the dancing."

Allixter shifted uneasily, glanced over his shoulder to the door. Sam Schmitz, the dispatcher, had been buzzing him for an hour and Sam was an impatient man. He lounged back against the bar, attempting an air of nonchalance. "Look at the colors the little rascal goes through — *there!* That red! Ever see anything so bright? Think how that would look hung around some lady's neck!"

Kitty, the sumptuous blonde hostess, said in a breathless contralto, "I think it's lovely. I'd be proud to wear it myself."

The bartender took up the bubble once more. "I don't know no ladies." He inspected it doubtfully. "It's a pretty little trinket. Well, maybe I'll spring twenty franks."

The screen at his back buzzed. He turned on audio and duovision together without first waiting for the caller's identification, then took his bulk to the side. Allixter had no time to duck. Sam Schmitz stared at him eye to eye.

"*Allixter!*" barked Schmitz. "You've got five minutes to report. After that, don't bother!" The screen went blank.

Allixter stared under thoughtful dark eyebrows at the bartender, who regarded him placidly. "Since you're in a hurry," said Buck, "I'll make it twenty-five franks. It's a cute little bobbet."

Allixter rose to his feet, still staring at the bartender. He juggled the bubble from hand to hand. Buck reached out in alarm. "Easy — the thing might break." He dived into the till. "Here's your twenty-five franks."

Allixter said, "Five hundred."

"Can't do it," said the barkeep.

"Make it four hundred."

Buck shook his head, watching Allixter from craftily narrowed eyes. Allixter turned, wordlessly walked from the bar. The bartender waited like a statue. Allixter's long dark face returned through the door. "Three hundred."

"Twenty-five franks."

Allixter screwed his face into an expression of agony and departed.

In the street he paused. The depot, a big cube of a building, rose like a cliff in the wintry sunlight, dominating the rather disreputable purlieus of the Hub. At its base spread warehouses, glittering aluminum banks, each a quarter-mile long. Trucks and trailers nuzzled at side-bays like red-and-blue leeches.

The warehouse roofs served as cargo decks where flexible loaders crammed airship holds with produce from a hundred worlds. Allixter watched the activity a moment, conscious that, for all the activity, nine tenths of the traffic passed unseen along the tubes — to continental Earth stations, to stations among the planets, among the stars.

"Rats!" said Allixter. He walked without haste to the corner transit, considering the little bubble. Perhaps he should have sold — twenty-five franks was twenty-four franks profit. He rejected the idea. A man was able to carry only so much along the tubes and expected a decent profit from his enterprise.

The bubble actually was a kind of sea-creature washed up on the pink beaches of — Allixter couldn't remember the name of the planet — 9-3-2 was the code to the station. He tucked it away in his pouch, climbed into the shell at the transit, swerved, rose, popped out into light. Allixter stepped out upon the depot administration deck.

A few feet distant was the glass-enclosed cubicle where Sam Schmitz, the Service Foreman and Dispatcher, sat on a high stool. Allixter slid back a pane, said, "Hello, Sam," in a kind voice. Schmitz had a round pudgy face, fierce and red. He had the undershot chin and general expression of a bulldog.

"Allixter," said Schmitz, "you'll be surprised. We're tightening up around here. You guys on the repair crew have picked up the idea that you're a bunch of aristocrats, responsible only to God. This is a mistake. You were due on standby three hours ago. For two hours the Chief's been chewing my rear end for a mechanic. I find you in Buck's bar. I want to be good to you guys but you've got to follow through."

Allixter listened without concentration, nodding at the right places. Where next to peddle the bubble? Maybe wait till he got a week's leave, take it down to Edmonton or Chicago. Or better yet, stash it away till he had accumulated a few other items and then make Paris or Mexico City, where the big money was. Schmitz paused for breath.

"Anything on the docket, Sam?" Allixter asked.

The response startled him. Sam's chin quivered in rage. "Blast it! What do you think I've been talking about the last five minutes?"

Allixter desperately sent his mind back, recalling a phrase here, a sentence there. He rubbed his thin cheek and jaw, and said, "I didn't quite catch all of it, Sam. Maybe if you'd go over it again…Just what's the complaint?"

Sam flung up his arms in disgust. "Go see the Chief. He'll give you the picture. I'm done."

Allixter crossed the deck, turned down a hall, stopped at a tall green door with bronze letters which read: SERVICE AND MAINTENANCE DIRECTOR. ENTER.

He pushed the button. The door slotted and he entered the outer office. The secretary glanced up. Allixter said, "The Chief's expecting me."

"That's no secret." Then she said into the mesh, "Scotty Allixter's here." She listened to her ear-plug, nodded at Allixter, keyed back the lock on the inner door. He slid it aside, stepped into the office. The air, as always, had a harsh medicinal odor which irritated Allixter's nose.

The Chief was a small man, built to an angular design. His skin was wrinkled and yellow, parched like an old lemon. His eyes were small black balls, snapping with some kind of inner electricity. A few wisps of kinky hair rose from his head, some white, some black, without apparent design. The skin of his neck was corrugated like an alligator's and the right side was marred all the way to his knobby chin by a heavy welt of scar tissue. Allixter had never seen the Chief laugh, had never heard him speak other than in a dry monotonous twang.

The Chief said without preliminaries, "Schmitz probably gave you the picture on this job."

Allixter took a seat. "To be frank, Chief, I didn't quite get it."

The Chief spoke as if he were explaining table manners to an idiot — softly, with careful enunciations. "You've been through to Rhetus Station?"

"Code six minus four minus nine. Sure thing. They've got a new Mammoth installation."

"Well, six minus four minus nine is coming in out of phase."

Allixter's thick straight eyebrows rose in an arch. "So soon? Why, we just —"

The Chief said drily, "Here's the story. The tube came in, just barely scraping over the bitter edge of the tuner. I computed thirty-one-hundredths-of-a-percent slack in the phase."

Allixter scratched his chin. "Sounds as if there's a leak in the selector unit."

"Possibly," agreed the Chief.

"Or maybe they've got a new dispatcher and he's playing with the adjustments."

The Chief said, "To make sure we hit the unit dead-center I'm sending you out on six minus four minus nine, slacked down the same percentage that it came in."

Allixter winced. "That sounds dangerous. If the code doesn't sock home in the contacts I'll come out something pretty poor on Rhetus."

The Chief pushed himself back in his chair. "Job for a service man. You're on standby. So it's yours."

Allixter frowningly looked through the window, across the misty reaches of the Great Slave Lake. "There's something fishy here. That's a new Mammoth and they work close."

"True."

Allixter shot a narrow glance at the Chief. "Sure it was Rhetus?"

"I never said it was in the first place. I said the code was six minus four minus nine."

"Got a picture of that code?"

The Chief wordlessly tossed him an oscillograph pattern.

Allixter said, "Amplitude six, frequencies four and nine." He frowned. "Almost six, almost four and nine. Not quite. Close enough to sock into the contacts."

"Correct. Well, get your gear, climb through the tube, service that installation."

Allixter anxiously pulled at his wedge-shaped Gaelic chin. "Maybe..." He paused.

"Maybe what?"

"Do you know what I think?"

"No."

"Looks like it might be an amateur station or a hijacking outfit. The Rhetus tube runs valuable cargo. Now if some outfit could divert the tube to their own station..."

"If you think so, you can take a gun with you."

Allixter rubbed his hands together nervously. "Sounds like a police job to me, Chief."

The Chief raked him with his snapping black eyes. "It sounds to me as if the code is thirty-one-hundredths-of-a-percent slack. Maybe some silly bloke is punching wrong buttons on that Mammoth. I want you to go straighten it out. What do you think you're drawing a thousand franks a month for?"

Allixter muttered something about the infinite value of human life. The Chief said, "If you don't like it I know better mechanics than you who will."

"I like it," said Allixter.

"Wear Type X."

Allixter's thick black eyebrows became question marks. "Rhetus has a good atmosphere. Type X is anti-halogen —"

"Wear Type X. We're not taking unnecessary chances. Suppose it is a hijack installation? Take along the Linguaid too. And a gun."

"I see we're of the same mind," said Allixter.

"Don't forget spare power and check your breather unit. Evans reported a leaky tube on the extra unit. I had it condemned but maybe they're all that way."

II

The mechanics' locker room was deserted. In glum silence Allixter pulled on the Type X — first a thick neck-to-toe coverall webbed with heating elements, then a thin sheath of inert film to seal him from a possibly dangerous atmosphere, then high boots of woven metal and silicone impervious to heat, cold, dampness and mechanical damage. A belt strapped around his waist and over his shoulder supported his tool kit, a breather and humidity-control unit, two fresh power packs, a sheath knife, a JAR, and a heat-torch.

In the corridor he met Sam Schmitz. "Carr's at the buttons. He's checking you out on the adjusted code…"

A door labelled DANGER, KEEP OUT slid aside for them and they entered the central depot, a long hall filled with sound, activity, dust and, most notably, a thousand odd odors, whiffs of spicy reeks, balms and fetors from the thousand off-planet commodities coming in on the near belt.

The luminous ceiling gave off a cold white glare which searched out every shadow. There was no glamour or concealment in this light — every item on the belts minutely described itself to the eyes of the checkers. The walls were painted in ceiling-to-floor blocks of various colors, the better to designate the bays, where various shipments, temporarily stacked, awaited re-routing.

A narrow glass-fenced platform cut the depot in two. Back and forth from platform to the belts jumped the clerks in blue and white smocks, checking the merchandise in-coming on the near side, out-going on the far — crates, sacks, boxes, bales, bags, racks and cases.

Machinery, metal parts in ingots and machined shapes, consignments of Earth fruit and vegetables going out to the colonies, the homesteads, the mines. Other consignments of off-world exotics incoming to entice and stimulate the sophisticates of Paris, London, Benares, Sahara City. Tanks of water, oaken casks of whiskey, green bottles of wine.

Prefabricated houses, flyers, automobiles, speed-boats for the lakes of the Tanagra Highlands. Beautiful woods, richly mottled and marked from the hardwood swamps of a jungle planet. Ores, rocks, minerals, crystals, glasses, sands — all riding the belts, either approaching or leaving the twin curtains of dark brown-gold, shot with flickering streaks of light, at the far end of the hall.

At the curtain end of the out-belt a big blond man sat in an elevated box, viciously chewing gum. Allixter and Schmitz ducked across the in-belt, stepped over the clerks' platform, rode the out-belt to the operator's box.

Carr hauled back a lever and the belt eased to a stop. "All ready to go?"

"Yep, all set," said Schmitz cheerfully. He hopped up into the box while Allixter stood glumly eyeing the curtain. "Howza wife, Carr?" asked Schmitz. "Heard she took a dose of dermatitis from something you carried home on your clothes."

"She's okay," said Carr. "It was that kapok stuff from Deneb Kaitos. Now let's see — I've got to set up this phony code. Hey, Scotty," he called down to Allixter, "made your will yet? This is like stepping out of an airplane holding your nose and hoping you'll hit water."

Allixter made a nonchalant gesture. "Everyday stuff, Carr, my boy. Set those dials — I want to be back sometime tonight."

Carr shook his head in rueful admiration. "They pay you a thousand franks for it — brother, it's yours. I've seen some of the stuff that's come out of the tubes when the settings were a little out of phase. Plywood panels come through looking like cheese-cloth handkerchiefs — a turbine agitator makes about a gallon of funny-looking rust."

Allixter's mouth tightened over his teeth and he cracked his knuckles.

"There she is," said Carr. A bulb on the panel flared red, flickered, wavered through smoky orange, glared white. "She's through."

Schmitz leaned down over the box. "Okay, Allixter, all yours."

Allixter pulled the hood over his head, sealed it, inflated the suit. Carr chuckled into Schmitz' ear, "Scotty's gloomy for sure over this one."

Schmitz grinned. "He's afraid he's walking into some hijacker's warehouse."

Carr turned him a blankly curious side-look. "Is he?"

Schmitz spat. "Hell no. He's going to Rhetus, to set adjustments on the coder. That's how I figure it." He spat again. "Of course, I might be wrong."

Allixter lifted up his hood, yelled to Schmitz, "You better get me down the Linguaid."

Schmitz asked with a grin, "Can't you talk English? That's all you'll hear on Rhetus."

"The Chief says take the Linguaid. So roll her out."

A buzzer sounded on Carr's panel. Carr grunted. "Get him his analyzer. I can't tie up the belt all day. Old Hannegan's hollerin' to get his grapes off to Centauri."

Schmitz snapped a few words into a mesh and moments later a runner from the shop appeared, rolling the Linguaid ahead of him, a black case slung between two wheels.

"Be careful of that job," said Schmitz. "It's expensive and it's the only decent outfit we got left since Olson burnt out the Semantalyzer. Don't leave it on Rhetus."

"You worry a confounded lot about that Linguaid," muttered Allixter, "and not a cent for old Scotty Allixter."

He sealed the hood over his head and, trundling the Linguaid ahead of him, stepped through the curtain.

Allixter stood on a bone-white platform, bare to the heavens. He felt a stir of morose triumph. "I'm still alive. I'm not a cheese-cloth handkerchief, not a gallon of rust. I guess the Chief figured okay — got to give the old cuss credit. But..."

Allixter stared around the landscape, a gray and black plain. At precise intervals massive concrete rotundas rose from the ground, most of which had been shattered as if by internal explosions.

"This isn't Rhetus — nowhere near Rhetus. And those aren't men and they aren't Rhets..." He turned an anxious look to the tube installation — it was of a type strange to his eyes — a cylinder of dark gold-brown fog. It seemed to be swirling slowly around a vortex.

Where in creation was he? He looked at the sky — a hazy violet spangled by a myriad distant suns, random gouts of colored fire. Was it day or was it night? He searched the horizon with anxious eyes, sweating inside his air-film. Perspectives were strange, the lighting was strange, the shadows were strange. Everywhere he looked, everything was strange with the un-human wildness of the remote worlds.

"I'm in a fix," thought Allixter. "I'm lost."

It was a dreary landscape, a dingy plain studded with tremendous gray wrecks. Where the shattered walls had fallen machinery could be seen — wheels, shafts, banks of complex gear and circuits, squat housings and cases. All were broken, silent, corroded.

Allixter turned his attention back to the cylinder of brown-gold fog. This was the in-curtain but where was the installation to send him back? Usually the two went together. The creatures who stood along the outer edge of the white platform approached, apparently with indecision and puzzlement. Allixter made no move for his JAR. He thought that if it were possible to cross-breed a seal and a man and plant a palmetto thatch of red-green quills on the scalp of the issue — here would be the result.

As they approached, watching him from big dull-surfaced eyes, they made sounds of communication — squeaks, windy whistling tones, hisses — forming these sounds by trapping a pocket of air under their arm-pits, squeezing it past a flap of skin.

Allixter said, "How do you do, my friends. I'm the representative of Tube Maintenance and it looks to me as if I've crossed over into an entirely different mesh, a million light-years gone from Earth if not farther. I fear that I'm entirely divorced from my own set of stations and Old Nick himself couldn't tell me how to find my way home."

The natives ceased their noise as he spoke, then commenced once more. Allixter chewed his lips, laughed in tart amusement. He rocked the Linguaid back and forth affectionately, murmured, "And Sam Schmitz wanted to send me out half-naked!"

He dropped a pair of legs to steady the Linguaid, swung the shutter away from the screen. "Come on over, Joe," he said, motioning to a creature who stood slightly in the lead. "Let's get to understand each other."

He set the controls for Cycle A. The screen glowed white. Geometric figures appeared — a circle, a square, a triangle, a line and a point.

Joe looked intently, and the others crowded around his back. Allixter pointed to the circle and said, "Circle," to the square — "Square," likewise for the other shapes. Then, motioning to Joe, he pressed the record key and pointed to the circle.

Joe was silent.

Allixter released the key, went through the priming routine again. Again he set the banks to record, pointed to the circle. Joe squeezed a skirl of a sound from under his armpit. Allixter pointed to the other figures and Joe made other sounds.

Encouraged, Allixter proceeded to Step Two — Enumeration. The screen depicted symbols representing the agglomerative numerals — a series of lines, one dot in the first line, two dots in the second line, three in the third, four in the fourth, in such fashion up to twenty. Joe, alive to his task, made sounds for the numbers. Then the screen displayed a random multitude of dots and Joe created another sound.

Now Allixter tried colors. Joe stared at the screen impassively. Red — no response. Green — no response. Violet — no response. Allixter shrugged. "We'll never get together here. You see by infra-red or ultra-violet."

The cycle passed on to more complicated situations. A dot moved swiftly across the screen, followed by a dot moving slowly. The sequence was repeated and Allixter pointed to the first dot. Joe created a sound. Allixter indicated the slow dot and Joe made another sound.

From the bottom of the screen a line rose nearly to the top. Another line lifted about an inch. Joe made sounds which Allixter hoped were "tall" and "short" or "high" and "low".

A circle swelled almost past the outer verge of the screen and beside it appeared a minute dot. Joe's sounds for "large" and "small" entered the memory banks.

Presently the comparative situations were exhausted and the screen depicted noun objects — mountains, an ocean, a tree, a house, a factory, fire, water, a man, a woman. Then came more complicated objects — a turbine in a plastic housing to convey the idea of machinery — a conventionalized drawing of a dynamo with an exterior circuit first coiled around a bar, from which a magnetic field radiated, then continuing to a point where the circuit was broken and lightning-like flashes jumped the gap. Allixter pointed to these flashes and the Linguaid recorded Joe's sound for electricity.

Two hundred basic nouns were so recorded. Then the cycle turned to inter-person relationships. The machine had been designed for use by men — the stock situations depicted men. Allixter hoped confusion would not arise.

First a man was shown attacking another man, striking him with a club. The victim fell with a crushed skull. Allixter pointed; the analyzer filed the words for dead and corpse. Then the murderer turned a savage face out of the screen, rushed forward with club upraised to strike. Joe jumped back, squeaking. Allixter, grinning, ran the sequence again, and the analyzer noted the word for enemy or assailant, or possibly attack.

An hour passed — a score of situations were pictured and analyzed. It seemed to Allixter as time went by that the natives showed signs of nervousness. They cast restive glances in all directions, gestured with agitated flutters of their hand-members.

Allixter searched the landscape but no menace was evident in the perimeter of his vision. However, by a kind of sympathy, he found his own nerves growing taut, found it difficult to concentrate on the Linguaid.

Cycle A was completed — all the words and situations of the basic vocabulary had been recorded, although more useful and near-essential abstractions, such as interrogatives and pronouns, were still absent from the file.

Allixter switched the machine from Cycle A to Converse. He spoke into the mike, careful to use only words of the basic vocabulary. "Desire return through machine. Lead to out-machine."

The Linguaid absorbed the words, found their counterparts in the recorded squeaks, hissings, trumpetings and voiced them from the speaker.

Joe listened with attention — then he looked blankly at Allixter. His shoulders quivered. Air creaked and sputtered past the skin at his armpits.

The Linguaid searched the files, voiced the words: "Call to machine… Desire… Machine man… Broken machine… Man come through machine… Bad…"

There had obviously been more words spoken. The Linguaid translated only the sounds it could match against its recorded patterns.

Allixter said, "Use words given machine."

Joe stared with great dull eyes. His tall thatch of red and green plumes drooped dejectedly. He made a further effort. "Man call for distant machine builder. Man come. Desire friend to build machine."

Allixter looked in frustration around the drab horizon, looked up into the spangled violet sky where there would never be night or day. He considered running Cycle B on the Linguaid — a process which would tax the patience of both himself and Joe but which might enable him to locate the installation to send him back to Earth.

He tried once more. "Desire return through machine. Lead to out-machine." He gestured to the brown-gold curtain. "See in-machine. Desire out-machine."

Something was wrong. The nervousness which Allixter had first noticed became marked. The natives crouched on the bone-white platform in smooth balls with their crests folded around them like partly-closed umbrellas. Allixter looked for Joe. Joe was at his feet, as huddled and compact as his mates.

In sudden anxiety Allixter snapped the iris across the Linguaid screen, closed the lid down over the controls. A nearby building caught his eye. The machinery within was moving — grinding, pounding, snapping. Electricity or some other flow of energy arced across old contacts.

Corroded shafts shuddered and twisted and strained. Wheels moaned and whined around dry bearings. Without warning the building exploded. Chunks of concrete and metal flew up in a crazy tangle, fell clattering in all directions. Smaller material scattered across the platform, and the natives trumpeted in terror.

Some small fragments struck Allixter, bounded off his resilient air-film. It occurred to him that as yet he knew nothing of the atmosphere, that if the film had been punctured he might be poisoned.

From his pouch he brought a spectrometer and let air in the vacuum chamber. He pressed the radiation button and read the dark lines on the ground glass off against a standard scale. Fluorine, chlorine, bromine, hydrogen fluoride, carbon dioxide, water vapor, argon, xenon, krypton — not a salubrious environment for the likes of him, he thought. He gazed speculatively at the structures. If he could get a few analyses of those metals he'd revolutionize the anti-corrosive industry — make a million franks overnight.

He looked back to the exploded building, now in utter ruin. It suddenly glowed white hot and the heat did not seem to dissipate but increased. The wreckage melted into a pool of seething slag. The ground in the immediate vicinity steamed, scorched, slumped into the widening pool of lava.

Allixter thought — That's hard energy and if it's dangerously radio-active it's time for me to blow.

He pushed the Linguaid ahead of him to the edge of the platform, prepared to jump down to the surface of the gray-black ground about two feet below. Behind him the natives still huddled, balls of seal-soft flesh, neatly covered by their thatch.

Joe stirred, looked up, saw Allixter. He scampered forward on flex-ible short legs, making urgent sounds. Allixter turned the switch on the Linguaid.

"Danger, danger, bad, deep, death," said the Linguaid, the intona-tions calm and matter-of-fact.

Allixter jerked back from the edge. Joe stopped alongside, tossed a fragment of rock to the ground. It cast up a puff of feathery dust, settled quickly out of sight. Allixter blinked.

There but for the grace of God went Scotty Allixter, he thought. It was an ocean of ashes out there — soft fluff. With new eyes he gazed across the flat gray plain, where the blasted buildings rose like islands. He shrugged. It was beyond his understanding. He knew of many Earthmen who had lost their minds trying to comprehend the para-doxes and peculiarities of the outer stations.

A sudden intuition struck him. He swept his eyes around the circumference of the bone-white platform. It was like a raft on the gray sea, with the slow-whirling cylinder at the center. How then had the natives made their way here? Could it possibly be that they too had arrived through the cylinder from an out-world?

Joe's soft fingers fumbled at his arm. He squeaked, pumping his shoulders loosely, expertly, and the Linguaid translated, "Off. Come. Lead toward large machine."

Allixter said hopefully, "Desire out-machine. Desire return. Lead to out-machine."

Joe squeezed out further sounds. "Come — follow. Friend to large machine corpse. Large machine wreck friend. Large machine desire friend. Come — follow. Build large machine."

Allixter thought that whatever it was, it could be no worse than standing on this platform.

Joe fumbled with a grating, pulled it aside, descended a steep flight of steps. Trundling the Linguaid ahead of him Allixter followed.

The corridor became dark. Allixter flicked on his head-lamp. Ahead he saw a pair of gold-brown curtains, the 'in' distinguished from the 'out' by a subtle difference in their golden flicker.

Joe stepped through the out-curtain, disappeared. As Allixter hesitated, he bobbed through the in-curtain, beckoned with a certain querulous insistence, once more popped back through the out-curtain.

Allixter sighed. Pushing the Linguaid ahead of him, he stepped through.

III

Allixter stood in a wide corridor tiled with vitreous white squares. Ahead of him Joe slid through a tall vaguely Romanesque archway. He followed and came out on a pavilion open to the sky. The floor was the same vitreous tile, squares six feet on a side. It was innocent of furnishings or fittings. Around the edge of the floor pipe-stem columns supported a disproportionately heavy pediment and Allixter paused in trepidation, half-expecting the whole construction to buckle and fall crashing at his feet.

He walked cautiously out into the center of the pavilion, noting a trembling underfoot as of heavy machinery. In renewed apprehension he estimated the stability of the columns and was not reassured to find them quivering and swaying. Joe seemed oblivious to the danger. Allixter gingerly approached the edge of the pavilion, every instant expecting the precariously-perched pediment to land on his head.

The view was different from the outlook across the drab sea of ash. From here the panorama, if strange and unearthly, had a certain haunting charm. A long murky valley lay cradled between two low hills. Two or three miles distant, at the bottom of the valley, lay a glass-calm lake and the mirror of its surface reflected the swarm of many-colored suns.

Along the hills purple shrubs grew almost like Earthly vines and in the valley black-green paddies lay in rectangular blocks to the limit of his vision. He noticed what appeared to be a village about halfway to the lake — a row of neat sheds open at front and rear under a line of spindle-shaped lime-green trees like Lombardy poplars.

There was a sharp sound, a terrific crack which reverberated across the valley. Joe screeched, ducked back, huddled trembling in the middle of the pavilion. Allixter, all goose-flesh lest the pediment topple and crush him, nevertheless could not tear himself from the spectacle in the valley.

The hill to his right had opened in a vast split at least a mile long and perhaps a hundred yards wide. A sheet of white flame issued from this seam and blasted up at a slant clear across the valley. Heat seared Allixter's face and he dodged behind one of the slender columns, which shuddered and swayed before his face.

"Phew!" said Allixter to himself. "This planet is a poor place to plan a vacation. No wonder it's a wreck!"

Joe came cringing up beside him like a frightened dog in search of comfort. Allixter grinned in spite of himself. "I can see why these boys act like they're scared to death. No telling where the next outburst takes place."

He studied Joe with a new concentration. Round dull-eyed face under a ludicrous head-dress, face without expression, coincidentally human. Round arms fringed with black hair, round sinuous legs joining the torso like pipes to a boiler.

Allixter speculated as to Joe's ultimate motives. Whatever they might be, whatever thoughts passed through the creature's organ for thinking, they were certainly indescribable in Earth terms. "We've got something in common, Joe," said Allixter. "Neither one of us wants to be blown to smithereens."

There was one vestige of cheer to be derived from the situation, thought Allixter — Joe's mental patterns were not those of an evolutionized predator. By Gram's Theorem the carnivore that evolved to civilization retained the ferocity and callousness of his prototype. The herbivore tended to placidity, discipline and convention — while the omnivores were erratic, prone to nervous disorders and unpredictable emotion.

Joe tugged at Allixter's arm. Allixter held back a minute, then relaxed and followed. "There's no point in thwarting you; I'll never get home. Perhaps even now you're taking me to the out-tube — and that reminds me, I must watch for any small trinkets to take back with me. A man can't get rich on a thousand franks a month."

He swept the spangled sky with curious eyes. "I must be in the heart of a cluster — maybe past the Milky Way. I'm a long way from home. It's avarice which has brought me out here, the old fault. Oh well, let's see what good old Joe wants."

Joe led him around the side of the pavilion along a walk built of thin stone slats. Allixter felt them vibrate and throb under his feet as if to the impulse of powerful machinery nearby. Behind the pavilion rose a hill. A stone building thrust forward, its after end under the slope.

The walls were great rusty gray-yellow masses of masonry, studded and strapped with metal bars like a fortress. The walkway of stone strips came to an end. They trod on the bare ground and it thudded and throbbed with an ever heavier pulse. Joe stopped at a heavy door which, slightly ajar, vibrated on its hinges.

Joe squeaked, Allixter turned on the Linguaid.

"Large machine bad. Build good. Danger. Large machine wreck friend one. Friend two," here he tapped Allixter's chest. "Friend two. Build man come through hole. Go see large machine. Danger. Wreck friend. Large danger. Large machine enemy. Make large wreck."

Allixter gingerly approached the door. "You don't make the project sound very inviting." He squinted through the slit into a large bare hall. The floor was flagged with great squares of polished red stone eight feet on a side. The walls were faced from floor to ceiling with rectangular panels, evidently removable. Where one of the panels had been swung aside Allixter glimpsed masses of exquisitely complicated and delicate machinery.

A track appeared to make a circuit of the hall; at the range of Allixter's vision a trolley supported a high black case. From the controls and dial-settings at one side this mobile case appeared to be another massive mechanism.

Such were the inorganic aspects of the hall and Allixter noted them with a single glance. Then he gave his attention to another object, at once more interesting and fuller of implications regarding his own future. It was a corpse on the floor — a man with a crushed skull.

The face of the dead man was gaunt and greenish-yellow. His body was thin, his skin stretched taut over sharp bones. The entire effect was that of an exotic bird cruelly stripped of its feathers, murdered and flung in a heap.

The body had apparently lain in its present state for several days and Allixter was glad that in his air-film he was not forced to breathe the air of the hall.

Breathing — he scrutinized the corpse once more. No air-suit or head-dome was in evidence. The man had been able to breathe the halogens which poisoned the atmosphere for an Earthman. Odd, reflected Allixter. Joe pushed him forward. "Go. Large machine wreck. Danger."

Allixter held back. "Desire life. Desire avoid danger. Fear."

Joe said, "See." He opened the door, slid inside with a sidewise motion. As he loped around the hall, he pumped his shoulders furiously, squeezing forth a steady flow of shrill sound.

"Joe," said Allixter admiringly, "if we were back on Earth I'd take you to Scotland and list you with the Queen's Own, where you'd play lead bagpipe without the bagpipe."

Joe never halted his trumpeting till once more he joined Allixter outside the door.

"Go," said Joe. "Talk, danger absent. Silence, danger." He tapped Allixter's chest. "Large machine build-man come through hole, build large machine."

The first glimmerings of enlightenment came to Allixter. "I think I see it. There's some kind of machine in there you want me to fix. It's dangerous if it's not fixed and it's dangerous while I'm in there unless I keep talking." He uttered a sharp bark of laughter.

"Schmitz should see me now. He calls me the Silent Scot and now I'll be talking and prattling like a jay. Oh well." He sighed. "A thousand franks a month is security for my old age — so long as I survive my job. And I'll never starve…"

He looked into the hall once again, chewing his lip in frustrated silence and wishing he had established the interrogatives in the native language.

"I may be the world's best mechanic," said Allixter, "but coming cold-turkey on an off-planet machine, not knowing what's wrong with it, not even knowing what it's supposed to do in the first place — this is the stuff old Willy Johnson died from."

Joe prodded him anxiously. Far in the distance he heard a great thud, a blast as of an enormous explosion. Joe quivered, squeaked in agitation, fanned the quills of his headdress in all directions.

"A man dies but once," reflected Allixter, "and if it's my time to go at least the Chief and Sam Schmitz won't have the satisfaction of hearing about it."

He pushed the door wide and was about to step into the room when Joe pointed over his head, squeaked, "Danger."

Allixter looked up. Overhead a great hammer, swinging from a ball and socket joint in the center of the ceiling, hung cocked back against the wall — apparently the agency by which the corpse on the floor had been crushed.

"Danger," said Joe. "Talk many."

Allixter entered the hall, pushing the Linguaid before him. "I wish I was home," he said in a loud voice. "I wish I knew where the tube came out. So near and yet so far and here I am depending on my voice for my life like a canary."

The Linguaid, picking up translatable words, squeaked and groaned so that the hall rang with mingled sounds.

Allixter thought, "Why should I have to talk when there's a perfectly good mechanical talker right here under my hand?" He pushed the Linguaid to the middle of the hall, set the index so that Cycle A was repeated, together with Joe's recorded interpolations. Now, he thought, there should be sufficient sound to distract anyone.

Warily eyeing the poised hammer Allixter scrutinized the hall. Beyond doubt repairs to the machinery had been underway when death had stopped the hand of the mechanic. Panels had been removed from the wall and the face of the mobile unit had been demounted. Various cams, gears, shafts, assemblies of indescribable nature mounted in small cases, lay neatly in a tray beside a rack of tools. Apparently the mechanic had barely started when — Allixter turned an anxious glance at the poised hammer.

No, thought Allixter, too precarious — too chancy.

He climbed up the side of the mobile unit. Perching on the top he took from his belt the heat-torch which served him both as weapon and tool. Stretching across the gap he played the torch on the shaft. Fire spattered, the metal melted in a shower of sparks, the hammer dropped with a clatter, missed the Linguaid by inches. Allixter clapped a hand to his forehead, jammed the torch back in his belt.

A voice cried out in the native tongue, screaming, hissing, groaning, protesting. Allixter hurriedly descended to the floor, stood searching for the source of the voice. The sweat running off his back made small rivulets down his spine.

He was alone in the room.

The voice continued, and after a moment he located its source — a metal diaphragm at the far end of the hall. Directly above a many-faceted lens about six inches in diameter was mounted so that it projected slightly into the room.

He wheeled the Linguaid close, said, "Friend, friend. Come out, see." It must be a fellow to the corpse, thought Allixter — perhaps one who watched by remote vision through the many-faceted lens.

The speaker said in English, "Build across many words. Build words through machine."

Evidently the watcher was an intelligent being, thought Allixter. Very well, Cycle B. He started the sequence but the voice made no attempt to supply words for the automaton. It said, "Man talk. Man talk."

"Ha-hmm," said Allixter to himself. "The chap is sensible enough, wants to learn English. It seems that I do the talking rather than he. I suppose this is covered in my salary although it's true that I signed on as a mechanic and no blooming linguist. Ah, well…"

He settled to the task and supplied English words for the depicted sequences and relationships.

Cycle B, with the pronouns, was complete. He started Cycle C. The voice said, "More words, faster. All comes understood and remembered."

"Hmm," muttered Allixter, "I've got a ruddy genius on my hands. The chap has a mind like a sponge. Very well, I'll give him as much as he can take." And he described the screen situations in great detail, supplementing the prime concepts with additional nominal and verbal materials.

In two hours he had completed Cycles C, D, E and F — normally the work of a month.

As he flicked off the switch he said, "Now, my friend, wherever you are, you should be able to talk to me and maybe you'll answer a few questions."

IV

His own voice returned from the speaker. Allixter stared in surprise. "Ask — the files will return information. That is their function."

"First..." Allixter paused. What was first? As he considered he heard a grind, a swish. Overhead the stump of rod swung toward him. If the hammer had yet depended Allixter would have been mate to the corpse on the floor.

Allixter crouched in alarm. "Who's trying to kill me? Why? All I want is to get back to Earth."

The speaker said with disarming calmness, "The protective instruments try to kill you because the inhibitor circuit is disorganized."

Allixter said with a worried glance at the corpse, "How am I supposed to survive?"

"A constant impulse from the attention units drains ergs from the B-sub C monitor and holds the relay open. As long as you supply material that occupies the attention banks the automatic protective devices will not function."

"I'll try as hard as I can," said Allixter. "Is conversation safe?"

"As long as attention is occupied. Three seconds is the critical lapse. This is the time required to leak the charge past the relay condensers."

"Who are you? Who's speaking?"

"This voice is the courtesy unit of the Planet Machine."

"What's that again?" asked Allixter in puzzlement.

The message was repeated. Allixter stared in bewilderment and awe. "As I get it then you're a kind of — robot?"

"Yes."

Three seconds passed swiftly. Hurriedly Allixter asked, "What's your function? What do you do?"

"When repair machine directs world-wide installations which collect energy from the suns, apply this energy to the designated uses."

"Which are?"

"Machine mines ore, smelts, refines ore, alloys and shapes metal parts, manages photo-synthetic tanks producing fluoro-silicon and fluoro-carbon compounds, combines and fabricates items in Classification Zo, Schedules Ba-Nineteen through Pec-Twenty-five. When complete, products are delivered to the master-planet Plagigonstok through the transfer."

Allixter found a hint of enlightenment in the explanation. "I understand then that this planet is a colony of another world? Plagi — Plagi — something or other? And the natives, where do they fit in?"

"The natives supply what unskilled and flexible labor may be necessary. They are paid in commodities."

Allixter glanced at the corpse. "Where are all the — what do you call them?"

"Question is inexact."

"What kind of man is that dead creature on the floor — what race?"

"He is a Plag, a Lord of the Universe."

Allixter snorted. "Are there any others nearby?"

"There are twelve similar in condition to this one."

A small chill ran along Allixter's neck. "What do you mean — similar condition?"

"Bodily functions disrupted by disorganization of mental centers."

"Dead?"

"Dead."

"You killed them?"

"Protective instruments killed them."

"Why?"

"Inhibitor circuit is not functioning. Machine is fundamentally ordered not to kill Plags. This order is occluded. Now machine kills Plags freely without inhibition and destroys Plag installations at random."

"Then why don't you kill the natives?"

"Inhibitors concerning autochthones are still in place. Machine protects autochthones. Machine kills alien life-forms who enter this room, the mental center of the machine. You survive only by accident — attention units, draining from B-sub C monitor, shunt out exterminators."

Allixter grimaced. "There's a serious oversight somewhere."

The machine was silent. Allixter waited for a reply. One second — two seconds — he realized with a prickle of urgency that the machine responded only to questions, that the circuits were not set up to exchange small-talk with casual passers-by.

He blurted, "Yes. No. I've seen robots and calculating machines and automatic mechanisms but I've never seen anything like you. You're a pretty big piece of machinery — er, aren't you?"

"Yes."

One second — two seconds. Allixter's mind was blank.

"Ah — the Plags built all this machinery?"

"The Plags organized the nucleus, consisting of planning, engineering, mechanical, energy and operating segments, delineated the ultimate ends desired. Subsidiary elements were conceived by the planning segment, designed by the engineering segment, constructed in the central factory. The entire planet is now noded with various agencies which the planning segment considers useful."

"Why all the blasting? The exploding buildings, the hillsides spitting out fire?"

"Installations benefiting Plags are being destroyed. Destructive agencies exist. Inhibitors formerly restrained them. Now inhibitors are cut out. Destructive agencies go into effect at random."

Allixter grinned. "The Plags won't like this — will they?"

"Accurate information unavailable."

"How will the Plags fix the machine?"

"No information. As soon as Plags arrive, they are killed."

"How come the natives were waiting for me at the in-curtain?"

"Precise information unavailable. Possibility exists that they dispatched message to Plagigonstok requesting service crew, and awaited reply."

"Ah!" Allixter nodded sagely. "How long has the machine been out of order? And why did not the Plag service man repair it at once before it went out?"

"When machine is in disrepair the maintenance unit moves along tracks to the rupture and makes the necessary renewals. The service mechanic never repairs the machine. It is too complex. In this case the maintenance unit was out of order and the mechanic was occupied in repairing it. Then the inhibitor circuit fused. The fundamental orders went into effect and the exterminators killed the Plag."

Allixter sighed. Then, remembering that sighs occupied time, he said, "How can I extend this three-second time limit? I can't stand here forever asking you questions."

"You can supply problems to occupy the attention units or better you can repair either the inhibitor circuit or the maintenance units."

"And while I'm working, you kill me?"

"Yes."

"Why does a chicken cross a road?"

"Presumably the motivations and restraints in reference to the prospective action settle into an equilibrium which prompts the motion rather than the stasis."

"When do two and two make three?"

The voice said, "Attention bank will be occupied with the problem for six minutes. This is the time necessary to explore all possible conditions in all the various regimens of mathematics built into my nucleus."

Allixter glanced at his watch. "Good. I'll have time to think up some corkers in the meantime."

He relaxed, dented the film of his head-bubble to rub at his forehead. Six minutes — would he ever sleep again? And the old life back on Earth! With longing and nostalgia he thought of Buck's Bar at the Hub, the familiar faces around the walnut oval, the big glass steins foaming over the top...

He brought himself back to the present. Apparently his future would be occupied in entertaining this planetary robot in puzzles, riddles and mathematical recreations. At least, thought Allixter with a sour grin, he knew how to tie it up for more than three seconds. The thing to do was to get to the source, repair the machine. What the devil was wrong with it? The inhibitor circuit? The maintenance unit? Both out — a sorry situation. The repair system exists to keep the machinery operating but there was nothing to repair the repair system.

He sauntered across the floor, examined the interior where the side panel had been removed. Complexity upon complexity, unfamiliar shapes, conductors and leads, rank on rank. There'd be a month's work merely tracing down a corner of the mechanism.

He picked up one of the tools. My word, thought Allixter, there's some fine equipment here. Now if I could patent this little pocket winch, I'd make myself a cool million. And what's this? It's a saw, by golly. I'd never have believed it…Why I could poke this arm a yard into nowhere and the teeth would slice through hard alloy. Clever, these Plags.

But this conductor appliance, we've got the same thing on Earth. Same design, identical — strange. One of those odd coincidences you notice when you run back and forth world to world…My Lord, the time. He looked at his watch. Five seconds.

But he was in no immediate danger. The robot had much to report. "Filed under solubility indices there exists a number of situations where two units of one substance and two units of another substance, mixed, result in three units of an end substance. These are not rigorous cases and may be dismissed. However in the case of…" The voice droned into mathematical terminology which meant nothing to Allixter.

He listened five minutes but the flow of symbology showed no signs of coming to an end. Attending with half an ear he paced back and forth, examining the hall. The red tiles of the floor were of a rubbery substance, laid with microscopic precision.

Allixter hacked out a sliver with his knife, dropped it in his pouch. There'd be a fortune in it, back on Earth — rubber to resist fluorine. His fingers hit a hard round object, an unfamiliar shape. He drew it out.

Ah, the little sea-crystal which shone with such intriguing shafts of radiance. Only twenty-four hours before he had picked this little ball off the beach of — what was that planet? — and now... Allixter grinned sourly. A thousand franks a month to nurse lunatic robots to sanity, to wander a strange gray planet, looking for the tube back to Earth. It might be underfoot, it might be ten thousand miles north, east, south, west.

He noticed the door. It hung a trifle ajar. He walked forward to open it. If things got rough he could retreat. The door moved. *Click!*

Allixter cursed. Deceitful little devils! There was silence in the hall. He became aware that the voice had ceased. In its place sounded a sharp hissing.

He twisted anxiously. "What's going on?"

His own voice from the speaker said, "Protective system has been engaged. You are being smothered by an atmosphere of pure nitrogen."

"I see," said Allixter. He gingerly felt the surface of his air-film. "I don't care to be killed. Maybe we had better concentrate on —"

An explosion shook the machinery, jarred him from head to foot. Outside he heard the anguished squeaks of the indigenes. "Good God, what's that?"

"The scavenging and rural simplification program, uninhibited by safety precautions, is leveling useless relics of past operations. A great number of fabricating and —" the voice whirred and gurgled. "No word on file for concept. Plag industrial plants are being destroyed. There is no order on file to contravene demolition —"

Allixter said hastily, "For God's sake, don't wreck the space-tube. That's how I get home!"

"Orders placed in appropriate file," said the dry voice.

"We'd better get your inhibiting circuit back in order before —" A staccato burst of explosions like the discharge of a string of firecrackers cut him off short. Allixter continued shakily, "I was going to say, before you do any real harm."

V

Allixter asked, "What's the fastest way that circuit can be put back in working condition?"

The robot said, "The maintenance unit is designed to adjust, tune, lubricate and replace the worn parts of the circuit in four-point-three-six minutes. A Plag mechanic can perform the same routine in twenty-six hours."

Allixter scowled at the mobile repair unit. "What's the best way to get the repair machine going?"

"No data on extent of damage."

Allixter said sarcastically, "You're a fine robot — don't even know what's going on in front of your nose."

Was there a trace of near-human tartness in the reply? "Machine's optical system cannot penetrate opaque panel."

"Whereabouts on the track can you see?"

"Radian two-point-six-seven, as indicated in white characters, is optimum."

Allixter sniffed. "I can't read those characters. They're in Plag writing."

"Information filed appropriately," came the toneless acknowledgment.

Allixter said, "I'll move the unit — tell me when you can see. In the meantime," he said thoughtfully, "you can compile a list of prime numbers ending in the digits seven-nine-seven."

The speaker made a bleating sound which once more seemed to carry near-human overtones. Allixter set his shoulder to the mobile unit.

It moved slowly around the track. At last the speaker said, "Optimum." Then, "The list of the first hundred prime numbers ending in the digits is as follows —"

"File them," said Allixter, "Give your attention to this machine. And don't try to kill me while I'm busy. Do you agree to that?"

The toneless voice said, "Protective mechanism acts independently."

"Okay," said Allixter. "You seem to be interested in mathematics. Suppose you make a list of prime numbers which when multiplied by the prime numbers immediately before and after, and the product taken to the sixth power, divided by seven and the remainder dropped, yield a prime number ending in the digits one-one-one."

The speaker stuttered, rumbled.

"These calculations will be performed," said Allixter, "when your attention is not given to the repair job. Now, what's first?"

"Remove panels from both sides."

Allixter obeyed.

"Unclip copper band from half-inch stud, pull pin from cam shaft, cut welding away from bearing clamp…"

The machine was well-lubricated, well-engineered. After a half-hour's work Allixter discovered the cause of the breakdown — an L-toggle which had failed at the joint.

"Spring back double spirals with tool in corner of tray. Grip shaft with clamp, turn ninety degrees — prongs will separate, releasing ruptured part."

Allixter did as he was bid and the offending part came loose.

"Material is all standardized," said the machine. "Spare toggle will be found in third locker at opposite end of hall."

"Keep busy on that little list of numbers while I'm getting the bearing," said Allixter.

"Memory banks have capacity for eight billion digits," announced the robot. "Bank is half-full now."

"When the unit is full, discharge it and start over."

"Instructions filed."

Allixter crossed the floor, passed the crumpled body of the Plag. In sudden curiosity, he turned it over with his foot, looked down the front. It was definitely human in all the primary characteristics, though the nose and chin were long and gnarled, the skin a peculiar plucked-chicken yellow, the hair like steel-wool. The creature wore a garment of dark green velvet, lustrous and rich where the light struck fair.

"That's odd," said Allixter to himself, reaching down, tugging at a small metal loop. "A zipper. First one I've seen on an off-Earth garment. Now if he was only equipped with something *better* — I could take it back, patent it, make a million — and then when the Chief says, 'Run this blasted errand, fix that blasted tube, wipe the nose on that starving Mafekinasian,' I'll say, 'Chief, that thousand franks you insult me with every month…'"

He stared at the dead Plag, scrutinized the face, the zipper, and then, pulling his lip back in distaste, searched the body.

There was nothing in the pocket save a pair of small metal objects like keys and a fiber-bound notebook inscribed with green-black ink. In the pouch were a few small hand-tools.

Allixter, whistling softly, found the L-toggle, returned to the repair unit. "Robot."

"Attending."

"This inhibitory circuit — was it entirely blown out, totally inoperative?"

"No."

Allixter waited but the robot, having answered the question, found no reason to expatiate. "I didn't think so. Any organism with as much power and responsibility as you would need almost as many positive inhibitors as there are possibilities for action. Right?"

"Right."

"For instance, the inhibitor against killing the natives holds. So does the inhibitor against burning out all your own fuses. And it seems that if you really had a powerful urge you would find little difficulty killing me. In other words the mere exciting of your attention units would not disturb a deep-seated impulse to kill a presumably hostile alien."

The robot asked, "How many times do you wish the memory banks filled with prime numbers ending in one one one and discharged?"

"Are you getting bored with the problem?"

"Concept incomprehensible."

"Well — just for the sake of novelty consider each square foot of the planet in turn, compute the chances of a ten-pound meteor plus or minus six ounces striking each of these square feet in the next ten minutes."

The speaker was silent except for a faint buzzing. Allixter continued with the pattern which was gradually forming in his mind. It was large, it was of such great scope and implication that he found it incredible — at first.

Allixter went back to the corpse, looked in the frozen face once more. He turned toward the speaker. "What sections of the inhibitor are burnt out?"

"Shreds R eight-sixty-six-ninety-two through R nine-eleven-ninety-one."

"And these refer to the Plags?"

"Yes."

"To such an extent that in the place of the inhibitor preventing you from harming a Plag or a Plag construction you are now more than likely, if not certain, to destroy everything Plag on the planet?"

"Yes."

Allixter mused a moment. "Where is the out-leading space-tube?"

"On the north side of this building a door of yellow metal opens into a large warehouse. At the rear of the hall is the terminal."

"What is the setting for Plagi — Plagi —" Allixter shook his head. "The Plag planet?"

"Phase ten, frequencies nine and three."

"In what kind of units?"

"In Plag units."

"Translate these into Earth units."

"Phase eight-point-four-two, frequencies seven-point-five-eight and two-point-five-three."

Ha, thought Allixter. There'd be some surprises — lots of surprises in high places. When they started to pull wool over human eyes, they should have selected someone other than Scotty Allixter. There was still another aspect to be considered. "What are the dial settings for the Earth station?"

The speaker made a series of squeaking sounds.

"Describe the settings in English."

"Dial one on top — set at the symbol resembling a B on its flat side. Dial two — set at the symbol resembling N inside oval. Dial three — set at symbol consisting of two concentric triangles."

Allixter searched in his pocket for a convenient piece of paper, brought forth the bubble with the changing colors, put it back, found the notebook, scribbled the information, tucked it back in the pouch.

"Now," said Allixter, "I'm going to the inhibitor bank. I want to excise the particular inhibitions which are now burnt out entirely and permanently. What is the easiest method?"

"Beside the panel is a series of dials and a plunger. Set the dial correctly, press the plunger. This act erases significance from the shreds."

"Fine," said Allixter. "Then when the circuits are repaired, they'll still be blank?"

"Correct."

"Excellent." Allixter went to the dials. "Now tell me how to find the right settings."

The robot described the symbols, Allixter set dials, punched, set dials, punched, set dials until his wrist ached.

"Now — those inhibitions are permanently erased?"

"Yes."

"And you'll destroy every Plag who sets foot on the planet?"

"Machine has no instructions to the contrary. Plags will be obliterated."

"How do I create new inhibitions?"

"Connect with a vacant shred, voice the order."

"Connect me with a vacant shred."

"Contact made."

"It is forbidden to kill me."

"Command conflicts with basic order. Command has been held up by monitor circuit."

Allixter gritted his teeth in vexation. "How the devil can I get home then? As soon as I leave you alone you will take steps to kill me."

"Problem contains variables without predictability."

"Thanks for nothing," said Allixter. "In other words I figure it out for myself. Okay — let's see. You're still working that problem I gave you?"

"Yes."

"How near done are you?"

"Approximately half done."

"You're swift."

"Computation of such material is largely automatic."

"Hmm." Allixter rubbed his chin through the air-film. "Contact with a vacant inhibitor shred."

"Contact made."

"Do not destroy any installation which will harm the natives or interfere with their livelihood."

"Instructions noted."

Allixter hesitated, eyed the mobile repair unit, looked it up and down with a doubtful eye. "If I put this machine back together will it hang that big hammer in place again?"

"Yes."

Allixter grimaced. "Well — let's get on with it."

He replaced the mechanism of the repair unit according to the instructions from the robot, set the facing panels back in position. The mobile unit remained quiet and lifeless. "How do we start her going?" asked Allixter.

"The control box at the back is fitted with a primary switch. Throw it down."

Allixter hesitated. There were too many unpredictable possibilities. He asked cannily, "What is the first job the repair unit will handle?"

"It will replace the damaged sections in the inhibitor banks."

"But they're blank now?"

"Yes."

"Then what?"

"It will lubricate bearing KB-four-hundred-eight, which is warm, and replace a chafed insulation in the Paradox Resolving System."

"When will it hang up the hammer?"

"In eighteen-point-nine minutes."

"Hm," mused Allixter. "That's time enough to get me out of this hall but otherwise…Will I be able to set the dial on the transfer tube and leave the planet before some other violent action occurs?"

"Problem contains unpredictable variables."

Allixter paced back and forth. "If I fix the machine's attention I'll get away. If not, I'm executed as an undesirable alien. All robots should have hobbies, something to keep them occupied, out of mischief. Now maybe…" He hesitated. "It'll cost me money." He considered carefully. "But what's a few franks compared to the value of my life?"

He pulled the quartz sphere from his pocket and the little crystalline creature inside glowed, glanced, sparkled in changing colors — hyacinth, rose, sea-green. Allixter set the sphere on the lip of a chin-high molding. "Can you see the little sphere?"

"Yes."

"You see those colors?"

"Yes."

"Observe this sphere and those colors. This is to be a hobby for you, to amuse you through the lonely hours of the night. You're to predict the color next to appear. When you are wrong review your computations and predict once more."

"Instructions noted," said the robot.

Allixter touched the smooth quartz ball. "Now, my little jewel, be as erratic as you like. I'll bet on any free-will tippet of life to beat down and confuse a machine, no matter how complex and how wise. So shine all your pretty colors and shine 'em as wild and clever as you know how." He flung the switch on the mobile repair unit.

The door was still locked. Allixter burnt it open with his heat torch, stepped out on to the path of stone slats overlooking the hazy gray valley. Overhead burned the myriad suns — colored balls of various flames, near and far in the violet sky.

"North is up here," said Allixter. "There's the warehouse and there's the golden door…"

VI

The depot back at the Hub was quiet when Allixter pushed through the tube. The out-belt carried only a few-score lugs of green-white grapes, a dozen green-painted tanks of oxygen — the lot bound for a mining station on an ore-rich but airless asteroid.

The in-belt was empty and the operator, after letting Allixter through, returned to his magazine.

Allixter ducked past the dispatcher's office but Schmitz spotted him, slid back the glass panel. "Hey, Scotty," he bellowed. "Come back here and turn in your report. You think this is Liberty Hall? Aint'cha read the rules?"

Allixter paused, then turned back.

"Here," said Schmitz, tossing over a yellow form. "Fill 'er out — and after this let's do it without me riding herd on you. After all, I got my job to handle too. You guys run me ragged, ducking in, ducking out, like a bunch of fillies at a tea-house. Then when they come and ask me who's been where and who's done which —"

"Look here, Sam," said Allixter, "I want to use your phone."

Schmitz looked up in surprise. "Go ahead, use it. I don't care. Just so long as you treat me right anything goes. Use my phone, anything.

Do like you're supposed to do, I won't kick. My God, man! Where's the Linguaid? The Chief will chew us green and blue if —"

"I left it in the depot." Allixter thumbed through the directory. He looked up. Schmitz was watching him intently, bright blue eyes gleaming like galvanized washers in the round red face.

Allixter closed the book. "No, I think I'll wait. Good day to you, Sam Schmitz."

"*Hey!*" roared Schmitz. "The report!"

"I'll be back shortly."

"When's shortly? Don't forget, I'm responsible for all this. It's me who gets reamed when you guys foul off..."

Allixter said in a voice like silk, "Give me fifteen minutes, Sammy old dear. I'll write you a report you'll wish you could take home and frame."

Fifteen minutes passed. Schmitz fidgeted, growled, looked through his assignment sheet. "That damn Allixter, he's the worst. Them Scotchmen is all crazy, drink too much of that brown smoke they call whiskey. Thank God for beer... Hey now, I believe he's back."

The four men with Allixter wore gray uniforms and they looked curiously alike. All were tall, spare of form, controlled of motion. Their faces were uniformly blunt, their eyes sharp and probing, their mouths tight.

"Heaven forbid!" barked Schmitz. "It's the World Security Intelligence. Now what's Allixter gone and done?" Automatically he reached for the button to the Chief's phone.

"*Hold it*, Schmitz!" yelled Allixter. "Leave that phone alone!"

One of the WSI men opened the door into Schmitz' cubicle, motioned. "I think you'd better come with us."

Protesting volubly Schmitz followed, hopping and bounding on his short legs to keep pace. The WSI men stood, two on each side of the big green door with the bronze letters. Allixter pushed the button, the door slid back, he entered. The secretary looked up. Allixter said, "Tell the Chief I'm back."

She hesitantly pushed the button. "Scotty Allixter reporting."

There was a pause. "Send him in."

She keyed back the lock, Allixter went to the inner door. Now the

WSI men entered the office. One strode to the desk where the secretary had made a swift movement for the speaker controls, caught her arm.

Allixter slid back the door. The air, smelling like a laboratory, wafted in his face. He entered with the WSI platoon at his back.

The Chief, sitting at his desk, his back to the light, stirred a trifle, then sat quiet. "What does this mean?" he asked tonelessly.

The WSI lieutenant said, "You're under arrest."

"On what grounds?"

"Grand theft, espionage, illegal entry to begin with. There may be further charges when a complete investigation is made."

"Got a warrant?"

"Sure have."

"Let's see it."

The lieutenant stepped forward with a blue-bound folder. The Chief glanced down the printed page, his mouth curled sardonically. Allixter thought — all the years I've come into this office, talked with the man, watched him, and only now do I see him as he is, the creature of an outer world with yellow goose-flesh skin and a breath of poisonous gas.

Allixter suddenly noted that the atmosphere, characteristically sharp and medicinal, had acquired a new harsh bite. He yelled, "Get clear, the devil's poisoning us!"

The Chief moved swiftly now, jumped to his feet.

The Lieutenant came forward. "Stop, or I'll shoot."

Allixter flung the door wide and saved his life. From the edge of the Chief's desk a plane of smoky yellow fire slashed out, burnt four men in half. Allixter shuddered back from the crackling ions which, deflected by the metal wall, scorched past an inch from his waist.

Allixter had shed his tools. He was weaponless. He ran to the secretary's phone. She pressed back against the wall, numb and glass-eyed. Allixter pushed the emergency button, bellowed, "Murder, the tube terminal maintenance office —" He heard stealthy motion inside the Chief's office, looked desperately toward the outer door. To escape he must cross the line of fire from the inner office.

Slow footsteps from inside were approaching. The Chief was edging close to the far wall to snap an angling shot through at Allixter. He was on the opposite side of the doorcase from the slide button. Allixter pressed the button, the door slid shut. Allixter dashed for the outer door. As he passed out a JAR rang behind him and the wall across the corridor shattered.

Allixter ran across the corridor into the still quiet depot. He ducked between fifty-gallon drums of acetone, sprang across the near-vacant clerks' platform, jumped up into the operator's box.

Breathless, fighting to make himself speak slowly and distinctly, he said, "This is an emergency. WSI business...Open the in-contacts as far as they'll go, set this code — phase eight-point-four-two, frequencies seven-point-five-eight and two-point-five-three."

The operator turned him a wondering glance. "What the hell kind of code is that? I never heard —"

"Shut *up!*" snarled Allixter. "Set the code! And route whatever you get into depot delivery."

The operator shrugged, turned the dials. "Eight-point-four-two — what was those other readings?"

"Seven-five-eight! Two-five-three! For God's sake, get moving!"

The operator pushed home the activation switch. Allixter jumped down, went to stand by the gold-brown curtain at the point where the belt rolled up out of the floor.

Ten seconds...fifteen seconds. He stared into the brown roil, flickering and shot with gleams of light, until — motion. The Chief appeared, looking over his shoulder. He turned his head, his mouth fell open.

Allixter jumped, caught him from behind, flung him to the belt. The Chief's JAR thudded free. Allixter seized it, rose to his feet.

"Now, old man — take it easy. You're caught, fair and square. I'd hate to jar you apart."

VII

Allixter was the center of a respectful audience in Buck's Bar. Beer flowed freely, the finest imports from Germany and the Netherlands, and there was always a ready hand to cover the tab.

The story had been told several times but among the audience were those to whom some feature of the episode was not completely clear. Of these Sam Schmitz was the most insistent.

"Allixter, look here," he said plaintively. "You come barreling into my office and I never say a word. I'm square with you, like always, but you could of got me in a gang of trouble. You was right, now I admit it, but suppose you was wrong? Then we're both in the stew. Doesn't seem quite the thing to do somehow."

"Schmitz," said Allixter with lofty good nature, "you're talking rubbish."

"But how could you be so sure it was the Chief? I don't see how you even figured there had to be somebody here at the Hub. You say you deduced this and figured that — but it still don't make sense."

"Look at it this way, Sam." Allixter refreshed his throat with a half-pint of Hochstein Lager. "I was sent out on a phony call. For a while after I landed on that planet I thought it was an honest mistake. But I began thinking. A lot of little peculiarities kept nagging at me. The Chief insisted I take the Linguaid. Why would I need a Linguaid on Rhetus? The answer was the Chief knew I'd be running into natives who spoke from under their arms.

"Then why did he make sure my air-film was Type X, halogen-proof? Rhetus is carbon dioxide, argon, helium, a little oxygen, and we only wear head bubbles. Why? Because he knew the atmosphere where I'd be going was full of fluorine.

"And when I saw the dead Plag on the floor I was bothered by a few other angles. He was dressed in clothes with an Earth-style zipper. Not only *like* Earth-style, but a zipper identical in every respect."

"Might have been coincidence," said Buck, the big red-faced bartender.

Allixter nodded. "Might have been. But how about the ball-point pen the guy wrote with and the squirt he carried in his tool-kit?"

"What's a squirt?" asked Kitty, the blonde square-jawed hostess.

Barnard, another maintenance mechanic, said quickly, "New tool, brand new. We carry it now instead of wire. When we want to run current between two posts, we squeeze the trigger on the squirt, the goo comes out, seals itself to the first post. We draw it up, down, around, anywhere we want it to go, touch it to the second post, cut off the trigger and we've got a permanent bond. The outside oxidizes to a good insulator, it sticks where it touches."

Kitty drank Schmitz' beer as a signal of comprehension.

"Anyway," Allixter continued, "when I saw all these items lying around, I thought to myself that sure enough, there's been some kind of contact with Earth. And it's been one-way because I knew I'd never seen any of them long-nosed yellow Plags on Earth.

"And then I thought of the Chief. He looked just like the corpse, maybe a little bit more alive. And I thought awhile. I remembered these other peculiarities. Then when the robot told me his circuits were so jammed that he killed Plags automatically, I figured it all out."

"So?" asked Schmitz.

"The Plags wanted to keep the tube open to the planet — I don't know what the name of their place is. I wouldn't be surprised if they operated a number of these subsidiary worlds, all equipped with robots, each milking the planet for all its worth, shipping the produce to Plag — Plagi — cripes, I never did know how to pronounce that word. *Plagigonstok* — That's it.

"Well, the robot was now adjusted to kill Plags as soon as they appeared. So it was necessary to get a mechanic of another race in to fix the computer. I was the lad."

"Sounds like a case of last resort," growled Buck.

Allixter spread his hands out. "What could they lose? Either I'd fix the robot or I'd be killed. The only other course open was to send a warship to destroy the robot — and there went one of their assets. So they made contact with the Chief, told him to send his best mechanic out to the place with everything he needed to fix the robot."

Schmitz thoughtfully lifted his glass to drink, found it empty. He shot a glance at Kitty, who was fluffing out her hair. "Buck — draw me another beer. Seems to me the Chief might have given you some kind of hint as to what you might expect."

"And have me coming back with the magoo? Not on your life. This way, if I got back, I'd think the whole affair a remarkable accident."

Barnard asked, "How come you knew the code the Chief would try to escape on?"

Allixter cocked his thick black eyebrows knowingly. "Well — I told you when I saw all the Earth-style equipment lying around I thought

I'd make sure. Maybe I'd made a mistake — maybe we did run a tube out to this Plag planet. So I asked the robot what the code was.

"He gave it to me and I knew it wasn't on our list — wasn't even in our units. The Plags evidently had discovered the tube system independently and set up a network of their own. Somehow they discovered we had a tube set-up and they smuggled in a representative, who became the Chief. Maybe there's more of them around."

"There's one thing I don't figure," said Barnard. "How did the Chief breathe? This kind of air should have smothered him."

Allixter drained his stein before replying. Buck slid it to the spigot, slid it back brimming with foam. Said Allixter, "Did you ever notice the scar along the Chief's neck?"

"Sure. Nasty thing. Must have got in the way of a long sharp Barlow."

"That was no scar. That was a breather tube, running under his skin into his throat. It supplied him with fluorine, carried hydrofluoric acid gas back to a filter for absorption. Not that our air would hurt him but it wouldn't do him any good."

Schmitz shook his head. "Should think it would burn out his throat."

Barnard laughed. "Remember the time you offered him one of those crooked black toscanis?"

"Yeah," gloomed Schmitz. "He said he didn't see how I could smoke one of those things and live."

Allixter said, "He wouldn't need anything like the volume of oxygen we breath. A few pounds would last him a long time. Of course there was an unavoidable leak up through his mouth and nose —"

Barnard struck the bar with his fist. "I always claimed the Chief's office smelled like a hospital!"

Schmitz said dolefully, "I wonder what's going to happen now? Is the government going to send a commission out to Plag — Plagi — you know where?"

"Well," said Allixter, who now found himself regarded as the font of all knowledge. "I can't be sure. They've been robbing us blind, those Plags. All our ideas, tools, techniques — all going out. That's not so bad in itself but they made sure we were getting none of their stuff in return.

"So there was the Chief's function. Send out merchandise — he could get into the depot when no one else was around, or else he could send it out the private escape hatch in his office — send out merchandise, pay for it through some figurehead corporation in platinum or uranium they mined cheap on some robot planet. Or maybe they printed up counterfeit money. The WSI says they found a case of brand new hundred-frank notes in the Chief's office."

"So that's who's been flooding my till!" roared Buck. "I've lost a thousand franks in bum bills!" The enormity of the Chief's crimes now seemed to dawn upon him. He writhed his shoulders, each the heft of a sack of wheat. "Why, the miserable long-nosed lizard, I'd like to — I'd like to tear him apart with my own hands! A thousand *franks* he's cost me!"

"Tough," said Allixter in a faraway voice. "He cost me five hundred franks too when I had to leave that valuable little jewel behind. But thank goodness I happened to pick up this scarab out there on that gray planet. Prime yellow fluorspar, a lovely piece, and it's the sacred seal of the indigenes. There's only one like it. The Curator of the Out-world Museum told me he'd give eight hundred franks for it but I'd have to wait a month till he could put through a purchase order. Buck, I'll let you have it for six hundred and take the profit yourself."

Buck picked up the octahedron. "Sacred seal? *Humph!* Looks like a lot of chicken-scratches. I'll give you five franks for it and maybe I can unload it on a drunk for ten."

Allixter rescued the fluorspar with an expression of hurt indignation. "Five franks? I'd sell you my right ear off my head first!"

Dover Spargill's Ghastly Floater

Dover Spargill, age twenty-one, paced the hearth, slapping his jodhpurs with a riding crop. Hunched in a wingback chair to the side, Attorney James Offbold turned up his eyes as if seeking divine support.

Dover paused in midstride; Attorney Offbold's expression at once became attentive: this insufferable young ass represented thirty thousand dollars a year in fees. Otherwise, Mr. Offbold would have sweat in Gehenna before crossing the street at Dover Spargill's bidding.

"That's the whole affair, then?" inquired Dover with a smart slap at his boots.

"That's the entire document, Mr. Spargill, and may I offer my heartfelt congratulations?"

Dover paused in his stride, turned his head in inquiry. "Congratulations? What for?"

"The fact that, now you are of age, you become one of the richest men in the world."

"Oh, the money." Dover flicked his riding crop to the side. Wealth occupied small place in his thoughts, the gesture implied. "Certainly it's a help; I won't have to worry about making it myself. Although I sometimes think my father was rather unimaginative; time and time again I've pointed out ways of doubling his fortune."

Offbold coughed, recalling tiger-eyed old Howard Spargill and his canny manipulations. "Well, I can't quite agree with you, Mr. Spargill; your father was certainly the smartest business man of his day. He started out a prospector and wound up owning Moon Mines, almost a third of the entire moon."

Dover shook his head, pursed his lips. "He also allowed Thornton Bray to organize the other holdings into the Lunar Mineral Cooperative, when he could easily have bought up the claims himself."

Offbold remarked rather loftily, "Don't you think that gaining title to a third of the moon is enough? An area larger than all of Europe?"

Dover frowned. " 'Enough' is a word inapplicable in modern commercial context, as I think you should be the first to acknowledge, Mr. Offbold."

Offbold made a grumbling noise in his throat, sat staring glumly into the fire while Dover proceeded to develop the argument, emphasizing salient points with motions of the riding crop. He explained that in the upper financial reaches, the accumulation of wealth was a game requiring little more skill than the manipulation of a pin-ball machine. Offbold nodded jerkily, finally snapped the lock on his brief-case and rose to his feet.

"Now then, Mr. Spargill, I'll say goodby; you'll probably have plans for dinner."

Dover conducted him to the door. Offbold turned for a last set of reminders.

"No doubt, Mr. Spargill, you'll be approached by promoters and confidence men; I scarcely need recommend caution to one of your —" he winced "— acumen."

Dover nodded briskly.

"But in any event, I will perform the formality. The mines are capably managed by the existing staff; the terrestrial interests are under the stewardship of Calmus Associates. I strongly advise against any changes or any new undertakings. If you are approached by anyone wanting money on any pretext whatever — refer him to me, and I will tick him off properly."

Offbold continued on these lines for a moment or two, while Dover, listening with half-closed eyes, swung his riding crop back and forth.

Offbold finally shook hands and departed. Dover watched him out to his cab.

"Bumbling old idiot..." He slapped at his boots. "He means well, no doubt."

✳

Thornton Bray, chairman of the Board of Directors for Lunar Mines Cooperative, was a large man, florid and moist as half a watermelon. He had prominent eyes without lashes; his cheeks were smooth and plump as a baby's buttocks. Tucking the signed agreement in his pocket he shook his head with a rueful smirk.

"Yes sir, a chip off the old block. I'm afraid I overshot myself trying to out-deal you."

Dover let the smoke of an expensive cigar trickle from the corner of his mouth. He adopted a careless manner, as if to deprecate his victory over Bray and Lunar Mineral Cooperative.

"Yes, sir," went on Bray, "you're a big man now. You'll go down in history. First man holding title to an entire world. Think of it! Fifty-nine million square miles! Lord of all you survey!"

Dover glanced to the three-foot globe of the moon on his desk. The surface was divided into irregular areas tinted in gray-blue and gray, distinguishing Moon Mines from the Lunar Mineral Cooperative.

"Yes, she'll be all one color now. I wonder…" He paused. "I supposed it would hardly be in good taste."

"What's that?"

"Change the name from 'Moon' to 'Spargill'."

Bray reflected. "You'd have your work cut out for you." He shook hands, with a hearty jerking motion. "Well, I wish you luck, Mr. Spargill." He gave his head an admiring shake. "Not that you need it, with that whipsaw brain of yours."

Dover gestured affably with his cigar. "I see a good thing, I go after it, I get it."

"Good-day then, Mr. Spargill."

Dover twitched his hand in a jaunty salute, turned back to the globe.

A moment later the visiphone buzzed.

Dover spoke over his shoulder. "Yes?"

"Mr. Offbold, sir," came the voice of his confidential secretary.

Dover yawned, returned to his desk. "I'll speak to him."

The screen revealed a face contorted by anger and desperation. "Quick," cried Mr. Offbold, "you haven't signed any papers, have you?"

Dover put his feet on the desk, flicked the ash from his cigar. "I've just concluded an advantageous deal, if that's what you mean. Very far-reaching."

Offbold's face sagged. "Tell me the worst..."

"Moon Mines Company now is legal owner to 59 million square miles, 42 billion cubic miles, 5×10^{19} tons of satellite. In short, we've bought out the Cooperative. I'm sole owner to the moon."

Offbold's eyes brimmed with tears. "Tell me, what did you pay? How much?"

"No small sum," admitted Dover. "But I've been to the moon, I've seen the ore reserves on our land and on the Cooperative land and I'll tell you, Offbold, we've come out to the good."

"How much?"

"Oh —" Dover puffed hard at his cigar "— 200 million cash."

Offbold put his hand to his forehead.

"And the Antarctic Energy interest."

"*Oh!*"

Dover inquired with asperity, "What's the matter with you, Offbold?"

Offbold heaved a deep sigh. "Now you own the moon, what are you going to do with it?"

"Why, continue mining it, naturally."

"You young fool!" roared Offbold. "Don't you ever read the papers?"

"Certainly, whenever I have time."

"Well, take time now!" The screen went dark.

"Miss Foresythe," called Dover.

"Yes, Mr. Spargill?"

"The afternoon journal, if you please."

The screen glowed. Dover's eyes went to the lead story.

SCIENCE UNVEILS NEW BOMBSHELL
Transmutation Process Announced

A method for mass conversion of one element into another has been announced today by Frederick Dexter, chairman of the Applied Research Foundation. Eminent minds claim the discovery will bring about social changes comparable to the Industrial Revolution.

Dexter made the historic announcement at a press conference this morning. "The device operates on a self-sustaining principle; that is to say, no outside energy is required, provided that a correct internal balancing according to established atomic theory is maintained. A condition equivalent to a temperature of hundreds of millions of degrees is used, but the energy produced — by either fusion or fission — is absorbed by the balancing process, and the cell remains at near-room temperature."

Dexter revealed that the Foundation itself will manufacture and distribute the transmutation units. Production will begin at once, Dexter announced, in sizes varying from household devices up to monsters capable of gulping many tons a minute.

Dexter was asked as to the technological and economic effects of the discovery. "It is my opinion," he said, "that we are entering a new Golden Age. Platinum will be as cheap as iron; we can now utilize the wastes and slag piles of the already antiquated chemical purification systems to obtain an abundance of pure materials. Mines of course will be —"

Dover said politely, "You may turn off the screen, Miss Foresythe."

He walked slowly to the three-foot globe, caused it to spin, and the pocked surface rasped the palm of his hand. "59 million square miles," mused Dover. "42 billion —"

"Mr. Spargill," came the voice of his secretary. "Mr. Offbold is back on the screen."

"Yes," said Dover. "I'll see him."

Mr. Offbold had himself under restraint; only the swelling of his neck betrayed the cost at which control had been achieved. He spoke in a labored voice, each word carefully enunciated.

"Mr. Spargill, it is my duty to reveal to you the exact state of your affairs. First, Moon Mines is worth nothing. Nil. Your new acquisition, the Lunar Mineral Cooperative, is likewise valueless."

"But — I own the whole satellite!" protested Dover.

Mr. Offbold's eyes glittered, his lip curled tartly. "You could show title to the entire Magellanic Cloud, and it wouldn't affect your bank credit a nickel's worth."

Dover mulled over the situation.

"You could not sell the entire moon for ten dollars," barked Offbold. "No, excuse me, I take that back. No doubt there are spendthrift college boys who would offer you ten, perhaps twenty dollars, if only for the unique distinction of owning the moon. If you receive any such offers, I advise you to close; it is the only wise in which the moon has transactional value. So. We write off Moon Mines, Lunar Cooperative, and Antarctic Energy from your assets. Now — 200 million dollars cash.

"There is perhaps 70 or 80 million dollars fluid, in various depreciation, building, amortization funds, etcetera. I have made a rough calculation, and find that when you have sold other holdings sufficient to pay the balance you will have left —" he paused impressively "— the South Sahara Pest Control Agency at Timbuctoo, and a considerable acreage in North Arizona, both taken by your father in payment of otherwise uncollectible debts."

"Sell them both," Dover directed him. "Sell everything. Pay all the bills and deposit the balance to my personal account." He added in a brave voice, "Everything is turning out very well, just as I planned, in fact..."

"I fail to understand you," declared Offbold icily.

Dover's voice came hollowly. "Well, every once in a while a shaking down is good for a great organization. Tones it up, so to speak..."

Offbold lapsed into the vernacular. "You got shook down, Mr. Spargill, you got shook down."

Roger Lambro, during a mid-afternoon conversation with Miss Deborah Fowler on the Tivoli Terrace, asked, "Where in the world is Dover Spargill these days? Haven't seen the chap in ages."

Miss Fowler absently shook her head. "He's dropped out of the picture. I've heard rumors..." She stopped short, unwilling to pass on unpleasant gossip.

Roger Lambro was not quite so delicate. "Oh?"

She twirled the stem of her Martini glass. "Well — they say that after he pulled that ghastly floater, he went out to live on his property." She raised her beautiful eyes to where the moon hung pale as an oyster in the afternoon sky. "Just think, Roger, perhaps he's up there right now, looking down on us..."

Thornton Bray stood on the marble plaza of his villa at Lake Maggiore, an after-dinner Armagnac in one hand, a Rosa Panatela Suprema in the other. He was entertaining a group of business associates with an anecdote of his business career.

"—I might have been more charitable except this young ass, not dry behind the ears, thought all the time he was doing me. *Me*, Thornton Bray!" Bray laughed quietly. "Thought he was getting something for nothing. So I played him along; after all, business is business. He made the break, I followed through...Yes, sir, I wish I could have seen his face when he first felt the clinch."

"Speaking of the moon," said one of his friends, "she certainly looks fine tonight. Can't say as I've ever seen her looking quite so —well, calm, pearly."

Thornton Bray glanced up to the full moon. "Yes, she's beautiful. From down here, that is. If you've ever mined up there, you come back to Earth with different ideas. A devilish place, bleak, arid."

"Funny color to it," observed another member of the party. "Green and blue and pink, all at once."

Bray remonstrated playfully. "Come now, Jonesy. You've been dipping your beak more than is good for you...Have another? By Golly, I think I'll join you."

Cornelius Armitage, professor of Astronomy at Hale University, muttered waspishly under his breath, wiped the eyepiece of the telescope with a bit of floss.

A teaching assistant sat nearby counting stars in a sky-sample. "What's the trouble?"

"Steam in the lens, a frightful condition. The moon looks all fuzzy." He inspected the glass. "There, that's better."

He bent once more to his observations.

The teaching assistant looked up at a new sound. Professor Armitage was sitting bolt upright, his eyeglasses on the table, rubbing his eyes, blinking. "I've been reading far too much; got to take it a little easier."

"All done for the night?" inquired the teaching assistant.

Professor Armitage nodded wearily. "I'm just too tired and bleary-eyed."

Lieutenant MacLeod, overlooking a student's work at the Maritime Institute, shook his head indulgently. "Those figures would set us three hundred miles inland. You've probably failed to correct for refraction."

Cadet Glasskamp set his lips rebelliously. The problem was futile in any event; celestial navigation was seldom used in this day of loran and automatic piloting. Lunar occultation of stars to determine Greenwich time was three centuries antiquated; the exercise was no more than drudgery.

Lieutenant MacLeod admitted as much, but he claimed that working the difficult old systems clarified the primary concepts of hour angle, declination, right ascension, local time, and the like, as did none of the modern short-cut methods.

Cadet Glasskamp bent over his problem. Twenty minutes later he looked up. "I can't find anything wrong here. Might have been an error in the observation."

"Nonsense," said the lieutenant. "I caught the sight myself." Nevertheless he checked on Glasskamp's figures, once, twice, a third time, and finally opening the Nautical Almanac, calculated the time of occultation.

He chewed his lip in amazement. "Twenty-two minutes? I don't believe it. That shot was right on the nose."

"Perhaps you didn't allow for refraction of the star's light around the moon."

Lieutenant MacLeod gave Cadet Glasskamp a pitying look. "Refraction occurs when light passes through an atmosphere. There's no atmosphere on the moon — although if there were —" he calculated under his breath "— the moon moves half a degree an hour, that's thirty minutes. Earth atmosphere refracts a thousand seconds; if there were an atmosphere dense as Earth's on the moon, you'd have to double it, light passing through twice. Two thousand. Say twelve hundred — that's twenty minutes. If so — that would create forty chronological minutes, at half a degree per hour. Apparently," said the lieutenant jocularly, "we've discovered that the moon has an atmosphere roughly half as dense as the Earth's."

Sunday morning breakfast in the home of Sir Brampton Pasmore moved along its usual lazy routine. Sir Brampton read a favorite technical journal with his kippers; Lady Iris scanned the *Times Magazine*.

Lady Iris uttered an amused exclamation. "Here's something in your field, my dear." She read. " 'Does the Moon Have an Atmosphere? Strange Signs and Portents'."

"Pooh," scoffed Sir Brampton. "I marvel at the *Times* for publishing that yellow sensational balderdash. Expect that stuff from the Americans..."

Lady Iris knitted her brows. "They seem perfectly serious. They speak of meteor trails appearing."

"Ridiculous," said Sir Brampton, returning to his paper. "It hasn't been ten years since the moon was extensively explored for minerals, before transmuters, of course. There certainly was no atmosphere then; why should there be now?"

Lady Iris shook her head doubtfully. "Couldn't someone give the moon an atmosphere?"

"Impractical, my dear," Sir Brampton murmured.

"I don't see why."

Sir Brampton laid aside his paper. "It's a scientific matter, dear, that I'm not sure you'd understand."

Lady Iris bridled sharply. "Are you by any chance suggesting —"

"No, naturally not," Sir Brampton said hurriedly. "What I meant was...Oh, well, it's a matter of escape velocity of a celestial body, and the molecular motion of gases. Lunar gravity is insufficiently powerful to retain an atmosphere, at least for any length of time: the molecules move at sufficient speed to escape into space. Hydrogen would whiff off at once. Oxygen and nitrogen — well, I believe they'd probably last longer, perhaps years, but eventually they'd escape. So you see, an atmosphere on the moon just isn't practical."

Lady Iris tapped her paper with a stubborn finger. "It says in the

Times there's an atmosphere. That means it's there. The *Times* is never wrong. Why doesn't somebody drop by and find out for sure?"

Sir Brampton sighed. "The moon doesn't interest anyone any more, my dear. Martian ruins are the current excitement. The moon is uncomfortable and dangerous, there's nothing to be learned, and now that transmutation supplies all our mineral wants, there's no reason whatever to visit the moon... Besides, I understand that some crank with legal title discourages trespassing; he has a special patrol that turns back visitors."

"Well, well, well," breathed lovely Deborah Fowler Lambro to her husband Roger. "Remember Dover Spargill? Just look at this!"

She handed across the bulletin from the news-facsimile.

"Moon being readied for habitation, announces Dover Spargill, owner of the moon..."

Lady Iris looked at Sir Brampton with glowing eyes. "I told you so," said she, and Sir Brampton crouched behind the *Report of the Royal Astrophysical Society.*

Thornton Bray walked back and forth, hands behind his back. Was it possible... No, of course not. And yet... Dover Spargill had been so innocent a sheep, so succulent for the plucking.

He reached for the visiphone, dialled his attorney. "Herman, remember when we first organized the Lunar Cooperative?"

"All of twenty-five years ago," mused Herman Birch, a tall lemon-colored man with the flat-topped face of a falcon.

"There was an old duffer, dead now, who refused to sign up. He only held a few square miles, in Aristillus crater, I believe. When we sold Lunar Co-op to Spargill, that particular parcel was not included. I wonder what the status of that claim is now?"

Birch turned his head, spoke a few words to someone out of the range of vision, returned to Bray. "What do you make of this atmosphere talk?"

Bray curled his lips. "Eyewash. Where would it come from? Moon surface is a thirteenth of Earth surface; there'd be billions and billions of tons."

"Spargill might be using transmuters."

"Suppose he is? Do you have any conception of the size of a project like that? The moon's a big place. The heaviest transmuter I know of has a capacity of a hundred tons a minute and that's chicken feed."

"He might have built special installations."

"Where would he get the money? I know on reliable information that he was cleaned out when he took over Lunar Co-op...Just a minute, I'll call the Applied Research Foundation and make some inquiries."

He dialled rapidly, and a moment later was looking into a cautious round face. "Hello, Sam."

Sam Abbott nodded. "What can I do for you, Bray?"

"I want a little confidential information, Sam."

"What's on your mind?"

"Has Applied Research sold Dover Spargill any transmuters?"

Sam Abbott's face crinkled in a sudden broad grin. "I'll give you a straight answer, Bray: not a one. Not a single one."

Bray blinked. "How do you account for the talk of an atmosphere on the moon?"

Abbott shrugged. "I don't account for it; that's not my job."

Bray, muttering in irritation, returned to Herman Birch. Birch nodded a wise head. "That claim was open. I've just filed in your name."

Bray clamped his heavy mouth. "Good. Now I've got a legal right to visit my claim. Rent me a fast boat..."

The radar alarm sounded eighty thousand miles out from the moon. The pilot threw down the switch. A harsh voice said, "You are approaching my property."

Bray pulled himself to the speaker. "I'm going out to my own property, the Niobe claim in Aristillus Crater. If you interfere with me, I'll call the Space Patrol."

The voice made no answer; Bray visualized the frantic search through block maps and title deeds. Ten minutes passed.

A new voice said, "Aboard approaching boat: who is claimant to the Niobe claim?"

"Me. Thornton Bray."

"Oh. Bray," said the voice in a different tone. "This is Spargill. Why didn't you say who you were? Drop on down to home camp."

"Where are you?" inquired Bray cautiously.

"We're in Hesiodus, at the south point of Mare Nubium — beside Pitatus. The old Goldenrod workings."

The camp in Hesiodus Crater occupied a typical old mining compound: a big dome of plastic anchored into the rock by a web of cables which also served to contain the air-pressure from within. The pilot landed the boat and Bray, already clad in a space-suit, jumped out to the surface.

Three men approached; under the dome of the first Bray recognized the face of Dover Spargill.

Dover waved. "How are you, Bray? Nice of you to drop out…What's all this about the Niobe claim?"

Bray explained. "And since the land was ownerless, I decided I had better snap it up."

As he spoke he examined his surroundings. The lunar sky, which he remembered as black, was a deep hyacinth blue. "Looks like all the talk of a moon atmosphere is true."

Dover nodded. "Oh yes…Come along over to the dome." He led Bray across a flat of crushed pumice. A mile behind rose the walls of the crater, tall irregular spires. At the base of the walls Bray discerned a row of black cubes.

"What's the pressure here now, Spargill?"

"Got her up to seven pounds."

"Barometric? That is to say, against a mercury column?"

"Oh my no. A misleading statement. Seven pounds against a spring scale."

Bray snorted delicately. "Tremendous waste of money, Spargill."

"Do you really think so? I'm sorry to hear you say that; I rather hoped something useful might eventuate…Look there." He pointed against the wall of the dome. "Geraniums. Growing outside on the moon. Never thought you'd see a sight like that in the old days, did you, Bray?"

"Mmmph. What good are geraniums? Monumental waste. As fast as you make atmosphere it'll dissipate into space. Not enough gravity here."

Dover closed the outer hatch on Bray and himself. They removed their suits, and Dover conducted Bray to the main lounge, where a dozen men and women sat reading, talking, playing cards, drinking beer.

"You've got quite a colony here," said Bray in a mystified voice. "Do they work for nothing?"

Dover laughed shortly. "Of course not…This is only a small part of our operation. We've got units going at almost all the old mines…Have some coffee?"

Bray declined brusquely. "Exactly what are your plans, if I may ask?"

Dover leaned back in the chair. "It's a long story, Bray. First, I hope you'll let bygones be bygones. I suppose I fleeced you pretty thoroughly when I took Lunar Co-op away from you, eh?"

Bray said in a strangled voice, "You fleeced *me?*…Well, let it ride. I want to hear about this—" he jerked a thumb toward the sky "—this mad stunt of yours."

Dover said soothingly, "It's probably not so impractical as you think. Consider the future, Bray. Do you see what I see?

"Forests, meadows, grass-lands. Moon, the green planet! Trees five hundred feet tall! We're filling craters with water right now. Moon, the world of a million lakes! In five more years we'll have thirteen pounds pressure, and we'll be living out-of-doors."

"Waste, waste, waste," intoned Bray. "You'll never get a stable atmosphere."

Dover scratched his head. "Well, of course I may be mistaken—"

"Sure you are," said Bray bluffly. "I hate to see you making a fool of yourself, Dover. For old time's sake, I'm willing to—"

"My theory," explained Dover, "was that the composition of the atmosphere determined how fast it dissipated. Naturally we expect to make adjustments for a long time to come."

"Well, of course—"

"But actually, we're building a special kind of atmosphere, rather different from Earth's."

Bray's nostrils flared in interest. "How so?"

"Well, in the first place, xenon replaces nitrogen. Specific gravity of 4.5, as against 1 for nitrogen. Then we're using the heaviest possible isotopes for oxygen, carbon and nitrogen, and deuterium rather than hydrogen for our water. It all works out to a pretty dense atmosphere —

physiologically identical to Earth air, but about three and a half times as dense. So our vapor loss into space will be minimized to almost nothing."

Bray cracked his knuckles. Something must be wrong. Dover was saying, "We could easily make the atmosphere even denser, if we so desired — by substituting radon for the xenon."

"Radon! My God — you'd fry!"

Dover smilingly shook his head. "Radon has many isotopes, not all significantly radioactive. On Earth we're familiar only with the breakdown product of radium, thorium, actinium. But radon's disadvantage is that it's too heavy. A gust of wind would bowl a man off his feet, like hitting him with a sack of sawdust."

"Hm…Interesting," remarked Bray absently. Some means must be found to repair what he now recognized as an error in judgment: allowing Dover to become sole owner of the moon. Not quite sole owner; Bray, as a lunar property holder, was entitled to a certain advisory status. Reason, sweet reason, was the phrase.

He explored the ground cautiously. "What do you propose to do with all this property?" He winked slyly. "Sell it at a fancy figure?"

Dover made a deprecatory motion. "I suppose that an unprincipled man, by subdividing and selling, could easily become a multi-billionaire…Did you say something?"

"No," said Bray, swallowing hard. "I just coughed."

"But I have a different end in view. I want to see the moon become a garden suburb of Earth — a park, a residential area. Certainly I want no housing projects on the moon, no tourist hotels…"

"Naturally you're using Applied Research transmuters?"

"Of course. Are there any other kind?"

"No, not that I know of."

"These are special mammoth units built specially for this project. We've got two thousand in operation already. We push them under a mountain, bulldoze rock into the hoppers. Every week two more units go into operation; there's a tremendous amount of material to transmute, and we're on a fifteen-year schedule. That means that we've got to average three billion tons a day, for atmosphere alone; so far, we're up to the mark."

Bray grimaced, clenched his fist. Observing Dover's questioning look, he blurted, "Sam Abbott at Applied Research is a damn liar. Said he never sold you any transmuters."

"But that's correct, we're using them free, on a loan basis."

"Free!"

Dover turned out his hands in a gesture of frankness. "That's the only way I could undertake the project. Buying out Lunar Co-op took almost everything I had. But my father originally endowed the Foundation, and there was a certain sense of obligation. In a way, we're partners in the deal." He nodded toward the other occupants of the lounge. "All Foundation staff. They're sinking the profits from producing the transmuters into the scheme; of course they'll get it all back ten-fold."

"But you still retain control?"

"All except the Niobe claim." Dover laughed jovially. "You slipped one over on me there. I thought that I was sole owner, and now I fear that…Well, no matter."

Bray cleared his throat. "As you say, we're the sole owners, you and I. I imagine we should form some kind of supervisory board to protect our interests so to speak."

Dover seemed surprised. "Do you think that such a formality is necessary? After all the Niobe claim —"

Bray said portentously, "I'm afraid I'll have to insist."

Dover frowned. "I don't think the claim will impose as much of a burden on your time as you fear."

Bray raised his eyebrows. "How so?"

"Well —" Dover hesitated "— you haven't visited your holdings yet?"

"No. All I know that it's a ten-mile-square block in the floor of Aristillus."

Dover got up. "Perhaps we had better fly up and take a look at it."

In a small stub-winged air-craft they rose up out of Hesiodus, flew north along the shore of Mare Nubium.

"All good basalt," said Dover. "A few years of weathering should produce a magnificent red soil. We're experimenting with bacteria to hasten the process."

Sinus Medii passed below, and the eastern littoral of Mare Vaporum. Ahead loomed the great crags of the Apennines, a little to the left was the great crater Eratosthenes.

Bray craned his neck. "Surely that's not water?"

"Oh yes," smiled Dover. "Lake Eratosthenes. We're using Eratosthenes and one other for primary evaporation points. Water will come rather slower than the air; the moon will be a dry world for quite some time yet."

Bray said bluffly, "I believe I'll put up a big resort hotel on my property — amusement park, big casino, dog-racing." He nudged Dover waggishly. "Thank God, there's no blue laws out here, eh Dover?"

Dover said stiffly, "We hope to govern ourselves, with the aid of our native good taste."

"Well," said Bray, "if I had a bit more land, I wouldn't be forced to make do on so little. Personally I don't like the idea, but what'll you have? There's just the Niobe claim, and no more. I hope it doesn't turn out an eyesore... Perhaps if you'd make me a good deal for old time's sake, let me buy back a chunk of Lunar Cooperative for, say —"

Dover shook his head. "I'm afraid that's impossible."

Bray snapped shut his jaw. "Then I'll have to do the best I can at Aristillus. A sky-scraper, maybe. We'll make it the hot-spot of the moon. Sort of a Latin Quarter, a Barbary Coast."

"Sounds interesting."

The Apennines stabbed up at them from below. "Beautiful mountain scenery," said Dover. "Remarkable. Wait twenty or thirty years, and you'll really see something. That's Palus Putredinus below, and ahead, those three craters —"

"Archimedes, Autolycus and Aristillus," said Bray. "Aristillus — future hot-spot of the moon."

"Lake Aristillus," said Dover absently.

Bray froze in his seat. The gleam of water was unmistakable.

"A beautiful crater," said Dover. "And it makes a beautiful lake, ten thousand feet deep, I believe."

The airplane circled over the placid blue surface. A small island protruded from the center.

Bray found his voice. "Do you mean to say," he demanded, "that you've submerged my property under ten thousand feet of water?"

Dover nodded. "See there..." He pointed to a cascade of water tumbling down the eastern wall. "Back along that rill sixty units are turning out water and xenon. I'll name the river after you, if you'd like. Bray River... From your point of view, rather a sad coincidence that we decided on Eratosthenes and Aristillus for our first lakes. I didn't have the heart to break the news to you back at the camp."

Bray roared, "This is insufferable! You've flooded my property, you've —"

Dover said in a conciliatory voice, "Naturally we had no idea that the property was not ours; if I had known that you wanted to build a 'hot-spot' — as you call it — I'd never have planned the lake."

"I'll sue, I'll collect damages!"

"Damages?" asked Dover in a pained voice. "Why surely —"

Bray rolled his eyes in fury. "I can prove that the property was worth millions, that —"

"Er — how long ago did you come into possession of the Niobe claim?"

Bray subsided suddenly. "Well, as a matter of fact — It makes no difference! You're guilty of —"

"Surely it's obvious, Mr. Bray, that you filed claim on property already under water." Dover scratched his head. "I suppose the claim is legal enough. Can't see what you'll do with your property, Mr. Bray. You might try stocking it with trout..."

SABOTAGE ON SULFUR PLANET

I

NOLAND BANNISTER, SUPERINTENDENT of Star Control Field Office #12, was known at the space-port and along Folger Avenue as a hell-roarer — a loud-voiced man of vigorous action. He made no secret of his dislike for administrative detail and attacked paper work with a grumbling rancor. Negligence in his staff he dealt with rudely. Mistakes of a more serious nature left him grim and white with rage.

It was Robert Smith's misfortune to commit the most striking blunder of Bannister's long and varied experience.

As usual, at four o'clock Friday afternoon Bannister sat in his office reviewing the week's work: ships cleared for passage, ships inspected and cleared for discharge of cargo, contraband seizures, crews screened for hijackers and known performers. Last he inspected a *précis* from the logs of ships which had surfaced during the week; skimming for information of possible economic or scientific value.

Near the end of the *précis* he found an informal note.

> Re SpS Messeraria. *Supercargo very drunk when ship's log was taken. Followed me back to the office rambling about planet inhabited by intelligent life-forms (obvious fabrication). Tossed him out of office on ear. Smith.*

Bannister blinked in amazement, stiffened in his chair. He switched the film back to the *Messeraria*'s log, examined it with flinty attention. It appeared ordinary enough, although Captain Plum's reputation offered no surety against falsification. He checked the ship's roster against a master index.

Jack Fetch, mate. One-time member of the Violet Ray Association. Never convicted.

Abe McPhee, chief steward. Moral deviant, refused de-aberration.

Owen Phelps, quartermaster. Expert gambler and game-rigger.

Don Lowell, supercargo. Known embezzler; a brother refused to prosecute.

"Mmmph," said Bannister to himself. "Nice bunch." He continued. First and second engineers, wiper, mess boy. Pasts stained to a greater or lesser degree.

Bannister re-read Smith's breezy message. Anger rose in his throat like the aftertaste of cheap whisky. Suppose Supercargo Don Lowell had been drunkenly babbling the truth? He punched a button on his desk.

"Yes, Mr. Bannister?"

"Who the devil is Smith? There's a report here — just a few casual lines — signed 'Smith'. Who the devil's Smith?"

"That'll be Robert Smith. A front-office man we hired last week."

Bannister said in a metallic voice, "I want to see him."

There was a wait of five minutes, while Bannister drummed his fingers on the desk. Then the door slid back a few inches, remained in this position, revealing a hand on the latch, while the owner exchanged a bit of final banter with Bannister's secretary.

Bannister barked, "Come in, come in!" He glared at the young man, still grinning, who swung the door open.

"Smith?" Bannister spoke with steely gentleness.

"Yes, sir."

"Can you guess why I want to see you?"

Smith raised his eyebrows. "Not unless it's about the suggestion I made the other day to the office manager."

"A suggestion? Well, well," said Bannister, catlike. "How long have you been with us now?"

"About a week. I'm not complaining — don't get me wrong. I just think the work I'm doing could be handled more efficiently by machine."

"What are your duties, Smith?"

"Well, I've been collating reports, reviewing similar information in Central Intelligence Bank, and appending or amending. If we had a scanner machine to grade and append the material automatically, I'd be free to tackle more important duties."

Bannister inspected Smith under lowered eyebrows. "Interesting. What do you imagine to be the price of the machine you visualize, Smith?"

Smith frowned. "I'm really not sure. That's out of my line. Twenty or thirty thousand, I suppose."

"Who would service the machine, who would code the material?"

Smith smiled at the question. "A cyberneticist, naturally."

Bannister looked toward the ceiling. "And what, I wonder, is the salary such a technical expert commands?"

Smith likewise raised his eyes in calculation. "Perhaps five or six hundred. Seven hundred possibly for a good man. You'd want the best."

"And how much are we paying you for performing identical work?"

"Well — three hundred."

"Are there any conclusions to be drawn?"

Robert Smith said candidly, "It must be that I'm worth seven hundred dollars a month to the bureau."

Bannister cleared his throat, but managed to continue in the same gentle voice. "May I direct your attention to the matter on the screen?"

"Oh, certainly." Smith swung his gaze to the three lines of neat typescript. He nodded. "I remember the man very well. In terrible shape, dead drunk. Vicious stuff, alcohol." And he confided, "I myself don't drink; it rots the brain."

Bannister was fond of whisky and beer. Once more he cleared his throat. "What exactly did this man say to you?"

Smith settled himself into Bannister's most comfortable chair, stretched out his legs. "He was clearly subject to delusions and also victim of a well-established persecution complex. Assured me the captain and mate of his ship were intent on his death."

"Did he mention why he was in danger?"

Smith laughed easily. "Typical paranoia. A man in bad shape. He claimed that the *Messeraria* had landed on an unknown planet and discovered an intelligent race of beings. He made a full account in his diary — so he insisted — but the captain tore it up and obliterated passages in the ship's log."

Bannister nodded sagely. "And why did all this take place?"

"He said something about —" Smith knit his brows "— I believe it was jewels. Rather trite." He chuckled. "He could at least have given us something bizarre for our trouble — energy from the air, a paradise of beautiful women, clairvoyant dragons. But no — just jewels."

Bannister nodded. "Drunk, eh?"

"Drunk as a lord."

"Crazy to boot?"

"Well, Mr. Bannister, you've heard his story. You can judge for yourself."

Bannister's fury and contempt had taken him past the stage of invective. He said in a sibilant voice, "Smith, you're a remarkable man."

Smith looked up in surprise. "Why, thank you, sir."

"A museum piece. A man with a head full of corn cobs."

Smith stared in confusion.

"We've been exploring space a hundred and fifty years," Bannister intoned. "We've found hot worlds and cold worlds, big ones and little ones. We've found dead planets and planets swarming with life, there've been insects and fish and lizards and dinosaurs and god-awful things you'd hate to see under a microscope. But never — not once, Smith — has there been the report of an intelligent race, a civilized people."

Smith nodded. "That's why I was quick to see through the man."

"You ineffable damn fool," roared Bannister, "you pitch out a man who claims first-hand information, and meanwhile you have the brass to sit here grinning like a cuckoo! Where's your conscience? You feel no twinge when you accept your salary?"

"Well," said Smith hesitantly, "it still seems to me that you're grasping at straws. I sized this man up when I first picked up the log book. I'm an excellent judge of character, Mr. Bannister. I can usually predict a man's actions fairly well."

"Ah," said Bannister. "Then in that case perhaps you can predict my next sentence?"

Smith looked worried. "Is it 'You're fired'?"

"Right. You're fired."

Smith said in a weak voice, "I told you I was good at it."

✳

All was not lost, thought Smith as he walked along Folger Avenue toward the space-port. If he were able to confront Bannister with the supercargo, Bannister could see for himself how completely addled was the man. No doubt there would be reinstatement, a handsome apology, promotion, a raise in pay…

Smith returned to his surroundings. Folger Avenue presented a solid five-story front of ancient wooden houses, painted mud color. The ground levels housed saloons and eating-places in almost continuous succession; the few stores intervening were given to the sale of cheap clothing, second-hand goods, weapons, souvenirs of space, medicinal preparations and specifics against out-world ailments; in the upper stories were cheap hotels, warehouses, an occasional Class 12B brothel.

In spite of much that was squalid, Folger Avenue was rich with a certain swashbuckling charm, and equally rich with odor: the musty scent of the warehouses, stale spirits from the taverns, garbage in the gutter, perfume from an oil adulterator.

At last the wooden houses fell away, and Folger Avenue gave into the space-port, a great seared oval bordered by the Evan River. Three spaceships occupied the far end of the field; on the lapstrake of the nearest Smith read the silver letters: *Messeraria*.

He trotted across the field, dodging crazy lenses of mottled green glass burnt into the soil by departing ships, mounted the ladder into the *Messeraria*.

A quartermaster on the gangway sat reading a paper: a gray-skinned little man no more than five feet tall, thin as a heron. He put down his paper. "Yes, sir, what is it? If it's bills, you'll have to see either the captain or the supercargo, and neither one's aboard."

Smith nodded carelessly. "Where can I find the supercargo?"

"He's liable to be any place. Might try the Bobolink in Rafferty Alley, off Folger Avenue."

"I'll do that," said Smith. "Er — were you aboard last trip?"

The quartermaster squinted sharply. "What if I was?"

"Just curious," said Smith hastily. "I hear you made a pretty good trip."

"Fair. Chow was distasteful."

"May I ask, what planets did you close?"

"Who wants to know?"

"Just curiosity."

"Take it some other place."

Smith descended the ladder, started back across the field. A voice halted him. The quartermaster was looking down from the port. "This curiosity — don't go taking it near Captain Plum. He's a big rough man. Like to be unhealthy. I'm telling you out of kindness."

II

Smith returned to Folger Avenue to search for Rafferty Alley. Every twenty steps revealed another little side-street. After wandering a hundred yards Smith came to a standstill, looking around helplessly.

A fat man wearing a remarkable green- and white-striped garment stood by the wall, observing him with speculative interest. Smith approached, made a polite inquiry.

"Rafferty Alley?" said the fat man. "Directly behind you, young fellow."

Smith turned, noted the street marker, and, a hundred feet down the alley, a bird outlined in green fluorescent tubing. "That must be the Bobolink."

The fat man was inspecting him, Smith thought, with more than ordinary interest.

"New to these parts, young fellow?"

Smith cleared his throat. "Well, yes and no."

"Gotta be careful along in here. There's strange characters watching and waiting for patsies." He laid a soft hand on Smith's arm. "Come along, I'll take you down to the Bobolink, we'll have a drink, and maybe I can do you a good turn."

It occurred to Smith that the fat man would provide him with protective coloration; he would be less conspicuous with someone known to the district. He nodded. "Very well. It's only fair to warn you, I'm not a drinking man."

"Well, well," said the fat man. "Fancy that. Say," he nudged Smith with his elbow, "ever think you'd like to make a trip? You look like you might be good at figures. And it just so happens I know of a vacancy that wants to be filled quiet-like without any red tape."

Smith reflected a moment. The idea had many ramifications. Life in space was by no means easy and he would have to forget the supercargo of the *Messeraria*. He thought of the far worlds, the strange sights to be seen, the naked beauty of the stars seen in their native element. "I'd have to know more about it," he said cautiously. "I've never given the idea serious thought."

The fat man nodded, and pushed open the door into the Bobolink. When Smith paused, adjusting his eyes to the dimness, the fat man took his elbow and conducted him to a table where three men were sitting.

The fat man addressed the central of the three figures, a giant of a man with a low forehead, a coarse overhanging shock of hair, a splayed nose with tufts of hair sprouting from the nostrils. These the man had freakishly waxed and shaped into tiny mustaches. There was also a peculiar rancid odor, which reminded Smith of the bear pen at the Haight Memorial Zoo.

"Captain, sir," said the fat man, bending over the table with doggish servility, "here's a young fellow says he can figure pretty well and maybe he'd like to make a trip."

The giant turned clever little eyes up and down Smith's crisp gabardines. "Well, well, a dude. You ever been to space before?"

"Well, no, but —"

"Don't make too much difference. I need a man that knows how to add, how to take orders, how to keep his mouth shut. This damn fool here can't do any of the three."

Smith followed his glance to the man at the captain's left. He sat morosely, with his back half-turned to Smith: the supercargo who had staggered drunkenly after him into the Star Control office.

Smith turned back to the captain. "You must be Captain Plum."

"That's me. Meet Bones, my steward —" he pointed to the fat man "—Jack Fetch, the mate, and —" he jerked a thumb at the supercargo "— this is Bilge."

The supercargo straightened in his chair. "My name is Lowell."

"Harrup!" roared Plum. "If I say your name is Bilge, that's your name."

Smith conceived that a year with Captain Plum in the welded steel tube of a spaceship might be trying. He rapidly diagnosed megalomania in Plum, sado-masochism in the hatchet-faced Jack Fetch and a shifted valence in Bones, the steward; a set of ship's officers over-rich and over-ripe even in the unreal atmosphere of Rafferty Alley. Captain Plum and his nose-mustache. Bones and his green- and white-striped suit. Bilge Lowell and his delusions of an intelligent race in the far places. Did he recognize Smith as the clerk from Star Control? Smith felt the brush of the hot black eyes, saw Lowell's pale brow furrow in thought.

Smith turned uneasily to Plum. "What's your ship?"

"The *Messeraria*. My own property." Captain Plum looked him over coolly. "Know her?"

"Never heard of her."

"A good ship," said Plum. "Good quarters, good chow." He winked slyly; the great brush of his eyebrow made near-contact with his cheek. "Maybe a little extra money at the end of the trip, if things go right."

"It sounds very interesting," said Smith. "I'd have to think the proposition over." He looked toward Lowell. "Er — your present man is leaving you?"

"Yes," said Plum. "He's leaving us."

Lowell said in a hoarse voice, as if his throat were lined with bark, "I've just been thinking. I've just been making myself up a philosophy, and I've come to the conclusion that there's nothing in the world as good as a good drink. What do you say to that, Captain?"

"I say that you've been following that philosophy too close, and it's liable to stove you in before you're much older."

"Pah. Nothing's as good as a good drink, unless it's one of them pretty jewels you carry in that big pocket of yours."

The captain swung a burly arm and there was a sound: half slap, half thud. Blood dribbled down the supercargo's chin. He grinned a wide, toothless grin. "No more teeth, Cap. You're a mighty rough man."

Smith asked ingenuously, "Just what jewels are these? I'm interested in off-world minerals."

Plum's eyes glowed. "First thing you learn on my ship, son, is to ask no questions. Jump to it when orders are given, and you're fine as wine."

"Speaking of wine," said Lowell, "I'm now going to mix us a drink such as you've never tasted in the history of the world. Just like our last trip, eh, Captain?" He ducked back before Plum could strike. "Now then, don't hit a sick man. Hey, Bosco!" He called to the bartender. "Come over here."

"You got legs."

Lowell staggered over to the bar, returned with a tray full of bottles and measuring glasses.

"Watch close," said Lowell. He looked deep into Smith's eyes. "Watch close. This is important."

Smith stirred uneasily, glancing at Captain Plum, who leaned back, watching Lowell's motions like a cat fascinated by a bit of twitching paper.

Lowell picked up a bottle, waved it in the air. "Here's arrack, good white arrack. But it should be red arrack. Well, we'll pretend it's red arrack. The recipe calls for: Red Arrack — twenty-six and a half cc. Very well. I put it aside. Next, the Dubonnet. I pour the bottle into the pitcher. Now I take away — take away, mind you — ten cc. Seem strange to you?" He eyed Smith searchingly. "No? Good."

Captain Plum chuckled indulgently. "Bilge is cooking you up some of the Fountain of Youth."

"A jag of that slop and age means nothing," said Jack Fetch.

Lowell ignored them. "Now this stuff is Fleur de Lys liqueur. Just Lys is good enough; I never was much at this European lingo." With a sudden clutch he tore the label in such a way that only the 'Lys' remained.

Lowell was rambling insanely, thought Smith; a wink from Captain Plum confirmed the diagnosis. If only Bannister were here now!

In his husky voice Lowell said, "This is important. I'm a sick man not long for the world. It's as well that the knowledge survives me. So: Lys — ninety-four cc." He heaved a great sigh; his shoulders slumped. "There, that's the body of it. Now the trimmings." He laid out an orange and a lemon, three black olives and a green one.

Bones the steward suddenly bent forward, whispered into Plum's heavy ear. Plum's eyebrows shot upward; he struck out, swept the tray, bottles, glasses to the floor. The crash and clatter of breaking glass brought conversation throughout the Bobolink to a dead halt.

Lowell sat back grinning wearily at Captain Plum. "Who's the crazy one now?" He coughed. Plum surged forward, raised his arm; in sudden pity Smith reached out, pushed him back into his seat. "For Heaven's sake, Captain, take it easy! The man's not well!"

Bosco the bartender had been sweeping up the broken glass. "Who's going to pay for the good liquor and glassware? Three bottles, arrack rum, wine and liqueur — that's twenty dollars — and five for the glass."

"Take it out of Lowell," said Plum with a heavy-lidded stare. "He ordered the drinks."

Smith said sharply, "The arrack and the liqueur weren't broken; you picked them up and carried them off. And that glassware isn't worth a dollar. Here — two dollars for half a bottle of wine, a dollar for the glass." He shoved bills at the bartender. "That's all you'll collect here; if you want more —" He paused, feeling the baleful weight of Captain Plum's eyes on his skin.

Bosco said spitefully, "You're sure a smart snipe, ain't you?" He took the money and went muttering back to the bar.

Plum said, "Does seem like you're pretty big for your britches. Minute ago you pushed me; can't say as I like it." He came to his feet suddenly, as if snapped up on a spring. A hand slammed around, struck with a crushingly sick impact.

Smith tottered limply back, caught himself with his elbows over the bar. His eyes went dim, something strange clamped at his brain. Faintly he heard Jack Fetch say in a pleased breathless voice, "The young fool's gonna challenge you, Cap; the — young — fool…"

Smith whirled through nightmare, through a fury of thudding blows that seemed to diminish in intensity. From a great distance he heard sounds, but the impression most vivid was Captain Plum's great face, swollen and turgid, with the ridiculous nose-mustache, the eyes staring, wide open, the mouth working up and down as if he were chewing.

His own arms and feet were moving; he felt the jerk and strain; he felt the breath burn in his throat. His knuckles stung; he saw Captain Plum stumble awkwardly, trip on a chair, fall flailing to the floor. From his pocket rolled a green ball.

Smith stared stupidly down at Plum, who sat staring back, his eyebrows a bar across his face.

The green ball glittered, sparkled. On a sudden impulse Smith seized it, turned, ran out of the Bobolink and pell-mell down Rafferty Alley. He turned into Folger Avenue, hearing the thud of steps behind him.

First came Jack Fetch, running like a weasel. Behind was Captain Plum, yelling hoarsely.

Smith turned the corner, stopped short.

Jack Fetch came swiftly around. Smith hit the saturnine gray face as hard as he could; Jack Fetch tottered blindly toward the gutter. Smith turned, ran up on Folger Avenue.

A taxi stanchion rose from the street; a cab was moored to the davits. Smith jumped on the lift; the chain moved, he slid up the tube. From the platform he glimpsed the hulk of Captain Plum striding like a mad colossus down Folger Avenue.

He jumped into the cab. "Star Control Field Office," he directed.

Bannister sat with the jewel between his fingers, fascinated by the delicate snowflake light-spangles forming, building, expanding, varying, dissolving, one after the other. "It's like nothing I've ever seen before. I'll have the mineralogist look at it. Or —" he hesitated, inspected the jewel more closely "— maybe it's a matter for the biology department."

Smith hitched himself forward in his chair. "Now what? Do you think we'd better send the patrol out for Captain Plum?"

Bannister flicked Smith's face with a cool glance. "Right now he's probably in the patrol office, signing a complaint against you for stealing his jewel. I can't say that you've handled this very well." He turned back to the jewel. "I had already assigned two men to check up on Plum; now there's no telling what he'll do."

The visiphone buzzed; Bannister leaned forward, punched a button. "Yes?"

"Sergeant Burt here, sir. We've picked up Lowell, the supercargo, in Chenolm Way, off Folger Avenue. He's been aratinized. Face yellow, eyes and tongue hanging loose. We've sent him to the hospital, but I'm afraid there's nothing more to be done."

Bannister cursed softly. "Damned scoundrels. How about Plum?"

"He's dropped out of sight."

Bannister nodded grimly. "Keep looking for him." He snapped off the visiphone. For a moment he sat motionless, then sighed heavily.

"Well, that's that. Lowell is done for. He'll never talk to anybody again. As good as dead."

"He was lucid enough in the Bobolink," said Smith doubtfully.

"That was an hour ago. He's been dosed with aratin since, and his brain is bubbling like a pot of hot mush." Bannister sat back, looking thoughtfully at Smith.

Smith moved uneasily in his chair.

Bannister said, "I have in mind a job I think you can do. If you carry it off, you'll get a promotion."

Smith frowned. "I'm not so sure that —"

"You're a good Star Control man?"

"I was, until I was fired this morning."

Bannister gestured impatiently. "That's all water under the bridge; you're hired again. You understand that this hint of contact with an intelligent race is unprecedented? How important it is that we either verify or disprove it?"

Smith nodded. "Certainly."

"A Star Control man is resourceful and daring — right?"

"Right."

Bannister pounded the table. "We can't let Plum antagonize this race, if it exists, or destroy it with Earth diseases. If it exists, we've got to find it. And you're the man to do it, Smith!"

Smith blinked.

"Here's how I see it," said Bannister. "If there's money to be made looting this planet, Plum will be out and away as soon as he organizes a trip. Once in space, under sky-drive, he's gone. We can't trace him. Unless of course we have a representative aboard. There's where you come in. He's practically hired you already. You return the jewel to him, tell him you're sorry you ran off with it, and that you want a chance to pick up a few yourself."

Smith sat hunched in his chair. "You don't think he'll be angry with me?"

"You've brought his jewel back; why should he be?"

"He won't —" Smith paused, tried to gauge the temper of Plum's mind. "Won't what?"

"Well," said Smith, "don't you think that if he got me out in space, aboard his ship, that he might take advantage of the situation to — well, beat me up?"

"I don't see why," argued Bannister.

"But I knocked him down in the Bobolink."

"He respects you for it."

"You don't think he might use that aratin stuff on me?"

"What good is a man dosed up with aratin? He needs you as a member of his crew."

Smith chewed his lips.

"I'll give you a packet of hyolone," said Bannister heartily. "Out in space, when you go into sky-drive, drop it into the thrust-box. The ship will leave a trickle of luminescence behind that we can follow at a safe distance."

Smith still seemed uncertain. Bannister eyed him under half-closed lids. Suddenly he turned to the visiphone. "Codge, get credentials ready for Sergeant Robert Smith —" He looked sidewise at Smith, calculated rapidly. There was nothing to lose. "Make it Lieutenant Robert Smith, of the Extraordinary Squad."

Smith sat back in his chair. Lieutenant Smith of the Extraordinary Squad! He rolled the words around his tongue. Bannister watched covertly a moment, then rose to his feet, motioned to Smith.

"Come along, Lieutenant. I'll drop you off at the field."

They flew out across Lake Maud, circled Mount Davidson, dropped low across the Graymont district, and presently flew along the taxi lane only a few hundred feet above the mud-colored old buildings of Folger Avenue.

Below was the space-port. Polished black hulls lay quiet around the field like enormous dead beetles.

Smith pointed. "There's the *Messeraria*. Or rather —" he hesitated, frowned, searched the field. "It was about there, near that new glass blister."

"New glass blister, eh?" Bannister spoke in a strained voice. "Well, Lieutenant Smith —" he laid heavy stress on the title "— it appears the bird has flown the coop."

Smith drew a deep breath. "Perhaps it's all for the best, I never was completely comfortable with the plan. But there'll be other jobs."

III

Returning toward the Star Control Office, Smith pointed to a landing plat on a terrace above St. Andrews Place. "There's the Odd Angle Club, that blue blazon with the green bars. I happen to be a member. Would you care to lunch with me, by way of celebration?"

Bannister gazed at him blankly. "Celebration? What for, in God's name?"

"My promotion."

"Oh," Bannister smiled grimly. "Your promotion, indeed."

He landed the boat and a moment later Desdumes, the maître d'hôtel, ushered them to a seat.

Smith signalled the bar-boy. "A drink before lunch, perhaps?"

Bannister grudgingly relaxed his aloofness. "A good idea."

"I'm not a drinking man myself," said Smith. "Alcohol corrodes the intellect. But naturally there's not an objection in the world to your enjoying yourself."

"Very decent of you," said Bannister dryly. He looked Smith up and down with dispassionate curiosity.

"What's the matter?" asked Smith uncomfortably.

"Nothing at all. I know a woman who can't stand the sight of feathers."

Smith was unable to trace the sequence of thought, and glancing sidelong at Bannister, seemed to notice a lack of warmth in his manner. Was it possible that Bannister considered him something less than a good fellow? Such a notion might militate against further advancement, no matter how efficient his work.

Smith said heartily, "Let me order you something a little different — a drink I imagine you've never tasted before."

Bannister made a wry face. "Camel milk, something of the sort? Thanks no, I'll stick to whisky."

"Just as you like," said Smith. "It was recommended rather highly by the *Messeraria* supercargo; he was so emphatic that I noted the recipe. Arrack — red arrack — Dubonnet, a liqueur —"

"What's this?" demanded Bannister. "Lowell telling you how to mix drinks?"

Smith found a soiled bit of paper in his pocket. "Red arrack, twenty-six and a half cc. Dubonnet — a half bottle less ten cc. Fleur de Lys liqueur, ninety-four cc. An orange, a lemon, four olives."

Bannister, sitting rigidly in his chair, asked, "Why haven't you mentioned this before?"

Smith made an indulgent gesture. "Just more of this alcoholic stuff."

Bannister asked in a steely voice, "Could it possibly be that he was attempting a secret communication?"

Smith considered, "I will say this much," he admitted uneasily. "Immediately afterward, Captain Plum became violent."

"Exactly what happened? Try to remember every detail."

Smith described the episode to the best of his recollection.

Bannister, frowning, scanned the formula. "Undoubtedly he recognized you and was trying to tell you about this secret planet. The orange and the lemon seem to refer to a double star, the three black and the green olives tell us that the planet in question was fourth from the sun."

"And the numbers must be position coordinates for the double star."

Bannister nodded shortly. "So it would seem."

"Take the first figure along the x-axis," said Smith excitedly. "Twenty-six and a half light years toward Polaris. The second figure — now I see, it's negative. A negative ten light years along the equinoctial axis, or ten light years, roughly, toward Denebola. The third figure, along the solstitial axis — ninety-four light years toward Betelgeuse. Combine the three —" He scribbled on a bit of paper. "Square root of the squares of twenty-six and a half, ten and ninety-four. Somewhere near a hundred. The direction would be roughly —" he paused, chewed his pencil "— probably in the direction of Procyon. That would be fairly close. A hundred light years in the direction of Procyon."

Bannister made an impatient motion. "Please let me think."

Smith sat back with injured dignity. Lunch was served; they ate almost in silence.

Over his coffee Bannister leaned back with a sigh. "Well, it may be a wild-goose chase. But I'm going to stick my neck out, requisition a cruiser."

"I suppose I'd better wind up my affairs," Smith said tentatively.

"No need at all," replied Bannister. "You'll be travelling no farther than the sub-basement storeroom."

"Mr. Bannister, I hardly think you're being reasonable."

"Reasonable or not," growled Bannister, "I can't risk another of your fiascos." He rose to his feet. "And now I'll have to be back to work. Thanks for the lunch."

Smith watched the broad back retreating, then ordered more coffee.

After a few minutes' thought he rose to his feet, went to the visiphone, called Harry Codge at the Star Control Office.

"Harry," he said to the ruddy face, "have you made up those credentials for me yet?"

Codge nodded sourly. "You must be related to Bannister."

Smith ignored the implication. "Drop them into the tube, will you please? I'm at the Odd Angle Club, St. Andrews Place."

He took himself to the club office and a moment later a little cylinder thudded into the receptacle.

Smith pinned the badge inside his coat, tucked the plastic card into his wallet, ordered a cab and flew to the Bureau of Registry hard by the space-field.

He displayed his new credentials to the girl at the front desk. "Bring me the card on the SpS *Messeraria*."

"Yes sir." She went to a file, thumbed through once, twice. "That's strange."

"What's the trouble?"

"The card's not in place. Unless —" She crossed the room, flipped through a small stack of pink and blue cards. "Here it is. Change of ownership."

"Let's see the card," said Smith in high excitement.

He ran his eye down the form. "Built twenty years ago. First owners — Vacuum Transport. Sold to R. Plum and Chatnos Widna. New owner — Hermetic Line. Well, well."

"Anything wrong, Lieutenant? The Hermetic Line is very conservative —"

"No," said Smith hastily. "Nothing at all."

He turned away engrossed in his thoughts. It would be a fine feather in his cap to drag the sullen but cowed giant before Bannister for questioning. And evidently he had not departed with the *Messeraria*.

Smith crossed the space-field, climbed the ramp into Folger Avenue.

There was Rafferty Alley, and there the Bobolink. It was unlikely, thought Smith, that Plum would still be in evidence after the events of the morning; still it represented a starting place for an investigation.

He felt for his badge, strode down Rafferty Alley, entered the Bobolink.

There was confusion, which Smith later was never able to sort out into component events; it was as if everything occurred in a single timeless clot.

He remembered a scraping of chairs, voices, a bull-bellow; he saw Plum's great angry face, the lips drawn back over yellow horse-teeth; he felt a clutch at his knees, an eye-watering jar at the side of his head, a buffet in the pit of his stomach.

Reality floated upward, like a picture rising on a screen leaving black beneath. Light, motion, sound, color went completely out of his perception; there was nothing.

Captain Plum's face, large as a house, seemed to fill the sky. A black velvet beret hung rakishly past one ear; his nose-mustache was preened and twisted to a fare-thee-well. He was so close that Smith could see the small corrugations of his skin, the blemishes, the ropy muscles of the cheeks, stubble on the massive rectangular chin.

The little eyes peered cunningly into Smith's face. "You alive, fellow? Yes? You're lucky. Now, what did you do with my little trinket?" He took Smith's chin between his thumb and forefinger. "Hey? Where's my little gem?"

Smith became aware of a curious lightness in his limbs. He focused his eyes on the background. Metal. Suddenly terrified, he sought to rise to his feet. A belt around his middle restrained him.

Captain Plum set heavy feet to the wall, pushed his bulk out at right angles, stood in apparent defiance to sanity.

"We're in space!" shouted Smith. "You've kidnapped me!"

Plum grinned enormously, like a bear. "Shanghaied, they used to call it. Young fellow, you don't know how lucky you are. I could have put you away simple as squeezing a bug, but I used my head. You're one of them Space Control hoop-te-doos; still, I need a man to do my paper work, and you happened in at the right time. Just right. I kill me two birds at one lick. Three birds, as it may be." Plum ticked the points off his fingers. "I get me an honest worker. He better be honest. I get a Control snooper off my tail. And I get myself a bit of exercise sparring you now and again; rather handy you showed yourself."

"But," cried Smith, "you don't own a ship any more! You sold —"

"This ain't the old *Messeraria*, young fellow." Plum showed the inside of his maroon maw in a soundless gust of laughter. "This here's the *Dog*, a little boat more suited to our good purposes. And now you've rested on your lowers long enough; it's go to work for you, earn your way."

"I didn't ask to be brought aboard," grumbled Smith.

Plum's mouth compressed; his hand caught Smith a buffet on the cheek. Smith felt his teeth creak; before him came a vision of Lowell's toothless mouth. He sat quietly, staring at Plum.

Plum grinned slowly. "Sure, I know what you're thinking, that you'll bide your time and come at me when I least expect it. Well, I say try ahead, try ahead. Better men than you have gone that path, and it keeps me lively. Now, young fellow, on your feet. And remember I'm a hard man to please; there can't be a red cent over or under on the books; it all must come out so."

Smith silently unfastened the belt at his waist. The cruiser that Bannister had ordered out, he thought, must surely run down Plum's ship. But if there were a battle, he might easily be lost with the ship. And in the meantime — A threatening move by Plum cut short his reflections. "Are you done dreaming?" growled the giant.

Smith tried to rise to his feet; instead set himself floundering awkwardly into the air.

Plum's guffaw stung him almost beyond endurance. He bit his lips, and steadying himself on a stanchion, turned to Plum. "What is it you want done?"

"Up forward, my lad, up in the chart room: that's your nook. First you'll sort out my old charts, arrange them in the projector. When I press for a sector, I want to get that sector and none somewhere fifty parsecs distant. Very important. That's fair warning. Up forward!"

Smith pulled himself forward, aching in every joint. The *Dog*, he perceived, was a small advance ship, one of the exploration 'terriers' built for maneuverability, landing ease and cheap maintenance, a type in vogue among the sun-duckers of outer space. But no matter how fast, how shifty, how desperately Plum drove his ship, once the cruiser thrust out a magnetic finger it would never win free. Smith shot a look through the forward port, seeking Procyon, past which the course must lead.

Nowhere in the field of his vision was there such a star. The sky appeared more like the region north of Scorpio — the constellation of Ophiuchus, in a direction exactly opposite to Procyon. He stared. There was some dreadful mistake. "Where are we headed for?"

"None of your damn business," snarled Plum. "Get forward into the chart room, and thank yourself I'm a merciful man."

Smith pushed himself into the chart room, numbly began to sort the star-charts. This was death, he thought, and he was in hell. Before his eyes was a black and gray panel, a bank of dials, a mesh, a row of switches. Smith focussed his attention. Radio! Long-distance radio — launching its meaningful radiation in a parallel-sided bar, to take it hot and sparkling across space.

How far had they come? Little more than a light-week or two; he could hear the whir of motors still building up acceleration.

He glanced out into the bridge; Captain Plum stood by the door bellowing back toward the engine room.

With trembling hands Smith twisted dials, aimed the antenna dead astern, flipped the switch. In a fever of impatience he waited for the circuits to warm into full power, meanwhile listening to Captain Plum's salty condemnations of the engine-room gang.

Once more he checked the direction of the beam. Dead astern, to hit Earth on the nose. He set the frequency to standard space-band. A hundred monitors were tuned to the frequency.

Now.

He spoke into the mesh. "SOS — Star Control attention. SOS. This is Lieutenant Robert Smith aboard Plum's ship the *Dog*. SOS. Attention, Bannister, Star Control Field Office Twelve. This is Lieutenant Smith. I have been kidnapped." The edge of his attention sensed that Plum's voice had quieted; he heard the rustle of heavy movement in the bridge. Desperately he bent to the mesh; he might not have another chance. Power on, direction right, frequency right. "SOS. This is Lieutenant Robert Smith, Star Control, kidnapped aboard Plum's ship, headed toward Rho Ophiuchus." He became aware of a great shadow in the doorway. "Kidnapped aboard Plum's ship, headed toward Rho Ophiuchus, Robert Smith speaking —" He could bear it no longer; he looked up. Plum stood watching him from the doorway.

"Ratting on me, hey?"

Smith said with feeble bravado, "I got the message through. You're washed up, Plum. If you're smart you'll pull about."

"My, my, my," Plum jeered mincingly. "Me and my Aunt Nellie. Go ahead, call again if you like."

With one eye on Plum and suddenly anxious, Smith leaned toward the mesh. "This is Lieutenant Robert Smith, aboard Captain Plum's ship, *Dog*, bound for Rho Ophiuchus —"

Plum moved carelessly forward. His hand struck Smith's face with a sound like beef liver dropping on a butcher's block.

Smith, crumpled in a corner, looked up at Plum, standing in his favorite pose, legs spraddled wide, arms behind him.

"Damn addle-brained snooper," snarled Plum.

Smith said weakly, "It'll go just so much the worse for you when you're caught."

"Who's going to catch me? How am I going to be caught? Hey? Answer me that!" He prodded Smith with his toe.

Smith slowly drew himself to his feet. He said in a tired voice, "I sent the message three times. It's bound to be picked up."

Plum nodded. "You sent it out — dead astern. Sure the monitors will pick it up. At the speed we're leaving Earth, the frequency they get will be so they can count the cycles on their fingers. That radio isn't much good unless we're stopped."

Smith numbly considered the radio. The speed of the ship would make his message completely unintelligible.

"Now," said Plum harshly, "get back to your work. And if I catch you fooling with the equipment again, I'll treat you fairly rough."

IV

It was as if the ship lay motionless, the center of all, and the galaxy flowed past in a clear dark syrup, the stars like phosphorescent motes in sea water — lost and lonesome sparks.

Two points were steady: a wan star astern and an orange-yellow glint ahead which gradually resolved into a doublet. So the days passed. Smith slunk about the ship as inconspicuously as possible, dreading the daily drubbing Captain Plum administered under the guise of calisthenics.

During the bouts both men wore magnetic slippers and twelve-ounce gloves, the exercise lasting until Captain Plum was winded or Smith too dazed to afford further entertainment.

As time went on, Smith became increasingly familiar with Plum's style of combat: a full-chested prancing forward, arms thrashing. Perforce Smith learned the elemental tricks of defense, but in a sense this proficiency defeated its own purpose. The more adroitly he fended off the punches, the more cleverly he rolled and ducked with the blows, so did Captain Plum's violence wax, and Smith saw clearly that the end would lie at one of two extremes: either he would achieve an impregnable defense or else Captain Plum would kill him with a single terrible blow.

To avoid such an impasse, Smith tentatively went on the offensive, jabbing at Plum after his tremendous swings had thrown him off balance. The ruse was successful to such an extent that when Captain Plum found himself unable to land effective blows, with Smith darting in at will to pummel his nose and eyes, he insisted on the exercise at ever-longer intervals. At the same time his aversion to Smith reached the point of obsession.

The last few bouts were terrible episodes, in which Captain Plum, red-eyed and roaring, charged like a bull, lashing out in wide roundhouse sweeps, any one of which would have broken Smith's bones. Half-measures were worse than none, Smith now realized; he must either become a supine wad of flesh for Plum to pound at his pleasure, or he must hurt Plum badly enough to discourage him — again a dangerous undertaking.

The final bout lasted for half an hour. Both Smith and Plum reeked with blood and sweat. Plum's nostrils flared like a boar's, his great chin hung lax and limp. Smith, seizing an opportunity, struck as hard as he could, on a downward slant at the loose-hanging jaw. He felt a snap, a crush, and Plum staggered back clasping his face. Smith stood panting, half expecting Plum to go for his gun.

Plum rushed from the cargo hold, while Smith, full of foreboding, made his way to the cubby-hole which was his quarters.

Captain Plum appeared at the mess table, his jaw taped, his lips suffused with violet. He brushed Smith with his eyes, nodded with grim menace.

Later Smith was in the chart room, calculating fuel consumption against distance traveled. Plum lurched close up against him. Smith turned his head, looking close into the hairy face.

"You're a mean son of a gun, ain't you?" said Plum.

Smith saw that Plum was toying with an eight-inch blade. Smith said in a low voice, "Anybody's mean when he's driven to it."

"You talking about me, young fellow?"

"Take it any way you want."

"You're walking on thin ice."

Smith shrugged. "I don't see how I've anything to gain by being polite. I don't expect much out of this trip."

The speech seemed to appease Plum; he slowly put his knife up. "You asked for it when you started that schoolboy Star Control stuff."

"I don't see it that way. Somebody's got to be at the top. In this case it's Star Control. You'd be better off if you'd turn back and make an honest report on this planet, whatever it is."

"And lose all that money? What do I care for Star Control? What have they done for me?"

Smith leaned back against his workbench, with a curious sense of speaking in an incomprehensible language. "Don't you care for your fellow-men?"

Plum vented a gruff bark of a laugh. "Humanity never bust itself open working for me. And even supposing I did, what difference does it make what goes on out here eighty miles past nowhere? Just a bunch of fuzzy yellow things."

"Do you really want to know what difference it makes?"

"Go ahead, spill it."

Smith gathered his thoughts. "Well, in the first place, human knowledge is only a small fraction of what can be learned about the universe; we've concentrated on the subjects which fit our kind of minds. If we find another civilized race, we'd meet an entirely different complex of sciences."

Plum used a coarse expression. "We know too much as it is; if we knew any more we'd be clogging our brains. Anyhow, there's nothing out here on Rho that we don't know already."

"Maybe yes, maybe no. But if there's a civilized race, men with the proper knowledge ought to be the first to make contact."

"Then where'd my cut be? I've gone through lots to get where I am. I've taken it on and I've given it back, just to get a crack at a chance like this. Those jewels are novelties, worth plenty on Earth. I can get out to Rho, I can clip the fuzz-balls loose of the jewels, I can get back to Earth — and my fortune's made. If the scientists found Rho, they wouldn't tell me, would they? Why should I spill my guts to them? You got things twisted all screw-wise, young fellow."

"If these things are intelligent, perhaps they're on their guard now. You'll find it dangerous taking any more of the jewels."

Captain Plum threw back his head, then winced at the wrench to his jaw. "Not a chance. We're safe on Rho as we are in our own bunks. And why? It's easy. These fuzz-balls is blind, deaf and dumb. They walk around holding up jewels like they was offering 'em to us on velvet pillows. A clip of the knife, fuzz-ball flips over, the jewel comes rolling home. And that's the way it goes."

Leaving Smith chewing his lip nervously, Captain Plum slapped the chart table with the flat of his knife and turned away.

The *Dog* coasted up at the big orange sun, with the small yellow sun hanging beyond, no more than a cusp visible. Nearby were the planets, yellow motes — one, two, three, four.

Through the port Smith watched the fourth planet, a world smaller than Earth, with an oily yellow atmosphere, and which possessed an arid surface.

From the bridge came the voices of Plum and Jack Fetch, disputing where best to set the ship down. Fetch was inclined to caution. "Put yourself in their shoes, make as if it's Earth."

"Cripes, man, this ain't Earth. This is Rho Ophiuchus."

"Sure, but think of it like this: a few months ago there's an epidemic of heists; if they've got the brains of a turtle, they'll take precautions. Suppose we set down beside one of the big castles. Suppose they come along, discover the ship. Then the jig is up."

Plum spat disgustedly. "Hell, them fuzz-balls live in a dream world. They come along, feel the ship, they think it's a new kind of rock. They don't even know they've got a sun or that there's other stars; like that lightheaded supercargo says, they got a way of looking at things that's different from ours."

"That's right. And maybe they'll know we're back by some different kind of sense, and then there'll be hell to pay. Why take the risk? Set down out in that little desert; then we can work up to the castles in the boat."

"Too complicated," growled Plum. "There'd be men getting lost and the boat breaking down."

Compromise was reached: the ship would be landed in desolate country as near as possible to the castles, close enough to allow its use as a base of operations.

The greasy yellow atmosphere swirled up around the ship. Jack Fetch sat at the controls while Plum stood spraddle-legged at the telescopic viewer. "Slow," he called to Fetch. "We're getting low. Take her north a bit, I see a whole settlement of big castles. Now straight down; we'll land in that little arm of desert."

Smith, standing at the chart-room port, glimpsed a series of large yellow cubical structures. From a liquid gleam at their centers it seemed as if they might be tanks.

A low ridge cut off the view; the ship grounded. Almost immediately he heard the exit port jar open, and Captain Plum, in a heavy space-suit, crossed the foreground, walking out of his vision.

Knees shaking under unaccustomed gravity, Smith joined Fetch on the bridge. Fetch threw him a swift side-look and turned away.

Smith asked, "What's Plum gone out for?"

"See how the land lies. If it's not safe we'll take off."

Smith peered up into the smoky yellow sky. "What's the atmosphere?"

"Hydrogen sulfide, sulfur dioxide, SO_3 oxygen, halogen acids, inert odds and ends."

"My word," murmured Smith. "Rather unpleasant stuff to breathe."

Jack Fetch nodded. "Last trip the atmosphere ate holes in our spacesuits; that's why we left so soon. This time we've got specials."

"What were those square tanks?"

"The fuzz-balls live in them."

Plum's lumbering form came into view over the brow of the hill.

"Look," said Jack Fetch, "there's a fuzz-ball. Plum doesn't see him yet."

Following Fetch's finger, Smith saw a mustard-colored creature on the hillside. It was four feet high, two feet thick — a hybrid of barrel cactus and sea urchin, with flexible feelers projecting from all sides, ceaselessly squirming, reaching, feeling. A glint of green came from the tip of its body.

"Blind, deaf, dumb." Fetch grinned like a fox. "And there goes Plum. Looks like he wants to start work at once. Never saw a man so keen after the loot."

Plum had paused in his stride; now he turned, moved cautiously toward the yellow-brown creature.

Smith leaned forward like a man at a drama. "Blind, deaf, dumb," he heard Fetch say again. Plum sprang forward, the blade of a knife flashed in the murky air. "Like taking candy from a baby." Plum held up the glint of green in a gesture of triumph, and the fuzz-ball was a toppled mass of brittle matter.

"Murderous brute!" said Smith under his breath. He felt Fetch's sardonic scrutiny and froze into himself.

Plum stood in the locker. Smith heard the hiss of the rinses: first a sodium carbonate solution, then water. The inner door opened; Plum stamped up to the bridge.

"Couldn't be better," he announced, with vast gusto. "Six big castles over the hill. We'll clean up fast and get out."

Smith muttered under his breath; Plum turned, looked him over. Fetch said maliciously, "Smith isn't convinced we're doing the right thing."

"Eh?" Plum stared at Smith blankly. "More of your damn belly-aching?"

"Murder is murder," muttered Smith.

Plum scrutinized him with eyes like black beads. "I'm planning another this minute."

Smith raised his voice recklessly. "You'll have all of us killed."

Plum twitched, took a step forward. "You damn croaker —"

"Just a minute, Cap," said Jack Fetch. "Let's hear what he's talking about."

"Put yourself in the place of these creatures," said Smith rapidly. "They can't see or hear; they have no idea what's destroying them. Picture a similar situation on Earth — something invisible killing men and women." He paused, then asked vehemently, "Would we sit back and do nothing about it? Wouldn't we strain every ounce of brain-power toward destroying the murderers?"

Plum's face was wooden. He twirled his nose-mustache.

"You don't know the mental capacity of these creatures," Smith continued. "It might be high. Because you can kill them so easily means nothing. If an invisible monster dropped down on Earth, we'd be as helpless as these things here seem to be. But for just a short time. Then we'd start devising traps. And pretty soon we'd catch one or two of our visitors and deal pretty roughly with them."

Plum laughed rudely. "You've talked yourself into a job, young fellow. Get into a suit."

Smith stood stiffly. "What for?"

"Never mind what for!" Plum snatched a weapon from his belt. "Get into that suit, or you've had the last breath of your life!"

Smith went slowly to the locker.

Plum said, "Maybe you're right, maybe you're wrong. If you're wrong — well, we'll figure out something else to do with you. If you're right — then, by Heaven!" and he cackled a throaty laugh "— you'll be doing us a good turn."

"Oh," said Smith. "I'm to be the stalking horse."

"You're the decoy. You're the lad that moves in front."

Smith went to the locker and donned a space-suit. On sudden thought he felt at the belt where hung a holster for a gun. It was empty.

Fetch was slipping into his own suit, lithe as an eel. Bones the steward and the men from the engine room were likewise dressing themselves. The quartermaster took up his perch at the gangway.

Plum motioned. "Outside."

Smith went to the double chamber with Fetch. A moment later they stood on the surface of Rho — a brown-yellow hardpan, sprinkled here and there with bits of black gravel and little yellow chips, like cheese parings. Condensations in the atmosphere swirled like dust devils.

This was Smith's first contact with alien soil. For a moment he stood looking around the horizon; the strangeness of the world weighing upon him almost as a force. Yellow, yellow, yellow — all tones, from cream to oil-black. Right, left, up, down — no other color occurred in his range of vision except the varicolored space-suits.

Plum's voice rasped through the earphones. "Up the hill — spread out. Every one of the fuzz-balls you see, carve him. We can't have any spreading of the news."

Spreading the news? thought Smith. How could these creatures, blind and deaf as they were, communicate? Although it was inconceivable, this must be a civilization — no matter how crude — without communication. He twisted the dial of the space-suit radio. Silence up the band. Up — higher, higher, almost to the limit of the set's sensitivity. Then a harsh crackle, a sputtering of a million dots and dashes.

He listened an instant, turned the knob further. The sputtering fluctuated, then cut off abruptly. Smith twisted the dial back to Captain Plum and just in time.

"—Bones next, and where's that supercargo? Smith, you come along the outside right; if you want to wander off and lose yourself, that's your own damned lookout."

Smith thought dourly, it might be just as well; there was nothing in his future but the ultimate dose of aratin, or a bullet.

The line of men moved forward, up the slope. Smith looked tentatively back toward the ship. If it were deserted, if he could get inside, lock the port, he would have Plum at his mercy. But the outer door was clamped, and through the bull's-eye he caught the white flash of the quartermaster's face.

Smith sighed and trudged up the slope. He heard Plum's harsh cry of satisfaction. "Two by God — two at once. Keep your eyes open, men. The sooner we make up a cargo and get off, the better."

Smith twisted the dial up to the band he had discovered. Clicking sounded loud and sharp, so loud that he came to a surprised halt.

He now stood among a tumble of sharp brown boulders a hundred feet from Bones and slightly to the rear; it was unlikely, he thought, that any of the others were watching him. He scanned the ground in his immediate vicinity. There was nothing. He climbed the slope; the noise grew louder. He veered left toward Bones. The noise lessened. He turned off to the right.

Behind a jagged black and yellow pinnacle he found the fuzz-ball — an aimless thing, groping a slow way up the hillside. In the very apex of its torso the green jewel winked and blinked like an electronic eye.

Smith bent close, fascinated. He noted that as the spangle of light formed in the green jewel, so did the radio sputter and sound. Each spangle was different from the one previous; Smith suspected that if the radio wave-pattern were made visible on an oscilloscope, there would be concordance with the pattern of the spangle.

The fuzz-ball seemed harmless enough; Smith decided to experiment. With his transceiver tuned to the fuzz-ball's frequency, he clicked his tongue into the microphone. "Ch'k, ch'k, ch'k."

The fuzz-ball made a series of odd sidewise jerks and came to a halt, as if puzzled. The feelers waved querulously. Smith said, "Take it easy, fellow." The fuzz-ball teetered dangerously to the side; the feelers performed a disorganized throbbing. From the speaker came an angry clicking. The fuzz-ball stood stock-still. Smith watched in amazement.

He said again, "Take it easy, fellow."

The fuzz-ball behaved exactly as before, tottering awkwardly to the side. Smith watched narrowly. The feelers seemingly had clenched in the precise pattern as before.

Once more he said, "Take it easy, fellow," in identical tones.

Once more the fuzz-ball reacted, in identical fashion.

Smith counted. "One, two, three, four, five."

The fuzz-ball twisted to the left, writhed certain of its feelers.

Smith counted again. "One, two, three, four, five."

The fuzz-ball twisted to the left, writhed the same feelers in the same way.

"This is odd," muttered Smith to himself. "The thing seems geared to radio stimuli, as if—"

He stared at the ground. A heavy black shadow showed, motionless.

He whirled. Silhouetted on the yellow sky was Captain Plum.

Plum's face was set in pale rage. He was speaking. Smith hurriedly turned the dial back to intercommunication.

"—lucky I came over to look. You was talking to the thing, you was ratting on us. Well, it's the last time." His hand went to his belt, came up clamped around his gun.

Smith feverishly dodged behind the black and yellow pinnacle. A bolt left a flickering, smoky trail in the atmosphere.

No use playing peek-a-boo, thought Smith desperately. He was a goner anyway. He clambered up the pinnacle in a frenzy, over a bit of a saddle, looked down at the back of Captain Plum's neck, advancing around the rock.

Bones' voice rang in his ear. "Look out, Cap'n; he's over your head."

Plum looked up. Smith jumped into his face.

Plum stumbled, sprawled. Smith fell staggering to the ground, jerked himself to his feet. Plum was hauling himself erect. Smith ground his foot on Plum's wrist. The fingers opened, the gun lay loose. Smith grabbed. In his ear sounded voices, anxious questions. "You okay, Cap?"

Smith aimed the gun at Plum. Plum dodged and fell. Smith caught movement from the corner of his eye—Jack Fetch. Rapidly he backed into the clutter of rock. Captain Plum lay quiet. Jack Fetch showed himself cautiously. Smith raised his arm. Fetch saw the motion, and as Smith pulled the trigger he fell to the ground. The nose of the gun sputtered, melted to a blob of metal. The crystal had broken when Plum fell.

Fetch came crouching, sidling forward, and Smith retreated behind the rocks.

Plum roared, "Don't shoot him; let him be. Shooting's too fast for the skunk. He likes the place so much, he can make his home here, for a few hours anyway." Irrationally he raised his voice. "Smith, you hear me?"

"Yes, I hear you."

"You show your face, we'll shoot it off; we'll be watching for you. You're on your own now, snooper. You take it from here."

V

From a crevice between crags of black sulfur, Smith watched the men march up the hill. He glanced at the oxygen indicator. Six hours.

Cautiously he rose to his feet, looked back toward the *Dog*. The port was still locked and impregnable.

He watched the crew march up over the rise, looming on the sky. He had one chance: ambush one of them, get his gun, kill the others. One chance — dangerous, desperate, bloody.

He scrambled swiftly up the slope and peered over the ridge. There were no men in his immediate range of vision. But there were the castles — six great blocks sixty feet high, built of a dull tufa-like substance.

Smith circled to the right, around the ridge. He climbed a mound of granular stuff, like lemon-yellow sugar, and slid down the other side.

He caught a glimpse of Bones a quarter of a mile distant. No good — Bones was out in the open, and in any event Bones carried no gun. It had to be Plum, Jack Fetch, or one of the engine-room gang.

He dialed his radio up the band. A loud crackling told him he was near a fuzz-ball. There it was, a hundred feet distant. Smith watched it, fascinated. If it responded to the random noise he made, was he to assume that it had no mind of its own? If so, who or what guided it? What was its purpose?

Smith cautiously approached the creature. It moved over the ground, and now Smith saw that from its underside hung a tube which swept over the ground. When it passed over one of the yellow flakes that sprinkled the ground, it jerked, and the flake was gone.

Smith reached for one of the flakes. It came free of the ground with a trace of resistance; Smith saw a trailing mesh of dependent fibrils — a small sulfurous plant. The fuzz-balls walked abroad, gathering little bits of Rho Ophiuchus vegetables. For their own consumption?

Smith surveyed the valley. From where he stood, an easy way led down the hill, across a saddle, up a kind of rough ramp to the lip of the nearest castle, which was perhaps two hundred yards distant. Smith descended slowly into the saddle; and here the crew of the *Dog* came into view.

Down the valley they strode, along a rude road. They were busy. From time to time Smith saw the glitter of knife, the quick flash of green, the suddenly brittle mass toppling to the side.

Smith ran up the ramp to the top of the castle, watching the five men over his shoulder. His hand strayed toward the radio dial. Why not apologize to Captain Plum, ask to be given back his life? Surely something so precious was worth the humiliation. Smith shuddered. In his mind he saw Plum's gloating, blood-charged face, saw the lips twisting in a grin. There would be no mercy from Plum. Better a desperate ambush, or perhaps a boulder of glassy brown sulfur rolled down one of the slopes.

The castle beside him was full of turgid brown liquid. Water? Acid? It was more than ever like a tank from his present vantage point. The liquid boiled and swirled as he looked.

Down in the flat, Plum, Bones, Jack Fetch and the two engineers were proceeding along the crude road, overtaking and killing fuzz-balls which were strung out along the road about a hundred feet apart.

Something brushed Smith's legs; he started, swung around. A fuzz-ball wandered past him, lax as a somnambulist, and stopped beside the liquid. The surface boiled; a great arm rose up, wound around the fuzz-ball, lifted it, and dragged it under the surface. Smith stood transfixed, too startled to move. He backed slowly to the ramp.

On another ramp across the hollow suddenly appeared black forms: Jack Fetch, Bones, the two engineers. Where was Captain Plum?

Smith saw him by the foot of the castle, looking up. Tuning into the communication band, he heard Fetch's voice. "Nothing up here, Cap — just dirty water. Some kind of cistern or blow-hole."

Plum roared back, "Don't you see no fuzzies? That's where they seem to live; there ought to be a whole swarm of them inside. Come on back down; let's split one of these castles open, see what's —"

A huge pale shape rose in the tank, four arms wrapped around the four men. Frantically, unbelievingly, they fought; Smith saw their desperate shapes black on the yellow sky. They tottered; the arms jerked them into the liquid. For a second or two the communication channel rang with their agony.

Then came Plum's bellow. "What's going on, what's —" his voice died suddenly, and a black silence followed.

Smith stumbled blindly down the ramp, away from the tank. These were terrible things, a terrible world. He paused, peering around the crumbling tufa. His sight misted and blurred through the sulfurous atmosphere; it was as if he were trying to peer into a dream. He saw Plum, standing silent, as if thinking.

Smith looked at his oxygen gauge. At normal respiration, he had four hours of life. He valved it as low as possible, tried to breathe shallowly, moved with the utmost efficiency.

Suddenly he knew how to deal with Captain Plum.

Plum turned, searched the landscape. Smith saw that he carried only a knife.

Smith slowly descended the slope, making no attempt to avoid discovery. Plum turned his head sharply and hefted his knife. Smith said mildly, "Do you think the knife will help you, Plum?" He picked up a cubical chunk of pyrite, heavy, compact, and continued slowly down the slope. It occurred to him that he was breathing hard; he saw that Plum was panting. He forced himself to breathe shallowly, to control his slightest unnecessary movement.

Plum said in a guttural voice, "Keep away from me, if you value your health."

"Plum," said Smith, "you're on your last lap, whether you know it or not."

"Says you."

Smith spoke in a half-whisper, with power turned high on his transmitter. Spend the power, save the oxygen. Keep Plum talking, the longer the better. "I was green when you dragged me aboard your ship. I'm not green now."

Plum cursed him in a thick voice. Excellent, thought Smith; anger increased the rate of his respiration. "I've seen gorillas as fat as you are," said Smith, "but none so ugly."

Plum's face burnt brick-color; he took a step toward Smith. Smith flung the pyrite; it struck Plum's head-dome, jarring him. Plum said, "I'm going to cut you open, Smith."

"Lumbering ape," said Smith. "You'll have to catch me first."

Plum lurched forward, and Smith retreated uphill. Plum weighed two hundred sixty pounds, Smith weighed one-seventy. Plum carried another twenty pounds slung over his back — knapsack and jewels.

Smith, keeping a few feet ahead of Plum, evading Plum's sudden dashes forward by virtue of his agility, led Plum ever away from the *Dog*.

Plum stopped short. "You think you're going to get me up on top of that rim," he panted. "Think again, Smith. I don't know what happened up there, but I'm not gonna let it stop me."

"I saw what happened. I saw the whole thing. It worked out just as I told you it would."

"Don't try to play me for a sucker, Smith."

"You've *been* played for a sucker, Plum, but not by me. By whatever it is that lives inside the tanks."

Plum laughed jeeringly, slapped his knapsack. "I've got about thirty of those jewels right here. If that's what you call being played for a sucker —"

"Those aren't jewels. They're beautiful little radio receivers — better than anything we have on Earth. That's what I meant when I told you that there were things for us to learn here."

Plum's eyes narrowed. "How did you figure that?"

"If I'm right," said Smith, "the fuzz-balls that you've been chasing up and down the planet aren't essentially living creatures." Plum was craftily edging forward, his knife concealed behind him. Let him come. Let him make a rush. "They act more like machines — half-living robots, if you want to use the word, designed to gather food for the tank builders."

Plum, taken momentarily aback, blinked. "That's silly. Machinery don't look like that. Them things is alive."

Smith laughed. "Plum, you're not only unpleasant; you're stupid."

"Yeah?" said Plum softly, creeping a step closer.

"All you know is what you've seen on Earth — metal, glass, and wire. There's no metal here, just sulfur. They use sulfur in ways we've never conceived — something else Earth scientists would like to know. Sulfur, oxygen, hydrogen, traces of this and that. They make their machines differently than we make ours, perhaps breed them out of their own bodies. So if it's any pleasure to you, you're not a murderer — you're a saboteur. You've been wrecking machines and stealing the spark plugs. You've been a damned nuisance, and the people here set a trap for you. Got four out of five. Good hunting, I should —" Plum lunged forward. Instead of dodging, Smith charged forward and hit Plum with his body crouched.

Off balance, Plum clutched at him; they went down together. Plum brought his knife into play, trying to pierce the tough fabric of the space-suit. Smith ignored him, groped for Plum's oxygen hose. He caught it, yanked it loose.

Oxygen spewed out at a tremendous pressure, flapping the hose wildly. Plum cried out crazily, dropped the knife, caught the hose, kinked it, fitted it back over the nipple. Smith picked up the knife, threw it far out into the boulders.

Plum was coughing; some of the atmosphere had been carried into his head-dome.

Smith stood back, grinning. "Plum, you're as good as dead. I've got you where I want you."

Plum looked up, his eyes watering. "How do you figure, you got me? All I have to do is go back to the ship, take off, leave you waving good-bye with your handkerchief."

"How much oxygen you got left?"

"I got plenty. Two hours."

"I've got four hours." Smith let the idea sink in for a moment, then said softly, "I'm not going to let you go back to the ship. Three hours from now I'm going back — by myself."

Plum stared at him, then snorted in vast contempt. "How you gonna stop me?"

"We might do a little fighting. Don't forget, you've taught me a lot this trip."

"You think you can hold me off for two hours?"

"I know damned well I can."

"Good enough. Go ahead, try it." Plum backed warily down the slope. Smith came after him and stepped in close. Plum beat his fist on Smith's head-dome, then brought up his knee, as Smith had expected. Smith grabbed the knee, jerked; Plum staggered, fell heavily on his face. Smith snatched at the oxygen tube. Oxygen thrashed out, flailing the tube back and forth. Feverishly Plum fitted it back in place, sat looking up at Smith with a strange, pale expression.

Carefully he rose to his feet. "You keep away from me, young fellow. Next time I get you, I'll bust your neck."

Smith laughed. "How much oxygen do you have left, Plum?"

Plum glanced quickly, made no answer.

"You're lucky if there's an hour's worth. It's half an hour to the ship. Still think you can make it? All I need to do is grab that tube just once more."

Plum said hoarsely, "Okay Smith, you win. You got me licked; I'm man enough to admit it. We'll forget the bad blood, we'll go back and there'll be no more talk of anyone being left here."

Smith shook his head. "I wouldn't trust you if you were Moses on a raft. That's something else you taught me, Plum. In a way, I'm sorry. I don't want to be responsible for anybody's death, not even yours. But once aboard that ship, with you and Owen against me, two to one, how long would I last? Not very long."

"You got me wrong, Smith."

"No, Plum. One of us is going to stay here. You."

Plum rushed him. Smith backed away easily out of reach, leading Plum away from the ship. Plum pounded on, arms outstretched grotesquely, and Smith trotted ahead just out of reach.

Plum halted, red-eyed, then turned and ran in the other direction, toward the ship.

Smith brought him down with a tackle, and his hand found the oxygen tube. He hesitated. He could not pull it loose. It was too cold, too calculating, this slow stealing of a man's breath.

Only a moment. Revulsion or not, it was Plum's life or his. He jerked. Plum thrashed wildly to his feet, fitted the hose back in place. His fingers were trembling. The hose had not flailed so hard.

Motion entered Smith's field of vision — something black and big. Unbelievingly, he stared. Plum rose to his feet, stared likewise; together they watched the Star Control cruiser settle behind the hills, beside the *Dog*.

"Well, Plum," said Smith. "It looks like maybe you'll live after all. Spend quite some time in de-aberration camp, of course. How much oxygen you got left?"

"Half an hour," said Plum dully.

"Better get going…I don't want to have to carry you in…"

Noland Bannister nodded to Smith as if he had never been away. The Star Control office looked cool and dim and somewhat smaller than Smith had remembered it.

"Well, Smith, I see we brought you back alive." Bannister leaned back in his chair, stretching luxuriantly.

Smith said coolly, "I'd have made it back by myself."

Bannister's eyebrows rose. "Sure of that?"

Smith looked Bannister over carefully. He saw an efficient, hard-working man who resented office work, who unconsciously visited his irritation upon his subordinates. He saw a man no bigger, no brainier, no more resourceful than himself.

"Not that I wasn't glad to see the cruiser," he said. "It relieved me of the decidedly unpleasant job of killing Plum."

Bannister's eyebrows rose still higher.

"What I want to know," said Smith, "is how the cruiser trailed us out. Surely the coordinates Lowell gave me were wrong?"

Bannister shook his head. "The coordinates were correct. You merely applied them in the wrong system. You said, 'Lowell gives us figures; they must refer to navigational data — X-Y-Z coordinates.' If you had considered a little more deliberately, you would have seen that the figures applied not to the rectangular system, but to astronomical, or polar coordinates." He blew smoke briskly into the air. "'Red Arrack' obviously meant 'Right Ascension'. 'Dubonnet' meant 'Declination'. 'Lys' meant 'Light-years'. The figures hit Rho Ophiuchus right on the nose: a fine double star. We didn't waste much time." He leaned back in his chair.

Smith flushed. "I made a mistake. Very well. I won't make it again."

"That's what I like to hear," said Bannister approvingly.

"What about that rating? Do I still have it?"

Bannister contemplated him. "You feel you've learned something about Star Control work this last trip?"

"I've learned all Captain Plum could teach me."

Bannister nodded. "Very well, lieutenant. Take a week off to rest up, then I'll find another assignment for you."

Smith nodded. "Thanks." He reached in his pocket, laid a glittering green sphere in front of Bannister. "Here's a souvenir for you."

"Ah," said Bannister, "another of the jewels."

"No," said Smith. "Just a good receiving set."

THREE-LEGGED JOE

It might be well to make, in passing, a reference to old-time prospectors. Their experience has been gained through vast hardship and peril; no cause for wonder, then, that as a group they are secretive and solitary. It is hard to win their friendship; they are understandably contemptuous of academic training. Much of their lore will die with them and this is a pity, since locked in their minds is knowledge that might well save a thousand lives.

— Excerpt from Appendix II, *Hade's Manual of Practical Space Exploration and Mineral Survey.*

JOHN MILKE AND OLIVER Paskell sauntered along Bang-out Row in Merlinville. Recent graduates of Highland Technical Institute, they walked with an assured and casual stride in order to convey an impression of hard-boiled competence. Old-timers on porches along the way stared, then turned and muttered briefly to each other.

John Milke was rubicund, energetic, positive; when he walked his cheeks and tidy little paunch jiggled. Oliver Paskell, who was dark, spare and slight, affected old-style spectacles and an underslung pipe. Paskell was noticeably less brisk than Milke. Where Milke swaggered, Paskell slouched; where Milke inspected the quiet gray men on the porches with a lordly air, Paskell watched from the corner of his eye.

Milke pointed. "Number 432, right there." He opened the gate and approached the porch with Paskell two steps behind.

A tall bony man sat watching them with eyes pale and hard as marbles.

Milke asked, "You're Abel Cooley?"

"That's me."

"I understand that you're one of the best outside men on the planet. We're going out on a prospect trip; we need a good all-around hand, and we'd like to hire you. You'd have to take care of chow, service space-suits, load samples, things like that."

Abel Cooley studied Milke briefly, then turned his pale eyes upon Paskell. Paskell looked away, out over the swells of naked granite that rolled six hundred miles west and south of Merlinville.

Cooley said in a mild voice, "Where you lads thinking to prospect?"

Milke blinked and frowned. It was his understanding that such questions were more or less taboo, though of course a man had a right to know where his job would take him. "In strict confidence," said Milke, "we're going out to Odfars."

"Odfars, eh?" Cooley's expression changed not at all. "What do you expect to find out there?"

"Well — Pillson's Almanac indicates a very high density. Which, as you may know, means heavy metal. Then the Deed Office shows neither claims nor workings on Odfars, so we thought we'd survey the territory before someone beat us to it."

Cooley nodded slowly. "So you're going out to Odfars...well, I tell you what to do. Get Three-legged Joe to wait on you. He'll make you a good hand."

"Three-legged Joe?" asked Milke in puzzlement. "Where do we find him?"

"He's out on Odfars now."

Paskell came closer. "How do we locate him on Odfars?"

Cooley smiled crookedly. "Don't worry about that. Leave it to Joe. He'll find you."

From the house came a dark-skinned man five feet tall and four feet wide. Cooley said, "James, these boys are going prospecting out on Odfars; they're looking for a flunky. Maybe you're interested?"

"Not just now, Abel."

"Maybe Three-legged Joe is the man to see."

"Can't beat Three-legged Joe."

Paskell drew Milke out to the street. "They're joking."

Milke said darkly, "No use trying to get work out of those old bums. They get by on their pensions; they don't want an honest job."

Paskell said thoughtfully, "Perhaps it's as well to go out by ourselves; it might be less trouble in the long run. These old-timers don't understand modern methods. Even if we found a man that satisfied us, we'd have to break him in on the Pinsley generator and the Hurd; he'd have the aerators out of adjustment before we'd been out twice."

Milke nodded. "There'll be more work for us, but I think you're right."

Paskell pointed. "There's the other place — Tom Hand's Chandlery."

Milke consulted a list. "I hope this doesn't turn out to be another wild goose chase; we need those extra filters."

Tom Hand's Chandlery occupied a large dirty building raised off the ground on four-foot stilts. Milke and Paskell climbed up on the loading platform. A scrawny near-bald man approached from out of the shadows. "What's the trouble, boys?"

Milke frowned at his list while Paskell stood aside puffing owlishly on his pipe. "If you'll take us to your technical superintendent," said Milke, "I think I can explain what we need."

The old man reached out two dirty fingers. "Lemme see what you want."

Milke fastidiously moved the list out of reach. "I think I'd better see someone in the technical department."

The old man said impatiently, "Son, out here we don't have departments, technical or otherwise. Lemme see what you want. If we got it, I'll know; if we don't, I'll know."

Milke handed over the list. The old man hissed through his teeth. "You want an ungodly amount of them filters."

"They keep burning out on us," said Milke. "I've diagnosed the trouble — an extra load on the circuit."

"Mmph, those things never burn out. You've probably been plugging them in backwise. This side here fits against the black thing-a-ma-jig; this side connects to your circuits. Is that how you had 'em?"

Milke cleared his throat. "Well —"

Paskell took the pipe out of his mouth. "No, as a matter of fact we had them in the other way."

The old man nodded. "I'll give you three. That's all you'll use in a lifetime. Now for this other stuff, we got to go around to the front."

He led them down a dark aisle, past racks crammed with nameless oddments, into a room split by a scarred wooden counter.

At a table near the door three men sat playing cards; nearby stood the dark thick man called James.

James called in a jocular baritone, "Give 'em a jug of acid for Three-legged Joe, Tom. These boys is going out to prospect Odfars."

"Odfars, eh?" Tom scrutinized Milke and Paskell with impersonal interest. "Don't know as I'd try it, boys. Three-legged Joe —"

Milke asked brusquely, "What do we owe you?"

Tom Hand scribbled out a bill, took Milke's money.

Paskell asked tentatively, "Who is this Three-legged Joe?... A joke? Or is there actually someone out there?"

Tom Hand bent over his cash box. The men at the table snapped cards along the green felt. James had his back turned.

Paskell put the pipe back in his mouth, sucked noisily.

On the way back, Milke said bitterly, "It's always been the same way; whenever these old-timers have a laugh on a stranger, they play it for all it's worth..."

"But who or what is Three-legged Joe?"

"Well," said Milke, "sooner or later, I suppose we'll find out."

Odfars ranked fourteenth in a scatter of dead worlds around Sigma Sculptoris, drifting in an orbit so wide that the sun showed like a medium-distant street lamp.

Paskell gingerly handled the controls, while Milke scanned the face of the planet with radar peaked to highest sensitivity. Milke pointed to a mirror-smooth surface winding like a fjord between axe-headed crags. "Look there, an ideal landing site — perfect!"

Paskell said doubtfully, "It looks like a chain of lakes."

"That's what it is — lakes of quicksilver." Milke turned Paskell a chiding glance. "It's absolute zero down there; it can't help but be solid, if that's what's on your mind."

"True," said Paskell. "But it has a peculiar soft look to it."

"If it's liquid," scoffed Milke, "I'll eat your hat."

"If it's liquid," said Paskell, "neither one of us will eat — ever again. Well — here goes."

The impact of landing substantiated Milke's position. He ran to the port, looked out. "Hmmph, can't see anything in this dark without booster goggles. In any event, we'll have a good level floor for our assay tent."

Paskell saw in his mind's eye a page from Hade's Manual:

> The assay tent is customarily a balloon of plastic film maintained by air pressure. Its use eliminates noxious, acrid or poisonous fumes inside the ship, formerly a source of great annoyance. Certain authorities advise a field survey before bringing out the tent; others maintain that erecting the tent first will facilitate examination of samples taken on the survey, and I generally favor the latter practice.

Milke said off-handedly, "Some of the boys like to wait before they put up their bubble; others set it out first thing to give them a place to drop off their samples. I generally like to get it up and out of the way."

"Yes, yes," said Paskell. "Let's get it up."

In space-suits, with booster goggles over their eyes, they left the ship. Paskell looked across the quicksilver lake, up into the jutting rock — icy bright and black through the booster goggles. The lake gleamed like buffed nickel, terminating nearby in a long finger pointing up a defile. In the direction opposite it dropped off around the curve of the horizon.

Paskell said in a tone of dubious humor, "I don't see Three-legged Joe anywhere."

Milke's snort sounded loud in the earphones.

"He's supposed to know we're here."

Milke said crisply, "Let's get to work."

From an exterior locker they took the assay tent, carried it fifty feet across the quicksilver to the length of the air hose. Milke turned the valve; the tent swelled into a half-sphere fifteen feet in diameter.

Milke tested the lock with a deftness attained on lunar field trips. He squeezed the lock compartment against the tent, forcing the enclosed air into the tent through a flap valve; then entering the lock, he sealed the outside entry, opened the inside valve, letting the compartment fill with air, and entered the tent.

"Works fine," he told Paskell confidently. "Let's get the equipment."

From the locker they brought the knock-down bench, carried it inside through the lock. Milke brought out a rack of reagents and the pulverizer. Paskell carried out the furnace, then went into the ship for the spectroscope.

"That should be good for a while," said Milke. He shot a glance up at distant Sigma Sculptoris. "It's a six hour day here — about two hours of light left. Feel like taking a quick look around?"

"It might be a good idea." Paskell fingered the empty loop at his belt. "I think I'll get my gun."

Milke chuckled. "There's nothing alive here; it's a vacuum, absolute zero. You've let that talk of Three-legged Joe get you down."

"Quite right," said Paskell. "In any event, I'll feel better with my gun."

Milke followed him into the ship. "Might as well get in the habit of wearing the thing." He holstered his own gun.

They set out across the lake, past the tent, up the narrow finger of quicksilver, into the defile. "Strange stuff," said Paskell chipping a fragment from the cliff. "Looks like chalk — gray chalk."

"Can't be chalk," said Milke. "Chalk is sedimentary."

"Whatever it is," said Paskell, "it's still strange stuff, and it still looks like chalk."

The fissure widened, the cliffs fell away almost at once; another quicksilver lake spread before them. "Makes for easy walking," observed Milke. "Better than scrambling through the rocks."

Paskell eyed the mirror-like surface which wound like a glacier past alternating bluffs, and in a perceptible curve over the horizon. "It might easily be connected all the way around."

Milke motioned to him. "See that pink stone? Rhodochrosite. And look down at the end — somehow it's been fused and reduced, leaving the pure metal."

"Very encouraging," said Paskell.

"Encouraging?" boomed Milke. "Why it's downright wonderful! If we found nothing else but this one vein, we're made…perhaps it might even be economical to mine the quicksilver…"

Paskell glanced at the sun, "There's not much daylight left; perhaps —"

"Oh, just around the next bend," said Milke. "It's easy walking." He pointed ahead to a massive knob of shiny black material projecting from the crag. "Look at that knob of galena — interesting."

Paskell felt a throb and hum at his side. He looked down to the dial, stopped short, walked to the left, turned, walked back to the right. He looked up toward the knob of shiny black rock. "That's not galena, that's pitchblende."

"By Jove," breathed Milke reverently, "you're right! As big as the Margan-Annis strike…Oliver, my boy, we're made."

Paskell said with a puckered brow, "I can't understand why the planet hasn't been developed…" He glanced nervously up into the deep shadows, perceptibly lengthening. "I wonder —"

"Three-legged Joe?" Milke laughed. "Fairy-tale stuff." He looked at Paskell. "What's the matter?"

Paskell said in a husky whisper, "Feel the ground."

Milke stood stock-still.

Thud-bump. Thud-bump. Thud-bump.

The sun dropped behind a crag; even the boosters found no light in the sudden shade. "Come on," said Paskell. He turned, paced hurriedly back up the lake.

"Wait for me," said Milke breathlessly.

At the ridge of chalky rock which divided the two lakes, they paused, looked back. The ground felt solid, immobile under their feet.

"Strange," said Milke.

"Very strange," said Paskell.

They crossed the ridge; the hulk of their ship caught the last flat rays from Sigma Sculptoris.

Paskell came to a sudden halt. Milke stared at him, then followed his gaze. "Our assay tent!"

They ran forward to where the fabric lay in a crumpled heap. "There's been a hole cut in it," muttered Paskell.

"Three-legged Joe?" inquired Milke sarcastically. "More likely there's a leak."

Paskell kicked at the material, now stiff as sheet metal with the cold. "We'll have a devil of a time finding it."

"Oh not so bad. We'll pump in warm air —"

"And then?"

"Well, there's a leak. As soon as the air hits the vacuum the water vapor condenses. So we look for a little jet of steam."

Paskell said in a precise voice, "There's no leak."

"No? Then why —"

"We never turned on the heat. The air inside liquefied."

Milke turned away to look out over the lake. Paskell quietly plugged in the cord; power circulated through elements meshed into the tent fabric.

Milke turned back, slapping his gloves together. "That's about all we can do until the air thaws out…" He looked at Paskell, who again was standing as if listening. Irritably he asked, "What's the matter now?"

Paskell made a furtive motion toward the ground. Milke looked intently down.

Thud-bump. Thud-bump. Thud-bump. Thud-bump.

"Three-legged Joe," whispered Paskell.

Milke looked hurriedly in all directions. "There can't be anything out there." He turned. Paskell had disappeared.

"Oliver! Where are you?"

"I'm in the ship," came a calm voice.

Milke backed slowly toward the port. Night had come to Odfars; starlight shone on the quicksilver lake, intensified by the booster goggles to near the power of moonlight. Was that a black shadow standing in the defile? Milke hurriedly backed against the port.

It was locked. He pounded against the metal. "Hey, Oliver, open up!"

He looked over his shoulder. The black shape seemed to have moved forward.

Paskell came to the port, looked carefully out past Milke, threw back the bolts. Milke burst into the air-chamber, on into the ship. He took off his helmet. "What's the idea locking me out? Suppose that damn whatever it is was hot on my tail?"

Paskell said in a practical voice, "Well, we'd hardly want him inside the ship, would we?"

Milke roared, "If he got me first I wouldn't care whether he got into the ship or not." He jumped up into the central dome, played the searchlight around the lake. Paskell watched from the sideport. "See anything?"

"No," grumbled Milke. "I still don't believe there's anything out there. Let's eat dinner and get some sleep."

"Perhaps we should keep watch."

"What do we watch for? What good would it do if we saw something?"

Paskell shrugged. "We might be able to deal with it, if we knew what it was."

Milke said, "If there *is* anything out there —" he slapped the holster at his belt "— I'll know how to deal with it... A couple ammo into its hide and we'll have to screen for its pieces."

The ship vibrated; from the tail came a harsh sound. The floor jarred under their feet. Milke looked askance at Paskell, who puffed rather desperately at his pipe. Milke ran back to the searchlight. But the central dome interrupted the backward path of the beam and the tail was left in darkness.

"I can't see a thing," fretted Milke. He jumped down to the deck, looked indecisively at the after port.

The vibrations ceased. Milke squared his shoulders, pulled the helmet back over his head. Slowly Paskell followed suit.

"You bring a flashlight," said Milke. "I'll have my gun ready..."

They stepped into the air lock. Paskell gingerly thrust his arm out, aimed the light toward the tent. "Nothing there," grumbled Milke. He pushed past Paskell, stepped down to the ground. Paskell followed, played the light in a circle.

"Whatever it was, it's gone," grunted Milke. "It heard us coming —"

"Look," whispered Paskell.

It was no more than a zigzag of shadows, a moving mass.

Milke held out his arm; his gun spat pale blue sparks. Explosion — a great splash of orange light. "Got him!" cried Milke exultantly. "Dead center!"

Their eyes adjusted to the pallid illumination of the flashlight. Nothing but the glistening sheen of the quicksilver and — a rumpled tumbled mess where the assay tent had stood.

Milke said in an outrage too deep for vehemence, "He's ruined our gear — our tent!"

"Look out!" screamed Paskell. The flashlight took lunatic sweeps over the lake. Milke sent shot after shot at a tall shape; the explosions smote back on their suits; the orange glare blinded their eyes.

Thud-bump... Thud-bump... "Inside!" gasped Milke. "Inside, we can't hold him off..."

The outer port slammed. A breathless moment later the hull was jarred, scraped along the quicksilver. Milke and Paskell stood haunted and pale in the center of the deck.

Metal creaked at the stern under pressure or torsion. Milke's voice came high-pitched. "We're not built to take that kind of stuff —"

The ship lurched to the side. Paskell put his pipe in his pocket, grabbed a stanchion. Milke jumped up to the controls. "We'd better get out of here."

Paskell cleared his throat. "Wait, I think it's stopped."

The boat was quiet. Milke thought of the searchlight, flicked the switch. "Hah!"

"What is it?"

Milke stared out the port. He said slowly, "I really don't know. Something like a one-legged man on crutches... That's how he walks."

"Is he big?"

"Yes," said Milke. "Rather big... I think he's gone, through that fissure —" He came down to the deck, split open his space suit, climbed nervously out. "That was Three-legged Joe."

Paskell took a sudden seat on the bunk, reached for his pipe. "Quite an impressive fellow."

Milke laughed shortly. "I can certainly understand how he scared the bejabbers out of those old bindlestiffs."

"Yes," Paskell nodded earnestly. "I can too." He lit his pipe, puffed reflectively. "He can't be invulnerable..."

Milke dropped leadenly upon his own bunk. "We'll get him — somehow or other."

Paskell craned his neck out the port. "There'll be light in a few hours... I suppose we might as well sleep."

"Yes," said Milke. "If Three-legged Joe comes back, I imagine he'll let us know about it."

✳

Sigma Sculptoris washed the quicksilver lake with the palest of lights. Milke and Paskell glumly examined the wreckage of the assay tent.

Milke's indignation brimmed over the restraints he had set upon himself. He clenched his fists inside the gloves, glared toward the defile. "I'd like to lay my hands on that three-legged devil..."

Paskell busied himself among the tatters of the tent. "Nothing but ribbons."

Milke said gloomily, "No use to think about mending it..." He watched Paskell curiously. "What are you looking for?"

"I wonder what possessed him to break into the tent."

"Sheer destructiveness."

Paskell said thoughtfully, "I notice one thing —" he paused.

"What?"

"All our reagents are gone."

Milke bent over the wreckage. "All of them?"

"All the acids. All the bases. He left distilled water, the salts..."

"Hm," said Milke. "What do you make of that?"

Paskell shrugged inside his suit. "It's suggestive."

"Of what, if I may ask?"

"I'm not sure." Paskell wandered out over the quicksilver, searching the surface. "He was about here when you shot at him?"

"Just about."

Paskell bent. "Look here." He held up a rough brownish-gray object the size of his thumb. "Here's a piece of Three-legged Joe."

Milke examined the fragment. "If this is all our weapons did to him — he's tough. This stuff is flexible!"

Paskell took back the fragment. "Let's take it in and run it through the works."

They returned into the ship. Paskell clamped the bit in a vise and after exasperating difficulty, succeeded in slicing free a brittle shaving. He forced it flat between a slide and a cover glass, examined it under the microscope. "Remarkable."

"Let's see." Milke applied his eye. "Hm...it's like a carpet — woven in three dimensions."

"Right. No matter which way you cut or tear, fibers mat up against you... now let's see what he's made of."

"You're the technician," said Milke.

Paskell looked up from the workbench an hour later. "It's a very complex silicon compound. The spectroscope shows silicon, lithium, fluorine, oxygen, iron, sulfur, selenium, but I can't begin to put a name to the stuff."

"Call it Joe-hide," Milke suggested.

Paskell blew into his pipe, looked solemnly down at the workbench. "I have a tentative theory about Joe's inner workings..."

"Well?"

"Obviously he needs energy to exist. His hide shows no radioactivity, so he must use chemical energy. At least I can't think of any other form of energy that he could be using."

Milke frowned. "Chemical energy? At absolute zero?"

"He's insulated. No telling how high his internal temperature goes."

"What kind of chemical energy? There's no free oxygen, no fluorine, nothing..."

"Presumably he uses whatever he can get — anything that reacts to produce energy."

Milke pounded his fist. "We could bait him into a trap, with, say, a chunk of solid oxygen!"

"I should certainly think so. But what kind of trap?"

Milke scowled. "A dead-fall."

"Here on Odfars gravity is not too strong... we'd have to stack ten thousand cubic yards of rock to make an impression."

Milke paced up and down the room. "I've got it!"

"Well?" said Paskell mildly.

"Perhaps you could make a detonator that we could set off from the ship."

"Yes, that could be done."

"Here's what we'll do. We'll set out about twenty pounds of myradyne, with the detonator in the center. Joe will come past, tuck this bundle into whatever kind of stomach he's got. We wait till he gets a few hundred yards from the ship, then set it off."

Paskell pursed his lips. "If events proceeded along those lines, everything would be fine."

"Well, why shouldn't they? You claim that Joe eats —"

"Not 'claim' — 'theorize'."

"— anything that produces energy. Well, the myradyne should look to him like ice cream and candy and cake all mixed up. It's nothing else *but* energy."

"It's a different kind of energy — the energy of instability. Perhaps he only digests energy of combination."

"You're quibbling," said Milke with disgust. "I say the idea's worth trying."

Paskell shrugged. "Get out your myradyne."

"How long will it take you to fix up a detonator?"

"Twenty minutes. I'll hook up a battery and a spare head-set to the cartridge…"

While Milke gingerly carried the packet of explosive across the lake, Paskell stood by the port watching. Milke surveyed the landscape with fine calculation, setting down the packet, moving it a few yards to the right, another few yards toward the defile. Finally satisfied, he looked back to Paskell for approval. Paskell signaled casually, and his hand fell against the detonation switch. He looked out toward Milke, hastily jumped into his suit, let himself through the port, ran across the lake.

Milke asked, "What's the trouble?"

Paskell said, "That remote detonator doesn't work. I'd better take a look at it."

Milke stared at him truculently. "How do you know it doesn't work?"

Paskell made a vague gesture, knelt beside the packet, unfolded the wrapping.

"You couldn't have just sensed it," Milke insisted.

"Well, as a matter of fact, my hand accidentally hit the switch, and it didn't go off — so I thought I'd better run out and see what was wrong."

Milke seemed to sink inside his suit. For a moment there was silence. "Ah," said Paskell. "Nothing very serious; I neglected to clip down the battery leads…now it's ready to go —"

"I'm going back to the ship," said Milke thickly.

Paskell glanced up toward Sigma Sculptoris. "Yes, there's only a few moments of daylight left…"

Inside the ship, without the booster goggles, night apparently had already come to the quicksilver lake.

Milke roused himself from his bunk where he had been quietly sitting, took his goggles, went up into the control blister. "Nothing in sight."

Paskell said mildly, "Maybe Joe won't be back."

Milke, with his back to Paskell, said nothing.

"Maybe he's been watching us all day," Paskell remarked.

Milke leaned forward. "There's something moving in the gulch… there goes the daylight. Blast it! Now I can't see anything… and the dome's in the way of the searchlight again."

In sudden inspiration Paskell said, "Use the radar!"

Milke ran to the screen, flipped some switches, set the key on Green, short range. Paskell swung around the antenna. "Hold it!" said Milke. "Right there!"

Paskell and Milke bent close to the screen. The plane of the lake, the bulk of the mountains, the gap were all clear. Three-legged Joe, much closer, was a blur. "Can't you adjust it finer?" demanded Paskell.

Milke ran to the workbench, came back with a screw-driver, set the Green adjustment to its limit. "How's that?"

"Turn off the lights. I feel like I'm in a peep-show."

"There, any better?"

"Yes, much better."

Milke came back to the screen. Three-legged Joe was a barrel surmounted by a keg. The legs were a blur; flickering wisps of light to either side of the trunk seemed to indicate arm-members.

"Look," sighed Milke. "He's stopping by the package."

The great trunk seemed to waver, collapse.

"He's reaching for it."

The shape once more reached its full height.

"He's stopped," said Paskell.

"He's eating the myradyne…"

Three-legged Joe came forward, and presently blurred out past the resolving power of the set.

The ship jerked tentatively. Milke and Paskell braced themselves.

Nothing more. Silence. The radar screen was empty. Paskell swivelled the antenna. Nothing.

"He's gone," said Milke. "Where's the detonator switch?"

"Wait!" Paskell whispered. He turned on the lights. "Look!"

Milke jerked back. Pressed close to the port beside his face was a rough silvery brown-gray substance.

The port suddenly showed black. A flicker of movement passed the stern port.

"Off with the lights," hissed Milke. "Back to the radar."

A blur of golden light resolved into an ambling barrel and keg.

"Now," said Milke, "press the button! Quick! Before he gets out of range."

"Just a moment," said Paskell. "Suppose he's smarter than we think?"

"No time for theorizing now," cried Milke. "Where's the button?"

Paskell pushed him away stubbornly. "First, we'd better take a look around." He climbed into his space suit while Milke fumed and ranted.

Taking no heed, Paskell left the ship. Out the port Milke could see the glimmer of his head lamp.

The outside port sighed open, thudded shut. Paskell came back into the ship. Milke had his finger on the switch. Paskell, unable to talk through the helmet, banged his glove against the wall. In his other hand he held up a brown packet.

Milke's fingers fell nervously away.

Paskell split himself out of the suit. "I didn't think he'd like myra-dyne," he said in modest triumph. "The wrong kind of chemical energy. He left it beside the ship."

"Gad!" said Milke huskily. "Twice on the same day I'm blown to smithereens…"

Paskell carefully removed the detonator. "Every day we're learning more about Three-legged Joe."

Milke's voice was warm with emotion. "Every day we come closer to killing ourselves."

"Tomorrow," said Paskell, "we'll try again."

✳

Over a cup of hot coffee Milke asked, "How do you mean, try again? So far as I can see, we're licked. Our guns are no good, he refuses to eat our explosives. Certainly nothing in the world could poison him."

"True." Paskell tamped black shag into his pipe. "The methods for killing human beings don't apply to Three-legged Joe."

"No wonder those old goats at Merlinville gave us the laugh."

Paskell puffed thoughtfully. "If we could concentrate enough heat on Joe, for a long enough time —"

"Nuts!" said Milke. "If we had an ocean we couldn't even drown him."

Paskell said through the cloud of smoke. "If we melted a puddle in the quicksilver and he fell in, and the quicksilver froze around him —"

"Impossible. Quicksilver at absolute zero is super-conductive. We'd have to heat half the planet."

"Super-conductive... Right. So it is." Paskell stared dreamily into the haze. "I wonder how far the quicksilver extends around the planet?"

"What difference does that make?"

"Maybe we'll electrocute Joe."

"Hah!" spat Milke. "With what? Our two thousand-watt generator?"

Paskell said, "First we'll have to check on the quicksilver."

"On foot? With Joe pounding along behind us, breathing down our necks?"

Paskell said carelessly, "I imagine we can move as fast as Joe."

"I'm not sure. Maybe he runs like a greyhound."

"We'll have our guns."

"Fat lot of good they'll do."

"Well — I suppose we could take up our ship and cruise around the planet. In fact it might be better..."

His companion had been completely absorbed in his theorizing when Milke called out in alarm, "You're setting down almost in that defile!"

"Good," said Paskell. "We want to have the ship as near to the gap as possible."

"I don't see why," Milke said petulantly. "In fact I don't understand what you're up to."

"We're planning to electrocute Three-legged Joe," said Paskell patiently. "We've been around the planet; we've established that the quicksilver is interconnected everywhere except at this fifty-foot saddle of gray chalk. We've got enough lead and copper aboard to bridge the gap with a fairly heavy cable — which we will do. We can melt a good connection into the quicksilver with thermite."

"So then?"

"While you're installing the cable, I'll be rigging up some kind of fancy induction coil to take power from our generator and build up watts in the round-planet circuit."

Milke stared incredulously at Paskell. "What good will that do?"

"You'll arrange the cable so that when Joe comes along the defile, he'll have to take hold of the cable to break it. As soon as he does, he'll get everything that we've been feeding into the circuit."

Milke shook his head. "It won't work."

Paskell puffed at his pipe. "And why not, pray?"

"Think of the hysteresis in all those miles of quicksilver — the inlets and bays and channels. There'll be a billion little whorls and eddies..."

"There's no energy lost," said Paskell. "There's no resistance, so there can't be any production of heat."

"There'll be field conflicts," insisted Milke.

"Only for a few hundredths of a second. After that the fields will necessarily enforce a flow pattern that minimizes the impedance."

Milke shook his head. "I hope you know what you're talking about... But —" he raised a finger "— we've got another problem."

"What's that?"

"The planet's natural magnetism. If we start current flowing around the planet, we're setting up artificial north and south poles. We'll be fighting the natural field."

Paskell blinked owlishly. "There is no natural field to this planet. I checked immediately."

Milke threw up his hands. "Go to it, Oliver. It's your party."

Milke and Paskell stood contemplating the defile, across which, at the height of their eyes, dangled a rude cable. Near the lake, the cable passed through a long box, from which came leads running to the generator inside the ship.

Paskell said solemnly, "There's a trillion amps running through the cable."

"A few more," said Milke, "it'll swell like a poisoned pup."

"There is a practical limit," admitted Paskell. "At absolute zero the resistance of super-conductive metals is infinitesimal, but still is greater than nothing. When the cable carries a load that generates heat faster than the heat radiates off, the temperature in the cable rises until it reaches the lower limit of super-conductivity."

"And then?"

Paskell flung up his arms. "No more cable."

Milke regarded his handiwork anxiously. "Perhaps we'd better check."

"How? We don't have a thermocouple aboard that sensitive."

Milke shrugged. "All we can do then is hope."

"Right. Hope that Joe comes down that pass before the cable goes." He looked up at the sun. "Still an hour or two of light."

Milke said doubtfully, "The set-up doesn't look very lethal. Suppose Joe grabs the cable and breaks it, and nothing happens — what then?"

"Something's got to happen. We're feeding a constant two thousand watts into that circuit. When Joe breaks the cable those watts have to go somewhere — they just don't evaporate. They keep on going — through Joe. And if Joe doesn't feel it, I'll personally go after him with a pocket-knife."

Milke turned Paskell a surprised glance: strong talk from modest Oliver Paskell.

Paskell was restlessly beating his hands together. "We're forgetting something."

Milke turned, looked toward the ship.

"Ah, yes," said Paskell.

Milke made a strange noise. His arm jerked up.

"The bait," said Paskell. "We want to set out some acid."

"Never mind the bait," rasped Milke. "We're the bait...Joe's behind us..."

Paskell sprang around. Three-legged Joe stood in front of the ship looking at them.

"Run," said Milke. "Up under the cable...And if it doesn't work — God help us..."

Three-legged Joe came forward, like a one-legged man on crutches.

Paskell stood frozen. "Run!" screamed Milke. He darted back, seized Paskell's arm.

Paskell broke into a shambling run.

"Faster," panted Milke. "He's gaining on us."

Paskell ran to the mountainside, tried to claw his way up the sheer rock.

"No, no!" yelled Milke. "Through the defile!"

Paskell turned, ducked under one of Joe's enormous arms, scuttled toward the defile.

Milke tackled him. "Under the cable — not through! *Under!*" He grabbed Paskell's legs, drew him under the cable. Three-legged Joe ambled casually after them.

Paskell rose to his feet, looked wildly around. "Easy," said Milke. "Easy…"

Cautiously they backed up the defile. Milke panted, "No use running now. If your contraption doesn't work, we might as well reconcile ourselves to death."

Paskell asked suddenly, "Did you turn on the generator?"

Milke froze. "The generator? Inside the ship? You mean the power out to the circuit?"

"Yes, the generator…"

"No, didn't you?"

"I don't remember!"

Milke said despairingly, "You'll know in a minute. Here comes Joe —"

Three-legged Joe paused by the cable. He walked forward. The cable touched his chest. He lifted up his arms. "Close your eyes," cried Paskell.

The sudden glare spattered darts of light through their eyelids.

"You turned on the generator," said Milke.

Three-legged Joe lay forty feet distant, twitching feebly.

"He's not dead," muttered Paskell.

Milke stood looking down at the silver-gray hulk. "We can't cut him up. We can't tie him. We can't…"

Paskell ran to the ship. "Get out the grapples."

✳

Returning from the Merlinville Deed Office, Milke and Paskell stepped into Tom Hand's Chandlery for a new tent and a replacement set of reagents.

Lounging at the table were Abel Cooley and his friend James. "Ah, here's the prospectors back from Odfars," said Cooley.

Tom Hand limped forward. His eyes were red, there was alcohol on his breath, and a series of black and blue bruises showed on one side of his face. "Well, young fellow," he said to Milke in a thick voice, "what'll it be?"

"First, we need a new assay tent."

From the table by the window came a chuckle. James called out in his jocular baritone, "Three-legged Joe maybe tried to bunk in with you?"

Milke made a noncommittal gesture; Paskell sucked at his pipe.

Tom Hand said, "Pick up your tent out on the loading platform. What else?"

"A set of assay reagents." Milke handed over a list.

Tom Hand looked at them from under his eyebrows. "You boys still going out prospecting?"

"Certainly. Why not?"

"I should think maybe you had a bellyful."

Milke shrugged. "Odfars wasn't too bad. We never expected an easy life from prospecting. Joe gave us a pretty hard time, but we took care of him."

Hand leaned forward, red eyes blinking. "What's that?"

"We don't mind letting it out. We've got everything in sight sewed up and recorded."

Abel Cooley said, "You took care of Joe, did you? Talk him to death maybe?"

"No. He's still alive. We've got him where he can't get away. A research team from the Institute is coming out to look him over."

James stepped forward. "You've got him where he can't get away? I've seen Joe break out of a net of two-inch cable like it was string. We blasted a mountain down on top of his cave. Twenty minutes later he pushes his way out... Now you tell me you've got him where he can't get away."

"Right," murmured Paskell. "Exactly right."

Milke turned to Tom Hand. "Give us about a hundred gallons of hydrogen peroxide, two hundred gallons of alcohol."

"We've got to keep Joe alive," Paskell told James.

Abel Cooley snorted. "Hogwash."

Tom Hand shrugged, turned away into the recesses of his shop.

James said, in an oil-smooth voice, "Suppose you break down and tell us just what you did to poor old Three-legged Joe."

"Why not?" said Paskell. "But I'm warning you — stay away from him."

"Never mind the jokes … I'm still listening."

"Well, first we electrocuted Joe. It stunned him."

"Yeah?"

"We couldn't kill him or tie him — so while he was still twitching, we threw grapples around his leg, hoisted him twenty miles out into space and gave him an orbit around Odfars. That's where he is now — alive and well and feeling rather foolish, I should imagine."

James pulled at his chin. He looked at Abel Cooley. "What do you think, Abel?" he asked.

Abel Cooley snorted, looked out the window.

James sat down by the table. "Yes," he said heavily, "Three-legged Joe *is* feeling rather foolish, I expect."

"About like the rest of you birds," came Tom Hand's voice from behind the shelves.

Four Hundred Blackbirds

I

AT THE SIGHT of the green-and-black uniform, the guard stiffened, stepped forward, a hand at his weapon.

Director Edvard Schmidt of the Institute said, "It's all right, Leon. Open up."

The guard hesitated, bristling at the short square man in the alien regalia.

"Open up," said the director, without heat, as if he had already passed through the same emotions.

The guard complied with a shrug, returning stare for flinty stare as the uniformed man passed in.

Beyond the wall, the director and his guest faced a number of white buildings irregularly placed on a grassy compound. Director Schmidt gestured with a lean old hand. "Undoubtedly the smallest, least pretentious national research station in the world."

The man in uniform turned him a quick look, pitiless rather than hostile. "And probably the farthest advanced."

When Director Schmidt made a deprecatory murmur, the visitor said with a meaningful smile: "You Suaredes have enjoyed the benefits of a neutrality many years; you have not expended your brainpower on tactics and military subservience."

The sallow lines of Director Schmidt's face momentarily deepened. "True enough," he said bitterly, "we have been content inside our own borders; we don't want to rule the earth. Our ways of life may seem peculiar, but they suit us. And we do not dragoon others into step."

The man in uniform smiled slightly. "An eloquent speech, Director.

However, I am uninterested in your doctrine; I consider it a relic of the past. A change has come over the world — and in the future I advise a discipline upon your emotions as rigid as that which you impose on your intellect."

Director Schmidt said nothing. He looked over and beyond the walls of the Institute to the face of Mt. Hellenbraun, where great green firs rose staunchly, where snow lay golden-quiet in the slanting afternoon sun. Here was the spirit of Suare, a tradition which the general and his kind seemed unable to understand.

The general continued. "You must know from your work in the fields of science that all knowledge evolves, gathers strength. We of Moltroy are applying newly-discovered methods of control to our people, to our future, and ultimately the future of the world. Fanatics, extremists, individualists —" he rolled the words "— they are today like dinosaurs in the Stone Age, creatures marooned in unsympathetic times."

The director turned his head slowly, with an effort looked into the eyes of the soldier Zoltan Vec. Zoltan Vec stared back into the old man's eyes, indifferent, faintly amused. He jerked his shaven head. "Come, let us view your famous center of learning."

Director Schmidt sighed. In regard to this, there was no argument; he had his orders.

"What will you examine first?"

Zoltan Vec consulted a notebook. "Your physics department."

Director Schmidt shook his head. "There is none."

The general said, "What?" Then, coldly: "Impossible."

"We do not lop knowledge into discrete segments, like links of sausage," the director told him. "Few of our men are specialists."

Zoltan Vec rubbed his heavy chin. "I do not understand your methods. Would you not achieve firmer results with better organization? Here — you have a problem: you classify it, you assign it to the man best acquainted with the field. In the army, I would never put a man trained in fusing-rockets to piloting a Jugger-tank. Why should a chemist be allowed to dabble in physics or biology?"

Director Schmidt had recovered his detachment. "The fields are closely related; there is no longer any such creature as a chemist."

Zoltan Vec shook his black-thatched head. "There are chemists in

Moltroy. I spoke to one yesterday; he is working on a material that will coagulate mud to a solid. He told me himself he was a chemist."

The director smiled coolly. "Doubtless, then, you have chemists in Moltroy. But here we have none."

Zoltan Vec regarded the thin old man with sudden suspicion. "Your orders were explicit — to conduct me through the laboratory; to assist me without hindrance or reservation."

Director Schmidt now reflected that non-committal cooperation might have been wiser, since eventual humiliation, of one sort or another, was inevitable... Perhaps he could preserve a little face.

"I have no reservations. I speak to you with perfect freedom. The hindrances, if such they exist, are in your understanding of our methods — and are possibly due, I may add, to your training, your viewpoint."

"Enough!" barked Zoltan Vec in a loud harsh voice. "I demand to be taken to your physics department. First I will inspect your newest nucleonic techniques."

"This way," said Director Schmidt. Zoltan Vec marched after with the air of a man who has crushed an opposing force.

Schmidt rapped on a door, opened it. "Good afternoon, Louis." He gestured to the soldier. "Here," drily, "we have General Zoltan Vec of the Moltroy Army. General Vec, Louis Maisan."

Vec nodded, glanced around the room. "And where is your equipment?"

"Equipment?" Louis Maisan shook a bald head. "We have little here. It is well known that most of our work is theoretical."

Zoltan Vec pointed to a litter of papers. "What do you do there?"

Maisan regarded him with raised eyebrows. "May I inquire your interest?"

Director Schmidt raised a hand. "We have orders, Louis."

"Orders, orders," growled Maisan. "The word itself is an indignity..." He jerked an arm at the papers. "The *papers* are the property of the Institute, and subject to orders; *I* am not. Inspect the papers as thoroughly as you wish, but please do not trouble me with your questions."

Zoltan Vec wordlessly strode forward, took up a clip of papers, held them at arms-length. After a moment he turned with a puzzled frown to the director. "Just what is this gibberish?"

"Louis Maisan is calculating the angular velocities of mesons in several non-physical dimensions…You might say he is determining how fast mesons turn themselves inside out."

Zoltan Vec returned the papers slowly to the table, made a note in a small book. Tucking the notebook in his pocket he swung a long slow glance around the room — blackboards, desks, Louis Maisan's indifferent profile, Director Schmidt, impassive, watchful.

"You may conduct me, if you will. I wish to interview every man in your employ; I have a list here which I will check against."

They entered a long cool room smelling of formaldehyde. A low bench along one wall, under a line of green-glass windows, held thousands of cotton-stoppered flasks. Three men sat at microscopes, rapt, like ants at a drop of syrup, only occasionally one moving or speaking in a low tone. They paid General Vec and the director little heed.

Zoltan Vec's voice seemed needlessly brusque. "And here?"

"We are studying photosynthesis — using radioactive tracers, atom-substitution, other techniques. The flasks contain solutions in some of which we hope to duplicate photosynthesis."

"Which means you will be able to make food from air and water?"

"Oh, ultimately perhaps… At the moment, we'd be satisfied with a trace of hydrocarbon."

Zoltan Vec turned away. "At our plant in the Morispill mountains we grow two thousand tons of protein yeast a day. Think of it! Rations for the entire army! Will your process ever equal that record?"

"Never," declared the director.

"If I were you," said Zoltan Vec, "I would discontinue the study; it is clearly not so practical as the yeast process."

The director paused at a door, whose panel bore a playful caricature in blue crayon, the square root of negative one representing each eye. "In here are a group of mathematicians." He laid a hand on the knob, looked back at Vec quizzically. "Would their studies interest you?"

A sudden braying arose within, an excited hubbub. Director Schmidt frowned. Zoltan Vec stood watching with an intent gleam in his eye. "What are they so excited about?"

Director Schmidt shrugged, opened the door. A tall young man with a pink face and wild black hair, stalking back and forth with a glass of wine in his hand, waved vehemently. "It is so beautiful, so simple, even as Fermat described...Edvard!—Edvard!—" to Director Schmidt. "Today we are part of history! The discovery of the century!"

Zoltan Vec was abreast of Schmidt now. "What's this? What's this?"

"Fermat's lost solution! 'It is impossible to partition a cube into two cubes,' said Fermat, 'I have discovered a truly wonderful proof of this,' said Fermat, but the margin was too narrow to hold it! Today I scribbled it in an instant! Now," and the tall young man drank his wine, "when they say Fermat, Euler, Gauss, Riemann, they will also say—" he beat his chest "—Jevinsky."

The director rubbed his chin. "You have checked for values of n above 14,000?"

Jevinsky waved his glass jubilantly. "No need! It is a general solution!"

"My congratulations!" came the sardonic compliments of General Zoltan Vec. He turned to the director. "Let us go on."

Director Schmidt hesitated. "This evening we will check together," he told Jevinsky. "In the meantime, don't call the press. In fact, better tell no one. We can't have the Institute in an uproar for nothing."

Jevinsky nodded, settled like a great crane on a bench, began munching a slab of cheese.

II

Schmidt joined Zoltan Vec beyond the door. "A genius, that Jevinsky. Still young, unpolished, but one of our best men."

The soldier said nothing, but marched at Schmidt's side, thinking his own thoughts. They crossed a court, entered an area around which a long low building curved like a U.

"Our newest addition," said Schmidt. "We still have some vacancies... Archaeology. Here is a specialist, General—a man after your own heart; his job will occupy him the rest of his life."

Zoltan Vec gazed through the half-opened door at the frail gray man, who at the moment was leaning back in his chair, smoking a pipe.

"He seems to be enjoying life," was the general's dour comment. "Indeed, no one connected with the Institute appears to take it seriously. In Moltroy men earn their pay." He nodded within. "What's his job?"

Schmidt said coldly, "He is reconstructing the language of the Neolithic European."

Zoltan Vec snorted. "An idle man lost in dreams — at government expense. In Moltroy he would be assigned work in the shoe combine."

Director Schmidt glanced outside to a flag riding the west wind, a flag blue, green and white. "Here in Suare, where we have no army, you, General, might likewise find yourself at a job ill-suited to your capabilities — a bouncer in a cheap cabaret, a horse trainer..."

General Zoltan Vec halted in mid-stride, searched Director Schmidt's lean old face with narrow eyes.

"Well, General?" inquired Schmidt. "What is it?"

Zoltan Vec said, "Let us continue."

They rounded a corner, crossed the compound to a large white building.

"This is our life-sciences building — biology, psychology, and the like."

They entered a large bright room, unoccupied. "In here," said Schmidt, "Professor Luka and his son, Dr. John Luka, of Midland University, are probing the consciousness of single-celled animals. The amoeba, they find, can see various colors, can hear, smell, detect warmth and cold. They wish to ascertain his awareness of this world."

Zoltan Vec stared a moment across the top of his notebook. "Just what can these men hope to gain by their studies? A thousand and one things we need more than such... such..."

"Tomfoolery?" suggested Schmidt. "Is that the word? Suppose you learned that germs were able to choose between men as to which it desired to attack? Suppose a germ, face to face with a Moltroy soldier, turned away and instead infected a Federate?"

Zoltan Vec stood with eyebrows knitted, a dubious twist to his hard dark mouth. "Are these things possible? Is that what your laboratory is actually engaged in — germ warfare?"

"By no means," said Schmidt. "You express skepticism as to the value of the Lukas' research; I indicated a line along which these studies might conceivably lead."

The general slowly turned away, wrote at some length in his notebook. Then: "Are you conducting any other investigations of this type?"

"Bacterial warfare? No," said Schmidt. "We have some rather interesting psychosomatic studies in progress, one of which might be termed a vast projection of the Lukas' work."

General Zoltan Vec endeavored to grasp the idea. "How is that?"

"Step through here," and Schmidt pushed through a stainless steel swinging door. Zoltan Vec, close at his heels, saw a room of gray metal lined with benches and surgical equipment. A pair of white pallets occupied the center of the room, and a pair of young men, very quiet, lay on these.

Abel Ruan stood between the pallets, a thin wispy man somewhere between youth and middle-age. He was sand-colored; his head was long and bald; his long thin nose supported a pair of rimless glasses. He jerked a glance at his visitors, then returned to the two lying asleep.

Schmidt and the general watched a moment. The general, seeing little of interest, showed signs of impatience. Schmidt appeared not to notice, but said behind his hand: "Abel Ruan is an extremely brilliant scientist, ingenious, resourceful. At the moment he is endeavoring to link the brains of two men through their spinal cords."

"Toward what end?" demanded Zoltan Vec flatly. "Another *tour de force*? Or is there some significance to his efforts?"

Abel Ruan's hearing was acute. "General," he said, without turning his head, "I am an extremely fortunate man."

Zoltan Vec inspected him a moment before replying. "How is that?"

"I am obsessed by many curiosities. They would nag me, make my life intolerable, if the Suarede government were not paying me to satisfy them."

"How will all this —" Zoltan Vec gestured abruptly "— make you the wiser?"

"I have wondered many times if one man sees the world in the same shapes, the same colors as another man. Would the color Franz calls 'red' evoke an entirely different sensation in Jean's mind — if Jean could experience Franz's mental pictures? If so, when I couple Franz's eyes to Jean's brain, Jean will experience a wonderful sensation, for he will be seeing colors heretofore unimaginable, shapes previously beyond his conjecture. He will be living in a world utterly new and strange."

"Humph," said Zoltan Vec. "Very interesting. And how —" here he grinned humorlessly "— will the Suarede government profit by Jean's amazement?"

Abel Ruan stretched his thin freckled arms, pushed the glasses up the bridge of his big nose. "We shall never know — since, unfortunately, contact between the two men is impossible to maintain."

Schmidt clucked. "Nothing, Abel?"

Abel shrugged. "A microvolt or two. Nothing to speak of. Insufficient to arouse images. And — in all probability — as we imagined — the brain would automatically compensate."

Schmidt shook his head. "A pity."

"However," said Ruan, "a set of equally interesting results has appeared."

Schmidt glanced uncomfortably toward Zoltan Vec, who had inclined his massive head forward. "Indeed?"

"The difficulty arose in the coupling," said Ruan, smiling in a broad display of long white teeth. "Each brain wished to generate the master cycle; there was no consonance. In an effort to circumvent this conflict, I joined the brain of a canary to Jean's brain."

"And —"

Abel Ruan shrugged his thin shoulders. "Nothing occurred — until, and mark this, gentlemen, until one of the other birds chanced to become excited, whereupon Jean exhibited signs of restlessness."

Schmidt's old face looked suddenly eager, passionate, with all the fatigue erased. "Telepathy?"

Abel Ruan nodded. "Consistently."

Zoltan Vec rubbed his chin. Schmidt, becoming aware of him, diminished, lost the zest he had displayed, became gray and old once more.

Vec inquired sarcastically, "Does your government pay you to dabble in spiritualism, too?"

Schmidt hunched his head between his shoulders; Abel Ruan flung his arms out, turned away.

Schmidt said, "You speak in ignorance, General. Here at the Institute we feel that any means to establish understanding between the two camps of the world deserves all attention. If men understood each other freely, there would be no tension, no hostility, no war...Telepathy would be the ideal means to this end."

Abel Ruan's glasses glinted as he tilted his narrow head back. He met Zoltan Vec's unsmiling gaze. "Doctor Schmidt, as you see, is an idealist. He believes in the essential decency of men."

Zoltan Vec nodded shortly. He noticed a chair, pulled it to him, seated himself, one booted leg advanced farther than the other. "Just how far have you progressed with these telepathy experiments?"

Abel Ruan leaned back against the wall, tapped his teeth with a pencil. "We've made a number of empirical discoveries, a few theoretical essays."

"Such as?"

"We find that birds are more sensitive, on the whole, than men. Possibly you have watched a flock of blackbirds, for instance, flying and suddenly all veering together as if guided by one brain."

Zoltan Vec nodded. "I was born on a farm in the Kerkhaz Valley."

"We've been using the idea of wavelength, loosely of course, since we are not aware of the fundamental nature of telepathy. Imagine telepathy as high frequency radiation, imagine the human brain as a transmitter and receiver only of low frequency, but a bird's brain as a transmitter and receiver of the correct wavelength. When we couple a bird's brain to the human, the bird's brain acts as an amplifier."

Director Schmidt coughed. "It's getting late, General. Perhaps you'd care to visit our observatory?"

Zoltan Vec made a brusque sign without turning his head. "Suppose there were two men, both with brains joined to the brains of birds?"

Abel Ruan smiled slightly. "We have made that experiment. The results are limited only to the conceptual faculties of the birds. Hunger, fear, curiosity, colors, numbers up to five — they may be sent into the bird's brain, transmitted, received and given to another human brain. Any ideas more complex than these are impossible to telepathize."

"Can these bird brains be housed in portable units?" inquired Zoltan Vec. "Is it necessary that the men involved be incapacitated?"

Abel Ruan said without interest, "Only a small nerve-graft is necessary — leading from the requisite chord to a — let us say — 'wall-plug' on the neck. Then the portable unit containing the bird's brain may be connected and disconnected at will…However, General," he added, glasses glinting sardonically, "for any military communication, I'm sure your radio equipment will provide better service."

Zoltan Vec rose to his feet. "Methods of war," he observed drily, "change as well as the frontiers of science. Any future victory will be won in the first hour of war, by that power which can concentrate sufficient offensive potential above the opponent's territory. If one combatant can devastate the other at will, while sealing off its own frontiers, the other power must instantly surrender."

"'Your money or your life'," suggested Abel Ruan.

Zoltan Vec paced several steps back and forth unheeding. "All our plans are directed toward winning this quick war. Then we shall reorganize the world on the Moltroy pattern, with order, discipline, purpose, replacing aimlessness —" the sweep of his hand included the environs of the Institute "— dilettantism, irresponsibility."

Director Schmidt had sagged. His mouth moved feebly. "But war? Why need there be war? At the Grenaden Conference Moltroy and the World Federation agreed…" His voice trailed off.

Zoltan Vec stared briefly at him, then past. Abel Ruan showed his teeth in the smile that seemed more a nervous mannerism than a reflection of inner enjoyment, and which made him appear like a dentist, or an accountant eager to ingratiate himself.

Director Schmidt was gazing into a far nothingness. "Even so," he muttered, "Suare will naturally retain its neutrality. That is traditional." He seemed to take comfort in the thought, and his voice became stronger. "Suare need not be involved, regardless of outcome."

Zoltan Vec finished writing in his notebook. "Continue with your work," he said to Abel Ruan. "You may find yourself richly rewarded." He turned to Director Schmidt. "Come, let us continue."

III

Head bent, Edvard Schmidt came walking, from his little cottage on the first slope of Mt. Hellenbraun, up the gravelled road to the gate.

The guard saluted.

"Good morning, Leon," said Schmidt in a flat automatic tone.

"Good morning, Director." Leon held up a newspaper. "Seen the news? Lesmond and Couch already have fled to Varly. The People's Rights party is in power, and they've jailed Renner."

Schmidt nodded dismally. "I just turned off the radio... A terrible thing, Leon. I don't know — I hope it won't affect us here."

Leon pointed high at a flight of three airplanes. "Look, they don't waste any time, the insolent scoundrels! Those are Blatchats — Moltroy fighters!"

Schmidt turned away. "I suppose we'll see a lot more of them. It's the new way of invasion, Leon — no longer armies storming the borders, but cunning minds festering like tumors in the body of the government."

The telephone in the guard's cabin rang. Leon said, "Hello." Then: "It's for you, Director."

"Hello," said Schmidt. "Yes... Ah, what?... Effective immediately, you say?... I see..."

He returned outside. "Orders from the new Minister of the Interior. No one is to be permitted to leave the Institute, under any circumstances, until the new director arrives."

"New director?" gasped Leon. "But...?"

Schmidt flung out his long arms. "That's the way it goes, and there are your orders; no one is to leave."

Baze Roseau, the new director, was a small fat man, with a reedy voice, small wide-set eyes which constantly seemed to be peering sidewise. Immediately on his arrival he summoned the personnel of the Institute to a conference, and without ceremony made a speech. He proved to be a quick incisive speaker.

"Friends, as you all know, the party of progress has assumed control in Suare, and our nation becomes a new dynamic entity. Now we must join the tide to the future, set our faces to the light, march against the forces of reaction and oppression. To this end the People's Rights central committee has formulated a new program for the Institute, one which will advance the cause. I'm sure you've all been dissatisfied with the previous aimless, irresolute policy; no longer will this be true. A goal will be set for us all to work toward, united and enthusiastic in our common devotion to the new life. I have here a number of changes which must be effected immediately; I will read them to you now, openly and for us all to know. That is the new policy at the Institute, no more interdepartmental jealousy and back-biting. We will all be working for our common goal, and if there are any shirkers or malcontents, I will be pleased to learn of them…Here then is our new program."

He unfolded a crackling sheet of paper. "First, Edvard Schmidt will be Assistant Director in Charge of Administration, while Abel Ruan is promoted to Assistant Director in Charge of Research. Everyone on the research staff will work under Ruan's orders, including a number of exchange students arriving today from Moltroy. Now that is all for the present. Let me say however, that while liberal bonuses will be awarded for good work and cooperation, there is no place in the new life for sluggards or reactionaries. We must all throw ourselves, heart and soul, into the struggle, all working for the inevitable victory over our enemies. That is all, thank you."

As the personnel filed silently, glumly, from the room, Baze Roseau signalled to Abel Ruan. When they were alone, the new director motioned Ruan to a seat, while he walked back and forth, rubbing his hands briskly.

"Ah, Ruan — it would hardly be fair to keep from you the fact that your work has made a great impression in higher quarters; you are well on the way to honor and wealth."

"Indeed?" Abel Ruan scratched the sparse hair at the back of his head.

Baze Roseau nodded. "It has been decided that your work on telepathy will be continued here at the Institute, to be concentrated on intensively. All else will be suspended."

"Hm." Abel Ruan removed his glasses, polished them musingly. "I see…It has been decided then, that there *is* a military application to my work?"

Roseau smiled craftily. "Between you and me, it might be said to be true. I understand General Zoltan Vec was impressed by the possibilities, and in this time of militancy anything which will contribute to our eventual victory over the imperialists must be utilized."

"Ah!" Abel Ruan nodded sagely. "And what, precisely, is desired?"

"Think of it this way," said Baze Roseau. "In the eventual war, the first hour is crucial. Our bombers and missile-carriers, our fighter swarm will take off. They will attack at several points, and will be met by the defenses of the enemy, and his offensive force will take to the air. There will be a monstrous air battle over the ocean, and the side that breaks through will win the war. Now the weakest spot in our attack, in any attack, is coordination — since both sides automatically jam the other's radio channels. If we could maintain absolute control over all elements of our attacking force, the organization thus achieved would give us a decisive superiority, and we would have won the war. Telepathy functioning to perfection would completely solve the problem."

"Quite true, quite true," said Abel Ruan. "But — as I pointed out to General Vec — the medium through which we must act, the brain of a bird, permits no precision to the messages."

"The objection has been noted in higher places, and the suggestion made that intensive breeding and selection be tried to improve the type of brains involved."

Abel Ruan grinned, drawing aside his lips. "Something of the sort has occurred to me; however it is a long-range program."

"How long?" inquired Baze Roseau, eyes sharp and cold.

"Impossible to say. Several years, at least."

Baze Roseau nodded, began to pace once more. "That, of course, is unavoidable. Well, we will advance along those lines, as rapidly as possible. You will be in charge of the entire program. No effort, no expense is too great. There will of course be a substantial increase in your salary. If you succeed in developing a workable system, you will receive a pension of ten thousand marks a year, elite status and the Order of Butin."

"But," Ruan put forward, "suppose the idea is unsound? Suppose I fail?"

Baze Roseau swelled his plump chest. "The Movement recognizes no such word...Let us not talk of unpleasantness..."

"Persuasive arguments," was Abel Ruan's comment. "On both hands. Well, we shall see; we shall see."

※

On the afternoon of the same day, Edvard Schmidt, knocking at the door and entering, found Abel Ruan seated in a chair leaning back on two legs with his own feet on a desk, arms clasped behind his head.

Schmidt quietly took a seat, leaned forward, sat bewildered when Ruan held up a hand for silence, picked up his portable phonograph, carried it to the wall, turned it on rather loudly.

Grinning his bare-toothed smile, Ruan returned to his seat. "That's where Roseau has installed his eavesdrop button. If he's listening he will be treated to the Moltroy anthem played *con brio*, with encores till you leave."

Schmidt shook his head. "I had no idea…"

"It pays to be suspicious," said Ruan, "even when you are working your soul out for them."

Schmidt leaned forward. "That's what I came to see you about. Abel, you'll succeed in this project!" And he eyed Ruan accusingly.

"Of course. That is my business, to make progress. They are paying me well, they offer me honors —"

"But heavens, man!" and Schmidt's old eyes glittered. "Do you mean to help those beasts? Do you understand what you are doing?"

Abel Ruan shrugged. "The sooner war comes, the sooner it will be over."

"But if you succeed — the slave state will be the model for the world."

Abel Ruan lit a cigarette. "Who knows? Moltroy may not win the war. After all, scientists work for the World Federation, too."

"But none of them are perfecting an instrument as decisive as the one you prepare…I ask you, Abel, do you intend to complete the project?"

Abel Ruan's eyes glinted warily as he watched the older man. "That is my job."

Schmidt pulled out a gun, levelled it, fired. Ruan ducked, toppled from his chair, reached under the desk, pulled at the old man's legs. Schmidt fell, and the gun clattered to the floor out of his reach. Ruan picked it up, returned to his seat.

Schmidt rose stiffly. "Well, why don't you call the guards?"

Ruan shook his head. "Edvard — you misjudge me. First and foremost, my guiding principle is — trust no one! Except now, perhaps you — for you have expressed your sentiments forcefully. I would like to point out that no man is indispensable; that if you shot me, there are a thousand who could fill my shoes with equal effect. That is one reason I'm pursuing these experiments. Here I control the situation. I am on top of it, I guide it. If I refused to cooperate — one of the other thousand would be in my shoes, and we would not be a whit the better off."

Schmidt had been absorbing as much of this as possible. "Abel, you cleverly avoid stating anything specific. Do I understand that you — you have some sort of plan?"

"Opportunities suggest themselves to a thoughtful man," said Ruan. "But not —" he held up the gun "— of this nature."

Schmidt stood stiffly. "I did what my conscience told me…I'm not sure that I'm glad I failed, because you promise nothing definite —"

"The universe, down to the most negligible electron, is indefinite, my dear director," was Ruan's cheerful statement. "Absolute decision is out of my hands. And never forget my motto is — trust no one."

"But in the meantime," remarked Schmidt glumly, "you perfect the weapon Moltroy will use to win the world."

IV

General Zoltan Vec unsnapped the clip at his neck, removed the high-domed helmet.

"Well?" demanded Marshal Koltig, chief of staff of the Moltroy armed forces.

"Perfect," said Zoltan Vec. "When I shut my eyes, I see the same scene the pilot sees. With my eyes open, I can transmit orders which need no acknowledgment, because I feel the impact in the pilot's mind."

"Excellent." Marshal Koltig turned to Abel Ruan, who stood quietly in the background. "How many of these have you prepared?"

"About four hundred and fifty, sir," replied Abel Ruan after a moment's hesitation. He appeared thin, tired, his color had become pasty.

Marshal Koltig pondered. "Four hundred and fifty…Hm. We are ordering two hundred flight-groups into action. That means four hundred helmets — one for each flight captain and one for his intermedium here at headquarters. That leaves fifty spares...Is it not possible to obtain another fifty?"

Abel Ruan shook his head. "Not for several months, sir. These brains are exceedingly delicate things, and for every brain large and complex enough to serve, we must discard ten thousand faulty ones."

The Marshal reflected further. "Well, we will make do. If necessary we can double up in non-critical areas, or use radio." He turned back to Zoltan Vec. "General, you will conduct exhaustive tests and report to me." Zoltan Vec bowed his head.

Abel Ruan cleared his throat. "I have some ideas for an improved model of the helmet. If I work hard, I possibly can complete a few in time for — an emergency. Perhaps enough for the top officers, or at least you and General Vec."

The Marshal gestured cordially. "By all means. Spare no expense; you have done handsomely so far, Abel Ruan, and will be well rewarded."

The scientist bowed, withdrew.

The morning of I Day. On a hundred fields bombers sat like great drone bees, gorged not with pollen but with nucleonic explosives, poison-foams and mists, violent bacterial cultures, propaganda leaflets prepared by renegade Federates. Fighter-jets and rockets ranged in long glinting rows, fueled, dangerous, willing.

Within the barracks, pilots sat smoking, talking or silent, as their temperaments prompted, while in the command centers flight captains donned their new high-domed helmets. And at the staff headquarters deeper within Moltroy, two hundred intermediums donned helmets each containing a brain habituated to the brain in a corresponding flight captain's helmet.

The intermediums took their numbered seats, these ranged around a dais and a great screen. Here would form a schematized picture of the battle, with different colors indicating the advances, retreats, with lights emphasizing emergency points. The whole play of this chart would be synthesized from the steady reports of the two hundred flight captains, relayed through the intermediums, and watching the chart, the staff, including General Vec and Marshal Koltig, would direct the strategy of the battle.

Marshal Koltig sat drinking coffee in a study nearby, brooding over intelligence reports — a large, brown, mustached man, full of bluff energy. "They know we've mobilized," he told General Vec. "We've kept it secret longer than I dared hope...They're calling up reserves."

Vec poured himself coffee. "I'll be interested to see the performance of the Mark IV Blatchats against their new Gladius Rams. I believe we've the better fire-power."

Koltig looked up. "That's right, the Blatchats are your special pets.

"... Better emphasize once again to the intermediums that there must be no individual actions, no dog-fighting. We are a vast overwhelming mass of precise machinery; that's important. No heroics. Drive home the fact that we will win through our unprecedented firmness and coordination. We cannot allow this advantage to be nullified by individual grandstanding."

Vec stood up. "I'll make it clear." He paused. "Let me see — Abel Ruan was to have special helmets for us. Has he arrived?"

"I believe he's in Suite C. You'd better send an orderly to check. Time's getting short. Twenty-two minutes now."

Zoltan Vec delivered his warning speech to the sighing body of intermediums, returned to the study. The orderly he had sent to Abel Ruan saluted.

"Abel Ruan requests that you come to Suite C for your helmet, sir."

"Very well," said Vec. "Tell the technicians to give the screen a final check."

"Yes, sir."

Vec found Marshal Koltig in Suite C, adjusting a domed helmet to his head, while Abel Ruan connected a clip to the nerve-graft on his neck.

"It would be better not to use the helmet until the battle is under way," said Ruan, in the tone of a doctor advising about the use of a salve. "The brain is particularly energetic, but it also must work harder than any of the others, so it is as well not to use it until there is a need."

"I see," said Marshal Koltig. "I just throw the switch, correct?"

"Right — the switch stimulates the brain, awakens it from what amounts to sleep. To select one whom you wish to communicate with, merely think of the color corresponding to the name." He produced a printed sheet. "Here is the list. General Vec, as you see, is light blue. You, Marshal, are maroon. So to make contact with General Vec, merely picture the color. The brain will do the rest."

"Marvellous, marvellous," exclaimed Marshal Koltig. "In the name of our leader, the great Butin, you shall be richly rewarded!"

Abel Ruan shook his long narrow head, and the glasses on his nose glinted. "No, I want no reward — merely the satisfaction of contributing to a great historical event."

"Oh, you scientists!" the Marshal chaffed. "Impractical visionaries!"

Abel Ruan smiled his wide long-toothed grin, turned to General Vec. "Here, General, is your helmet. You heard my instructions to the Marshal? Not to use the helmet until necessary?"

General Vec nodded, donned the helmet gingerly. Never had he quite accustomed himself to the use of this subsidiary brain. Grimly he clipped the lead to the nerve-graft on his neck.

"Now," said Abel Ruan, "you're all in order."

Marshal Koltig glanced at his wrist-watch. "We must hurry. The bombers took off nine minutes ago; in half an hour we will be over Federate territory."

An orderly entered. "Contact has been made, sir. Over Blorland, by Fighter Squadron 819."

"Results?" snapped Marshal Koltig.

"Unreported, sir."

"819," muttered Koltig. "That will be Flight 14." He dialed '14' on a communicator, was put through to the intermedium serving the squadron in question.

"14."

"What's going on?"

"F-S 819 encountered 12 Gladius Rams at 90,000 feet, sir. They are trying to break our formation, but have not succeeded and we have downed three — now four — without loss."

"Good," said Koltig. "Carry on."

A number of other contacts were made and reported, skirmishes, scout brushes.

"Looks like they're waiting for us somewhere over Ladomir," said Koltig, arising. "Well, Vec, perhaps we'd better take our places."

They passed through the door into the murmurous room, took their places on the dais. The screen above them now glowed, showing the Blorland–Ladomir boundaries, with a rim of the North Ocean in one corner. A flat black triangle slowly crossing the chart was the body of the Moltroy bombers, the great ships of strategic position. Once any number of these thunderous vessels had penetrated the enemy's defenses, he must surrender, or see his nation vanish in molten clods and hot gas. A fainter gray shadow indicated the supporting fighters, and already along the periphery spots of color indicated contact with the defending planes of the World Federation.

Far down, sweeping along the Glimmet coast came a blue shadow — vague because its composition was yet unknown — the World Federation offensive force. And at the bottom of the screen a chart noted the current casualties, so far nine Moltroy Blatchats, opposed to fifteen Federate Gladius Rams.

Koltig glanced out at the two hundred intermediums; each sat pale, intent in his seat, eyes half-closed, the thoughts from the flight captains far out over Ladomir winging home to the brains in the helmets and so to the human brain.

Vec said, "Here it comes — here comes their median sweep." A red line glared across the screen — the battle-front.

Koltig jumped to his desk, gestured to the screen operator. The map suddenly expanded, until the area of battle filled the whole screen, and the black triangle of bombers dissolved into its separate elements.

Vec said, "They're breaking through at 98, sir."

Koltig shouted, "Rocket-squadrons 12, 13, 14 to 98!" His voice boomed across the hall, the intermedium working with the flight moved, sent the order, the flight captain swerved his squadron, and a minute later the breach was healed. The casualty chart at the bottom clicked over furiously, but faster, much faster on the Federate side.

"The Blatchats are out-maneuvering them," cried Vec, as the triangle of bombers, momentarily slowed, forged ahead. But as they watched, the apex of the triangle glowed red, vanished.

"By our great Butin!" cried Koltig, astounded. "What's happened?"

Vec called sharply to the integrators. "2 — repeat."

"A new type of rocket, sir, evidently dive-bomb type. Estimated speed five thousand MPH."

"Get those heavy trackers above the fleet! Spot them as they come in!"

The order flashed across the windy distance, a segment in the rear rose, cast a panoply of accurate anti-fire above the bombers.

"Second rocket-attack repulsed, sir."

"Good, good!" Koltig clapped his hands. "Vec, so far, so good! We're gaining!" He suddenly became aware of the weight on his head, his helmet — forgotten in the tension of the battle. "Eh, Vec — we have our helmets. We can see this all ourselves."

"Of course," said Vec...

The room went mad with fear. The intermediums sprang from their seats, ran shrieking in circles, dove into corners, plunged from the room.

Koltig and Vec watched, rapt in the utmost dream-like wonder, unable even to feel dismay.

And on the battle-front, the flight captains screamed and flailed their arms, and likewise fled anywhere legs could take them.

And in a twinkling the armada from Moltroy became a mindless anarchy of expensive machinery.

Edvard Schmidt stopped the car, stared unbelievingly at the man in the vineyard — a thin wispy man wearing faded blue dungarees, a man with a narrow bald head, a thin toothy mouth.

Schmidt jumped from the car. "Abel! Of all things, to find you here!"

Ruan looked up with no surprise, indeed little reaction other than a slight narrowing of the eyes. "How are you, Edvard?"

"Well, of course! But you —" Schmidt indicated the vineyard.

"I own this land," said Abel shortly. "Now I live here — just over the hill."

"But your retirement — a young man yet!"

Ruan sighed, put his pruning shears in his pocket. "Evidently, my dear Edvard, you do not read the papers."

"What's all this?" demanded Schmidt. "What's in the papers concerning you?"

Ruan pinched his lips, snorted sardonically. "Today, my friend, the great leader Butin, as well as Marshal Koltig and your old acquaintance General Vec, is to be hanged... And but for my — let us say, anonymity — beside them would hang Abel Ruan. The mad scientist! The arch-fiend of the electrons! String him up!"

Schmidt sobered. In his surprise he had overlooked Ruan's record of cooperation with the Moltroy despots.

"Well — possibly. Of course, Butin and those others — after all they planned the whole thing..."

Ruan stared bitterly sidelong at old Schmidt. "Hang them then? When simple therapy would make them into different men entirely? No — human blood-thirst demands revenge. Revenge on poor Abel Ruan as well as Butin the leader... Revenge is pride. It's like saying no one's going to do that to me and get away with it!"

"Well — what about you?" inquired Schmidt cautiously. "Do you consider therapy a sufficient expiation for your part in the Moltroy crimes?"

Abel Ruan laughed a harsh loud laugh, with a genuine note of amusement.

"Edvard, it becomes necessary to mar your illusions. You are not aware but that for *my* work, *my* scheming, *my* risks — that Butin would not be hanging today, but rather the members of the World Federation Council!"

"It seems to me," said Schmidt coldly, "that you bent your best efforts to aid the Moltroy cause."

"How do you account for the remarkable Federate victory, when Moltroy was advancing at all levels?"

"Why — the breakdown of your telepathic system, of course."

"Bah!" Ruan suddenly bared his teeth, and the glasses perched on his long nose flashed in the sunlight. "The telepathic system functioned perfectly — from first to last, exactly as I had planned."

"Perhaps you had better explain."

Ruan smiled. "Why not?... From the time that the Moltroy general entered the Institute, it was obvious that telepathy would be used in war communications. All that was needed was the idea — the funds to develop it. Any one of a thousand Moltroy scientists could have done as well as I. But, as I told you one time, it was necessary for me to stay with the project, stay on top of it, control it...I went to work for the Moltroy army, even as you did."

Schmidt blinked. "I—I contributed nothing to their war effort."

"You detracted very little. Well, to get on; from the first, as you are aware, we used the brains of blackbirds, as being peculiarly susceptible to telepathic rapport. Even when the brains had been bred and refined to nearly the complexity of a human brain, with a blackbird's instincts...I built several special helmets secretly; I arranged for their use at exactly the critical instant. These helmets on the heads of Marshal Koltig and General Vec won the war for the World Federation."

"And these helmets—what was so remarkable about them?"

Abel Ruan smiled, showing long teeth. "They were built around the brains of sparrow-hawks."

Schmidt stared.

"The instant the blackbird-brains felt the hawk-brain, they reacted the same way four hundred blackbirds in the field react to a hawk in the sky. Panic."

Schmidt said after a moment, "Abel, this is hard to believe."

Ruan shrugged.

"However, I believe! I apologize to you. And I insist that you accompany me to Varly, and receive the recognition you deserve."

Ruan shook his head. "The Sunday-supplements would call me 'the Blackbird Hero'. And I have my vineyard to tend."

Schmidt said, "Once, Abel, you told Zoltan Vec that you were a man of many curiosities. Are you still curious?"

"Indeed I am. I am curious as to the nature of an animal that produces great works of music, atomic power, a united world, but nonetheless hangs its old enemies."

"That curiosity may be relieved in the new Suarede National Institute. A chair; a salary; and time for your vineyard, too."

Abel Ruan flung out his long thin arms. "You are right. I'm with you."

Together they climbed into Schmidt's car and drove off toward Varly.

SJAMBAK

HOWARD FRAYBERG, Production Director of *Know Your Universe!*, was a man of sudden unpredictable moods; and Sam Catlin, the show's Continuity Editor, had learned to expect the worst.

"Sam," said Frayberg, "regarding the show last night..." He paused to seek the proper words, and Catlin relaxed. Frayberg's frame of mind was merely critical. "Sam, we're in a rut. What's worse, the show's dull!"

Sam Catlin shrugged, not committing himself.

"*Seaweed Processors of Alphard IX* — who cares about seaweed?"

"It's factual stuff," said Sam, defensive but not wanting to go too far out on a limb. "We bring 'em everything — color, fact, romance, sight, sound, smell... Next week, it's the Ball Expedition to the Mixtup Mountains on Gropus."

Frayberg leaned forward. "Sam, we're working the wrong slant on this stuff... We've got to loosen up, sock 'em! Shift our ground! Give 'em the old human angle — glamor, mystery, thrills!"

Sam Catlin curled his lips. "I got just what you want."

"Yeah? Show me."

Catlin reached into his waste basket. "I filed this just ten minutes ago..." He smoothed out the pages. "'Sequence idea, by Wilbur Murphy. Investigate "Horseman of Space", the man who rides up to meet incoming spaceships'."

Frayberg tilted his head to the side. "Rides up on a *horse*?"

"That's what Wilbur Murphy says."

"How far up?"

"Does it make any difference?"

"No — I guess not."

"Well, for your information, it's up ten thousand, twenty thousand miles. He waves to the pilot, takes off his hat to the passengers, then rides back down."

"And where does all this take place?"

"On — on —" Catlin frowned. "I can write it, but I can't pronounce it." He printed on his scratch-screen: CIRGAMESÇ.

"Sirgamesk," read Frayberg.

Catlin shook his head. "That's what it looks like — but those consonants are all aspirated gutturals. It's more like 'Hrrghameshgrrh'."

"Where did Murphy get this tip?"

"I didn't bother to ask."

"Well," mused Frayberg, "we could always do a show on strange superstitions. Is Murphy around?"

"He's explaining his expense account to Shifkin."

"Get him in here; let's talk to him."

Wilbur Murphy had a blond crew-cut, a broad freckled nose, and a serious sidelong squint. He looked from his crumpled sequence idea to Catlin and Frayberg. "Didn't like it, eh?"

"We thought the emphasis should be a little different," explained Catlin. "Instead of 'The Space Horseman', we'd give it the working title, 'Odd Superstitions of Hrrghameshgrrh'."

"Oh, hell!" said Frayberg. "Call it Sirgamesk."

"Anyway," said Catlin, "that's the angle."

"But it's not superstition," said Murphy.

"Oh, come, Wilbur..."

"I got this for sheer sober-sided fact. A man rides a horse up to meet the incoming ships!"

"Where did you get this wild fable?"

"My brother-in-law is purser on the *Celestial Traveller*. At Riker's Planet they make connection with the feeder line out of Cirgamesç."

"Wait a minute," said Catlin. "How did you pronounce that?"

"Cirgamesç. The steward on the shuttle-ship gave out this story, and my brother-in-law passed it along to me."

"Somebody's pulling somebody's leg."

"My brother-in-law wasn't, and the steward was cold sober."

"They've been eating *bhang*. Sirgamesk is a Javanese planet, isn't it?"

"Javanese, Arab, Malay."

"Then they took a *bhang* supply with them, and *hashish, chat,* and a few other sociable herbs."

"Well, this horseman isn't any drug-dream."

"No? What is it?"

"So far as I know it's a man on a horse."

"Ten thousand miles up? In a vacuum?"

"Exactly."

"No space-suit?"

"That's the story."

Catlin and Frayberg looked at each other.

"Well, Wilbur," Catlin began.

Frayberg interrupted. "What we can use, Wilbur, is a sequence on Sirgamesk superstition. Emphasis on voodoo or witchcraft — naked girls dancing — stuff with roots in Earth, but now typically Sirgamesk. Lots of color. Secret rite stuff…"

"Not much room on Cirgamesç for secret rites."

"It's a big planet, isn't it?"

"Not quite as big as Mars. There's no atmosphere. The settlers live in mountain valleys, with airtight lids over 'em."

Catlin flipped the pages of *Thumbnail Sketches of the Inhabited Worlds.* "Says here there's ancient ruins millions of years old. When the atmosphere went, the population went with it."

Frayberg became animated. "There's lots of material out there! Go get it, Wilbur! Life! Sex! Excitement! Mystery!"

"Okay," said Wilbur Murphy.

"But lay off this horseman-in-space. There *is* a limit to public credulity, and don't you let anyone tell you different."

Cirgamesç hung outside the port, twenty thousand miles ahead. The steward leaned over Wilbur Murphy's shoulder and pointed a long brown finger. "It was right out there, sir. He came riding up —"

"What kind of a man was it? Strange looking?"

"No. He was Cirgameski."

"Oh. You saw him with your own eyes, eh?"

The steward bowed, and his loose white mantle fell forward. "Exactly, sir."

"No helmet, no space-suit?"

"He wore a short Singhalût vest and pantaloons and a yellow Hadrasi hat. No more."

"And the horse?"

"Ah, the horse! There's a different matter."

"Different how?"

"I can't describe the horse. I was intent on the man."

"Did you recognize him?"

"By the brow of Lord Allah, it's well not to look too closely when such matters occur."

"Then — you *did* recognize him!"

"I must be at my task, sir."

Murphy frowned in vexation at the steward's retreating back, then bent over his camera to check the tape-feed. If anything appeared now, and his eyes could see it, the two-hundred million audience of *Know Your Universe!* could see it with him.

When he looked up, Murphy made a frantic grab for the stanchion, then relaxed. Cirgamesç had taken the Great Twitch. It was an illusion, a psychological quirk. One instant the planet lay ahead; then a man winked or turned away, and when he looked back, 'ahead' had become 'below'; the planet had swung an astonishing ninety degrees across the sky, and they were *falling!*

Murphy leaned against the stanchion. " 'The Great Twitch'," he muttered to himself, "I'd like to get that on two hundred million screens!"

Several hours passed. Cirgamesç grew. The Sampan Range rose up like a dark scab; the valley sultanates of Singhalût, Hadra, New Batavia, and Boeng-Bohôt showed like glistening chicken-tracks; the Great Rift Colony of Sundaman stretched down through the foothills like the trail of a slug.

A loudspeaker voice rattled the ship. "Attention passengers for Singhalût and other points on Cirgamesç! Kindly prepare your luggage for disembarkation. Customs at Singhalût are extremely thorough. Passengers are warned to take no weapons, drugs or explosives ashore. This is important!"

✳

The warning turned out to be an understatement. Murphy was plied with questions. He suffered search of an intimate nature. He was three-dimensionally X-rayed with a range of frequencies calculated to excite fluorescence in whatever object he might have secreted in his stomach, in a hollow bone, or under a layer of flesh.

His luggage was explored with similar minute attention, and Murphy rescued his cameras with difficulty. "What're you so damn anxious about? I don't have drugs; I don't have contraband…"

"It's guns, your Excellency. Guns, weapons, explosives…"

"I don't have any guns."

"But these objects here?"

"They're cameras. They record pictures and sounds and smells."

The inspector seized the cases with a glittering smile of triumph. "They resemble no cameras of my experience; I fear I shall have to impound…"

A young man in loose white pantaloons, a pink vest, pale green cravat and a complex black turban strolled up. The inspector made a swift obeisance, with arms spread wide. "Excellency."

The young man raised two fingers. "You may find it possible to spare Mr. Murphy any unnecessary formality."

"As your Excellency recommends…" The inspector nimbly repacked Murphy's belongings, while the young man looked on benignly.

Murphy covertly inspected his face. The skin was smooth, the color of the rising moon; the eyes were narrow, dark, superficially placid. The effect was of silken punctilio with hot ruby blood close beneath.

Satisfied with the inspector's zeal, he turned to Murphy. "Allow me to introduce myself, Tuan Murphy. I am Ali-Tomás, of the House of Singhalût, and my father the Sultan begs you to accept our poor hospitality."

"Why, thank you," said Murphy. "This is a very pleasant surprise."

"If you will allow me to conduct you…" He turned to the inspector. "Mr. Murphy's luggage to the palace."

Murphy accompanied Ali-Tomás into the outside light, fitting his own quick step to the prince's feline saunter. This is coming it pretty soft, he said to himself. I'll have a magnificent suite, with bowls of fruit and gin pahits, not to mention two or three silken girls with skin like rich cream bringing me towels in the shower…Well, well, well, it's not so bad working for *Know Your Universe!* after all! I suppose I ought to unlimber my camera…

Prince Ali-Tomás watched him with interest. "And what is the audience of *Know Your Universe!*?"

"We call 'em 'participants'."

"Expressive. And how many participants do you serve?"

"Oh, the Bowdler Index rises and falls. We've got about two hundred million screens, with five hundred million participants."

"Fascinating! And tell me — how do you record smells?"

Murphy displayed the odor recorder on the side of the camera, with its gelatinous track which fixed the molecular design.

"And the odors recreated — they are like the originals?"

"Pretty close. Never exact, but none of the participants knows the difference. Sometimes the synthetic odor is an improvement."

"Astounding!" murmured the prince.

"And sometimes…Well, Carson Tenlake went out to get the myrrh-blossoms on Venus. It was a hot day — as days usually are on Venus — and a long climb. When the show was run off, there was more smell of Carson than of flowers."

Prince Ali-Tomás laughed politely. "We turn through here."

They came out into a compound paved with red, green and white tiles. Beneath the valley roof was a sinuous trough, full of haze and warmth and golden light. As far in either direction as the eye could reach, the hillsides were terraced, barred in various shades of green. Spattering the valley floor were tall canvas pavilions, tents, booths, shelters.

"Naturally," said Prince Ali-Tomás, "we hope that you and your participants will enjoy Singhalût. It is a truism that, in order to import, we must export; we wish to encourage a pleasurable response to the 'Made in Singhalût' tag on our *batiks*, carvings, lacquers."

They rolled quietly across the square in a surface-car displaying the House emblem. Murphy rested against deep, cool cushions. "Your inspectors are pretty careful about weapons."

Ali-Tomás smiled complacently. "Our existence is ordered and peaceful. You may be familiar with the concept of *adak*?"

"I don't think so."

"A word, an idea from old Earth. Every living act is ordered by ritual. But our heritage is passionate — and when unyielding *adak* stands in the way of an irresistible emotion, there is turbulence, sometimes even killing."

"An *amok*."

"Exactly. It is as well that the *amok* has no weapons other than his knife. Otherwise he would kill twenty where now he kills one."

The car rolled along a narrow avenue, scattering pedestrians to either side like the bow of a boat spreading foam. The men wore loose white pantaloons and a short open vest; the women wore only the pantaloons.

"Handsome set of people," remarked Murphy.

Ali-Tomás again smiled complacently. "I'm sure Singhalût will present an inspiring and beautiful spectacle for your program."

Murphy remembered the keynote to Howard Frayberg's instructions: *"Excitement! Sex! Mystery!"* Frayberg cared little for inspiration or beauty. "I imagine," he said casually, "that you celebrate a number of interesting festivals? Colorful dancing? Unique customs?"

Ali-Tomás shook his head. "To the contrary. We left our superstitions and ancestor-worship back on Earth. We are quiet Mohammedans and indulge in very little festivity. Perhaps here is the reason for *amoks* and sjambaks."

"Sjambaks?"

"We are not proud of them. You will hear sly rumor, and it is better that I arm you beforehand with truth."

"What is a sjambak?"

"They are bandits, flouters of authority. I will show you one presently."

"I heard," said Murphy, "of a man riding a horse up to meet the spaceships. What would account for a story like that?"

"It can have no possible basis," said Prince Ali-Tomás. "We have no horses on Cirgamesç. None whatever."

"But..."

"The veriest idle talk. Such nonsense will have no interest for your intelligent participants."

The car rolled into a square a hundred yards on a side, lined with luxuriant banana palms. Opposite was an enormous pavilion of gold and violet silk, with a dozen peaked gables casting various changing sheens. In the center of the square a twenty-foot pole supported a cage about two feet wide, three feet long, and four feet high.

Inside this cage crouched a naked man.

The car rolled past. Prince Ali-Tomás waved an idle hand. The caged man glared down from bloodshot eyes. "That," said Ali-Tomás, "is a sjambak. As you see," a faint note of apology entered his voice, "we attempt to discourage them."

"What's that metal object on his chest?"

"The mark of his trade. By that you may know all sjambak. In these unsettled times only we of the House may cover our chests — all others must show themselves and declare themselves true Singhalûsi."

Murphy said tentatively, "I must come back here and photograph that cage."

Ali-Tomás smilingly shook his head. "I will show you our farms, our vines and orchards. Your participants will enjoy these; they have no interest in the dolor of an ignoble sjambak."

"Well," said Murphy, "our aim is a well-rounded production. We want to show the farmers at work, the members of the great House at their responsibilities, as well as the deserved fate of wrongdoers."

"Exactly. For every sjambak there are ten thousand industrious Singhalûsi. It follows then that only one ten-thousandth part of your film should be devoted to this infamous minority."

"About three-tenths of a second, eh?"

"No more than they deserve."

"You don't know my Production Director. His name is Howard Frayberg, and…"

Howard Frayberg was deep in conference with Sam Catlin, under the influence of what Catlin called his philosophic kick. It was the phase which Catlin feared most.

"Sam," said Frayberg, "do you know the danger of this business?"

"Ulcers," Catlin replied promptly.

Frayberg shook his head. "We've got an occupational disease to fight — progressive mental myopia."

"Speak for yourself," said Catlin.

"Consider. We sit in this office. We think we know what kind of show we want. We send out our staff to get it. We're signing the checks, so back it comes the way we asked for it. We look at it, hear it, smell it — and pretty soon we believe it: our version of the universe, full-blown from our brains like Minerva stepping out of Zeus. You see what I mean?"

"I understand the words."

"We've got our own picture of what's going on. We ask for it, we get it. It builds up and up — and finally we're like mice in a trap built of our own ideas. We cannibalize our own brains."

"Nobody'll ever accuse you of being stingy with a metaphor."

"Sam, let's have the truth. How many times have you been off Earth?"

"I went to Mars once. And I spent a couple of weeks at Aristillus Resort on the Moon."

Frayberg leaned back in his chair as if shocked. "And we're supposed to be a couple of learned planetologists!"

Catlin made grumbling noise in his throat. "I haven't been around the zodiac, so what? You sneezed a few minutes ago and I said *gesundheit*, but I don't have any doctor's degree."

"There comes a time in a man's life," said Frayberg, "when he wants to take stock, get a new perspective."

"Relax, Howard, relax."

"In our case it means taking out our preconceived ideas, looking at them, checking our illusions against reality."

"Are you serious about this?"

"Another thing," said Frayberg, "I want to check up a little. Shifkin says the expense accounts are frightful. But he can't fight it. When Keeler says he paid ten munits for a loaf of bread on Nekkar IV, who's gonna call him on it?"

"Hell, let him eat bread! That's cheaper than making a safari around the cluster, spot-checking the super-markets."

Frayberg paid no heed. He touched a button; a three-foot sphere full of glistening motes appeared. Earth was at the center, with thin red lines, the scheduled spaceship routes, radiating out in all directions.

"Let's see what kind of circle we can make," said Frayberg. "Gower's here at Canopus, Keeler's over here at Blue Moon, Wilbur Murphy's at Sirgamesk..."

"Don't forget," muttered Catlin, "we got a show to put on."

"We've got material for a year," scoffed Frayberg. "Get hold of Space-Lines. We'll start with Sirgamesk, and see what Wilbur Murphy's up to."

Wilbur Murphy was being presented to the Sultan of Singhalût by the Prince Ali-Tomás. The Sultan, a small mild man of seventy, sat cross-legged on an enormous pink and green air-cushion. "Be at your ease, Mr. Murphy. We dispense with as much protocol here as practicable." The Sultan had a dry clipped voice and the air of a rather harassed corporation executive. "I understand you represent Earth-Central Home Screen Network?"

"I'm a staff photographer for the *Know Your Universe!* show."

"We export a great deal to Earth," mused the Sultan, "but not as much as we'd like. We're very pleased with your interest in us, and naturally we want to help you in every way possible. Tomorrow the Keeper of the Archives will present a series of charts analyzing our economy. Ali-Tomás shall personally conduct you through the fish-hatcheries. We want you to know we're doing a great job out here in Singhalût."

"I'm sure you are," said Murphy uncomfortably. "However, that isn't quite the stuff I want."

"No? Just where do your desires lie?"

Ali-Tomás said delicately, "Mr. Murphy took a rather profound interest in the sjambak displayed in the square."

"Oh. And you explained that these renegades could hold no interest for serious students of our planet?"

Murphy started to explain that clustered around two hundred million screens tuned to *Know Your Universe!* were four or five hundred million participants, the greater part of them neither serious nor students. The Sultan cut in decisively. "I will now impart something truly interesting. We Singhalûsi are making preparations to reclaim four more valleys, with an added area of six hundred thousand acres! I shall put my physiographic models at your disposal; you may use them to the fullest extent!"

"I'll be pleased for the opportunity," declared Murphy. "But tomorrow I'd like to prowl around the valley, meet your people, observe their customs, religious rites, courtships, funerals..."

The Sultan pulled a sour face. "We are ditch-water dull. Festivals are celebrated quietly in the home; there is small religious fervor; courtships are consummated by family contract. I fear you will find little sensational material here in Singhalût."

"You have no temple dances?" asked Murphy. "No fire-walkers, snake-charmers — voodoo?"

The Sultan smiled patronizingly. "We came out here to Cirgamesç to escape the ancient superstitions. Our lives are calm, orderly. Even the *amoks* have practically disappeared."

"But the sjambaks —"

"Negligible."

"Well," said Murphy, "I'd like to visit some of these ancient cities."

"I advise against it," declared the Sultan. "They are shards, weathered stone. There are no inscriptions, no art. There is no stimulation in dead stone. Now. Tomorrow I will hear a report on hybrid soybean plantings in the Upper Kam District. You will want to be present."

Murphy's suite matched or even excelled his expectation. He had four rooms and a private garden enclosed by a thicket of bamboo. His bathroom walls were slabs of glossy actinolite, inlaid with cinnabar, jade, galena, pyrite and blue malachite, in representations of fantastic birds. His bedroom was a tent thirty feet high. Two walls were dark green fabric; a third was golden rust; the fourth opened upon the private garden.

Murphy's bed was a pink and yellow creation ten feet square, soft as cobweb, smelling of rose sandalwood. Carved black lacquer tubs held fruit; two dozen wines, liquors, syrups, essences flowed at a touch from as many ebony spigots.

The garden centered on a pool of cool water, very pleasant in the hothouse climate of Singhalût. The only shortcoming was the lack of the lovely young servitors Murphy had envisioned. He took it upon himself to repair this lack, and in a shady wine-house behind the palace, called the Barangipan, he made the acquaintance of a girl-musician named Soek Panjoebang. He found her enticing tones of quavering sweetness from the *gamelan*, an instrument well-loved in Old Bali. Soek Panjoebang had the delicate features and transparent skin of Sumatra, the supple long limbs of Arabia and in a pair of wide and golden eyes a heritage from somewhere in Celtic Europe. Murphy bought her a goblet of frozen shavings, each a different perfume, while he himself drank white rice-beer. Soek Panjoebang displayed an intense interest in the ways of Earth, and Murphy found it hard to guide the conversation. "Weelbrrr," she said. "Such a funny name, Weelbrrr. Do you think I could play the *gamelan* in the great cities, the great palaces of Earth?"

"Sure. There's no law against *gamelans*."

"You talk so funny, Weelbrrr. I like to hear you talk."

"I suppose you get kinda bored here in Singhalût?"

She shrugged. "Life is pleasant, but it concerns with little things. We have no great adventures. We grow flowers, we play the *gamelan*." She eyed him archly sidelong. "We love...We sleep..."

Murphy grinned. "You run *amok*."

"No, no, no. That is no more."

"Not since the sjambaks, eh?"

"The sjambaks are bad. But better than *amok*. When a man feels the knot forming around his chest, he no longer takes his kris and runs down the street — he becomes sjambak."

This was getting interesting. "Where does he go? What does he do?"

"He robs."

"Who does he rob? What does he do with his loot?"

She leaned toward him. "It is not well to talk of them."

"Why not?"

"The Sultan does not wish it. Everywhere are listeners. When one talks sjambak, the Sultan's ears rise, like the points on a cat."

"Suppose they do — what's the difference? I've got a legitimate interest. I saw one of them in that cage out there. That's torture. I want to know about it."

"He is very bad. He opened the monorail car and the air rushed out. Forty-two Singhalûsi and Hadrasi bloated and blew up."

"And what happened to the sjambak?"

"He took all the gold and money and jewels and ran away."

"Ran where?"

"Out across Great Pharasang Plain. But he was a fool. He came back to Singhalût for his wife; he was caught and set up for all people to look at, so they might tell each other, 'thus it is for sjambaks'."

"Where do the sjambaks hide out?"

"Oh," she looked vaguely around the room, "out on the plains. In the mountains."

"They must have some shelter — an air-dome."

"No. The Sultan would send out his patrol-boat and destroy them. They roam quietly. They hide among the rocks and tend their oxygen stills. Sometimes they visit the old cities."

"I wonder," said Murphy, staring into his beer, "could it be sjambaks who ride horses up to meet the spaceships?"

Soek Panjoebang knit her black eyebrows, as if preoccupied.

"That's what brought me out here," Murphy went on. "This story of a man riding a horse out in space."

"Ridiculous; we have no horses in Cirgamesç."

"All right, the steward won't swear to the horse. Suppose the man was up there on foot or riding a bicycle. But the steward recognized the man."

"Who was this man, pray?"

"The steward clammed up…The name would have been just noise to me, anyway."

"*I* might recognize the name…"

"Ask him yourself. The ship's still out at the field."

She shook her head slowly, holding her golden eyes on his face. "I do not care to attract the attention of either steward, sjambak — or Sultan."

Murphy said impatiently. "In any event, it's not who — but *how*. How does the man breathe? Vacuum sucks a man's lungs up out of his mouth, bursts his stomach, his ears…"

"We have excellent doctors," said Soek Panjoebang shuddering, "but alas! I am not one of them."

Murphy looked at her sharply. Her voice held the plangent sweetness of her instrument, with additional overtones of mockery. "There must be some kind of invisible dome around him, holding in air," said Murphy.

"And what if there is?"

"It's something new, and if it is, I want to find out about it."

Soek smiled languidly. "You are so typical an old-lander — worried, frowning, dynamic. You should relax, cultivate *napaû*, enjoy life as we do here in Singhalût."

"What's *napaû*?"

"It's our philosophy, where we find meaning and life and beauty in every aspect of the world."

"That sjambak in the cage could do with a little less *napaû* right now."

"No doubt he is unhappy," she agreed.

"Unhappy! He's being tortured!"

"He broke the Sultan's law. His life is no longer his own. It belongs to Singhalût. If the Sultan wishes to use it to warn other wrong-doers, the fact that the man suffers is of small interest."

"If they all wear that metal ornament, how can they hope to hide out?" He glanced at her own bare bosom.

"They appear by night — slip through the streets like ghosts..." She looked in turn at Murphy's loose shirt. "You will notice persons brushing up against you, feeling you," she laid her hand along his breast, "and when this happens you will know they are agents of the Sultan, because only strangers and the House may wear shirts. But now, let me sing to you — a song from the Old Land, old Java. You will not understand the tongue, but no other words so join the voice of the *gamelan*."

"This is the gravy-train," said Murphy. "Instead of a garden suite with a private pool, I usually sleep in a bubble-tent, with nothing to eat but condensed food."

Soek Panjoebang flung the water out of her sleek black hair. "Perhaps, Weelbrrr, you will regret leaving Cirgamesç?"

"Well," he looked up to the transparent roof, barely visible where the sunlight collected and refracted, "I don't particularly like being shut up like a bird in an aviary... Mildly claustrophobic, I guess."

After breakfast, drinking thick coffee from tiny silver cups, Murphy looked long and reflectively at Soek Panjoebang.

"What are you thinking, Weelbrrr?"

Murphy drained his coffee. "I'm thinking that I'd better be getting to work."

"And what do you do?"

"First I'm going to shoot the palace, and you sitting here in the garden playing your *gamelan*."

"But Weelbrrr — not *me!*"

"You're a part of the universe, rather an interesting part. Then I'll take the square…"

"And the sjambak?"

A quiet voice spoke from behind. "A visitor, Tuan Murphy."

Murphy turned his head. "Bring him in." He looked back to Soek Panjoebang. She was on her feet.

"It is necessary that I go."

"When will I see you?"

"Tonight — at the Barangipan."

The quiet voice said, "Mr. Rube Trimmer, Tuan."

Trimmer was small and middle-aged, with thin shoulders and a paunch. He carried himself with a hell-raising swagger, left over from a time twenty years gone. His skin had the waxy look of lost floridity, his tuft of white hair was coarse and thin, his eyelids hung in the off-side droop that amateur physiognomists like to associate with guile.

"I'm Resident Director of the Import-Export Bank," said Trimmer. "Heard you were here and thought I'd pay my respects."

"I suppose you don't see many strangers."

"Not too many — there's nothing much to bring 'em. Cirgamesç isn't a comfortable tourist planet. Too confined, shut in. A man with a sensitive psyche goes nuts pretty easy here."

"Yeah," said Murphy. "I was thinking the same thing this morning. That dome begins to give a man the willies. How do the natives stand it? Or do they?"

Trimmer pulled out a cigar case. Murphy refused the offer.

"Local tobacco," said Trimmer. "Very good." He lit up thoughtfully. "Well, you might say that the Cirgameski are schizophrenic. They've got the docile Javanese blood, plus the Arabian élan. The Javanese part is on top, but every once in a while you see a flash of arrogance…You never know. I've been out here nine years and I'm still a stranger." He puffed on his cigar, studied Murphy with his careful eyes. "You work for *Know Your Universe!*, I hear."

"Yeah. I'm one of the leg men."

"Must be a great job."

"A man sees a lot of the galaxy, and he runs into queer tales, like this sjambak stuff."

Trimmer nodded without surprise. "My advice to you, Murphy, is lay off the sjambaks. They're not healthy around here."

Murphy was startled by the bluntness. "What's the big mystery about these sjambaks?"

Trimmer looked around the room. "This place is bugged."

"I found two pick-ups and plugged 'em," said Murphy.

Trimmer laughed. "Those were just plants. They hide 'em where a man might just barely spot 'em. You can't catch the real ones. They're woven into the cloth — pressure-sensitive wires."

Murphy looked critically at the cloth walls.

"Don't let it worry you," said Trimmer. "They listen more out of habit than anything else. If you're fussy we'll go for a walk."

The road led past the palace into the country. Murphy and Trimmer sauntered along a placid river, overgrown with lily pads, swarming with large white ducks.

"This sjambak business," said Murphy. "Everybody talks around it. You can't pin anybody down."

"Including me," said Trimmer. "I'm more or less privileged around here. The Sultan finances his reclamation through the bank, on the basis of my reports. But there's more to Singhalût than the Sultan."

"Namely?"

Trimmer waved his cigar waggishly. "Now we're getting in where I don't like to talk. I'll give you a hint. Prince Ali thinks roofing-in more valleys is a waste of money, when there's Hadra and New Batavia and Sundaman so close."

"You mean — armed conquest?"

Trimmer laughed. "You said it, not me."

"They can't carry on much of a war — unless the soldiers commute by monorail."

"Maybe Prince Ali thinks he's got the answer."

"Sjambaks?"

"I didn't say it," said Trimmer blandly.

Murphy grinned. After a moment he said, "I picked up with a girl named Soek Panjoebang who plays the *gamelan*. I suppose she's working for either the Sultan or Prince Ali. Do you know which?"

Trimmer's eyes sparkled. He shook his head. "Might be either one. There's a way to find out."

"Yeah?"

"Get her off where you're sure there's no spy-cells. Tell her two things — one for Ali, the other for the Sultan. Whichever one reacts you know you've got her tagged."

"For instance?"

"Well, for instance she learns that you can rig up a hypnotic ray from a flashlight battery, a piece of bamboo, and a few lengths of wire. That'll get Ali in an awful sweat. He can't get weapons. None at all. And for the Sultan," Trimmer was warming up to his intrigue, chewing on his cigar with gusto, "tell her you're on to a catalyst that turns clay into aluminum and oxygen in the presence of sunlight. The Sultan would sell his right leg for something like that. He tries hard for Singhalût and Cirgamesç."

"And Ali?"

Trimmer hesitated. "I never said what I'm gonna say. Don't forget — I never said it."

"Okay, you never said it."

"Ever hear of a *jehad*?"

"Mohammedan holy wars."

"Believe it or not, Ali wants a *jehad*."

"Sounds kinda fantastic."

"Sure it's fantastic. Don't forget, I never said anything about it. But suppose someone — strictly unofficial, of course — let the idea percolate around the Peace Office back home."

"Ah," said Murphy. "That's why you came to see me."

Trimmer turned a look of injured innocence. "Now, Murphy, you're a little unfair. I'm a friendly guy. Of course I don't like to see the bank lose what we've got tied up in the Sultan."

"Why don't you send in a report yourself?"

"I have! But when they hear the same thing from you, a *Know Your Universe!* man, they might make a move."

Murphy nodded.

"Well, we understand each other," said Trimmer heartily, "and everything's clear."

"Not entirely. How's Ali going to launch a *jehad* when he doesn't have any weapons, no warships, no supplies?"

"Now," said Trimmer, "we're getting into the realm of supposition." He paused, looked behind him. A farmer pushing a rotary tiller bowed politely, trundled ahead. Behind was a young man in a black turban, gold earrings, a black and red vest, white pantaloons, black curl-toed slippers. He bowed, started past. Trimmer held up his hand. "Don't waste your time up there; we're going back in a few minutes."

"Thank you, Tuan."

"Who are you reporting to? The Sultan or Prince Ali?"

"The Tuan is sure to pierce the veil of my evasions. I shall not dissemble. I am the Sultan's man."

Trimmer nodded. "Now, if you'll kindly remove to about a hundred yards, where your whisper pick-up won't work."

"By your leave, I go." He retreated without haste.

"He's almost certainly working for Ali," said Trimmer.

"Not a very subtle lie."

"Oh yes — third level. He figured I'd take it second level."

"How's that again?"

"Naturally I wouldn't believe him. He knew I knew that he knew it. So when he said 'Sultan', I'd think he wouldn't lie simply, but that he'd lie double — that he actually was working for the Sultan."

Murphy laughed. "Suppose he told you a fourth level lie?"

"It starts to be a toss-up pretty soon," Trimmer admitted. "I don't think he gives me credit for that much subtlety... What are you doing the rest of the day?"

"Taking footage. Do you know where I can find some picturesque rites? Mystical dances, human sacrifice? I've got to work up some glamor and exotic lore."

"There's this sjambak in the cage. That's about as close to the medieval as you'll find anywhere in Earth Commonwealth."

"Speaking of sjambaks..."

"No time," said Trimmer. "Got to get back. Drop in at my office — right down the square from the palace."

Murphy returned to his suite. The shadowy figure of his room servant said, "His Highness the Sultan desires the Tuan's attendance in the Cascade Garden."

"Thank you," said Murphy. "As soon as I load my camera."

The Cascade Room was an open patio in front of an artificial water-fall. The Sultan was pacing back and forth, wearing dusty khaki puttees, brown plastic boots, a yellow polo shirt. He carried a twig which he used as a riding crop, slapping his boots as he walked. He turned his head as Murphy appeared, pointed his twig at a wicker bench.

"I pray you sit down, Mr. Murphy." He paced once up and back. "How is your suite? You find it to your liking?"

"Very much so."

"Excellent," said the Sultan. "You do me honor with your presence."

Murphy waited patiently.

"I understand that you had a visitor this morning," said the Sultan.

"Yes. Mr. Trimmer."

"May I inquire the nature of the conversation?"

"It was of a personal nature," said Murphy, rather more shortly than he meant.

The Sultan nodded wistfully. "A Singhalûsi would have wasted an hour telling me half-truths — distorted enough to confuse, but not suf-ficiently inaccurate to anger me if I had a spy-cell on him all the time."

Murphy grinned. "A Singhalûsi has to live here the rest of his life."

A servant wheeled a frosted cabinet before them, placed goblets under two spigots, withdrew. The Sultan cleared his throat. "Trimmer is an excellent fellow, but unbelievably loquacious."

Murphy drew himself two inches of chilled rosy-pale liquor. The Sultan slapped his boots with the twig. "Undoubtedly he confided all my private business to you, or at least as much as I have allowed him to learn."

"Well — he spoke of your hope to increase the compass of Singhalût."

"That, my friend, is no hope; it's absolute necessity. Our popula-tion density is fifteen hundred to the square mile. We must expand or smother. There'll be too little food to eat, too little oxygen to breathe."

Murphy suddenly came to life. "I could make that idea the theme of my feature! Singhalût Dilemma: Expand or Perish!"

"No, that would be inadvisable, inapplicable."

Murphy was not convinced. "It sounds like a natural."

The Sultan smiled. "I'll impart an item of confidential information — although Trimmer no doubt has preceded me with it." He gave his boots an irritated whack. "To expand I need funds. Funds are best secured in an atmosphere of calm and confidence. The implication of emergency would be disastrous to my aims."

"Well," said Murphy, "I see your position."

The Sultan glanced at Murphy sidelong. "Anticipating your cooperation, my Minister of Propaganda has arranged an hour's program, stressing our progressive social attitude, our prosperity and financial prospects..."

"But, Sultan..."

"Well?"

"I can't allow your Minister of Propaganda to use me and *Know Your Universe!* as a kind of investment brochure."

The Sultan nodded wearily. "I expected you to take that attitude... Well — what do you yourself have in mind?"

"I've been looking for something to tie to," said Murphy. "I think it's going to be the dramatic contrast between the ruined cities and the new domed valleys. How the Earth settlers succeeded where the ancient people failed to meet the challenge of the dissipating atmosphere."

"Well," the Sultan said grudgingly, "that's not too bad."

"Today I want to take some shots of the palace, the dome, the city, the paddies, groves, orchards, farms. Tomorrow I'm taking a trip out to one of the ruins."

"I see," said the Sultan. "Then you won't need my charts and statistics?"

"Well, Sultan, I could film the stuff your Propaganda Minister cooked up, and I could take it back to Earth. Howard Frayberg or Sam Catlin would tear into it, rip it apart, lard in some head-hunting, a little cannibalism and temple prostitution, and you'd never know you were watching Singhalût. You'd scream with horror, and I'd be fired."

"In that case," said the Sultan, "I will leave you to the dictates of your conscience."

Howard Frayberg looked around the gray landscape of Riker's Planet, gazed out over the roaring black Mogador Ocean. "Sam, I think there's a story out there."

Sam Catlin shivered inside his electrically heated glass overcoat. "Out on that ocean? It's full of man-eating plesiosaurs — horrible things forty feet long."

"Suppose we worked something out on the line of Moby Dick? *The White Monster of the Mogador Ocean.* We'd set sail in a catamaran —"

"Us?"

"No," said Frayberg impatiently. "Of course not us. Two or three of the staff. They'd sail out there, look over these gray and red monsters, maybe fake a fight or two, but all the time they're after the legendary white one. How's it sound?"

"I don't think we pay our men enough money."

"Wilbur Murphy might do it. He's willing to look for a man riding a horse up to meet his spaceships."

"He might draw the line at a white plesiosaur riding up to meet his catamaran."

Frayberg turned away. "Somebody's got to have ideas around here…"

"We'd better head back to the space-port," said Catlin. "We got two hours to make the Sirgamesk shuttle."

Wilbur Murphy sat in the Barangipan, watching marionettes performing to xylophone, castanet, gong and *gamelan*. The drama had its roots in proto-historic Mohenjō-Darō. It had filtered down through ancient India, medieval Burma, Malaya, across the Straits of Malacca to Sumatra and Java; from modern Java across space to Cirgamesç, five thousand years of time, two hundred light-years of space. Somewhere along the route it had met and assimilated modern technology. Magnetic beams controlled arms, legs and bodies, guided the poses and posturings. The manipulator's face, by agency of clip, wire, radio control and minuscule selsyn, projected his scowl, smile, sneer or grimace to the peaked little face he controlled. The language was that of Old Java, which perhaps a third of the spectators understood. This portion did not include Murphy, and when the performance ended he was no wiser than at the start.

Soek Panjoebang slipped into the seat beside Murphy. She wore musician's garb: a sarong of brown, blue, and black *batik*, and a fantastic headdress of tiny silver bells. She greeted him with enthusiasm.

"Weelbrrr! I saw you watching..."

"It was very interesting."

"Ah, yes." She sighed. "Weelbrrr, you take me with you back to Earth? You make me a great picturama star, please, Weelbrrr?"

"Well, I don't know about that."

"I behave very well, Weelbrrr." She nuzzled his shoulder, looked soulfully up with her shiny yellow-hazel eyes. Murphy nearly forgot the experiment he intended to perform.

"What did you do today, Weelbrrr? You look at all the pretty girls?"

"Nope. I ran footage. Got the palace, climbed the ridge up to the condensation vanes. I never knew there was so much water in the air till I saw the stream pouring off those vanes! And *hot!*"

"We have much sunlight; it makes the rice grow."

"The Sultan ought to put some of that excess light to work. There's a secret process...Well, I'd better not say."

"Oh come, Weelbrrr! Tell me your secrets!"

"It's not much of a secret. Just a catalyst that separates clay into aluminum and oxygen when sunlight shines on it."

Soek's eyebrows rose, poised in place like a seagull riding the wind. "Weelbrrr! I did not know you for a man of learning!"

"Oh, you thought I was just a bum, eh? Good enough to make picturama stars out of *gamelan* players, but no special genius..."

"No, no, Weelbrrr."

"I know lots of tricks. I can take a flashlight battery, a piece of copper foil, a few transistors and bamboo tube and turn out a paralyzer gun that'll stop a man cold in his tracks. And you know how much it costs?"

"No, Weelbrrr. How much?"

"Ten cents. It wears out after two or three months, but what's the difference? I make 'em as a hobby — turn out two or three an hour."

"Weelbrrr! You're a man of marvels! Hello! We will drink!"

And Murphy settled back in the wicker chair, sipping his rice beer.

"Today," said Murphy, "I get into a space-suit, and ride out to the ruins in the plain. Ghatamipol, I think they're called. Like to come?"

"No, Weelbrrr." Soek Panjoebang looked off into the garden, her hands busy tucking a flower into her hair. A few minutes later she said, "Why must you waste your time among the rocks? There are better things to do and see. And it might well be — dangerous." She murmured the last word offhandedly.

"Danger? From the sjambaks?"

"Yes, perhaps."

"The Sultan's giving me a guard. Twenty men with crossbows."

"The sjambaks carry shields."

"Why should they risk their lives attacking me?"

Soek Panjoebang shrugged. After a moment she rose to her feet. "Goodbye, Weelbrrr."

"Goodbye? Isn't this rather abrupt? Won't I see you tonight?"

"If so be Allah's will."

Murphy looked after the lithe swaying figure. She paused, plucked a yellow flower, looked over her shoulder. Her eyes, yellow as the flower, lucent as water-jewels, held his. Her face was utterly expressionless. She turned, tossed away the flower with a jaunty gesture, and continued, her shoulders swinging.

Murphy breathed deeply. She might have made picturama at that...

One hour later he met his escort at the valley gate. They were dressed in space-suits for the plains, twenty men with sullen faces. The trip to Ghatamipol clearly was not to their liking. Murphy climbed into his own suit, checked the oxygen pressure gauge, the seal at his collar. "All ready, boys?"

No one spoke. The silence drew out. The gatekeeper, on hand to let the party out, snickered. "They're all ready, Tuan."

"Well," said Murphy, "let's go then."

Outside the gate Murphy made a second check of his equipment. No leaks in his suit. Inside pressure: 14.6. Outside pressure: zero. His twenty guards morosely inspected their crossbows and slim swords.

The white ruins of Ghatamipol lay five miles across Pharasang Plain. The horizon was clear, the sun was high, the sky was black.

Murphy's radio hummed. Someone said sharply, "Look! There it goes!" He wheeled around; his guards had halted, and were pointing. He saw a fleet something vanishing into the distance.

"Let's go," said Murphy. "There's nothing out there."

"Sjambak."

"Well, there's only one of them."

"Where one walks, others follow."

"That's why the twenty of you are here."

"It is madness! Challenging the sjambaks!"

"What is gained?" another argued.

"I'll be the judge of that," said Murphy, and set off along the plain. The warriors reluctantly followed, muttering to each other over their radio intercoms.

The eroded city walls rose above them, occupied more and more of the sky. The platoon leader said in an angry voice, "We have gone far enough."

"You're under my orders," said Murphy. "We're going through the gate." He punched the button on his camera and passed under the monstrous portal.

The city was frailer stuff than the wall, and had succumbed to the thin storms which had raged a million years after the passing of life. Murphy marvelled at the scope of the ruins. Virgin archaeological territory! No telling what a few weeks digging might turn up. Murphy considered his expense account. Shifkin was the obstacle.

There'd be tremendous prestige and publicity for *Know Your Universe!* if Murphy uncovered a tomb, a library, works of art. The Sultan would gladly provide diggers. They were a sturdy enough people; they could make quite a showing in a week, if they were able to put aside their superstitions, fears and dreads.

Murphy sized one of them up from the corner of his eye. He sat on a sunny slab of rock, and if he felt uneasy he concealed it quite successfully. In fact, thought Murphy, he appeared completely relaxed. Maybe the problem of securing diggers was a minor one after all...

And here was an odd sidelight on the Singhalûsi character. Once clear of the valley the man openly wore his shirt, a fine loose garment of electric blue, in defiance of the Sultan's edict. Of course out here he might be cold...

Murphy felt his own skin crawling. How could he be cold? How could he be alive? Where was his space-suit? He lounged on the rock, grinning sardonically at Murphy. He wore heavy sandals, a black turban, loose breeches, the blue shirt. Nothing more.

Where were the others?

Murphy turned a feverish glance over his shoulder. A good three miles distant, bounding and leaping toward Singhalût, were twenty desperate figures. They all wore space-suits. This man here... A sjambak? A wizard? A hallucination?

The creature rose to his feet, strode springily toward Murphy. He carried a crossbow and a sword, like those of Murphy's fleet-footed guards. But he wore no space-suit. Could there be breathable traces of an atmosphere? Murphy glanced at his gauge. Outside pressure: zero.

Two other men appeared, moving with long elastic steps. Their eyes were bright, their faces flushed. They came up to Murphy, took his arm. They were solid, corporeal. They had no invisible force fields around their heads.

Murphy jerked his arm free. "Let go of me, damn it!" But they certainly couldn't hear him through the vacuum.

He glanced over his shoulder. The first man held his naked blade a foot or two behind Murphy's bulging space-suit. Murphy made no further resistance. He punched the button on his camera to automatic. It would now run for several hours, recording one hundred pictures per second, a thousand to the inch.

The sjambaks led Murphy two hundred yards to a metal door. They opened it, pushed Murphy inside, banged it shut. Murphy felt the vibration through his shoes, heard a gradually waxing hum. His gauge showed an outside pressure of 5, 10, 12, 14, 14.5. An inner door opened. Hands pulled Murphy in, unclamped his dome.

"Just what's going on here?" demanded Murphy angrily.

Prince Ali-Tomás pointed to a table. Murphy saw a flashlight battery, aluminum foil, wire, a transistor kit, metal tubing, tools, a few other odds and ends.

"There it is," said Prince Ali-Tomás. "Get to work. Let's see one of these paralysis weapons you boast of."

"Just like that, eh?"

"Just like that."

"What do you want 'em for?"

"Does it matter?"

"I'd like to know." Murphy was conscious of his camera, recording sight, sound, odor.

"I lead an army," said Ali-Tomás, "but they march without weapons. Give me weapons! I will carry the word to Hadra, to New Batavia, to Sundaman, to Boeng-Bohôt!"

"How? Why?"

"It is enough that I will it. Again, I beg of you…" He indicated the table.

Murphy laughed. "I've got myself in a fine mess. Suppose I don't make this weapon for you?"

"You'll remain until you do, under increasingly difficult conditions."

"I'll be here a long time."

"If such is the case," said Ali-Tomás, "we must make our arrangements for your care on a long-term basis."

Ali made a gesture. Hands seized Murphy's shoulders. A respirator was held to his nostrils. He thought of his camera, and he could have laughed. Mystery! Excitement! Thrills! Dramatic sequence for *Know Your Universe!* Staff-man murdered by fanatics! The crime recorded on his own camera! See the blood, hear his death-rattle, smell the poison!

The vapor choked him. *What a break! What a sequence!*

"Sirgamesk," said Howard Frayberg, "bigger and brighter every minute."

"It must've been just about in here," said Catlin, "that Wilbur's horseback rider appeared."

"That's right! Steward!"

"Yes, sir?"

"We're about twenty thousand miles out, aren't we?"

"About fifteen thousand, sir."

"Sidereal Cavalry! What an idea! I wonder how Wilbur's making out on his superstition angle?"

Sam Catlin, watching out the window, said in a tight voice, "Why not ask him yourself?"

"Eh?"

"Ask him for yourself! There he is — outside, riding some kind of critter…"

"It's a ghost," whispered Frayberg. "A man without a spacesuit… There's no such thing!"

"He sees us… Look…"

Murphy was staring at them, and his surprise seemed equal to their own. He waved his hand. Catlin gingerly waved back.

Said Frayberg, "That's not a horse he's riding. It's a combination ram-jet and kiddie car with stirrups!"

"He's coming aboard the ship," said Catlin. "That's the entrance port down there…"

Wilbur Murphy sat in the captain's stateroom, taking careful breaths of air.

"How are you now?" asked Frayberg.

"Fine. A little sore in the lungs."

"I shouldn't wonder," the ship's doctor growled. "I never saw anything like it."

"How does it feel out there, Wilbur?" Catlin asked.

"It feels awful lonesome and empty. And the breath seeping up out of your lungs, never going in — that's a funny feeling. And you miss the air blowing on your skin. I never realized it before. Air feels like — like silk, like whipped cream — it's got texture…"

"But aren't you cold? Space is supposed to be absolute zero!"

"Space is nothing. It's not hot and it's not cold. When you're in the sunlight you get warm. It's better in the shade. You don't lose any heat by air convection, but radiation and sweat evaporation keep you comfortably cool."

"I still can't understand it," said Frayberg. "This Prince Ali, he's a kind of a rebel, eh?"

"I don't blame him in a way. A normal man living under those domes has to let off steam somehow. Prince Ali decided to go out crusading. I think he would have made it too — at least on Cirgamesç."

"Certainly there are many more men inside the domes..."

"When it comes to fighting," said Murphy, "a sjambak can lick twenty men in spacesuits. A little nick doesn't hurt him, but a little nick bursts open a spacesuit, and the man inside comes apart."

"Well," said the Captain. "I imagine the Peace Office will send out a team to put things in order now."

Catlin asked, "What happened when you woke up from the chloroform?"

"Well, nothing very much. I felt this attachment on my chest, but didn't think much about it. Still kinda woozy. I was halfway through decompression. They keep a man there eight hours, drop pressure on him two pounds an hour, nice and slow so he don't get the bends."

"Was this the same place they took you, when you met Ali?"

"Yeah, that was their decompression chamber. They had to make a sjambak out of me; there wasn't anywhere else they could keep me. Well, pretty soon my head cleared, and I saw this apparatus stuck to my chest." He poked at the mechanism on the table. "I saw the oxygen tank, I saw the blood running through the plastic pipes — blue from me to that carburetor arrangement, red on the way back in — and I figured out the whole arrangement. Carbon dioxide still exhales up through your lungs, but the vein back to the left auricle is routed through the carburetor and supercharged with oxygen. A man doesn't need to breathe. The carburetor flushes his blood with oxygen, the decompression tank adjusts him to the lack of air-pressure. There's only one thing to look out for; that's not to touch anything with your naked flesh. If it's in the sunshine it's blazing hot; if it's in the shade it's cold enough to cut. Otherwise you're free as a bird."

"But — how did you get away?"

"I saw those little rocket-bikes, and began figuring. I couldn't go back to Singhalût; I'd be lynched on sight as a sjambak. I couldn't fly to another planet — the bikes don't carry enough fuel.

"I knew when the ship would be coming in, so I figured I'd fly up to meet it. I told the guard I was going outside a minute, and I got on one of the rocket-bikes. There was nothing much to it."

"Well," said Frayberg, "it's a great feature, Wilbur — a great film! Maybe we can stretch it into two hours."

"There's one thing bothering me," said Catlin. "Who did the steward see up here the first time?"

Murphy shrugged. "It might have been somebody up here skylarking. A little too much oxygen and you start cutting all kinds of capers. Or it might have been someone who decided he had enough crusading.

"There's a sjambak in a cage, right in the middle of Singhalût. Prince Ali walks past; they look at each other eye to eye. Ali smiles a little and walks on. Suppose this sjambak tried to escape to the ship. He's taken aboard, turned over to the Sultan and the Sultan makes an example of him..."

"What'll the Sultan do to Ali?"

Murphy shook his head. "If I were Ali I'd disappear."

A loudspeaker turned on. "Attention all passengers. We have just passed through quarantine. Passengers may now disembark. Important: no weapons or explosives allowed on Singhalût!"

"This is where I came in," said Murphy.

PARAPSYCHE

I

JEAN MARSILE, FIFTEEN YEARS OLD, blonde and pretty, jumped at the chair where her father sat. "Boo!"

Art Marsile turned his head with provoking calmness. "I thought you were going out on a date."

Jean tugged at her blue jeans, smoothed the seams of her pale blue sweater. "I am."

"Where are you going?"

"Out on a weenie-roast. We're going to the haunted house, because it's Hallowe'en."

From across the room came a snort of derision and contempt. Jean ignored the sound.

Art Marsile, tall, tough as harness-leather, parched and coffee-brown from years of Southern California sunlight, looked Jean up and down with unconvincing sternness. "What haunted house is this?" he asked curiously while Jean finished getting ready.

"The old Freelock house."

"So now it's haunted."

"That's what everybody says. Ever since Benjamin Freelock killed his wife."

"What everybody *says*, eh? Has anyone seen anything?"

Jean nodded. "Lots of people. The Mexicans who live down the hill. They say there's lights and noises."

From across the room came a mocking bray of laughter. "Stupid bunch of wetbacks."

Art Marsile turned a brief glance toward his son Hugh, the child of his first wife, then looked back to Jean. "You're not scared?"

Jean calmly shook her head. "I don't believe any of it."

"I see." Art Marsile nodded thoughtfully. "Who's going with you?"

"Don Berwick. And —" Jean named others of the party.

Hugh spoke from across the room, his voice rich with disgust. "They call it a weenie-roast. All they do is go up there and neck."

Jean performed an impudent dance-step. "We've got to neck somewhere."

Art Marsile grunted. "Just don't get in a jam."

"Father!"

"You're human, aren't you?"

"Yes, but I'm — well..."

Hugh said, "They go out in the country and drink beer."

"I don't either!"

"The guys do."

"I know they do," growled Art Marsile. "And you know how I know? Because I used to do the same thing. And I'd do it again if I could get some pretty young girl to go with me."

"Father!" cried Jean. "You're *bad*!"

"Probably no worse than Don Berwick. So you be careful."

"Yes, Father!"

The door-bell rang; Don Berwick, a stocky square-shouldered lad of seventeen, entered, spent a few minutes in civil small-talk with Art Marsile and Hugh; then he and Jean went to the door. Art followed them out on the porch. "Look here, Don. I don't want no boozing. Not when you're driving a car with Jean inside. Understand?"

"Yes sir."

"Okay. Have yourself a good time." He went back inside the house. Hugh was standing near the door, at eighteen already taller than his father. He was big-jointed and thin, with hands the size of steaks, his long bony face sour and mulish. "I don't see why you let her get away with it."

"She's only young once," said Art Marsile evenly. "Let her have her fun...You should be out yourself, instead of staying home complaining about other people."

"I'm not complaining. I'm saying what ought to be."

"What 'ought' she be doing?" asked Art in a dry voice.

"There's schoolwork."

"She can't do much better than straight A's, Hugh."

"There's the revival meeting tonight."

"That's where you're going?"

"Yes. It's Walter Mott preaching. He's a great inspirational leader."

Art Marsile turned back to his magazine. "Walter Mott the Devil-Buster."

"That's what they call him."

"If you get a kick out of hell-fire and damnation," said Art Marsile, "that's your business. I wouldn't go, I wouldn't make Jean go."

"If I had anything to say, she'd go, and like it. It would do her good."

Art Marsile looked at Hugh in a wonder which had grown rather than lessened over the years. "It would do you good to drink some beer and kiss a few girls yourself. But I wouldn't make you do it. I'm damned if I'll make anybody do anything for their own good."

Hugh left the room, presently reappeared wearing limp gray slacks and a black sweater with the block letter he had won at basketball. "I'm going," he said.

Art Marsile nodded, Hugh departed. Art read his magazine, switched on television, watched a late movie, his mind more on his children than the superannuated flickerings. Hugh might or might not be his own flesh and blood; Jean was the child of his second wife. His first wife had decamped with a hillbilly musician shortly after Hugh's birth. Hugh resembled the musician more than Art. Art knew nothing for certain, but tried to give Hugh the benefit of the doubt. The second wife had died in an automobile collision, returning from the New Year's Day Rose Parade in Pasadena. If Art felt grief, no one knew it. He worked his orange grove with all-consuming intensity; he prospered; he bought new land, he made money which he showed no disposition to spend. Jean and Hugh grew into adolescence, treated with as much fairness as Art was capable of. Since Art could not bring himself to show affection to Hugh, he tried to conceal his love for Jean. But Jean would not be fooled. She hugged and kissed Art, rumpled his hair, and had no secrets from him.

Hugh lived in a different world. Hugh played basketball with tremendous zeal, joined all the school's organizations, became an officer in most of them. He bought a manual of parliamentary procedure, studied it with much more thoroughness than his mathematics texts. At sixteen Hugh had gone to an open-air evangelist rally, and from this time forward, whatever faint linkage existed between his mind and Art Marsile's disappeared.

Hugh worked summers in the orange grove. Art Marsile paid him scale for whatever work he did, and got his money's worth: Hugh was a hard and tireless worker. With his wages he bought a car, and then a portable loud-speaker: a megaphone-shaped instrument, powered by a battery. "What on Earth do you want that thing for?" asked Art. Hugh looked at the device as if he were seeing it for the first time. He made a list of the uses to which the instrument could be put: messages across the orange grove, emergencies and rescues, announcements at basketball games, talking to people in general. Art made the request that the implement should not be employed to address him, nor used at the dinner table to say grace — an innovation which Hugh recently had introduced into the household, and which Art tolerated with non-committal patience. Jean was less complacent and teased Hugh unmercifully, until Art quieted her. "If he feels he wants to say grace, it's his business."

"Why can't he say it to himself then? God doesn't need to be thanked every time we eat a meal."

"That's irreverent," Hugh remarked.

"It's not either. It's sense. If God hadn't arranged that we become hungry, we wouldn't have to eat. Why should we give thanks for doing something we have to do to stay alive? You don't say grace every time you breathe."

Art let them wrangle: why stop a good argument? It's something everybody's got to work out for himself, he thought. The argument had continued sporadically, Hugh's growing religiosity colliding with Jean's skepticism. Art kept his views to himself, intervening only when the argument became name-calling. And tonight, Hallowe'en, Hugh was off to a revival meeting and Jean to a weenie-roast at a haunted house.

Art expected Jean home around midnight, but at eleven she burst in the door, eyes glowing in excitement. "Father! We saw the ghost!"

Art rose to his feet, turned off the television.

"You think I'm fooling! We saw it! We really did! As close as from here to you!"

Don Berwick came in. "It's true, Mr. Marsile!"

"You kids been drinking?" Art inquired suspiciously.

"No, sir!" said Don. "I promised you I wouldn't."

"Well, what happened?"

Jean reported. They had driven up Indian Hill to the Freelock house, a desolate weather-beaten hulk, shrouded among cypress and ragged cedar, the doors hanging on their hinges, the windows broken. The original plan had been to build a fire in the fireplace, but the inside of the house was so dirty and unpleasant that the girls objected. The fire was built in the backyard, on a patch of gravel still bare of weeds. The supplies were unloaded, the girls spread blankets; the normal processes of a weenie-roast got under way.

Jean reminded Art of the Freelock murder: beyond question, a horrible affair. Benjamin Freelock, a crabbed old man of sixty, suspected his young wife, twenty-eight years old, of carrying on with his nephew. He gagged her, hung her by her wrists from a beam in the living room, presently brought in the corpse of the nephew, which he hung by the wrists six feet in front of her. He stripped both bodies, the living and the dead, of their clothes, then went about his normal business as a real-estate agent. Two days later he revived the barely-conscious wife, inquired if she were ready to confess. She was unable to speak coherently. He poured kerosene over her, set her afire, and departed the house.

The house smoldered and smoked but failed to catch fire. A Mexican living in a shack a hundred yards down the road called the fire department. Freelock, apprehended, made a sober and detailed confession and later died at a home for the criminally insane.

The affair had occurred five years previously. The house was abandoned and — perhaps inevitably — there was talk of haunting. Jean explicitly corroborated these reports. The group had been jocular, skylarking, inviting ghosts to the feast: all ostensibly casual and careless, but all inwardly thrilling to the spooky look of the house, and the memory of the macabre killing. Jean had noticed a flickering of red light at the window of the living room. She had assumed it to be a reflection of the fire, then had looked again. There was no glass in the window. Others noticed; there were squeals and squeaks from the girls. All rose to their feet. Inside the living room, clearly visible, hung a body, twisting and writhing, clothed in flames. And from within came a series of agonized throat-wrenching sobs.

At this point Art snorted. "Somebody was playing a trick."

"No, no!" Jean and Don both protested.

"We're not that dumb," said Jean indignantly. "Betty Hall and Peggy were hysterical — I admit that — and Johnny Palgrave wasn't any better. The rest of us were perfectly sensible!"

Don laughed shortly; Jean turned an indignant look on him. "We were excited," she explained. "Of course! Who wouldn't be? But it didn't interfere with our eyesight. Not mine! Anyway, that's not all. Don went inside."

"What?" Art was truly surprised. "You went inside? What for?"

"To investigate."

"You thought it was a trick, eh?"

"No. It couldn't have been a trick. All of us knew that. It wasn't only the flames and the groans — they were real but not *quite* real. It was a feeling. A kind of — well, I can't describe it. A sad lonely feeling, deep as a pit. A coldness — golly, I can't describe it. But it must have been what the woman felt while she was hanging, during the night. That place is *haunted*, Mr. Marsile!"

"So you went inside. Wasn't that kinda rash?"

"Maybe... But all my life I've told myself if I ever saw a ghost, I was going to walk right up to him, and check him. Tonight I got the opportunity." Don grinned. "It was like jumping into cold water."

"What did you see? You kids keep a man in suspense!"

"Well, we'd run back a ways, and were standing by the car. These two girls were still yelling, and Johnny Palgrave had fled. I came to life and went to the front door. I was scared. It was so strong I could hardly move my legs — but it seemed as if most of it was outside of me. The atmosphere of the place. I went up the front door, and told Jean to wait —"

"Oh," said Art. "You were there too."

"Certainly. I wanted to know too."

"Go on."

"We looked through the door. It wasn't quite as bright as it had seemed through the window. A double-exposure sort of thing. But the fire was bright enough to see the other body hanging there."

"He was naked," said Jean primly, as if the apparition should have exhibited a greater sense of propriety than at that moment.

"We stood watching. Nothing happened. I went inside, picked up a stick, tried to touch the burning thing. The stick went right through."

"And then," said Jean, "everything faded. The groans and the fire. Everything."

"Hmmf. You're telling me the truth? You're not pulling your old dad's leg?"

"No, Father! My word of honor!"

"Hmmf…Then what did you do? High-tail it for home?"

"Heavens no! We hadn't eaten yet. We went back to the fire, and ate, and then we came home. Don's going back tomorrow night with a camera."

Art looked at Don speculatively. He cleared his throat, then said gruffly, "Mind if I come along?"

"No, Mr. Marsile. Of course not."

"You want to go back right now?"

"Sure, if you like."

"Can I come, Father?"

Art nodded. "You got clear once. I guess whatever's there ain't gonna hurt you."

II

They stopped by Don's house for his camera, then drove south into the country, through sweet-smelling orange groves, past dim white houses. At the edge of the desert, they turned up Indian Hill. The road twisted and wound, through sagebrush, half-wild oleander, scrub-oak. Ahead, in the light of a late-rising moon, stood the Freelock house.

"It's spooky enough," said Art.

He turned into the overgrown driveway. "There's where we parked," said Jean. "There's where we had our fire." The headlights picked out the circle of dead gray ash. Art stopped the car, set the brakes, took his flashlight from the glove-compartment.

They sat in the dark a few moments, watching and listening. Cricket sounds came out of the night; the half-moon rode pale and lonely through the ragged black trees. Art opened the door, got out. Don and Jean followed. They went to the patch of gravel, wan and gray in the moonlight. The rocks crunched under their feet. They halted, disinclined to make sounds so incongruous and intrusive.

"We were right here," Jean whispered. "See that window there? That's the living room."

They stood staring at the dark old house. Far away a dog barked, lonesome and mellow. Art muttered. "I've always heard that if you come out looking for these things, they never happen. They come when you don't expect them...I'm gonna take a look inside."

He went around to the front porch. The yard was a waste of dead milk-weed stalks and feathery fox-tail, bone-color in the moonlight. Jean and Don came behind. Art mounted the steps, paused.

Jean and Don stopped. After a moment Don asked, "Do you feel it, Mr. Marsile? Something cold and lonely?"

"Yeah. Something like that."

Art continued more slowly. The feeling of grief, of desolation, of precious remembrance lost and gone, grew stronger.

They entered the house. The room was dark. Was that a glow? A flicker of red? A whimper, a sob? If so, it came and went; the woe vanished abruptly. Art drew a deep breath. "That's how it was before," whispered Jean. "Only worse."

Art flicked on his flashlight. Don pointed. "That's the stick I used. That's where the thing hung."

Outside a car turned into the driveway: the State Highway Patrol. A searchlight swept up the steps, picked up Art Marsile on the porch with Don and Jean close behind him.

A trooper got out of the car. "Hello Art...What's going on?"

"I'm trying to find out."

"We got a report of a disturbance up here, thought we'd take a look."

"I thought I'd look too."

"See anything?"

"Nothing I'd swear to. It's quiet now, that's for sure."

"Yeah. Well, sergeant told me to check." The trooper climbed the steps, flashed his light around the room. He turned back to Jean and Don. "You kids were in the bunch up here tonight?"

"Yes."

"You saw those ghosts?"

Don told him what they'd seen. The trooper listened without comment, flashed his light around the room once again. He shook his head. "Looks to me like somebody was playing a trick." He went to the patrol car. Hisses, crackling, a voice from the radio. He spoke into the microphone, made his report. "Well, I checked. I'll be on my way."

The patrol car backed out, drove away. Art, Jean and Don went to their own car, followed. They drove down the hill in silence.

"What do you think, Dad?" Jean asked presently.

Art made a non-committal sound. "Lots of funny things happen in the world. I guess this is another of them."

"But you believe us, don't you?"

"I believe you, all right."

"But *why*?" asked Don. "Why should there be ghosts?"

Art shook his head. "Nobody knows, nobody seems to care. It's not fashionable to believe in ghosts. Let alone see them."

"I know what I saw," said Don. "It was *there*."

"But what was it?" asked Jean. "A spirit? A ghost? A memory?"

"It's just one of the things nobody knows the answers to — and doesn't want to know."

"I want to know," said Don. "There's got to be a reason. Nothing happens without a reason. *Some* kind of reason."

Art agreed. "That's what we're brought up to believe. But whenever there's something out of the ordinary, people shrug their shoulders and pretend it didn't happen. Miracles, things being thrown around a house, ghosts, apparitions, spirit messages — you read about 'em all the time. The newspaper prints the news, people read it, then go back about their business. I don't understand it. There's a big field of knowledge here — as big as all of science, maybe bigger. And nobody dares to look into it. There's thousands of people digging for pots in Egypt and counting the field-mice in Afghanistan ... Why don't a few look into this stuff? Is it because it's too big, too scary? Maybe they're afraid to be laughed at. I don't know."

"I never knew you thought that way, Daddy," said Jean.

"Think what way?" asked Art. "I'm just a hard-headed working-man. When I see something I want to know why. And when something funny happens, I don't try to kid myself it doesn't exist...I'll tell you kids something I never told no one else. I don't want you spreading it either, you hear?"

"I won't say anything."

"I won't either."

"Well, you know what a dowser is? Some people call 'em water-witches."

"Sure," said Don. "They find water with a forked stick."

"Yeah. Well, I own quite a bit of land. Some good citrus land, some not so good. There's one tract I got out at the edge of the desert, about four hundred acres, dry as ashes. If I could get water, I might grow something, but it's out of the irrigation district. One day I heard of this dowser and hired him to walk over the four hundred acres. He walked back and forth and his stick bumped and jumped. He was kinda puzzled at first, then he said, 'Mr. Marsile, you drill here. You'll get water. It's about two hundred feet down, you should be able to draw about twenty gallons a minute.' Then he said, 'Over here, if you drill, you'll hit oil. It's deep, it'll cost you money to reach it, but it's there. Lots of it.' "

"Daddy — you never told me this!"

"I didn't intend to. Not just yet. Anyway I went down for the water, I hit her on the nose at two hundred feet. I pump just about twenty gallons a minute. As for the oil, I've had three geologists to check the ground. They all say the same. Nothing. Wrong formation, wrong lay of the land, the wind even blows the wrong way. I don't know. I can't get it out of my mind. It'll cost twenty or thirty thousand — maybe more — to run a test-hole...I could swing it, but I'd have to go into debt. I don't like to do that."

Jean and Don were silent. They passed through the main part of Orange City, crossed the Los Angeles freeway, and returned to Art Marsile's house, under the four big pepper trees.

"Come on in," Art told Don. "Jean can make us some hot chocolate. It's too late for coffee. We'd never get to sleep."

Hugh was sitting in the living room, reading. His feet, in black socks, were long and limp as dead salmon. "Where you all been?"

"We saw the ghost, Hugh!" Jean called out triumphantly.

Hugh laughed uproariously.

"It's true!" cried Jean.

"Of all the silly tripe!"

"Don't believe me then." Jean went haughtily into the kitchen to make hot chocolate.

Hugh, still grinning, looked at Art. "What're they trying to cook up?"

"They sure saw something, Hugh."

Hugh sat up straight in astonishment. "You don't believe in ghosts?"

Art said evenly, "I have an open mind. They saw something, that's for sure. Ghosts, spooks — what difference does it make what you call 'em? Nobody knows anything about the subject. The field's wide open."

Don said, "I wonder if there's anyplace you could go to learn about these things?"

"Certainly at none of the universities. None that I ever heard of, anyway. After all, what could they teach? Ghost-hunting? Mind-reading? There's not even a name for the subject."

Hugh laughed derisively. "Who'd want to take such ridiculous courses?"

"I would," said Don. "I never thought about it before, but it's like Mr. Marsile says; nobody knows anything about these things — and they're all around us. Suppose the government spent a hundred million dollars in research, like they did on the atom bomb? Who knows what they'd turn up?"

"It's not a proper field for investigation," said Hugh after a minute. "It conflicts with what the Scriptures tell us."

"It wasn't considered proper to teach evolution either," said Art. "I see now where the ministers are swingin' around to sayin' it's right after all."

"Not the real four-square preachers!" cried Hugh indignantly. "Nobody'll ever convince me I was descended from a monkey. And nobody'll ever convince me there's ghosts because the Bible is against it."

Jean brought in the chocolate. "I wish for once, Hugh, that every time we're trying to talk you wouldn't bring the Bible into it. I know what I saw tonight, whether it's in the Bible or whether it isn't."

"Well, all this to the side," said Art, "it's an interesting subject. Everybody's interested in it. But everybody's afraid to look into it scientifically."

"I wouldn't be," said Don. "I'd really like to."

Art shook his head. "You'd find the going mighty tough, Don. You'd need money, and nobody'd give you money. People would laugh at you. You'd be starting cold, from scratch; you'd even have to invent your tools. You've got such a big field you couldn't cover it all, and you wouldn't hardly know where to start. Does dowsing for water have any connection to ghosts? How does this telepathy business work? Can anybody read the future? If so, does that make time the same kind of stuff as telepathy? Is telepathy the same stuff as ghosts? Are ghosts alive? Can they think? Are they spirits or just imprints, like footsteps? If they're alive where do they live? What's it like where they live? If they give off light, where do they draw the power? There's thousands of questions."

Don sat silently, chocolate forgotten.

Hugh said huskily, "Those are things we were never meant to know."

"I can't believe that, Hugh," said Art. "Anything our mind is able to understand we got a right to know." He put down his cup. "Well, I'm gonna turn in. Don't you kids set up till all hours. Good night." He left the room.

"Golly," said Don, in an awed voice. "When you think of it, it almost takes your breath away — this tremendous knowledge that nobody knows."

Jean said, "There must be *somebody* studying it. After all, we're not the only people in the world with ideas."

"Seems to me I've read of a group in England," said Don grudgingly. "A society for psychic research. Tomorrow let's go to the library and find out."

"Okay. We'll start the Orange City Society for Psychic Research."

Hugh said coldly, "You ought to know better than talk like that. It's impious."

"Don't talk nonsense," said Jean crossly. "Why on earth is it impious to talk?"

"Because there's one authority on right and wrong — the Bible. If you sin and go to Hell, you suffer the torments of the damned. If you live a Christian life, you go to Heaven. That's the Gospel. There's nothing about spirits, or ghosts, or any of that other stuff."

"The Bible isn't necessarily right," said Don.

Hugh was astounded. "Of course it's right! Every word of it is right!"

Don shrugged. "Anyway, I'm going to check on this psychic research business. I'm going to be a scientist. I'm going to find out what ghosts are, what they're made of, what makes them tick. Nothing happens without a reason; that's common sense. I'm going to find out that reason."

"I am too," said Jean. "I'm just as interested as you are."

"It's evil knowledge," intoned Hugh. "You'll go to Hell. You'll live in eternal torment."

"How come you're such an authority on Hell and torment?" Don asked.

"I made my choice tonight," said Hugh. "I gave myself to Christ. I promised to preach the Holy Gospel, to fight the Devil and all his works."

Don rose to his feet. "Well, that answered my question...Good night, Jean."

Jean went with him out to the car; when she came back Hugh was waiting for her. "Good night, Hugh," she said, and slipped past him. "Just a minute," he said.

"What for?"

"I want to warn you about what you're doing. It's evil." His voice took on volume. "There's enough wickedness in the world without inventing more. Don Berwick is going to Hell. You don't want to join him there, do you?"

"I don't believe in Hell," said Jean sweetly.

"It's in the Bible, it's the Holy Word. They that sin shall suffer fire and pain without end, the furnaces shall open for them, they'll be doomed forever. That's the Christian gospel."

"It's no such thing," said Jean. "I know this much: Christ was kind and gentle. He tried to get people to be decent to each other. All this talk about fire and torment is a lot of nonsense. And I'm going to bed."

III

The school year came to an end; both Don and Hugh were graduated. The Korean War had started; both Don and Hugh received greetings from the President. Hugh won a medical exemption by reason of his pitifully flat feet and his extreme height — he now stood almost seven feet tall. Don was drafted and assigned to a paratroop battalion. Ten months passed, and Don's mother received news that Don had disappeared in action and must be presumed dead.

The years passed. Art Marsile prospered, but his mode of life varied little. Hugh studied at the Athbill School of Divinity at Lawrence, Kansas; Jean enrolled at UCLA.

Three years after Don's disappearance, Don's mother received an official letter from the Army Department in Washington, notifying her that Sergeant Donald Berwick was not dead, as had been presumed, and shortly would be arriving home.

Two weeks later Don Berwick returned to Orange City. He was reticent about his war experience, but it became known that he had been an undeclared prisoner-of-war, that he had escaped from a Manchurian labor camp and had made his way to Japan. He looked considerably older than his twenty-three years; he walked with a faint hitch in his stride, and his face was much more firmly modeled than anyone in Orange City had remembered it: the forehead low and wide, the nose straight and blunt, the cheekbones and jaw pronounced, the cheeks hollow.

On his second day in Orange City he went to see Art Marsile, whom he found a trifle thinner, a trifle more leathery. Art brought out beer from the refrigerator, told him what news there was to be told: that Jean was making good grades; that Hugh had become an evangelist, and had changed his name, now calling himself Hugh Bronny — which had been his mother's maiden-name. "And what do you plan to do, Don?"

Don settled himself back into the couch. "You remember the night we went up to the Freelock house, Art?"

"Yep."

"I've never forgotten that night. Afterwards I did a lot of reading —
all the books I could find on the subject. In Manchuria I had time to
do a lot of thinking. I did it. I still want to be a scientist, Art — a new
kind of scientist. I'm going to the University. I'm going to learn as much
mathematics, psychology, biology and physics as possible. I'm going
to read a lot more. Then I'm going to apply scientific techniques to the
so-called supernatural."

Art nodded. "I'm glad to hear that, Don. I'm going to ask you a personal question. How are you fixed for money?"

"Pretty good, Art. I got an awful whack of cumulative back pay. I'll
go to school on the GI Bill."

"Good enough. If you run short, I've got lots of money. Whatever
you need, it's yours."

"Thanks, Art. I'll sure call on you if I need help. But I think I'll make
out pretty well." He rose to his feet and shuffled uneasily.

Art said gruffly, "Why don't you stay to dinner? I telephoned Jean
you were here; she's due home in a few minutes."

Don sat down, a queer hard pounding under his ribs. Outside a car
door slammed. Feet came running up the walk, the front door opened.
"Don!"

"Seems like absence makes the heart grow fonder," observed Art
Marsile grinning.

"Father, don't you look while I'm kissing Don!"

"Okay. Just let me know when you're done."

Don applied for admission at Caltech, and was accepted. A year later he
and Jean were married.

There was news from Hugh meanwhile. He had established himself
in Kansas, and held weekly revival meetings in various parts of Texas,
Kansas, Oklahoma and Arkansas. Occasionally he sent home hand-
bills: "Monster Rally. Fighting Hugh Bronny, Leader of the Christian
Crusade."

On Easter of the year Don was to take his BS degree, Art drove out
to Don and Jean's apartment in Westwood. "I'm gonna make the jump,"
he announced as he came through the door. "In fact, I already made it."

"What jump, Father?"

"Remember my telling you about the dowser, how he told me there was oil?"

"Yes."

"Well, I'm going to do some wild-catting. I had a good year, I can blow whatever it's gonna take. If I hit it, fine. If I don't, it's out of my system."

Don laughed. "Either way, it'll be interesting."

"That's how I figure," said Art. "The geologists say no, the dowser says yes. We'll see who's right."

"How long before you know for sure?"

Art shook his head. "They start down next month. They drill till they hit oil — or until I run out of money. Whichever comes first."

"Here's hoping," said Don. "If hope will do you any good."

"We'll all hope. We'll drink a toast," said Jean. "If Hugh were here we'd ask him to pray."

"Hugh *will* be here," said Art. "That's another thing."

Jean made a face. "I thought he was established in Kansas."

"Well, he's coming west," said Art in the level voice he always used in connection with Hugh. "He seems to be a pretty big man in his field now. They've got him booked for meetings all over Southern California. He's going to make his headquarters in Orange City."

"Father! Surely he's not going to move in with you!"

"It's his privilege, if he wants to, Jean. It's his home."

"I suppose so. But I thought that later, after Don got his degree, we'd move back to Orange City."

Art grinned. "When Don gets his degree, you two are going to the Hawaiian Islands. It's a present from me. By the time you come back — then we'll see. Things may be cleared up. Maybe Hugh's got other plans in mind."

But Hugh had no other plans in mind. He arrived in Orange City the next week, tall, gaunt and solemn, wearing a pale blue suit, a Panama hat on his craggy forehead. Art received him with decent cordiality, and Hugh took up residence in his old home.

The drilling on Marsile No. 1 began. Don finished his undergraduate studies and received his BS; he and Jean flew to Honolulu for the month's vacation which had been Art's present to them.

During their absence they received two short letters from Art: the drilling was proceeding slowly and expensively. Nothing at five hundred feet; in the second letter, nothing at twelve hundred feet, with the drills scratching slowly through hard metamorphic rock. He made a dry comment that Hugh disapproved of the venture, on the basis that money being wasted on the drilling could be put to better use: namely, the Christian Crusade, an evangelistic movement which Hugh had founded.

The month passed; Don and Jean returned to Orange City. Art met them at the airport. His face was dour and drawn: Marsile No. 1 was still dry. "We're down to eighteen hundred," said Art glumly. "The rock gets harder and meaner every foot. And I'm running low of money."

Jean hugged him. "That's nothing to fret about. It was just a gamble — just a game."

"Damn expensive game. And I like to win my games you know."

They drove to the old house under the pepper trees, walked up the iris-bordered gravel path, entered the house.

"Good heavens!" cried Jean in wonder. "What's all this?"

"Some of Hugh's publicity," said Art drily.

Wordlessly Jean and Don examined the placards thumb-tacked to the wall. Most conspicuous was a large photograph of Hugh Bronny speaking into a microphone, fist poised in grim exultation. Four placards bore a picture of Hugh with scarehead printing: "March in the Christian Crusade with Hugh Bronny!" "Hugh Bronny, the Devil's enemy!" "Sweep America clean with Fighting Hugh Bronny!" A cartoon showed Hugh Bronny depicted as a muscular giant. He carried a broom labelled "The Fighting Gospel", with which he dispersed a rabble of half-human vermin. Some wore horns and bat-wings; others were characterized by bald heads, large hooked noses, heavy-lidded eyes; others were marked with the communist hammer-and-sickle. "Clean out the atheists, the communists, the deniers of Christ!" "Keep America pure!" cried another card. "Hear Fighting Hugh Bronny at the old-fashioned fundamental go-for-broke revival! Bring the children. Free soda pop."

Jean finally turned back to Art; she opened her mouth, then closed it again.

"I know," said Art. "It's kinda crude. But — well, it's Hugh's business. This is his home, he's got a right to hang up what he wants."

"But you live here too, Father!"

Art nodded. "I can stand it. I don't like the things, but what's the good of making Hugh take them down? That don't change Hugh, and it only makes things tough."

"Sometimes I think you carry tolerance too far, Dad."

"Now I don't know about that. Here comes Hugh now. I guess he's been asleep."

A door closed, slow steps sounded along the hall.

"He's changed quite a bit," said Art in an undertone.

Hugh came into the room. He wore an unpressed black suit, a blue shirt, a long gray necktie, long-toed black shoes. He seemed enormously tall, almost seven feet; his head seemed larger and craggier than ever; his eyes flamed blue from cavernous sockets. He had gained force since Don had seen him last — force and poise and intensity, and absolute assurance.

Hugh did not offer to shake hands. "Hello, Jean. Hello, Don. You both look well."

"We should," said Jean with a nervous laugh, "we've done nothing but lie in the sun and sleep for a month."

Hugh nodded somberly, as if frivolity and self-indulgence were all very nice, but that personally he could not afford the time.

"I'm glad you're here. I want to talk about this oil well business. Do you know how much money has gone into it?"

"No," said Jean. "I don't care."

"But there's no oil out there on the desert. That money could be put to a worthy Christian use. I could do wonderful things with it."

"No, you couldn't," said Art. "I told you once before, Hugh, I'm not putting any money into your Christian Crusade, whatever you say."

"Just what is a Christian Crusade?" asked Jean.

Hugh bent his head forward, swung his arms. "The Christian Crusade is a great and growing cause. The Christian Crusade aims to bring the power of the Bible against the evils of this earthly sphere. The Christian Crusade aims to make the United States of America a real Christian God-fearing community; we believe in America for the Americans,

Russia for the communists, Africa for the Negroes, Israel for the Jews and Hell for the atheists."

"I don't plan to finance it," said Art with a feeble grin.

Jean turned to Don, made a small helpless gesture. Don shrugged.

Hugh looked from one to the other. "I hear you've just graduated from college," he said to Don.

"Yes, that's right."

"And now you're a scientist?"

"Not quite. I've acquired some of the necessary background."

"So now what will you do?"

Jean said, "Father, take us out to the oil well."

"Don't call it an oil well yet," said Art. "It's dry as last week's biscuits. Around Orange City they call it 'Marsile's Folly'. But if I strike —"

Hugh made an unverbalized rumble of disgust.

"— if I strike there'll be lots of sick people around here. Because I quietly bought up mineral rights everywhere in sight. C'mon then, let's go. Coming, Hugh?"

"No. I'm working on my sermons."

They drove east from Orange City. The dark green foliage of the citrus groves came to an abrupt halt, with dun hills and the parched vegetation of the desert beyond.

They turned off at a side road, wound between balls of dry tumbleweed and gray-brown boulders, then suddenly came on another dark-green orange grove. Art stopped the car, pointed. "See that tank and the windmill? That's where the dowser told me to get my water. I got enough to irrigate that whole grove. Now look —" he started forward "— just around this little hill…" There was the derrick, the drill-rig, the drill crew in sweat-stained shirts and hard hats. Art called to the foreman. "I don't see no gusher, Chet."

"We're down to shale again, Art. Better going than the schist. But not a whiff of oil. You know what I think?"

"Yeah. I know what you think. You think I'm pouring money down a gopher hole. Maybe I am. I got another four thousand dollars to blow. When that's gone — we quit."

"Four thousand won't take us much farther. Specially if we hit any more of that schist, or that black trap."

"Well, keep biting at her, and when she blows, cap her quick; I don't want to lose a gallon."

Chet grinned. "All the oil you'll get out of that hole won't come to more'n a gallon."

IV

They returned to Orange City.

Jean said grimly, "I know we're going to argue with Hugh the whole time we're here. Darn it, Dad, he's a fascist! Where did he ever learn such things? Not from you!"

Art sighed. "I guess it's just Hugh. He's got a good mind, but — well, maybe it's his funny looks that he couldn't apply himself normally. And now he's found a place where his looks help him out... And it don't do no good arguing with him, because he doesn't listen."

"I'll try to behave myself."

But at dinner the argument started. Hugh insisted on knowing what field of investigation Don proposed to enter. Don told him, matter-of-factly. "I plan to study para-psychological phenomena — psionic research, some people call it."

Hugh frowned his great eyebrow-buckling frown. "I'm not sure as I understand. Does this mean you study black-magic, witchcraft, the occult?"

"In a certain sense, yes."

"It's all charlatanry!" said Hugh in vast disgust.

Don nodded. "Ninety-five percent of it is, unfortunately... It's the remaining five percent I'm interested in. Especially the so-called spiritualistic phenomena."

Hugh leaned forward. "Surely you consider that sort of study irreverent? Are the souls of the dead any concern of man?"

"I don't recognize any limitation to human knowledge, Hugh. If souls exist, they're made of some sort of substance. Perhaps not molecules — but something. I'm curious what that *something* is."

Hugh shook his head. "And how do you go about investigating the after-life?"

"The same way you investigate anything else. Isolate facts, check, reject. If there is life after death, it exists. Somewhere. If something exists somewhere, it can be examined, measured, perhaps even seen or visited — providing we find the proper tools."

"It's sacrilege," croaked Hugh.

Don laughed. "Calm down, Hugh. Let's talk without getting excited. You asked me what I was interested in, I'm telling you... If it's any comfort to you, I'm not at all sure there is an after-life."

Hugh glared from his cavernous eye-sockets. "Are you admitting to atheism?"

"If you want to put it that way," said Don. "I don't see why you make it out a bad word."

"An atheist and a communist!"

"Atheist yes, communist no. The ideas are at opposite poles. Atheism is the assertion of human self-reliance, dignity and individuality; communism is the denial of those ideas."

"You are forever damned," said Hugh in a hushed sibilant voice.

"I don't think so," said Don reasonably. "Of course I don't know anything for sure. No one knows the basic answers. Why is everything? Why is *anything*? Why is the universe? These are tremendous questions. They aren't answered by replying, 'Because the Creator so willed.' The same mystery applies to the Creator. And if there is a Creator, I'm sure he's not angry when I use the brain and the curiosity he endowed me with. In other words," said Don, smiling, "I'm trying to tell you that I'm not a dragon or a vampire. I'm a man honestly and decently puzzled about life, thought and the universe. I may never know the answers, but perhaps I'll make a start at finding out."

Hugh rose to his feet, nodded stiffly. "Good night." He left the room.

Jean broke the silence. "Well, that's that."

"I'm sorry if I caused any family trouble," said Don.

"Nonsense," said Art. "I've always liked a good argument. Hugh's got no call to get his feelings hurt. You didn't call him names or tell him he was damned."

"Hugh forgets that the constitution guarantees freedom of religion," said Jean indignantly.

Art chuckled, looked at the posters on the wall. "If this Christian Crusade really takes hold, Hugh'll change the constitution."

"He shouldn't use the word 'Christian'," Jean said indignantly. "Christianity stands for gentleness and kindness, and Hugh is a bigot."

Art drew a deep breath. "I'm not proud of Hugh…I'm not proud of myself, because I raised him."

"Hush Father, don't be foolish. Let's talk of more interesting things. Like how we're going to spend our first million when Marsile No. 1 comes in."

Art laughed. "You and Don can go about your ghost-hunting. Me, I'm going to buy some nice pasture-land and raise race-horses."

A week passed, two weeks. Marsile No. 1 remained dry, and Art Marsile reached the end of his bank-roll. He returned to the house, grim and dusty. "Well, that's it," he said. "I paid off the rig. I blew what loose money I had and I'm not going into debt."

Jean soothed him. "You're perfectly right, Dad, and now we'll forget all about it."

Art looked around the living room. "Why the suitcases?"

"You know we planned to leave today."

"You don't need to go anywhere. Your home is here, as long as you like living here."

"We do like it, but we've got to get to work. And we can't commute to Los Angeles every day."

"And how are you going to set about going to work?"

"First," said Don, "I've got to raise money. I'll apply for a Guggenheim Fellowship. I'll make contacts at the Society for Psychical Research, and see if I can sell some ideas to the finance committee. Perhaps one of the universities will set up a study group, like the ESP section at Duke. There's a number of possibilities."

Art shook his head in gruff vexation. "If Marsile No. 1 came through, you wouldn't have needed to worry."

"I know, Art. I was pulling for it as hard as you were."

They took their luggage to the car. Hugh came to the doorway, and stood watching. Jean kissed Art, waved to Hugh. "We'll be out next weekend, Daddy. Now you forget Marsile No. 1 and get back to oranges."

They drove to Los Angeles in a driving rainstorm, returned to their apartment in Westwood. Jean ran up the steps, opened the door; Don struggled up with the suitcases. He found Jean standing rigidly in the middle of the floor. "What's the trouble?" he asked, putting down the suitcases.

Jean made no answer. Don went to her. "What's wrong, Jean?"

"Don," she whispered, "something terrible's happened. To Art."

Don stared at her. "Surely not. We just left him, not an hour ago…"

Jean rushed to the telephone, called Orange City. The bell rang and rang. No one answered. Jean put down the receiver, stood up. Don put his arms around her.

"I feel it, Don," she whispered. "I know something's happened."

Half an hour later the telephone rang. Hugh spoke in a harsh babble. "Jean? Is this you? Jean?"

"Hugh! Father —"

"He's dead. A truck skidded into him — on the way out to that crazy oil well —"

"We'll be right out, Hugh."

Jean hung up listlessly. She turned. Don read the news in her face. She told him. He kissed her, patted her head. "I'm going to make you a cup of coffee."

Jean came out in the kitchen with him. "Don."

"Yes?"

"Let's go see Ivalee."

He stood looking at her, coffee-pot in his hand. "You're sure you want to?"

"Yes."

"All right."

"Right now."

Don put down the coffee-pot. "I'll telephone to make sure she's not busy." He went to the phone, made the call. "It's all right. Let's go."

Half an hour later they rang the bell of a neat white house in Long Beach. Ivalee Trembath opened the door, a slender woman of forty-five with steady gray eyes and silky white hair. She greeted them quietly, with simple friendliness, led them into the living room. If she noticed Jean's drawn face and over-bright eyes, she made no comment. Don said, "How do you feel, Iva?"

Ivalee looked from Don to Jean, then seated herself slowly in an arm-chair. "Sit down." Don and Jean seated themselves. "Do you want to speak to Molly?"

"Yes, please."

Ivalee lowered her head, looked at her hands. She began to breathe in long slow breaths. "Molly. Molly. Are you there?" There was silence. Outside a car whirred past over the wet macadam. "Molly?" Ivalee's head sank, her shoulders sagged.

"Hello, Iva," said a clear bright voice from Ivalee's mouth. "Hello, folks."

"Hello, Molly," said Don. "How are you?"

"Fine as rain. I see you got a little rain down below too. We sure could have used it in 1906. What a sight that was, dear old Frisco! Reeking up in flames like rags in a bonfire. Well, well. I've seen lots in my day." Molly's voice faded a little; there was a murmur, then another voice said harshly, "Come, come, enough of this nonsense! We're not having any more of this peeking and prying."

Ivalee Trembath whimpered like a sleeping puppy, rocked back and forth in the chair.

"Who are you?" asked Don, calmly.

A torrent of words in a foreign language pelted from Ivalee's mouth — hard, harsh gutturals that carried the sting of abuse.

Molly said good-naturedly, "Oh, get away, Ladislav... Silly creature — he's one of the bad ones. Always horsin' around."

Jean said in a husky whisper, "Is my father there?"

"Sure, he's here."

"Can he speak?" said Don.

Molly's voice was doubtful. "He'll try. He's not strong..."

A second voice interrupted, a low gravel voice that rasped in Ivalee's throat; for a second or two both voices were speaking at once.

"Hello, Jean. Hello, Don." The voice was distant.

"Art?" asked Don. "Are you there?"

"Yes." The voice was stronger. "Can't quite get the hang of talking through a lady. Well, I'm over here safe and sound, in spite of Hugh's predictions... Now don't you folks grieve. It's a little lonesome, but I'm fine and I'll be happy."

Jean was crying quietly. "It was so sudden…"

"That's the best way there is. Now don't cry, because you make me feel bad."

"It's so strange to be talking to you like this."

Art's dry laugh sounded in Ivalee's throat. "It's strange for me too."

"What's it like, Art?" asked Don.

"Hard to say. It's kinda hazy just now. It's something like home in a way."

His voice faded, as if it were coming from a radio tuned to a distant station. Molly's voice came bright and cheerful. "He's tired, dear. He's not used to life up here yet. But he's fine now, and we'll look after him. He wants to talk to you again."

The voice changed in Ivalee's throat, becoming not Art's voice, but using Art's clipped intonations. "Say, down there. You know where we was digging?"

"Marsile No. 1?"

"Yeah. Well, we stopped too soon. I just kinda pushed my head down and took a look. Don't quit, Don. Keep going, because it's there."

"How far, Art?"

"Hard to say; things is a little confused. I've got to go. I'll be talking to you again sometime. Say hello to Hugh…"

Molly's voice returned. "Well, that's all folks," she said brassily. "He's a nice man."

Don asked, "Molly — can I visit this land where you are?"

"Sure," said Molly. "When you die." And she chuckled. "Of course, we call it passing over."

"Can I visit your country while I'm alive, here on Earth?" he asked.

Molly's voice faded, waxed and waned as if winds were blowing. "I don't know, Donald. People like Iva visit us — but they always go back… I see that Ivalee's tired… So I'll be off about my business. Good-bye…"

"Good-bye," said Don.

"Good-bye," said Jean, softly.

Ivalee Trembath raised her head; her eyes looked tired; the cheek muscles sagged around her mouth. "How was it?"

"It was tremendous," said Don. "It couldn't have been better."

Ivalee looked at Jean, still softly crying. "What happened, Don?"

"Her father was killed tonight."

"Oh. Too bad...Did you reach him?"

"Yes. He spoke. It was wonderful."

Ivalee smiled faintly. "I'm glad when I can help."

"Thank you ever so much," said Jean.

Ivalee patted her shoulder. "You come to see me soon again...Do you still have the same plans?"

"Yes," said Don. "The same, only more of them. We'll start work as soon as we can."

"Tell me about it next time," said Ivalee. "You're anxious to go now."

"Yes," said Jean. "But I'm glad we came. Good night."

"Good night."

V

Don and Jean drove along the Freeway, through swift bright-eyed shoals of automobiles; past phosphorescent tangles of neon-tubing, filling-stations a-twinkle with banners and rotating glimmering tapes, cafes, bars, creameries, hamburger-stands, used-car lots draped and festooned with electric light-bulbs — hundred thousand-watt effulgences along the street, like a row of monstrous incandescent jelly-fish. It was splendor familiar to Don and Jean, a vibrant agitation of light and color and life to be seen nowhere else in the world; in any event their minds were elsewhere.

Jean said, "I don't know Ivalee as well as you do...I'm sure she's honest." She hesitated.

Don said, "She's more than honest. She's completely transparent. She's the most guile-less person I know. This is the fifth time I've sat at a seance with her. It was far and away the clearest and most direct."

"I wasn't questioning her honesty," said Jean. "But — do you think that was really Father?"

Don shrugged. "I don't know. It's possible that Ivalee unconsciously reads the minds of the people who visit her. That instead of spirits speaking through her mouth, she merely mirrors our own minds."

"But about the oil well — he said there's oil, to keep on drilling."

"I know. She wasn't mirroring my mind. Privately I've been

skeptical of Marsile No. 1. Dowsers aren't infallible, no more than anyone else."

Jean nodded. "I've never believed there'd be oil... But now father, or his spirit — whatever it is — says there's oil. What shall we do?"

Don laughed grimly. "Drill, I guess — if you're willing to risk it. If we can raise the money."

"I'm willing to risk it... But there's Hugh to be considered."

"Had your father made a will?"

"Yes. The property is divided equally between Hugh and myself."

"There may be difficulties... Speaking of Hugh — look at that." He pointed to an enormous billboard glaring under the illumination of six floodlights.

This appeared in red and black, on a white background, in heavy portentous letters.

:::::: GREAT NATIONAL GOSPEL REVIVAL ::::::
Fight Three Great Evils
with
FIGHTING HUGH BRONNY
Join the Christian Crusade
Keep America Clean, White and Christian
Fight Communism
Fight Atheism
Fight Blood Pollution
Massive Revival at the Orange City Auditorium
Two weeks starting June 19
⋮⋮

A picture depicted Hugh as a rock-jawed powerful giant, a hybrid of Abraham Lincoln, Uncle Sam and Paul Bunyan.

Don shook his head. "I never suspected Hugh had come so far!"

"He's always been a worker... It's rather revolting, isn't it?"

Don nodded. "I suppose people must come to listen to him."

"Evidently."

They arrived at Orange City, and were immersed in the inevitable melancholy details attendant on Art Marsile's death.

Art was cremated, his ashes buried in the orange grove, without funeral or formal ceremony, in accordance with his wishes. Hugh protested bitterly, until Art's attorney and executor of the estate brought forth the will, and indicated a paragraph giving explicit instructions as to the disposal of his body.

As Jean had informed Don, the estate was to be divided between Jean and Hugh, "in any manner mutually agreeable to the legatees." In the event that agreement could not be reached, the executor was instructed to sell the various properties of the estate at the highest possible figure and divide the proceeds between the legatees.

Jean, Don and Hugh discussed the situation the night Art's ashes were buried. There were nine parcels of property: the house, the four hundred acres of desert, and seven orange groves of various acreage.

Hugh had prepared a memorandum of the value of the various parcels, and was ready with a proposal. "I suggest that you keep the house, since my work takes me far afield, and I have no need of it. To compensate, I will take the Elsinore Avenue grove, which is roughly the same value. These other groves we can divide like this." He explained his plan. "The four hundred acres is worthless and I propose that we sell it and divide the proceeds."

Don said, "It's only fair to tell you, that we have reason to think there is oil on the property."

Hugh frowned. "What sort of reason?"

"A reason you may or may not take seriously. On the night Art died we stopped by the house of a friend, who is also a medium. While we were there, a voice, purportedly Art, spoke to us. The voice told us that there was oil on the four hundred acres, to proceed with the drilling."

Hugh chuckled hollowly. "And you are superstitious enough to give credence to this 'voice'?"

"Superstition is belief in something non-existent," said Don. "This voice existed. I heard it. It sounded like Art. Jean and I are willing to take the chance it was Art."

Hugh shook his great head slowly. "I can't agree with you."

"In any event," said Don, "I suggest that we sell one of the groves and use the money to continue drilling. It's a gamble, yes — but most of the hole is already there."

Hugh shook his head once more. "I have much better uses for money than pouring it into a hole."

"Very well," said Don. "You take the Frazer Boulevard Valencias, we'll take the four hundred acres, and we'll split the other parcels according to your system."

Hugh considered his list. "Very well. I agree. I hope that I may be allowed to reside in the house during my stay in Orange City?"

"Of course," said Jean. "If you'll please take those posters and placards off the wall."

Hugh rose to his full seven feet. "As you wish," he said coldly. "It is your house."

The division of the property was accordingly made. Don and Jean sold thirty-three acres of oranges, called the drill-crew back to work.

"Good money after bad?" inquired the foreman with genial good humor. "Take my advice, Mr. Berwick, don't waste your money. This just ain't the right formation. We've passed the Granville Blue shales — that's where the Rodman Dome came in — and according to the geology you'll be hitting granite in another five hundred feet."

"We want to see that granite," said Jean. "Drill on, Chet, and be ready to cap it when it comes."

"Yes, ma'am."

Three days later gas began blowing up the hole, and on the fourth day Marsile No. 1 came in.

Chet said sheepishly, "I gave you good advice. You shoulda took it. But if you had, you wouldn't be millionaires like you're gonna be."

VI

At ten o'clock in the morning Hugh came into the living room, wearing a cream-colored suit, long pointed yellow shoes. Jean looked up from the arm-chair where she had been sitting, lost in thought. Hugh put his Panama hat gently on a chair, slapped his leg with a newspaper.

"Well, sister," he said jocularly, "oil on the property, after all. Why didn't you let me know?"

"You weren't here when the news came."

"No. I was working with the Reverend Spedelius. It's wonderful, wonderful! God's gift to us. And we'll put it to God's work."

Jean sat up in the chair, a faint cool smile on her face. "What sort of fantasy is this, Hugh?"

"Fantasy?" He held up the newspaper. "Surely this is true?"

"We struck oil on the four hundred acres, yes."

"Then we're rich."

"It was the four hundred acres you didn't want, Hugh."

Hugh laughed hollowly. "What's the difference? Perhaps I spoke unthinkingly — but I'm sure that our father intended us to share. That was the tone of his last will and testament..." he looked around the room, picked up a book. "'A Compendium of Supernormal Phenomena', by Ralph Birchmill." He dropped it as if it were hot, glanced at Jean. "I don't see the Holy Bible in the room," he said, heavily jocose. He settled his great gaunt frame on the couch, knees almost as high as his chest. Don came in, sat down near Jean.

"Our father always insisted on an equal sharing of the good things," said Hugh. "I assume that we will continue to do so."

"Not in this case," said Jean. "You're a moderately well-off man right now, with your orange groves."

Hugh's hand slowly clenched on the newspaper. But his voice was gentle and low. "True, sister. But I have a need for money beyond mere material needs. I'm pledged to the furtherance of God's will, to spiritual enlightenment of the people, to the Christian Crusade."

"I'm sorry, Hugh. We've decided to put the money to other uses."

Hugh held out his hands ingenuously. "What use could be more important than spreading the Gospel?"

"It depends on your point of view. We plan to endow a research foundation."

"You mean this black magic, devil worship, occultism stunt?"

Jean said impatiently, "You know very well that we neither practice nor believe in black magic or devil worship."

Hugh glanced meaningfully at the book on Don's desk. He rose restlessly to his feet, paced back and forth across the room. "Exactly what kind of research do you intend, then?"

"I'll be glad to explain," said Don politely. "We want to bridge a very large gap in human knowledge. We want to attack what is commonly known as the supernatural with laboratory techniques. We want to make a large scale investigation of spiritualistic phenomena, with an eye to proving or disproving the existence of spirits, and perhaps the whole concept of the hereafter you see."

Hugh stood back with an exaggerated gesture of alarm that nearly bumped his head on the door lintel. "Proof of the hereafter? Isn't that rather beside the point? And presumptuous? Don't you read your Bible?"

"I don't care to argue theology with you," said Don. "You asked me a question; I answered you."

Hugh nodded. "Very well. I'll ask another question." He strode across the room, looked down at Jean. "This money, which you have acknowledged to be partly mine — do you intend to give it to me?"

"I haven't acknowledged it as partly yours and I don't intend to give you any."

Hugh nodded again. "Do you have the effrontery to suggest that this hocus-pocus is more important than the Christian Crusade?"

Jean, leaning back in the chair, looked up at him coldly. "Last night we went to your revival meeting. We listened to you. Do you know why?"

"Of course I don't know why. Unless —"

"No. We weren't planning to throw ourselves before the altar. We suspected that this matter would come up, we wanted to hear you, with our own ears. We heard you."

Hugh looked from Jean to Don, back to Jean. "Well?"

"I'll speak with complete frankness," said Jean.

"Of course," said Hugh stiffly.

"There's no point beating around the bush, or using ambiguous terms because they're more polite. So — to be brutally blunt — I think you're a fascist. You call yourself a preacher; you preach hate. You cloak your hatred in sanctimony, you bring out the worst in humanity. You asked people to come up and grovel, abase themselves for their sins — imaginary or otherwise. If there is a Creator, I'm sure you don't speak for him."

Hugh said ponderously, "That is not the truth. I preach the Lord's word."

"Whatever you call it, you sickened me. I won't let you go hungry, but I'll never give a cent to your Christian Crusade."

"Very well," said Hugh. "But what about the wishes of our father? He instructed us to divide the estate fairly between us." He held up his great hand. "I know what you're going to say. But surely you had secret information. You did not deal fairly with me."

"I gave you every bit of information we had," Jean said indignantly.

"You couldn't expect me to believe that story — about the medium," bleated Hugh.

"We took our chances. You refused to take yours. As far as I'm concerned the subject is closed."

Hugh danced back, stood with his fist in the air. "Very well! I warn you that I intend to fight you and your blasphemous program in every possible way. The money came from the minerals God put into the earth; you should not use it to derogate the Word of God!"

"Why not let God do his own worrying?" Jean wearily asked. "He can stop it anytime he wants with a thunderbolt."

"I am moving out of this sacrilegious place," cried Hugh. "I don't want your money. It stinks of the Devil!" He backed away. His voice boomed and rasped. "You will know punishment, you will know death and the awful agony of the hereafter!"

"Please go, Hugh."

Hugh departed. "He's a madman," said Jean. "Or — is he?"

Don was pulling Hugh's placards off the wall. "Filthy things... I don't know."

Jean put her arms around him. "Don — I'm afraid of Hugh."

"Afraid? Physically afraid?"

"Yes... He doesn't care what he does."

"I'm not so sure," said Don lightly. "I think he rather enjoys these dramatic scenes... But — I hope we don't see too much of Hugh. He's very wearing."

VII

At five o'clock in the evening the telephone rang. Jean answered, turned to Don. "It's a reporter from the Los Angeles *Times*."

"Let's talk to them. Publicity can't hurt us, and might do us some good."

Jean turned back to the phone, and twenty minutes later the reporter appeared at the front door. She gave her name as Vivian Hallsey — a young woman of twenty-five, not quite plump, with a round freckled face, alert eyes, a button nose and dark red hair, tightly curled. She stood in the doorway, looked from Don to Jean, smiled. "You certainly don't look as I expected you to look."

"What did you expect?" asked Don.

Vivian Hallsey shook her head. "Anything other than normality."

Jean laughed. "Why shouldn't we look normal?"

"I'm prejudiced," said Vivian Hallsey. "I understand that you were led to drill this oil well by communication with the spirit world. I've always thought that only neurotic old women patronized mediums and fortune tellers."

"Be that as it may," said Don. "Will you sit down?"

"Thanks. How *did* you find where to drill for oil? If it's through a spirit, which spirit? Because I'd like an oil well myself."

Don explained the circumstances which led to the tapping of Marsile Dome.

Vivian Hallsey looked around the room and shivered. "It makes me feel strange."

"What makes you feel strange?"

"The idea of spirits — everywhere. The spirits of the dead. Watching you. We're never alone. It's as if we all lived in glass cages…It's embarrassing!"

"Not so fast," said Don. "We still can't be sure."

"Sure of what?"

"That spirits exist. It's a pat answer."

" 'Pat answer'!" She looked at him incredulously. "You tell me this? You're the one who just brought in an oil well, with the help of spirits."

"I know," said Don. "That's the supposition. But it's possible there are other explanations."

Vivian Hallsey clutched her head in exasperation. "Exactly what *do* you think?"

"I don't know. We're going to spend the next few years finding out. Maybe the rest of our lives."

"I never believed in life after death before. You convince me, and then the next minute you try to un-convince me."

Don laughed. "Sorry. But it just might not have been life after death."

"I don't see how you can say that!"

"Ivalee Trembath might be highly telepathic. Without conscious effort on her part she might have been reading our minds — telling us things we wanted to believe."

Vivian Hallsey was silent a moment. "It all seems so fantastic… Isn't it more likely the other way?"

"I don't know. I'd like to know. If there is another world — it exists. That's just logic. If this other world exists, it exists *somewhere*! That's important. 'The Land of Nod' for instance — a figure of speech, meaning sleep. It exists — nowhere. Perhaps the after-life is also a figurative expression — something like the 'Land of Nod'. But if it *does* exist, I want to learn the truth. I have a right to know. Humanity has a right to know."

Vivian Hallsey looked doubtful. "Human beings derive a great deal of comfort from the hope of an after-life. Isn't it cruel to take that hope away from them?"

"Possibly," said Don. "New knowledge always comes as an uncomfortable shock to many people. And of course it's perfectly possible we might prove the reality of an after-life."

"You use the word 'proof'," said Vivian Hallsey. "Just how do you go about getting this proof?"

"The same way scientists try to get proof for any other matter in doubt."

"But how do you start?"

"First with a little deep thought. The problem is how to get evidence — scientific evidence — and parapsychology is a hard field to get definite evidence in."

"Why is that?"

"First, because the subject matter is so far out of reach. Second, good mediums are awfully scarce. Ivalee Trembath is one in a million. There probably aren't twenty people in the United States as efficient as she is. Incidentally, please don't use her name, as she isn't a professional medium — just a gifted woman who is interested in the subject. Third, there are thousands of convincing charlatans, and even more thousands of unconvincing ones. Fourth, good mediums are sensitive. Some of them are jealous of their gifts and don't want anyone investigating. Others resent laboratory checks. They think it's a reflection on their integrity."

"But surely there are mediums who'll cooperate."

"Oh, yes. With money anything is possible. There'll be lots of hard work involved, lots of sweat! If we got about a dozen mediums and held twelve simultaneous seances…" He paused.

"What would that prove?"

"I don't know. The results might suggest something. We've got to start somewhere."

"Would these simultaneous seances prove or disprove the after-life?"

"So far as I know," said Don, "nothing a medium does or says has completely ruled out the possibility of telepathy, clairvoyance, precognition, retrocognition, telekinesis. These of course are hypernormal — but they don't prove survival after death."

"How about ghosts — and things like that?"

"Ghosts," said Don. He looked at Jean. They both laughed.

"Why are you laughing?" Vivian Hallsey asked.

"Ghosts are how Jean and I became interested in parapsychology. It happened a long time ago…I wonder if the old Freelock place is still haunted…"

"What happened?" asked Vivian Hallsey. "Darn it, you're getting me interested. If I'm not careful — but never mind me. What happened at the Freelock house?"

Don told her.

"Do you think this ghost and the spirit which told you to drill for oil are the same sort of thing?"

"I don't know. I suppose they have certain qualities in common — assuming that the spirits aren't merely telepathic transferences. Even then there might be a connection. It's another thing we'll be checking. So far I haven't gone into it deeply. Various regions of the world have their unique type of ghosts. Very odd, when you consider it. You'd think a ghost in Siberia would be the same as a ghost in Haiti."

"Unless, of course, they're all hallucinations."

Don nodded. "With that proviso, of course. The degree of evidence for English ghosts, for instance, is stronger than the evidence for Irish fairies. The were-wolf is confined to the Carpathians and Urals. Although there are were-tigers in India, Malaya and Siam, and were-leopards in Africa. Kobolds and trolls live in Scandinavia, duppies and zombies in the West Indies. The Onas of Tierra del Fuego knew a terrible thing called a 'tsanke'. Assuming that these supernatural creatures exist, or at least are seen — isn't this localization suggestive?"

"Of what?"

"You think about it."

Vivian Hallsey laughed. "Are you trying to make a new convert?"

"Why not?"

"All right. You've got one. But now I've got to write a story on all this. One more question: what will you call this research foundation?"

"There's only one name possible," Don told her. "The Marsile Foundation for Parapsychological Research."

VIII

Eight more wells were sent down to tap Marsile Dome, and owners of adjacent property who had given up options and mineral rights gnashed their teeth in frustration. Representatives of six major oil companies approached Don and Jean Berwick with propositions of varying attraction. After six weeks of study and legal consultation, Don and Jean sold out to Seahawk Oil on a cash-royalty-stock transfer arrangement, and at last were able to devote their time to the Marsile Foundation for Parapsychological Research.

But there were still other delays. The mechanics of organizing the Foundation were more complicated than Don and Jean had anticipated. To qualify for tax-exemption benefits the Foundation was incorporated as a non-profit research institution, capitalized at a million dollars. "At last," sighed Jean. "We can get started. But how? We still haven't decided on a thing. Not even on where to establish ourselves."

"No," said Don, thoughtfully. "An institution with such an imposing name deserves an equally imposing headquarters — something concrete and glass, spread out over an acre — but how we'd use it at the present time — I haven't the slightest idea…We'd better try to organize a staff, work out a systematic program, and then we'll know better what kind of facilities we'll need." He picked up a letter from the table. "We should get some help here. This is from the American Society for Psychic Research. They're interested in coordinating programs. One of their associates is coming out to see us."

"That would be fine," said Jean. "Except that we don't know their program. We don't even know our own."

"But now we get down to business." Don took a notebook and pen, then looked up as the doorbell rang. He jumped to his feet, opened the door.

"Hello," said Vivian Hallsey. "I was in Orange City and thought I'd drop by to see you."

"Professionally or socially?" asked Don. "Come on in, in either case."

"It's a social visit," said Vivian Hallsey. "Of course, if you've done anything spectacular, like finding an Abominable Snowman or making contact with Lost Atlantis, I'd find it hard to restrain myself."

"We're just shifting into high gear," said Jean. "Have some coffee?"

"Thanks. Sure I'm not bothering you?"

"Of course not. We liked your story; you didn't make us out to be typical Southern California crack-pots. We're just now trying to organize a sensible program for ourselves."

"Go right ahead. I'm interested. In fact, that's why I'm here."

"Well, our first problem is deciding where to begin. There's plenty of literature, thousands of case-histories, bushels of more or less valid research — but we want to start where the others leave off. In other words, we're not planning to duplicate Dr. Rhine's experiments, and we don't want to make Borley Rectory-type studies. The field is enormous —" The telephone rang, Jean answered.

"It's Dr. James Cogswell, from the American Society of Psychical Research. He wants to call on us."

"Fine. Where's he phoning from?"

"He's in Orange City." She spoke into the telephone, hung up. "He'll be right out."

Vivian Hallsey started to rise; Jean said, "No, no, don't go. We like company."

Five minutes later Dr. James Cogswell presented himself. He was sixty years old, a brain surgeon: short, plump, with coal-black hair, combed in precise dark streaks across his balding scalp. He wore elegant clothes; his manners were highly civilized. Don thought of him as representing the old-fashioned school of psychic research, a man who might have been colleague to Sir Oliver Lodge or William McDougall. Dr. Cogswell looked about with interest and a faintly patronizing air, which at first irritated, then amused Don. It was, after all, the natural condescension of a veteran for a group of enthusiastic, and undoubtedly naive, beginners.

"I understand that you plan to conduct a large-scale attack on some of our mutual problems," said Cogswell.

"That's our purpose."

Cogswell nodded. "Excellent. It's exactly what's needed—a well-organized, well-financed—I understand that you're well-financed?" He looked searchingly at Don.

"Adequately so," said Don. "At least for all present possibilities and contingencies."

"Good. We need a central agency, a permanent full-time trained staff working at a definite program. My own organization is loose and undisciplined; we're on our own so far as investigations are concerned. However we do have access to a large library, and perhaps I can save you some duplication of effort." He looked around the room. "Is this your headquarters?"

"Temporarily. Until we know what we need—which depends on our program."

"And what is your program, may I ask?"

"We were just hacking it out when you arrived."

"Am I interrupting you?"

"By no means. You can help us."

"Fine. Go right ahead."

"I was explaining to Miss Hallsey that we have no intent of duplicating either Rhine's work or performing any ghost-laying in the classic tradition."

"Good. I approve heartily."

"What we want to do is attack the basis, the lowest common denominator, of all parapsychological phenomena. The simplest, or most common, effect of course is telepathy. It's part of our everyday lives, although probably none of us are aware how much or how little we use it. Telepathy exists, it links minds. How? Action at a distance without a link — of some kind — is impossible."

Dr. Cogswell shrugged. " 'Impossible' is a big word."

"Not too big. Don't forget, Doctor, we're operating as scientists, not mystics. Axiom One: action at a distance is unthinkable. Axiom Two: an effect has a cause." He raised his hand to quell Dr. Cogswell's objection. "I'm familiar with the Uncertainty Principle. But doesn't it describe the limits of our investigative abilities, rather than the events themselves? We can't determine both the position and velocity of an electron simultaneously — but this does not presuppose that the two qualities are non-existent. So far as we know there is nothing to differentiate a stable radium atom from one which is about to disintegrate. To the best of our present knowledge the process occurs at random. But obviously, if we were able to compare the two atoms carefully enough, we could decide which was about to disintegrate. The lack is in our abilities, not the radium atoms. If they were exactly alike, if they were identities, exposed to identical conditions, then they must act alike."

"I fear," said Dr. Cogswell, a trifle pompously, "that your analysis is based on human experience. You reason anthropomorphically, so to speak. Consider the increment of weight as an object approaches light-speed. Such a concept is completely beyond our experience — yet it exists."

Don laughed. "Your analogy doesn't contradict me, Doctor. Remember, I'm not postulating that all events are determined by Newtonian physics. Light-speed physics works by its own determinants, so do sub-molecular reactions, and so do parapsychological events."

"Very well," sighed Dr. Cogswell. "Continue."

"We consider the varieties of parapsychological events: telepathy, clairvoyance, precognition, retrocognition, telekinesis, spirit action, poltergeists, house-haunting, sympathetic magic. With precognition and retrocognition, a sort of time-travel occurs. This aside, the phenomena all involve or occur in some sort of medium definitely beyond the sensitivity of our instruments. For the sake of the discussion, we'll call it mind-stuff. Super-normal continuum, if you prefer."

"Mind-stuff suits me," said Dr. Cogswell.

Don nodded, leaned back in his chair. "So, it appears that our first objective is this mind-stuff, or continuum. What is it?"

Vivian Hallsey said, "Heavens, we don't even know what our own matter consists of."

Don nodded. "Right. My question was rhetorical. I should have asked, how does it work? How is it related to our own matter?"

"What if there isn't any relationship?" suggested Vivian Hallsey airily.

"There *has* to be some relationship. The two states have too many qualities in common. Time, in the first place. Second, energy. Ectoplasm reflects light, and certain ghosts give off light. Anything which radiates or reflects light must have some sort of relationship with normal matter. Third, the fact that a great deal of parapsychological phenomena is generated inside an undeniably material brain."

"Very well," said Dr. Cogswell. "So much is clear. Objective — mind-stuff. And how do you propose to proceed?"

Don smiled. "If I wanted to learn something about Timbuctoo, how would I do it?"

"Go there."

"And if I couldn't go there myself?"

"Talk to someone who's been there."

Don nodded. "Exactly. To this end I'd like to locate a dozen effective mediums of proved integrity, who don't object to scientific checks and corroboratory measures."

"Ah," said Dr. Cogswell sadly, "wouldn't we all? There may not be that many in the whole United States."

"After you get the mediums, after you contact the spirits — what do you ask them?" inquired Vivian Hallsey. "And after they tell you, how do you check?"

Don said sadly, "That's our first problem. And it's a hard one. Don't forget, we still aren't at all sure that spirits exist. There's a strong possibility that the mediums are highly, if unconsciously, telepathic. We've got to rule out that possibility first. We want to determine whether a departed spirit can give first, information unknown to any human mind, living or dead; and second, information predicting an event in the future whose existence has been determined by pure chance, or at least by no human intervention, such as the fall of a meteor, a volcanic explosion, a sunspot."

"Or two or three daily doubles at Santa Anita," said Vivian Hallsey. "That's what I need."

Dr. Cogswell ignored her, rather pointedly. "Those are the classic problems certainly," he agreed. "Personally, I know of no experiment to prove beyond dispute the existence of spirit control. There is always some combination of telepathy, clairvoyance, precognition or retrocognition to explain any apparently inexplicable knowledge."

"I'd even be satisfied to learn the mechanisms behind telepathy, as a starter," said Don.

"How about ghosts?" asked Vivian Hallsey. "If you could authenticate ghosts, you'd prove the existence of spirits."

"Not necessarily," said Cogswell. "Ghosts are probably the imprint of emotion on the supernormal continuum — about as alive as 3D movies."

"But aren't there cases of ghosts acting with intelligence? Of responding differently to different circumstances?"

Cogswell shrugged. "Perhaps. I can't think of any authenticated cases offhand. The Clactonwall Deacon, perhaps. Or the Wailing Lady of Gray Water."

"Poltergeists," suggested Jean.

"Yes. Poltergeists, of course."

"There's one sure way to find out the truth," said Don.

"Die," said Cogswell.

"I think I'll be going," said Vivian, "before I get elected guinea-pig."

"Perhaps I should have said two ways. The second is to go there — and return."

Cogswell started to speak, then paused. Then: "You mean, counterfeit death?"

"Something of the sort. Isn't it possible to die and be revived?"

Cogswell shrugged. "There have been rather remarkable rumors out of Russia... And some remarkable work being done at the local universities with low temperatures. The body can't take organic damage, of course. If large ice-crystals rupture the cells — finish. Then there's the matter of keeping the brain oxygenated. Ten minutes without oxygen — a man can never get his sanity back. It's not an easy situation."

"In the case of low-temperature catalepsy, is oxygenation so important?"

"No, not nearly... In fact — well, I'll admit it. I'm involved in some of these experiments myself. We've frozen a dog stiff, and revived him after twenty-two minutes."

Vivian laughed. "Now all you need is someone to be Bill the Lizard!"

Dr. Cogswell raised his eyebrows. "Bill the Lizard?"

"A character in 'Alice in Wonderland'. He was persuaded to perform some investigations with disastrous results."

"These experiments are only the first phase, of course," said Don. "If the other world exists, perhaps we can set up channels of communication. Possibly even material transfer."

Dr. Cogswell shook his head in respectful, if somewhat dubious, admiration. "You have remarkable ideas, Mr. Berwick."

"It's a remarkable world we live in," said Don. "Consider the sciences: astronomy, bacteriology, physics. Think how fantastic the contemporary scene would seem to the early researchers! And the old ideas of witchcraft and sorcery — how vastly more marvellous is our new knowledge! Think where it's leading us, this knowledge. Our lives change every week — never the changes we expect. This work we're dabbling in now — it's the foundation of a new body of knowledge as important as all the rest together. The men of the future — they'll use the word 'spiritualist' as we say 'alchemist', 'astrologer'. What we'll accomplish —" he shrugged. "Who knows? Perhaps a great deal, more likely not. We'll be lucky if we stumble on a few of the right tools. Still — someone has to start. Astonishing that humanity has waited this long."

"Not astonishing, really," said Vivian. "The after-life, the hypernormal — they're part of all the superstitions, the religions, and therefore taboo."

"They still are," said Dr. Cogswell. "I care nothing for any taboos, except those of the American Medical Association. And there I've got to be careful." He rose to his feet. "Now I must go. If I can be of any help, let me know."

"You can put us in touch with a dozen effective mediums."

Cogswell shook his head doubtfully. "They're scarce as hen's teeth... Exactly how do you plan to proceed with a dozen mediums? What do you hope to prove?"

"Mainly, I just want to see what'll happen. We'll try simultaneous seances — the mediums separate, then the mediums together. We'll try to send messages from medium to medium through their spirit controls. We'll try for exact knowledge of the physical nature of this after-life region."

Dr. Cogswell shrugged. "It sounds interesting and very ambitious, but there are also difficulties. For instance, you'd need optimum performances from all twelve mediums at the same time — which in such an atmosphere would be extremely lucky."

"All we can do is try," said Don. "We'll never know otherwise. Maybe this shot-gun technique will open up the problem."

Cogswell rubbed his chin. "When do you propose to begin?"

"As soon as possible. We'll call it — Exercise One."

IX

The day for Exercise One approached, arrived. At three o'clock the participants began to arrive at 26 Madrone Place, a large old house on the outskirts of Orange City, rented for the occasion. First came members of the Psychical Research Society, observers from the psychology departments of local universities, Vivian Hallsey, with a somber-appearing man in a dark suit. She introduced him somewhat mysteriously to Don and Jean as Mr. Kelso. Don hesitated, then said, "Are you a journalist, Mr. Kelso?"

"Of a sort, yes."

"Our policy here is freedom of the press — in general. We see no reason why the public shouldn't be informed of any progress we make. But I do object to sensationalization, because it impedes us. It's difficult to persuade sensitive people to undertake these experiments. If they become notorious or the subject of ridicule, it's impossible."

"I quite understand," said Mr. Kelso. "However I'm here today unofficially, an observer, a friend of Miss Hallsey's."

"Then you're very welcome."

At five o'clock the mediums began to arrive, and were taken at once to separate rooms. The floors were bare; in each was a small wooden table, a couch and arm-chairs for the medium and the observers. Inconspicuous in each room was a microphone, the leads of which ran to a central bank of speakers and tape-recorders in the old living room, now known as the control room. Don had considered installing closed-circuit TV within each room, connected to a screen in the control room, but could think of no advantage to the scheme, and had abandoned it.

Of fourteen mediums approached, only eight had agreed to participate in the experiments. In general they seemed to be persons of average intelligence and education, ranging in age from Grandma Hogart, sixty-two, to her grandson Myron Hogart, eighteen. Myron showed a timorous excitement; Grandma Hogart's comments were caustic and skeptical; Alec Dillon held himself aloof — a pallid thin-featured man, austere and taciturn; Ivalee Trembath maintained her crystalline serenity. They showed little interest in each other — all except Grandma Hogart, who labelled the others frauds. To prevent friction and any possible collusion, conscious or unconscious, Don arranged that each medium be kept isolated from every other.

At seven o'clock the exercise was scheduled to begin; but Alec Dillon, unmarried, middle-aged, and temperamental, developed nervous attenuation and asked for time to gain composure. The delay irritated the others; there was grumbling. The exercise threatened to collapse even before it started. Jean and Dr. Cogswell scurried from room to room, apologizing, soothing, easing the tension.

Don sat in the control room tapping his fingers nervously, watching the signal panel, where seven lights signalled "Ready". Vivian Hallsey and Kelso sat quietly to the side. There was nothing to do but wait. Don turned to Kelso. "Are you interested in this kind of thing personally or professionally?"

"Both," said Kelso. "It's frequently crossed my mind that telepathy, clairvoyance, etcetera, would confer a significant military advantage on the nation which systematized them."

Don reflected. "I suppose so. I hadn't considered that aspect of the situation. You're not a government official?"

Kelso shook his head. "I work for *Life*. We recently ran a picture-essay on haunted houses. Did you see it?"

Don nodded. "Beautiful pictures."

Minutes passed. At seven twenty-five Alec Dillon sank with a sigh into his arm-chair, ready to summon his control: Sir Gervase Desmond. In the control room all eight lights glowed. Don hunched forward, eight intercom speakers in front of him; also eight microphones connected to speaker-buttons in the ears of the operators. By this means Don could give signals and instructions without disturbing the mediums.

Don spoke into a master microphone which took his voice to all the eight rooms. "We're all ready. Remember, there's no pressure on any of us. This is for fun. We're not trying to prove anything; we're not trying to check on anyone — so everybody relax."

From Room 2 came a resentful mutter; this would be Alec Dillon, who had a poet's aversion to exactitude and scientific method. If there were four firm contacts, thought Don, he'd consider Exercise One a success. Under conditions at 26 Madrone Place even four contacts would be remarkable. "Let's go."

He switched on the tape-recorders, leaned back in his chair, and prepared for a wait.

From Room 4, Grandma Hogart's room, came the sound of the Lord's Prayer; in Room 7 someone was humming a hymn; from other speakers came snatches of uneasy conversation, jokes, complaints.

Don waited. Jean came into the room, sat beside him.

"There won't be anything for five or ten minutes," Don told Vivian and Kelso. "They have to get in the mood to begin with."

"Any chance of materializations, ectoplasm, things like that?" asked Kelso. "I've got a Canon F1 loaded with Tri-X that'll take stop-action of black cats fighting in a dark cellar."

Don shrugged. "Never can tell. Have it ready, if you like. None of these mediums, so far as I know, have ever materialized anything. An honest materialization is rare."

"Can a spirit materialize without the help of a medium?"

"If you wait long enough," Vivian told Kelso, "you'll have all the answers on your own."

Kelso laughed grimly, "But I won't be able to sell the pictures. I might not even be able to have them developed…What about it, Don? Do these spirits ever materialize on their own?"

Don grinned. "I've never been a spirit; I couldn't tell you…So far as I'm aware — no."

"But ghosts — they seem to come and go as they please. And poltergeists."

"Ah," said Don. "A different matter. I'm referring to the class of spirits which communicate through mediums. Ghosts and poltergeists are two other classes. Three distinct classes in all — at least three classes."

Kelso looked puzzled. "Isn't that rather confusing? How do you know there are three classes?"

"They behave differently. The spirits — I'll use the word to describe influences operating through mediums — the spirits act and think more or less as we'd expect the spirit of a human being to act. Ghosts seem to be mindless affairs, imprints of a great emotional disturbance on the parapsychological matrix, which reveal themselves under certain conditions — what these conditions are, no one knows. Poltergeists — 'noisy ghosts' to translate — are invisible and mischievous. They occur principally in houses where adolescent children live — and it's possible that they're no more than an unconscious telekinetic process of the adolescent mind. That's just a theory — no more. Poltergeists don't seem to fit anywhere else into the picture."

"Listen," said Jean. A voice came from Room 3: the clear voice of Ivalee Trembath's Molly Toogood.

"Hello."

"Hello," said the voice of the Room 3 observer, a divinity student named Tom Ward. "How are you tonight?"

"Very well. I don't think I know you."

"No, we've never met."

Jean signaled to Don; young Myron Hogart's wire, the line from Room 8 was coming alive; his control was rapping on the table. Almost at the same time a whistle came from Grandma Hogart in Room 4.

"Hello, sassy," said Grandma Hogart. "You're looking pert tonight — all cute in your little pink dress."

"Yes, ma'am," said the piping voice of a little girl. "I'm all fixed up because I'm glad to see you."

"This nice young man is Dr. Cogswell," said Grandma Hogart.

"How-de-do," said the control. "My name's Pearl; I'm a little colored girl; I was born in Memphis, Tennessee."

The other speakers all began to sound; there was suddenly too much to listen to.

Jean said, in a hushed voice of astonishment, "They've all made contact — every one of them!"

Two or three minutes passed. Chatter, gossip, greetings, small-talk came from the intercom speakers.

Don spoke into the subsidiary mikes, those which took his voice to the operator's ear-buttons. "Now — first question."

They listened to Room 3, as Tom Ward, the divinity student, put the first of the rehearsed questions to Molly.

"What does it look like where you are now?"

The various responses came in over the speakers and were recorded on the tapes.

"Second question," said Don.

In every room except No. 3 the question was asked. *"Do you know Molly Toogood? Can you see her now?"*

The answers came in slowly, dubiously, and were duly recorded.

As a second part of the same question, in all the rooms except No. 2, the observer asked, *"Do you know Sir Gervase Desmond?"*

This was Alec Dillon's control; while the responses came in from seven rooms, Sir Gervase, a Regency Buck, criticized Alec in a nasal supercilious drawl. Alec, not completely in trance, defended himself, and they quarrelled until the amused observer intervened.

Listening to the quarrel, Don thought that the two voices of Alec and Sir Gervase mingled and spoke together; the tape-recorder would corroborate his impressions. An interesting situation: two voices coming simultaneously from the same throat, the same larynx! Of course the diaphragm of any loudspeaker performed the same feat with no difficulty. But the vocal chords, the glottal passages, tongue, teeth and lips constituted a sound-producing mechanism rather more complicated than a diaphragm...Don shelved the line of thought; it had become too involved, and there was too much happening. He must guard against a marveling frame of mind, he told himself. Everything that he was seeing and hearing, everything in this universe and every other, had some kind of logic — some system of laws, some cycle of cause and effect. It might be far removed from classical physics and ordinary human experience — but the laws must be there, available for human brains to codify.

In the eight rooms the talk was becoming desultory.

"Third question," said Don.

In each of the eight rooms the observer asked: *"What does our world look like to you?"* And after the answers were recorded, *"What does your medium look like?"* For the words 'your medium' the observer substituted the name of the medium.

Then the fourth question: *"Is ex-President Franklin D. Roosevelt present? Can you contact him at the present moment? What does he think of the present administration?"*

The fifth question: *"Is Adolf Hitler present? Is he happy or unhappy? Is he being punished for his crimes on Earth?"*

The sixth question: *"Have you ever seen Jesus Christ? Mohammed? Buddha? Mahatma Gandhi? Have you ever seen Joseph Stalin?"*

Then the seventh question: *"In the year 3244 B.C. an Egyptian scribe by the name of Mahnekhe died in Thebes. Is it possible to communicate with him? Is he present now?"*

The eighth question: *"Do you think of yourself as a soul? A disembodied spirit? A person?"*

The ninth question: *"How do you know when your medium is ready to make contact? Why do you respond?"*

The tenth question: *"Is there anything on Earth that you feel the need of? Can some living person bring it to you?"*

The eleventh question: *"Do you eat, sleep? What kind of food do you eat? In what kind of shelter do you sleep?"*

Twelfth question: *"Do you have a day and a night? Is it night or day now?"*

Thirteenth question: *"Does this type of questioning bother you? Are you willing to help us learn more about the after-life?"*

X

At 7:25 Exercise One began, with all eight mediums in touch with their controls. The questions were not necessarily asked or answered with consistent precision or timing. In many cases, the control chattered inconsequentialities, mumbled, refused to speak, or was otherwise uncooperative; there was no means by which the operator could enforce order. At Question 10 Sir Gervase Desmond, in a huff, left Alec Dillon, who fell into a deep sleep. At Question 11 Grandma Hogart's vitality waned, and her voice faded; little Pearl respectfully said farewell. After Question 10 only Ivalee Trembath, young Myron Hogart, Mrs. Kerr (a placid fat woman), and Mr. Bose (a thin Negro mail-carrier), still maintained contact with the other world. These four showed no signs of fatigue until after Question 13 and the end of Exercise One. The time was 9:45.

Room	Medium	Control	Identity	Apparent date of birth
1	Kenward Bose	Kochamba	*Senegal Chieftain brought to New Orleans as slave*	1830
2	Alec Dillon	Sir Gervase Desmond	*English Nobleman*	1790
3	Ivalee Trembath	Molly Toogood	*Early California settler*	1845
4	Grandma Hogart	Pearl	*Little Negro girl*	1925
5	Mrs. Kerr	Marie Kozard	*Parisian demi-mondaine*	1900
6	Mrs. Vascelles	Lula	?	?
7	Joanne Howe	Dr. Gordon Hazelwood	*Massachusetts physician*	1900
8	Myron Hogart	Lew Wetzel	*Fictional character* (?)	?

Grandma Hogart, Alec Dillon were asleep, to be joined at once by Mrs. Kerr; most of the others were relaxing with tea, coffee, beer or highballs.

Don and Dr. Cogswell stepped into each room, thanked the participants; Jean paid Mrs. Kerr, Grandma Hogart and Mrs. Vascelles their professional fees. Only Myron Hogart seemed interested in the results of the exercise; to the others it had been merely another seance.

By eleven o'clock the house was clear. Don, Jean, Vivian Hallsey, Kelso, Dr. Cogswell and Godfrey Head, a professor of mathematics at UCLA, gathered in the library. The mood was convivial; the mass seance had come off with a success beyond the hopes of anyone.

"Don!" cried Dr. Cogswell. "We've got to play back those tapes and do some computing."

"If you like," said Don. "We can work up Question One tonight."

The tape recorders were arranged in a row; the response to Question 1 was played back for each room in turn, and a list made of significant elements.

Question 1: *What does it look like where you are now?*

1. *Kochamba*: "White plains" — "golden ramparts, the host of the Lord" — "shining in the pearly light of our Lord" — "the golden towers, the lawns and flower gardens like the most wonderful park in the world, with statues of the angels, and everywhere the great glory of Kingdom Come." — "Off in the distance there's the lower-class places, but you can't see 'em so good, and not too far away there's Hell." — "No, Hell ain't down below — at least not too far down."

2. *Sir Gervase Desmond*: "Why naturally, it's the finest of places; would I be here otherwise? Everyone wears elegant clothes; the gentlemen and their ladies, I mean. It's like a great race meeting. No horses, of course, and nobody runs a book, more's the pity. But lovely, lovely, and all melting away into gold, and all the silver and pearly water; jewels for the taking, by Jove! Far too good for you, Dillon."

3. *Molly Toogood:* "Seems like it's all they're interested in nowa-
days. I told 'em once, but I'll tell 'em again: it's like your
Earth, only much prettier. Of course we can see the old land
anytime we want to look."

4. *Pearl:* "Now, Grandma, I don't know as I can describe something like this, because it's too superior and wonderful for
words. But we're all up here, all waiting for you; all the great
men and women, all doing what they like to do. It's really
pretty, all gold and green and off in the distance there's the
great Light of God, and his wonderful city."

5. *Marie Kozard:* (no reply)

6. *Lula:* "Lovely, dear — I know you'd enjoy it. There's all the
people, all walking around in balls of light, and the greater
the man or woman, the brighter the light. And the gorgeous
palaces, and sunrises and sunsets, like great peacock tails
everywhere around the sky." (In response to question: what
costume do the great men wear?) "Just the clothes they
always wore. There's Napoleon in his cocked hat and white
breeches, and there's George Washington — he's got pow-
dered hair; he looks just like the pictures."

7. *Dr. Gordon Hazelwood:* (no comprehensible reply)

8. *Lew Wetzel:* "It's hard to say, because it's hazy-like.
Everywhere you look, all the palaces and big buildings —
they melt off into the haze. When I first came here it was
different — there wasn't any of those big skyscrapers; it was
more Frenchy-like. Now there's all these big steel and glass
things and streamline things."

The first question was tabulated; the time was two o'clock. Don
sighed, opened a can of beer. "Let's see. What do we have?"

Godfrey Head looked down the list. "The consensus seems to be
that the after-world is a bright, beautiful land full of palaces and golden
castles, with people walking around in fancy clothes."

"There's quite some talk of haze," said Dr. Cogswell. "Horizons melting away — and here: Lula says the skies are like peacock tails."

"Why can't spirits take photographs?" asked Kelso, in deep pain. "Think of it: big picture-essay on the after-life. Think we'd sell that issue?"

"Another thing about Lula," said Don. "Notice how the people 'walk around in balls of light', but the great men are the brightest."

"Great men seem very much in evidence," mused Jean. "Still, it's really rather queer the different ways they see the after-life. There they are, all together in the same place — at least, so we assume — and each gives us a description similar, but just a trifle different, from the others."

"Well," said Godfrey Head, "we don't want to take everything literally; we've got to make allowances, to consider the subconscious coloring of the medium, reconcile the various points of view, take the lowest common denominator, so to speak."

Don drummed his fingers on his beer-can. "I'm not sure that I agree — completely. I don't think it's good practice to select only the consistent statements. If we ignore whatever seems unreasonable, we're not learning anything, we're merely building our own picture of the hereafter — not the one which these controls have given us."

"What about Wetzel's 'skyscrapers' — 'streamlined shapes'? Incidentally, who was Lew Wetzel? The name's familiar."

"A character in a novel. 'The Deerslayer', by James Fenimore Cooper, I believe."

Head leaned back in his seat. "Now this really demands consideration. How can a character in a novel have a spirit?... It hardly seems credible!" He looked at Dr. Cogswell. "Are you convinced of the lad's responsibility?"

"Perfectly."

"Perhaps under the strain — the feeling of competition..."

"No," said Dr. Cogswell. "I've heard Wetzel talk half a dozen times."

"He's really the character from the novel?"

"That's right. I asked him about it. He says whatever or whoever he is he's there, and he can't account for himself any other way."

"Of course," said Jean, "his character might have been taken from life."

"Yes, that's possible. In fact, highly probable."

"But what about these chromium skyscrapers?" cried Head. "Certainly we've got to exercise some selection!"

"We've got to be very careful," Don insisted. "We simply can't throw out items because they're inconsistent, or don't agree with *a priori* theories."

"But these people can't all be right!" protested Head. "We've got to decide on a reasonable consensus — that's our function, after all!"

"They might be speaking from different parts of this after-world. To me Wetzel's comment about the skyscrapers is highly significant. It might mean that the after-world changes as our own world changes."

"Or reflects this one," said Jean.

"Or that the after-world and the control is nothing but the medium's subconscious fabrication," grumbled Head.

Don nodded. "That's certainly our big headache. The next question was designed to shed a little light."

Jean read the question: " 'Do you know Molly Toogood? Do you know Sir Gervase Desmond?' "

"We'd still face uncertainties," Don observed, "even if the answers were all 'yes', even if Molly and Sir Gervase were described with great consistency — because we might hypothesize telepathic communication between the mediums."

"Certainly not an unreasonable explanation," said Godfrey Head.

"As I recall," said Don, "the question gave us very little information; no one seems definitely to know anyone else." He looked at his watch. "It's late...Shall we call it a night?"

Head and Cogswell agreed. They rose to their feet. "Incidentally," said Head, "have any of you been over to hear the Fighting Preacher at the Orange City Auditorium?"

"Not I," said Cogswell. "What about him?"

"Dill, from our Political Science department, took me to hear him. Dill is alarmed. He says this Hugh Bronny is an alarming phenomenon, a nascent Hitler. He's got a force, a gift of gab, no question about it. But I only mention him because he's attacking 'devil-inspired scientists who're fooling around with God's business!' He says that they're trying to produce life in test-tubes and also trying to sneak sinners into

Heaven. He says places like the Parapsychological Foundation ought to be stopped — by force, if necessary. He really means business."

Jean sat rather limp. "He mentioned us — by name?"

"Oh, yes. In fact, he singled out the Parapsychological Foundation."

"Anything to constitute slander?" asked Don lightly.

"He called you a Godless scientist, in league with the Devil. If you can show that he acted in malice and that your reputation is injured — you can sue."

"First," said Don ruefully, "I'd probably have to prove I *wasn't* in league with the Devil."

"Maybe we can take our stable of mediums to court," suggested Dr. Cogswell, "and materialize the Devil for a witness."

"There'd be difficulties swearing him in," Don remarked.

"That does it," said Head. "Good night all."

Kelso, Vivian Hallsey, and Dr. Cogswell took their leave immediately after.

Don turned to Jean, took her hands. "Tired?"

"Yes. But not so tired that —" she stopped short, staring across his shoulder. Don turned. "What's the trouble?"

"There's someone outside — at the window."

Don ran to the door, opened it, went out on the porch. Jean came out behind him.

Don asked, "Did you see his face?"

"Yes … I thought it was —" she could not speak the name.

"Hugh?"

She pressed against his arm. "I'm afraid of him, Donald …"

Don raised his voice a little. "Hugh! Why don't you come out, Hugh? Wherever you're hiding …"

A tall shape materialized. Hugh stepped out onto the gravel path. The street-light shone yellow in his great angular face; shadows filled his eye-sockets and the pockets under his cheekbones.

Jean said in a sharp voice, "Why don't you press the doorbell, Hugh? Why do you look through the window?"

"You know why," said Hugh. "I came to see with my own eyes what goes on at this house."

"See anything worthwhile?" Don asked.

"I saw evil men and women leaving this place."

Don said in a voice that was light and dry and edged, like sandpaper, "I hear you've been including us in your invective."

"I've been preaching the Holy Lord God's word as I understand it."

Don studied him a moment, his mouth set in a disdainful smile. "You may be a power-mad hypocrite, Hugh — or you may just be a plain fool. One thing you're certainly not — that's a Christian!"

Hugh stared back, his eyes like kettles of hot blue glass. He said in a heavy voice, "I'm a Christian minister. I walk four-square down the Holy Path. And no sneering atheist like yourself can turn me aside."

Don shrugged, turned to go inside.

"Wait!" commanded Hugh hoarsely.

"What for?"

"You spoke ill of me just now. You reviled me. You denied my Christianity —"

"Christ taught kindness, the brotherhood of man. You're no Christian. You're a demagogue. A rabble-rouser. A hate merchant."

Now Hugh grinned, a painful uncomfortable grimace that showed long yellow teeth. "You'll be sorry," he said simply. Then he turned on his heel, his feet crunched down the gravel path.

Don looked back at Jean. "Let's go home."

XI

Instead of driving home Don and Jean drove out on the desert, passing Indian Hill. Jean looked up toward the invisible hulk of the Freelock house. Don slowed the car. "Want to go up and hunt ghosts?" he asked, wanly facetious.

"No thanks," said Jean decidedly.

"Scared?"

"No, not any more. I'm not afraid of the ghosts: it's the atmosphere which hangs around the house…" She hugged his arm. "I can't feel unkindly about the place — because that's where I decided to marry you."

Don laughed mournfully. "You probably thought you were picking a nice normal junior executive."

"No," said Jean. "I knew you were nice and — well, sufficiently normal — but I knew you'd never be the sort of man to plump for security and routine."

"Didn't you give up hope when the exaggerated report of my death came through from Korea?"

"In a way... But somehow I couldn't believe it. I had a feeling you'd turn up."

"Like a bad penny... That was a tough three years. I think I was half out of my mind the whole time... Mmf!"

"What's the trouble?"

"I've forgotten all the Russian and Chinese I learned so diligently. I doubt if I could ask for a drink of water now..."

They turned off on a side-road, drove two miles into the dark desert, parked, got out of the car.

The night was clear and quiet; constellations rode across the sky, the air smelled fresh of sage and creosote bush.

"We should be in bed," said Don.

"I know." Jean leaned back against him. "But I wouldn't be able to sleep... Not after tonight." She looked up into the sky. "Look, Don: all the stars, and the galaxies beyond — and beyond and beyond. Could the after-life world be as enormous as ours?"

Don shook his head. "We'll have to ask the question at another mass seance."

"And where is it, Don? In our minds? All around us? Off in another dimension?"

"All we can do is guess. I don't believe it's inside our minds, or in another set of dimensions. At least no dimensions with any formal or mathematical relationship to our own."

" 'If it exists — it exists somewhere!' — to quote that eminent student of the occult, Professor Donald Berwick." Smiling, she looked up over her shoulder into his face.

"Right! Where that somewhere is, is the problem. Perhaps we'll have to go there to find out."

She turned around, faced him. "Now look here, Mr. Berwick — I don't want you toying with such ideas... Such as dying in order to make a personal investigation."

Don laughed. "No. I don't want to die for a while." He kissed her. "It's too much fun being alive…But maybe it might be possible to tiptoe along the borderline — during a period of extreme stupor, or unconsciousness. Even sleep."

"Donald!" exclaimed Jean. "Sleep! Dreams! Do you think — ?"

Don laughed. "It *would* be amusing, wouldn't it? If every night everybody made little excursions into the after-world?…It's not impossible, not unthinkable. Our dream-world certainly is a world of the mind. It's palpable, sensible — we feel, hear, see, taste. But dream-worlds —" he thought, laughed. "I was about to point out that dream-worlds are a function of individual experience, and couldn't possibly be the afterlife…Then I remembered the results of Question One."

Jean took his shoulders in her hands, shook him. "If the after-world is the dream-world, I don't want you going. Because some terrible things happen."

"Sure! But we always wake up safe and sound, don't we? But I'm not convinced of this dream-world — after-world equation. The dream-world shifts so rapidly."

"How do we know that the after-world doesn't behave the same way?"

"We have the answers to Question One. And other reports, in the books of Eddy, Stewart Edward White, Frank Mason. They — or I should say, the spirits they contacted — describe the after-world as Utopia — more beautiful, more glorious, more happy than our own."

Jean nodded. "That accords, more or less, with what we heard tonight."

"More or less. There are differences. Peculiar differences." He took Jean's hand, they walked slowly along the pale ribbon of road. "These men are honest and intelligent, and they've tried to be objective. Stewart Edward White's Betty, Mason's Dr. MacDonald, Eddy's — I've forgotten his name — Reverend something-or-other; they give pictures of the after-world which are similar but not exact. Their hows and whys differ considerably."

"I suppose we have to make allowances for the medium, the control and even the predisposition of the author."

Don agreed. "Another point: consider the curious way in which the after-life seems to keep pace with contemporary sciences; never ahead, sometimes behind. For instance, Dr. MacDonald, a spirit, is asked to treat the medium Bib Tucker. He prescribes herbs which are unknown at the time, but used sixty years before. Still, in 1920 when Mason asks him about the nature of electricity, Dr. MacDonald gives a contemporary answer — describes it as a phase of atomic energy. It's inconsistent and unconvincing — if we assume Dr. MacDonald to be a true spirit."

They stopped. Don picked up a stone, tossed it out into the dark. "If we think of Dr. MacDonald as a function of the author Mr. Mason, the medium Bib Tucker, and the other members of the particular group — he becomes more credible."

"You mean that this Dr. MacDonald is an illusion — that Molly Toogood and all the others are illusions?"

"No. I think that they're real enough. Actually, I'm only speculating. But perhaps they've been created, brought into being...This may be the way ghosts, apparitions, spooks in general appear. Enough people believe in them — and suddenly they're real."

Jean maintained a dubious silence. Don slipped his arm around her waist. "Don't like it, eh?" They started back toward the car.

"No," said Jean. "There's so much that your theory doesn't explain. The acts of free-will — like my father coming to us, telling us to continue drilling."

Don nodded. "True. But on the other hand, consider young Myron Hogart's control, Lew Wetzel. So far as we know, he never existed outside of a novel. Think of ghosts — the grotesque ones: the chain-rattlers, the women in shrouds, the luminous monks, carrying their heads in their arms. Isn't it reasonable to suppose that these are the concreted product of minds? It may be possible."

"Whatever they are," said Jean, "I don't really want to see any...I must admit, that in spite of my brave words, two-thirds of the time I'm scared as blazes...I suppose we should be starting back."

"Cold?"

"A little...It's not the air...Sometimes the work we're doing frightens me. It's so remote from normal life. And death has such a close connection with it. I don't like death, Don."

Don kissed her. "I don't either...Let's go home."

XII

Don, Jean, Dr. Cogswell, Kelso, Godfrey Head and Howard Rakowsky, met at 26 Madrone Place at eight o'clock the next evening. Cogswell introduced Rakowsky, a short dark man of forty-five, resilient and active as a ping-pong ball, as a fellow member of the Society for Psychic Research from San Francisco. Don inquired as to Rakowsky's personal theories regarding spiritualistic phenomena, as he did of most people interested in the subject.

Rakowsky shrugged. "I've seen so much I'm confused. Ninety-five percent is fake. But that hard five percent —" he shook his head. "I suppose I take it at its face value: communication from the souls of the dead."

Don nodded. "I'm a hard-headed Scot. I was skeptical until I had an experience that practically rattled my teeth. Our teeth, I should say. Jean and I saw a beautiful fiery ghost one night. I was startled enough to do some reading. I found lots of honest accounts — but none of them conducted under what a scientist would call test conditions. Our Exercise One the other night, so far as I know, is the first of its kind."

"You were confounded lucky," said Rakowsky. "Good mediums are gold."

"Not to mention cooperative controls," said Cogswell.

"We did pretty well," said Don, "even though we still proved nothing, in a rigorous sense."

Kelso blinked. "Surely you've proved some sort of post-death existence!"

"I'm afraid not," said Don. "In fact I'd like to discourage that particular emphasis. The average dabbler in parapsychology, when he strikes a bit of evidence, thinks he's proved that death isn't final; that he's demonstrated life beyond the grave. Being human, he's overjoyed. He doesn't worry about verification, or if he does, he interprets it to corroborate what he wants to believe."

Rakowsky had raised his black eyebrows. "You sound as if you yourself have doubts."

"I don't think it's proved," said Don. "Not until there are no more alternative, equally consistent, theories."

"I've heard lots of 'em," said Rakowsky. "By and large it's simpler to postulate an after-life. Especially," he glanced impishly around the room, "since that's what we all want to believe. Including Mr. Berwick."

Don nodded. "Including me." He turned to the tape recorders. "I'll give you another theory as soon as we finish tonight's work." He looked at his list. "Question Three: 'What does our world look like?'"

Berwick turned on recorder No. 1. The voice of the observer asked the question; the rich heavy voice of Kochamba responded, as different from Henry Bose's dry husky tones as honey from vinegar. "We have left your world behind," said Kochamba. "We rejoice up here at the feet of the disciples." He said no more.

"Now," said Don, "Sir Gervase Desmond, on No. 2."

"*Your* world?" drawled Sir Gervase in contempt and astonishment. "Well, I must say I haven't turned back a second glance. I assume it's still there — but I assure you, old fellow, I haven't a farthing's worth of interest. 'What do you look like?' There you have me. I've never thought to notice…Ugly chap, now that I look. Face like a sick lizard."

Molly, speaking through Ivalee Trembath, was kindlier. "Why, just as it's always looked. And Ivalee herself — why, I hear her pretty voice; it comes to me along the vibrations, as they say, and the first thing I know I'm talking with strangers."

Such was the pattern for Question 3.

Don paraphrased Question 4: "'Is ex-President Franklin D. Roosevelt there? Can you see him, feel him? What does he think of the present administration?'" He looked around the faces. "The reason for the question is obvious. We want to find if a number of the controls can contact the same man simultaneously — and if they can, if they bring back identical messages from him."

"Still proves nothing, one way or the other," Godfrey Head pointed out. "Nothing is proven until we can rule out telepathy. Which is hard to do, if not impossible."

Cogswell laughed. "If we ever turn up evidence that satisfies you — then we'll know we're on solid ground."

Head said doggedly, "We can't pretend to be scientists if we lapse into mysticism."

"I quite agree," said Cogswell ponderously.

"No argument on that point," said Don. "Well—let's listen to the answer…"

He played the tapes. The responses were confused. Sir Gervase Desmond damned Alec Dillon's eyes for his insolence; other controls mumbled and muttered; Ivalee Trembath's equable Molly said that she saw him once in a while, off in the distance, wearing a black cloak, usually sitting at a desk or in a chair.

"Is he still crippled?" the observer asked.

"He's a great man," said Molly. "Full of power."

None of the controls reported Roosevelt's opinion of the current administration, nor showed any willingness to inquire.

The remainder of the tapes were played back, the data organized. Sometime after midnight the job was finished. The table was littered with beer-cans, ash-trays were full.

Don wearily took up the compilation, leaned back in his chair. "In outline here's what we've got. 'Is Hitler in the after-world?' Yes. According to two reports he appears as a shape of great solidity. Apparently he's being punished. Kochamba says he's in good old-fashioned Hell. Wetzel says he wanders the outer regions like a lost soul."

"Contradiction," muttered Head.

"Unless part of the time he's in Hell, and part of the time he wanders," Rakowsky pointed out. "Not impossible."

Don continued. "Question Six: religious leaders. Jesus is seen sometimes as a light of great radiance, sometimes as a man of great stature. He's wise, kindly, a great teacher. Mohammed, Buddha are also there, and seen in much the same manner. Gandhi the same. Now for Stalin the arch-atheist. There's two versions of Stalin apparently. One benign—the other evil. The benign shape, according to that little fragmentary sentence of Pearl's, is fading, dwindling; the evil shape is growing more solid. He seems to be enduring punishment, like Hitler." Don looked around the room. "I consider this significant. In fact, with the answers to the next question, it corroborates a suspicion that's been growing on me…"

Rakowsky, Cogswell, Head and Kelso looked speculatively at him; Jean smiled faintly into her beer.

"Suspicion?"

"I have a theory regarding the after-life which I'll presently expound."

"Theories are cheap," said Rakowsky.

"There may be a critical experiment to test this one. Well—let's go on. The Egyptian scribe. No one knows him. No one can produce him—if we discount Lula's vague and rather facetious remarks.

"Eighth question. It arouses amusement in those who gave an answer. 'Of course we're persons! Just like you!'

"Ninth question: 'How do you know when the medium is trying to make contact?' It's just like someone calling their name, so say Dr. Gordon Hazelwood, Molly and Pearl. Sir Gervase just knows."

"Superior son-of-a-gun."

"Tenth question — they need nothing, want nothing." Don was scanning the compilation rapidly.

"Eleven. Now they're starting to fold up. We rely on Molly and Wetzel mostly. They say that they rest, sleep; that they have houses. Molly lives in an old ranch-house, Wetzel lives in a cabin; sometimes he camps in the wilderness. It seems that they live much as they lived in life on Earth. Eating isn't important — not a routine affair — but they seem to eat on occasion. Bodily processes they aren't clear on … Pearl giggles. Molly is shocked and offended.

"Twelve. No agreement. Apparently there's both darkness and light. Molly says it's always day. Wetzel says there's day and night. Marie Kozard says the time's always more or less evening.

"Thirteen: 'Does investigation annoy you? Is it wrong for you to answer our questions? Do you want to help us learn more about the after-life?' No clear response. Molly says it's okay; she'll help. Wetzel doesn't want to be bothered; Kochamba thinks it's bad."

"Too bad Joanne Howe isn't a better medium," Cogswell grumbled. "We could learn a lot from Hazelwood. He's the most intelligent one of the lot."

Don threw the compilations down on the table. "That's it."

"By and large," said Cogswell heavily, "an impressive mass of evidence. We've had excellent luck."

Rakowsky grunted. "It tells us nothing new… There's neither striking divergence nor agreement."

"Well," said Don, "I'm newer to this game than any of you — maybe a disadvantage, maybe not. It seems to me that we turned up all kinds of significant material — assuming, of course, that our mediums are honest."

Cogswell eyed him patiently, Head shrugged. Rakowsky said, "What's this theory you were talking about?"

Don settled himself in his chair, looked from face to face. "You've all read Jung, naturally?"

"Naturally," said Dr. Cogswell.

"You're all acquainted with the idea of the collective unconscious."

"Yes."

"Jung uses the term to describe the reservoir of human symbols and ideas. I want to expand this phrase to take in all of human thought, memories, ideals, and emotions."

"That's your privilege," said Rakowsky. "It's your theory."

"I suggest," said Don, "that the so-called after-life is identical to the collective unconscious of the human race."

XIII

The faces wore different expressions. Godfrey Head pulled his chin thoughtfully; Rakowsky blinked half-angrily; Cogswell's heavy mouth was twisted into a skeptical S; Kelso appeared saturnine and disappointed.

"In that case, you definitely presume the absence of an independent after-life!" said Rakowsky.

Don grinned. "I knew I wouldn't get any applause."

Cogswell said sourly, "Your 'theory' is on its face illogical."

Don's grin became a little pained. "This 'theory' explains spiritualistic phenomena without recourse to personal immortality. Does that make it illogical? Are we trying to delude ourselves? Or are we trying to get at the truth, no matter how cheerless it may turn out to be?"

"We want the truth, of course," said Rakowsky. "But so far —"

Cogswell interrupted. "I maintain that the simplest explanation is the best — the usually accepted theory —"

Head said impatiently, "Let's hear Mr. Berwick out."

They all looked at Don, faintly hostile.

Don laughed. "Any theory that doesn't go to prove after-life runs into trouble. Let's be frank with ourselves. Most of us can't swallow religious dogma — but we still want to believe in after-life. That's why we're mixed up in this kind of research. We're trying to *prove* something to ourselves — not disprove it. It's pretty hard to be dispassionate. But if we're not — if we don't lean over backwards, we're not scientists. We're mystics."

"Go ahead," growled Rakowsky. "Let's hear some details to this theory of yours."

"Hypothesis is probably a safer word. It makes a minimum number of assumptions, and it applies to supernatural phenomena the same rationale that we apply to the traditional sciences. We need no occult propositions about the 'purpose of life', 'the pre-determined direction of evolution', 'the Ultimate Unknowables'. We can approach the problem with dignity, as self-determined men trying to systematize a mass of data, rather than humble seekers after an off-hand revelation or 'divulgences'."

"A fine speech," grumbled Cogswell. "Go on."

"Just one minute," interposed Godfrey Head. "I want to say that I heartily agree with Mr. Berwick in one respect. I've read some of the psychic research literature and a lot of it rather turned my stomach. Other-world beings are always making statements like 'this much I have been instructed to tell you —', 'you are not ready to learn more —', 'you are hardly at the threshold of knowledge'. I've always wondered, if they had any knowledge to impart, why they didn't impart it."

"Betty White described what she called 'the unobstructed universe'," said Rakowsky.

Head nodded. "So she did — with ostentatiously difficult terminology and ideas which she assured Mr. White were very, very difficult — and which Mr. White dutifully found difficult. They're really not so difficult. When Mr. White asks after matters which Betty thinks he's not entitled to ask about, he's reprimanded and told to keep to the subject…Excuse me for side-tracking. But it's a characteristic of spiritualistic writing which has always exasperated me."

Don laughed. "Me too. Well, to proceed. What does the collective unconscious contain? First, the actual contemporary scene: our cities, roads, automobiles, airplanes, the current celebrities. Second, imaginary places or localities distant in time and place which we're all more or less acquainted with: Heaven, Hell, Fairyland, The Land of Oz, the Greece and Rome of antiquity, Tahiti, Paris, Moscow, the North Pole. Third, famous men, or rather, stereotypes of famous men: George Washington as painted by Gilbert Stuart; Abraham Lincoln as on the dollar bill — or is it the five-dollar bill? Fourth, the concepts, conventions, symbols of the racial unconscious — as distinct from the collective unconscious. The American unconscious is naturally a part of the greater unconscious of the race. In turn it's built up of smaller blocks. The California unconscious is different from the Nevada unconscious. The San Francisco unconscious is different from the Los Angeles unconscious. The unconscious of the six of us is different from that of six people next door. So — we have this fabric. From a distance it appears uniform — the collective unconscious of Genus Homo. As we approach, it becomes variegated, till at its limit we find the unconscious mind of a single man. When a single man becomes aware of a person, the person takes his place as an image in the man's unconscious. The greater the number of men that know this person, the stronger their feelings toward him, the more intense becomes the image.

"Imaginary ideas become a part of the collective unconscious — such as ghosts, fairies. The images intensify with belief, until finally, under certain conditions, even people who don't believe can see these imaginary concepts.

"When a person dies, he figures strongly in the minds of the people who have loved him. By virtue of their devotion and faith the unconscious image gathers strength; he materializes, sends messages, and so forth. But we've got to remember that the spirit image is only a function of the living minds who knew the dead person. It talks and acts as the persons still alive think it should talk."

"But look here," cried Cogswell, "there are a dozen authenticated cases of spirits giving information outside the knowledge of any living person!"

Don nodded. "I'm hypothesizing that the spirits — call them spirits for lack of a better name — that they act by the personalities the living persons endow them with. Let's assume that John Smith is bad, in a hundred detestable secret ways. No one knows this. To his family and friends he poses as a man of benevolence and generosity. He dies; he's mourned by all. Statues are erected to him; his spirit sends back messages. But do these manifestations show John Smith's covert badness? No — they only corroborate John Smith's overt goodness."

Cogswell shuddered. "You picture a situation as detestable and incredible as the character of John Smith."

Godfrey Head said with a grin, "Dr. Cogswell is equating 'detestable' and 'incredible'."

Cogswell started to sputter; Don held up his hand for peace. "We've got to be sure in our own minds why we're engaged in psychic research. If it's only to reinforce our hopes we'd better get out, go join a church. If we're after the truth —"

Cogswell was angry, his round face was red. "Your theory is interesting, Berwick — but it's too pat. It's unconvincing."

Rakowsky laughed. "Take it easy, Doctor. Berwick's idea isn't unconvincing — what he says makes sense — but it just isn't in line with facts."

"'Facts'?" asked Don. "What facts?"

Cogswell pulled at his lips. "Betty White has given us a very circumstantial picture of the after-life. The details she presented are — incontrovertible."

"Well," said Don, "I don't want to argue the matter exhaustively... However, one point in regard to the 'Unobstructed Universe' — Betty White's spirit spoke to White; but she spoke as the idealized version of Betty White. She described the collective unconscious only as White and his friend Darby conceived it."

"I must concede," said Rakowsky, "that there are other equally substantial accounts of the after-life — and that Berwick's theory has ingenious elements to it... But like all the other theories — it gives no foothold for verification."

"I'm not so sure." Don rose to his feet. "Suppose a person wanted to explore this collective unconscious, this after-life; how would he go about it?"

"The classic response is: die," said Rakowsky.

"After he's dead — then what?"

"Then he's there."

"True. But exactly as the people still alive remember him. He suffers whatever weakness and hardships they endow him with."

"I see what you're getting at," said Head. "For a spirit — call it a spirit — to function at the optimum in this presumable after-life, he has to be remembered as a person with optimum qualities."

"Right! Strong, intelligent, resourceful!"

Jean grinned. "He's got to be curious — so that he'll want to investigate. Also he must be endowed with the will to communicate back."

Dr. Cogswell struck his fist into his palm. "What about Houdini? He had all these qualities. He was well-known. But he never showed himself."

"It's a good point," said Don. "But I think it can be circumvented. How was Houdini known? What was his reputation?"

"He was known as an intelligent resourceful man, certainly."

"Yes," said Don. "But he was known as a profound skeptic — a man who claimed that spiritualism was 100 percent falsity."

"Well, yes."

"A few men and women expected to hear from him. The public was beset by Houdini's own skepticism. Houdini to this day roams the after-life as the eternal embodiment of skepticism, believing nothing, not even in his own existence."

Cogswell gave Don a look of grudging admiration. "You talked yourself out of that one."

Don said, "I'm not just giving glib answers. I'm trying to show that my theory can meet objections."

"It hasn't met all of them. Just what, concisely, do you plan to do?"

"I want to explore the after-life. That means, I want to explore the collective unconscious. No doubt dangers exist: bogey-men, dragons, demons, television horrors, all the stereotypes of terror. They may even be dangerous; I don't want to go as a weakling."

"Don!" said Jean softly.

"'Go'? What do you mean 'go'?" asked Rakowsky. "In the classic sense?"

"Good heavens no!" said Don. "I'm not planning to kill myself. I'm talking about heavy unconsciousness, drugged or otherwise. Of course there are methods to kill a body — to make it legally, finally dead — and then revive it. Dr. Cogswell knows more about the subject than I do."

Dr. Cogswell spoke with care. "These processes exist — but they're purely experimental. We've only killed and revived dogs so far; no human volunteers have been available."

Don said, "Naturally we'll try the least drastic methods first...Incidentally, would anyone else care to make the journey? I'm only putting myself forward from a sense of responsibility."

"The honor's all yours," said Godfrey Head. "At least, so far as I'm concerned."

"What's the best way for attaining a deep stupor, the metabolism just barely ticking, the brain inert?" Don asked Dr. Cogswell.

"There's a new anaesthetic — Calabrisol — which meets your requirements."

"Do you have any objection to using it?"

"No. None whatever. When do you wish to — go? Is 'go' the right word?"

"It serves the purpose. Do you think we could be ready as soon as next Saturday?"

"I'll be in surgery Saturday," said Dr. Cogswell. "It would have to be Sunday."

"All right, Sunday, then."

Kelso broke in. "I don't understand this. When you awake from the anaesthetic, do you expect to remember your experiences?"

"No," said Don. "Whatever is discovered must be reported through the controls of three or four of our most dependable mediums — Ivalee, Myron Hogart, Mr. Bose, Mrs. Kerr. If I am able to leave my corporeal body and wander around the after-world, perhaps Kochamba or Molly Toogood or Lew Wetzel will notice. I hope so anyway."

"It sounds interesting," said Kelso. "I suppose there's no way you could take a camera along?" he added hopefully.

"You think of a way. I'll take it."

Kelso shook his head helplessly. Dr. Cogswell said, "We'll have to make certain preparations...The hospital would be most convenient. But there I'd fear for my professional reputation..."

"Eventually the Foundation will own the proper equipment," said

Don. "But in the meantime if we can perform the experiment here, so much the better."

"It'll cost money," said Dr. Cogswell.

"No trouble there," said Don. "Whatever it costs, we're good for it."

XIV

At eleven o'clock Sunday morning all was in readiness. In three of the upstairs bedrooms Ivalee Trembath, Myron Hogart and Mrs. Kerr sat relaxed, eyes closed, trying to make contact with their controls. With them were Godfrey Head, Rakowsky and Tom Ward. On a couch in the living room Don Berwick lay, with Jean sitting close beside him. Contacts were fixed to his chest, wrists and neck; his respiration, heart action and blood pressure were registered on nearby dials. Dr. Cogswell had arranged his equipment around the room: various drugs, hypodermics, an oxygen mask, oxygen tank and the flask of anaesthetic. He had hired a professional anaesthetist for the occasion, a mystified young woman who was unable to understand why a healthy man wanted to be rendered unconscious on a fine summer morning.

"Ready?"

"Ready."

Vivian Hallsey, at the control table, flashed signals to the upstairs rooms. Dr. Cogswell administered the hypodermic; the anaesthetist applied the mask.

In five minutes Don lay inert. Dr. Cogswell sat beside him, watching the dials which registered his vital processes. Respiration was shallow and slow; pulse and blood pressure were low.

Vivian Hallsey grimaced toward Jean, motioned above-stairs, shook her head. Ivalee Trembath had failed to contact the dependable Molly Toogood; Mrs. Kerr's Marie Kozard was off somewhere on business of her own. Only Myron Hogart had entered a trance. He lay almost as quiet as Don, lips twitching, fingers jerking.

Godfrey Head spoke quietly, gently. "Is Lew Wetzel there, Myron? Can we talk to Lew Wetzel?"

From Myron Hogart's lips came a cackle of harsh gibberish. Then a deep easy voice laughed. "Hear that? That was an Injun talking."

"Hello, Lew."

"Hello, mister. You understand that Injun talk?"

"No, I'm afraid not, Lew. How's everything up above?"

"'Bout as always. Nice day today."

"Do you see my friend Don Berwick there?"

"Don Berwick. Scout, is he? Or trapper?"

"He's from my own time. He's a scientist trying to learn things."

"Don't see him around."

"I guess he hasn't passed over to you yet. He's unconscious now, and will be up there temporarily. Look for him."

"Can't be bothered with them off-again gone agains. Why don't he handle himself more carefully?"

"He wanted to see you. He wants to shake hands."

"He's welcome, he's welcome."

"Look around for him, will you, Lew?"

"Can't worry too much about him, mister," said Lew fretfully. "If he hasn't passed over, he'll be hard to find. It sucks all a man's vitality out of him living down there with you folks...Yeah, there's someone here. He's pale and wan — too weak to talk."

"Ask him what his name is."

"He says his name is Donald Berman."

"Donald Berman, eh? Are you sure?"

"Course I'm sure, you scalawag."

"It wouldn't be Donald Berwick, would it?"

"I've heard enough of you, mister, and your doubtin' ways. I ain't talkin' no more to you."

Godfrey Head pleaded and cajoled, but Lew Wetzel remained obstinately silent. Myron Hogart twitched, whimpered, gave a jerk, opened his eyes. "Did you talk to Lew?"

Godfrey nodded. "He came; we talked a bit."

"Learn what you wanted?"

"He was a little touchy today."

Myron sighed. "He gets that way sometimes."

In the other rooms Ivalee Trembath and Mrs. Kerr still sat. Mrs. Kerr sang hymns, but Ivalee was quiet. Their controls refused to appear.

Two hours later Don returned to consciousness, assisted by a few whiffs of oxygen. He lay looking up at the ceiling, deep in thought, then turned his head, searched the faces standing over him.

"Do you remember anything?" asked Jean.

Don frowned. "It's like coming out of a dream. There were shapes, lights. There was a face: a man with pale blue eyes. He seemed to tower over me, as if I were a child. He wore fringed buckskin...Lew Wetzel?"

Jean nodded. "He's the only one who came through."

"What did he say?"

"You tell us what you saw first."

"That's all. Except I seemed to fly...It's completely vague. Like last week's dream."

XV

"Well, we can't expect dramatic successes every time," said Don. "Today was just a teaser...Confound that Lew Wetzel! Donald Berman!"

The group sat at the back of the old Marsile house in Orange City. Charcoal glowed in the barbecue pit; steaks marinated in oil, garlic, herbs and wine.

Kelso asked Dr. Cogswell, "Do you think some other anaesthetic might work better? One of the hypnotics?"

Dr. Cogswell shook his head. "I'm sure I don't know. We're just prodding around in the dark."

"How about opium?"

"Opium? You mean — opium?"

"Yes. According to the lore, it turns the mind out to canter through flowering fields. Or perhaps mescaline?"

Dr. Cogswell shook his head doubtfully. "Opium and mescaline induce hallucinations, true, but the mechanism is purely cerebral."

Don sighed fretfully. "Doctor, how much effort would be involved in setting up a simulated-death tank at 26 Madrone?"

"Considerable effort, a great deal of money."

Jean turned away quickly, went to fork the steaks out over the coals.

Dr. Cogswell's eyes took on a thoughtful glint. "Our present equipment is obsolete. We've a dozen ideas which we'd like to introduce into a new system. However, funds are short, and my colleagues would be delighted if I reported that funds were forthcoming."

"Okay," said Don. "You can take over the old dining room and kitchen — make any alterations you like."

Kelso asked, "You're seriously planning to try this artificial death, Don?"

"I don't plan to check out the new equipment, no. I want to see it tested backwards and forwards. If they kill and revive a dozen dogs, a dozen primates, including a few orang-utans, I might take a chance."

Kelso considered. "Isn't there any other way, that doesn't incur any risk?"

Jean looked hopefully over her shoulder.

"You name it, we'll try it."

Kelso rubbed his chin. "If we could train a chimpanzee —"

Don snapped his fingers. "A question we should ask: 'Are there animals in the after-world?' Excuse me; what would we train the chimpanzee to do?"

Kelso shook his head. "Darned if I know."

Don turned to Dr. Cogswell. "How long will it take you to set up a new tank?"

Dr. Cogswell considered. "A month and a half — in that neighborhood."

"And allow another two months for testing — say a total of three or four months. Right?"

Dr. Cogswell nodded.

"We can put the time to good use," said Don. "Kelso, maybe you can help us out here."

"I'll be glad to try."

"Granting my theory, that the mass unconscious generates an afterworld in the matrix of mind-stuff, that the characteristics of a spirit are determined by his reputation; that notoriety and fame strengthen the spirit — conceding all this to be true, it might benefit me to be planted in the public mind as a man of ingenuity and effectiveness."

Kelso nodded thoughtfully. "In other words — you want publicity?"

"Of a certain sort: as much as possible. The public should think of Donald Berwick as efficient, resourceful, insatiably curious, given to traveling to strange places, with a faculty for emerging unscathed. They must think of him as a lucky dare-devil who always wins."

"Well, well, well," said Kelso. He ran his fingers through his hair. "I wouldn't dare work a hoax."

"You wouldn't need to," said Jean in a muffled voice. "If you just printed a few facts."

"Facts? About the Foundation here? I'd like to. I've been kicking myself for not getting pictures of the mass seance — which of course we could re-enact."

Jean shook her head. "I'm not referring to the Foundation…Tell him about your escape from the Chinese prison-camp, Don."

Don grinned sheepishly. "It's a long story. It'll take a while."

"Let's hear it."

"The steaks are done," Jean said. "We'd better eat first."

Over coffee Don self-consciously settled himself in his chair. "I'm warning you, this is wild. At the time it seemed perfectly normal, but now —" he shook his head. "Once in a while I look at the photographs just to convince myself. I'll just give you the outlines; if you think there's anything in it, I can fill in the gaps.

"Toward the end of the Korean War I was captured, and for reasons best known to the Chinese shipped to a camp in Manchuria, near a town called Taoan, along with ten other Americans. We weren't listed with the Red Cross, and were never repatriated after the war. I think we were intended for super-special brain-washing, with an eye to making secret agents out of us.

"I was a prisoner for two years. We were brain-washed pretty thoroughly. I knew that if I got bored, I'd be lost, and to protect myself I learned Russian and Chinese. Studied hard at it — nothing else to do. They were glad to help, thinking the brain-wash was taking hold.

"The two years were tough. Six of the fellows died. Two were killed trying to escape, three from disease and undernourishment, one from a disciplinary beating. One day a Russian colonel visited the camp. He looked a bit like me…To make a long story short, I killed him, hid the body under the barracks, walked out in his uniform. In his jeep I drove to a place called Tsitsihar, on a feeder to the Trans-Siberian Railway.

"By this time there was hue and cry. I ditched the jeep, bluffed my way aboard a west-bound train. I stayed aboard two days and a night — past Chita, to a place called Ulan Ude, near Lake Baikal. Near Genghis Khan's Karakorum, as a matter of fact. Here my luck ran out — I was having visions of riding into Moscow and strolling to the American Embassy. I ran into a colleague, and gave him the wrong salute. I jumped off the train, ran through the yards. They were hot on my trail — a Keystone Kops sequence, but not funny. I jumped into the cab of a locomotive, pushed a gun into the engineer's back, and hid while the search-party ran past. We started back down the line to Chita, the fireman and the engineer convinced they were goners. I knew at Chita I'd be in trouble — but I couldn't see any way out. Twenty miles out of town I tied the engineer and fireman hand and foot, drove the locomotive into Chita. When we reached the yards I throttled down to about ten miles an hour, jumped out, let the train make its own decision. A hundred yards farther it ran into a yard engine.

"Here the story gets confused. I'll merely say I was chased through the streets of Chita. I hid in a bordello, stole a suitcase and some civilian clothes, mingled with a group of eighty Russian engineers, on their way to Harbin in a truck convoy. I couldn't get away from them; I was put to work installing machinery in a cement plant. I knew nothing about it, but the foreman working under me did. I watched him work for three months, drew pay, then felt the breath getting hot on my neck.

"I stole a car, drove north to a town near the Siberian border — Kiamusze on the Sungari River. I hid aboard a barge, was taken to Tunkiang on the border. I stole a skiff, paddled across the river into Siberia, and rode a local bus to Khabarovsk. At Khabarovsk, after a month of intrigue, I managed to scrounge air passage to Sakhalinsk on Sakhalin Island. I walked south to Korsakov, sneaked on a fishing boat. When the fisherman appeared, I made him take me south. He set me ashore on Hokkaido at four in the morning. I went to the police station; they took me to an American Army camp. In brief," said Don, "that's the story."

Kelso asked in a hushed voice: "You're giving it to me free?"

"If it'll do any good. I've got a few photographs that I took along the way. It was a Russian camera, not too good, but — they're pictures."

Kelso examined the pictures. "If this doesn't make the Great Adventure series, my name isn't Robert Kelso."

"Wait till you hear the details," said Jean. "You've just got the outline."

Donald Berwick appeared on the cover of *Life* wearing a Russian colonel's uniform. He was depicted gazing at a wall-map of East Asia, the path of his escape-route marked in black. His stance suggested capable masculinity; his acute hatchet-faced profile gave the impression of incisive virility. *Lucky Don Berwick* read the caption. He conspicuously carried a Polaroid camera, an incongruous note on which Kelso had insisted.

"If there's anything in this wildest of all schemes," said Kelso, "I want pictures of it. You've got to appear in the after-life wearing a camera. Because I want pictures!"

"What good are pictures?" argued Head. "He can't mail 'em back."

"He's got to materialize. I want him to show himself, holding out photographs like a man selling postcards. I'll have a cameraman ready, and if Henry Luce doesn't weep for joy, I'll jump in the ocean."

"Will he dare print the pictures?"

"Could he resist?"

"Don't forget to emphasize somewhere that the camera is self-developing," said Don. "Also, that I always carry it loaded; otherwise it won't do any good."

Jean brought him the issue. "Here — look it over. You're famous."

Don groaned ruefully. " 'Lucky Don Berwick'."

"You should read the story."

Don turned to the article, read. "Oh, Lord...They make me out a combination of Mr. Moto and Tarzan."

"Excellent!" said Jean. "Just what you want."

Don looked up with an embarrassed grin. "I suppose it's what I was asking for. But now — I feel a fool."

"You've made an impression," said Jean. "Look. Here's an article in the *Orange City Herald* — about 'Lucky Don Berwick, local hero'!"

Don read the article, grinning and blushing. "Here I'm a high school athletic prodigy, a war hero, a student who just barely missed a Rhodes scholarship, a petroleum engineer of uncanny wisdom." He ran his hand through his hair. "I feel the pressure of this contrived personality... It's gathering weight!"

Jean put her hand on his, squeezed. "It's not really as contrived as you might think. You really are like that."

"Rats."

"The picture is exaggerated — but it's you. Also — look at this." She pointed to a column on the other side of the page. Hugh Bronny's face stared challengingly forth at Don.

EVANGELIST ENTERS
POLITICAL PICTURE

Bronny Declares for Governorship
"Christian Crusade" as Third Party

Hugh Bronny, evangelist, and leader of what he calls the "Christian Crusade", today announced his candidacy for the governorship of California. At a press conference called at his Orange City headquarters he displayed a petition which he claimed bore the signatures of a million voters — enough to arouse attention and respect from both Democrats and Republicans. "I plan to make old-fashioned Christian principle the basis of government," declared "Fighting Hugh" Bronny. "The Christian Crusade is marching to bring the nation back to the fundamental idea of God — a clean white American God. We'll sweep the state this year; in two years we'll send Christian Crusade Congressmen to Washington and in 1964 we'll have a Christian Crusade President in the White House!"

"The man's off his rocker," said Don.

"Surely there can't be any chance of Hugh *becoming* governor!" protested Jean.

Don shook his head. "I imagine there's still more sane people than lunatics in California."

"I keep thinking of Hitler," said Jean. "How the Germans voted him into power, on something of the same basis."

"Yes. It's a good analogy. Hitler appealed to the worst instincts of the Germans; Hugh does the same for us. 'Clean white God'!"

The doorbell sounded. Don went to the window. "Speak of the devil. It's Hugh!"

Jean started to the door, then paused. "What on earth can he want?"

"Let's find out."

Jean opened the door. With a laugh that was half-hysterical, she cried out, "Hugh — you've got a new suit!"

Hugh was wearing a double-breasted black coat with great padded shoulders, gray flannel trousers, long limp black shoes.

"What of it?" asked Hugh grimly. "I'm the next governor of the State, and I've got to look the part." He swung his eyes suspiciously from Jean to Don. "What's behind all this publicity you're getting? War hero! Fantastic saga of escape! It's dishonest."

"You're wrong," said Don.

"You mean to say that all that guff is true?"

"I mean that the facts speak for themselves."

"Come on," said Hugh scornfully. "Let's have some details. I've known you too long, Don. You can't pull the wool over my eyes."

"It's the truth," said Don. "Take it or leave it. Do you think they'd print anything they couldn't verify?"

"Humph!" Hugh snorted. "Aren't you going to invite me in?"

"Hugh," said Jean, "you get crazier every time I see you."

Hugh's eyes glistened. "You're talking to a very important man, sister dear."

"What do you want?"

"Well —" Hugh hesitated. "As you know, I'm entering politics. I need money — you've got money that belongs to me. I want it."

"It doesn't belong to you and you won't get a cent," said Jean.

"What do you do with all the God-given money?"

"We're planning to build a laboratory and research center."

"For your Foundation of Atheistic Blasphemy?"

"Call it anything you like."

"What are you doing with all those animals at Madrone Place? Dogs, monkeys, apes?"

Don asked, "How do you know about these things, Hugh?"

"I keep my eyes open. What are you doing with them?"

"We are developing a new medical technique."

"You're killing them and bringing them back to life!"

"How do you know?" Don asked suspiciously.

"As I said, I keep my eyes open. I want to know why you're doing this? Are you going to try this unholy game with a man?"

"Haven't you asked enough questions?"

Hugh lowered his great head archly. "Just friendly interest."

"You're no friend of ours."

"I'm friend to all men. All God-fearing clean-thinking men."

"I don't fear anyone. So you're no friend of mine. Perhaps you'll do us the honor of leaving?"

Hugh serenely inspected the cuffs of his glossy new white-on-white shirt. "I came to visit my sister and my old home — which is my right. I came here taking valuable time, to get some information."

"If it concerns money," said Don, "you've got it. You don't get any."

"I'll sue."

"On what grounds?"

"You admitted that it was my money."

"When was this?"

"You knew the oil was there. You asked me to accept half of the property, because you knew it was due to me."

"How did we know oil was there?" asked Don.

Hugh looked at him blankly.

Don said drily, "Evidently you concede that your father's ghost directed us to continue drilling."

"No," said Hugh without moving a muscle of his face. "Spirits of the departed worship God, or suffer in Hell. They do not concern them-selves in earthly affairs. And however you learned of the oil, the money is mine. And now I need it." Jean said slyly, "Surely a candidate for governor has better things to do than stand on front steps wheedling money from his sister."

"It's my money," said Hugh doggedly. "If you think you'll keep it with impunity — you're wrong. Because I will fight back. Do you think I am called Fighting Hugh Bronny for nothing?" He fixed them in turn with a blue glare, then turned, stalked away.

Jean watched him go. "He's a different person, Don…It's something to do with changing his clothes…He's important now."

Don nodded. "He's building his own niche in the collective unconscious. Fighting Hugh Bronny…Let's go over to Madrone Place."

They drove across town, to the old frame building. From within came sounds of activity. An electric drill whined, a power-saw rasped through wood.

Don and Jean entered, walked through a new metal door into a large bare bright room. White-enameled cabinets lined one wall; opposite were oxygen tanks, an iron-lung, high-frequency electrical equipment. Through the floor came pipes, leading to a refrigeration unit in the cellar. A long glass-walled tank rested on a stainless steel box in the center of the room.

Don nodded to the tank. "There it is. Ferry to the after-world… What did Charon call his boat? Cerberus? No, that was the dog."

Jean's fingers were clenching his arm. Don looked down at her with a wry grimace. "What's the trouble?"

"I'm worried."

"It's Hugh. He's upset you."

"He's a maniac!"

"I suppose he is…Sometime I'm going to take an hour off and try to visualize the world as he sees it." He looked through a door into the next room. A man wielding an electric drill at the instrument panel nodded. He was about forty-five, round-bodied but sturdy, with a blond forelock hanging into his eyes. He finished drilling, came into the outer room.

"Doctor Clark," said Don, "I didn't expect to see you installing your own equipment."

"Just a small refinement," said Dr. Clark. "Everything's working beautifully — better than we had hoped."

"Then there's no danger?" asked Jean anxiously.

"No fatalities since our first two days. Last night we held a chimpanzee under for an hour and a half. She's bright as a dime this morning."

"Then we're ready to roll on the big one," said Don.

Dr. Clark nodded. "We're ready to roll."

Don peered into the tank. "Make it comfortable, Doctor — I've a long way to go."

XVI

The room was the same; the night was two weeks later. Nine men and three women sat or stood in their assigned positions.

Doctors Clark, Aguilar and Foley stood beside the glass-walled tank. Godfrey Head, Howard Rakowsky, Kelso, Vivian Hallsey and a cameraman sat in chairs to one side of the door; to the other sat Jean and Ivalee Trembath. Doctor James Cogswell stood by the foot of the tank and with him was Donald Berwick.

Don wore a blue terry-cloth bathrobe. His face was composed but the skin at his jawline shone pale. He turned his head, met Jean's eyes. He smiled, muttered to Cogswell, crossed the room, took her hand.

"I can't help but worry," she whispered.

"There's nothing to fear," said Don. "The technique has been practiced on dogs and chimpanzees till they can do it in the dark."

"I've heard that when men return to life, they're not always — sane."

"Nothing like that's going to happen."

"Another thing — that article in today's paper. Won't it prejudice some people, alter the archetype?"

Don shrugged. "Perhaps, perhaps not. It makes the archetype more exactly me. It focuses a lot more attention on me, from people who before paid small attention…"

At this moment Fighting Hugh Bronny stood in the Orange City Auditorium, reading the article to seventeen thousand rapt followers. He leaned his gaunt body forward over the podium, spoke with the sly breathless relish of a dog stealing garbage. As he read he raised his head to glance across the auditorium. To his eyes the scene appeared as an over-exposed photograph — burnt by glaring lights, marked by shadows and smoky air, and the mosaic of pale faces was blurred, out of focus. He no longer thought of the audience as human beings. They comprised a unique substance, malleable as candle-wax, but with a responsive fiber that stimulated and excited him like a bath-brush on his long bony back.

Fighting Hugh Bronny read in triumph. He finished the article. The audience was silent; Hugh could sense the seventeen thousand pulsing hearts, the prickle and minuscule multitudinous shine of thirty-four thousand eyes. He felt a great glow of power. These people were waiting for him to tell them, to lead them; he could fix and form their minds, whip them back and forth like a fisherman dry-casting.

"I'll read the article again," said Hugh in a throaty voice. "And as I read, ponder the audacity of these hermetic imps." He looked around his audience, raised his voice to oboe pitch. "These atheists." He peered into the blur of faces. "These nasty vandals, breaking a way even into God's own Heaven." He paused. Even the sibilant sound of breath and stirring cloth had stopped. There was as deep a hush as is possible when seventeen thousand people gather under a roof hung with bright lights.

Hugh's voice dropped an ominous octave. "If your blood doesn't boil like mine — then never call me Fighting Hugh Bronny, and never call yourselves Christian Crusaders."

He bent his head over the clipping and read.

LUCKY DON BERWICK
TO PLUMB PSYCHIC REGION
by Vivian Hallsey

Three months ago Lucky Don Berwick was a man known to comparatively few people; today his name is on everyone's tongue. Wherever men and women get together, chances are they're talking about Lucky Don Berwick. Now comes news of an adventure to pale all the fabulous exploits in Berwick's fabulous life — if it works. Tonight at nine o'clock Donald Berwick will be killed. By every medical and legal definition he will be dead. His heart will be still. His lungs will pump no air. There will be no sign of life in Berwick's body; there will be no spark of life in Berwick's body; he will have passed beyond.

At nine-thirty Drs. Cogswell, Clark, Aguilar and Foley of Los Angeles Medical Research Center will attempt to revive Donald Berwick by techniques conceived during World War II, improved upon, and now perfected. At ten o'clock it is hoped that Lucky Donald Berwick will be lucky enough to be once more alive.

What is the purpose of this experiment? Hang on to your seats, ladies and gentlemen; this is a jolt. Donald Berwick has volunteered to undertake the most daring exploration of his existence (although it's a journey all of us must make). He will endeavor to bring back a report on the land beyond the grave, if there be any.

Hugh looked up, carefully crumpled the clipping into a ball, cast it away with a gesture of revulsion.

"There, Christian Crusaders, you have it. You say with wrath in your hearts, God will punish these men. I say to you, God will certainly punish Donald Berwick and his kind! He has sent me —" Hugh became suddenly magnificent; he soared to his full height, an arm stretched high; his voice was a trumpet. "He has sent me! He has sent me as his strong right arm!" And in Hugh's voice was the sudden certainty, and every heart felt a pang, every throat contracted, gulped for air, expanded in a great guttural moan. "He has sent me! — and I will lead! — first against the Devil's Imp Berwick! — then against the vile forces that seek to befoul and destroy this dear America of ours! I can't tell you, go to 26 Madrone Place, make your wishes known. I can't urge you — as I might wish — to tear that cursed haunt of evil stone from stone. No! They'd say I was inciting you to riot! I can't say that! No, brothers! All I can say is that's where I'm going! Now is the time for Christian Crusaders to ask themselves to enforce the will of God. By fighting? Or by reading in the papers of blasphemy and sacrilege? The address, brothers and Crusaders! 26 Madrone Place. I will be there!"

XVII

Don looked at his watch. "Time grows short…I suppose I should be more alarmed, but I'm not." He grinned. "Just another dull evening."

Head said drily, "You're starting to take the exploits of Lucky Don Berwick seriously."

Don grinned. "It's hypnotic; I can't help it. The synthetic personality is taking me over." He caught Jean's half-alarmed glance, laughed. "I'll resist it."

Clark and Aguilar were giving the tank a final cursory inspection, looking without seeing, since the entire apparatus had been checked and re-checked during the day.

The cameraman walked here and there, taking photographs.

Don glanced around the faces, meeting the eyes that watched him with covert speculation. "Everybody looks comfortable." He prodded Cogswell's plump ribs. "Cheer up, Doctor. After all, it's me that's being killed."

Cogswell mumbled unhappily. "Do you think there'll be time for materialization?"

"I'll do what I can."

Dr. Foley touched Berwick's elbow. "Come on, Lucky; take the dive."

Don slipped out of the bathrobe. He wore the Russian colonel's uniform to identify himself as completely as possible with the archetypal image of himself in the mass mind. A Polaroid camera hung around his neck; at his hip, a holster held a .45 army automatic.

"Take a good look," said Don. "And remember — Lucky Don Berwick! Concentrate on it! The 'Lucky' part especially." He stepped into the tank, stretched out.

Foley started a timer; Clark and Aguilar gave him intravenous injections in the right and left thighs, then the right and left shoulders. At one minute Foley threw a switch; motors under the tank began to whine. The glass was quickly frosted, Don's shape became indistinct.

At two minutes Clark and Aguilar repeated the injections, while Foley clamped a soft band around Don's wrist, looped a metal ribbon around his neck. Dials on the panel indicated pulse and body temperature. The pulse indicator quivered, sank: 60, 55, 50, 45; the temperature gauge hovered at 98.6 for thirty seconds, then began to dive. When it hit 90 degrees Foley threw in another switch; the motors below the cabinet sang.

Don was now unconscious. His pulse sank swiftly: 20 — 15 — 10 — 5…It quivered to a stop. The temperature gauge began to plummet: 80° — 70° — 60°. Dr. Clark and Dr. Foley reached into the tank, flexed

Berwick's legs, arms. The temperature dropped: 50° — 40° — now far below room temperature.

Dr. Aguilar worked a knob; the motor sound declined in pitch. The temperature gauge moved more slowly, came to a halt at 34°.

Drs. Foley and Aguilar slid a glass cover over the tank, Clark opened a valve; there was a sound of pumps.

Dr. Cogswell turned to the spectators. "At this time — he's dead. The pumps are drawing the air out of his lungs; the tank will be refilled by an atmosphere of nitrogen."

Foley reached through a port, rubber gauntlets over his hands. He put a bracket against the waxy temples, pressed contacts against various parts of Don's close-cropped scalp. Aguilar watched a dial muttering, "No — no — no...No — no — nothing. No activity." Cogswell turned to the others. "He is now dead."

Kelso said, "Okay to take pictures into the tank?"

Dr. Cogswell nodded shortly.

Kelso motioned to the photographer.

Jean was looking at Ivalee Trembath. "Can you get anything?"

Ivalee shook her ice and silver head. "No...Not in here. There's too much infringement — disturbance."

"Want to leave the room?" Rakowsky asked her.

"Yes, please."

Rakowsky and Jean took her to one of the upstairs bedrooms. Suddenly conscious of noise, Rakowsky looked out the window. He touched Jean's arm. "The street — all of a sudden it's full of cars."

The cars crowded bumper to bumper along the street, glowing-eyed black fish. They roared and groaned and choked to a halt. The doors opened; men and women with twisted faces squeezed out, struggled and sidled to the sidewalk. They started to chant — off-key, off-beat. The tune suddenly emerged.

"Listen," said Jean.

"'Onward Christian Soldiers,'" said Rakowsky.

Jean shuddered. "It sounds weird — music from the future...What are they doing here?...A convention? A gathering?"

"A demonstration," said Rakowsky.

"An attack," said Ivalee Trembath.

The voices rose into the night, the faces looked up, pale as clam-shells. A tall figure, larger and more definite than the faceless crowd, stalked to the door.

Rakowsky muttered, "I'm going to call the police."

Hugh's bony knuckles echoed on the door. "Open up, open up, in the name of the Lord God Most High. Open this cursed door!"

Jean suddenly snapped out of it to find Ivalee's hands clutching her. Ivalee was crying. "Jean! Jean! Don't!" Jean had a heavy earthenware vase in her hand; the window was open in front of her. She stopped struggling, put down the vase. "What a horror!" she whispered. "I would have killed him…"

The knocks were sounding again. "For the last time!" blared Hugh's voice; then the door swung open. Godfrey Head's calm quiet voice rose up to them.

"I have called the police. You're disturbing a delicate scientific experiment. I advise you to leave before you get in serious trouble."

"Anti-Christ!" crackled Hugh's voice. "Stand aside." He put a great hand on Head's thin chest, pushed. Kelso stepped out on the porch. Hugh attempted to thrust him aside. Kelso swung a bony fist into Hugh's mouth, sent him reeling off the porch.

From the distance came the eery moan of sirens. It seemed to stimu-late the crowd, to heighten their mood.

Hugh staggered around, faced them. His mouth oozed black blood, his shirt was befouled. "They have drawn my blood! In the name of my blood, forward! The time is now! Such a great fire we will kindle to carry us across the world! Onward, you Crusaders, you soldiers of Christ! With fire and sword — onward!"

The crowd roared, surged. Jean caught a horrifying glimpse of Godfrey Head being yanked by his necktie, flung down from the porch, disappearing under the dark rush.

An enormous baby-faced young man with side-burns wearing a leather jacket charged into the hall, clamped Kelso's arms; they fell heavily, Kelso on the bottom.

Hugh stalked forward, kicked. The young man jumped up, kicked too, again and again with booted feet.

Hugh looked about him, majestic, flaming-eyed. "Fire and sword!"

came the cry behind him; and a woman who looked like a consumptive stenographer began keening "Onward Christian Soldiers!" And the baby-faced young man yelled, "Kill the devils! Kill the atheists!"

At the foot of the staircase, the cameraman snapped pictures — one, two, three — then prudently retreated down the hall. Hugh ignored him. The four doctors came forward, so cool and inquiring that Hugh was momentarily taken aback.

"Will you kindly get that beastly mob out of here?" asked Dr. Aguilar testily.

Rakowsky marched forward. "I'm placing you under arrest. If you attempt to escape, I'll shoot you."

" 'Escape'?" roared Hugh. "Stand aside!"

The doctors were disconcerted; the authority which served in hospital and laboratory had failed; they suddenly became ordinary men. They fought.

In the living room there was a sudden crackle, a roar and babble of voices. Hugh sidled against the wall, fended off Dr. Aguilar with one great hand. Jean met him at the door; he slapped her face, backward, forward; she staggered back.

Hugh stood a moment in the doorway. Cogswell, his face twisted by fear, lurched forward. "Go away, get out of here!"

Hugh looked contemptuously from Cogswell to the tank. Donald Berwick lay cold, impassive, dead. The dials showed no pulse. The temperature was 34°.

Jean stood with her back to the tank; Ivalee Trembath gripped a chair to one side; to the other Dr. James Cogswell stared at Hugh like a hypnotized frog.

"Get out of here, Hugh," whispered Jean. "I'll kill you..."

Hugh's eyes blazed. "No one can stop me...I am the new Messiah!" He took a step forward. Cogswell, screaming hoarsely, charged. Hugh swung his long lank arm, slapped Cogswell's red cheek. Cogswell thumped to the wall, slid down to the floor. Hugh stepped forward.

Jean ran around behind the tank. Ivalee swung the chair. Somebody behind Hugh fended it off.

Jean slid back the glass cover, seized the automatic from Don's holster; the cold stung her hands. She aimed it, pulled the trigger.

Nothing happened. Hugh laughed. He reached under the tank, heaved. The tank was bolted to the floor. Hugh grunted foolishly. Jean looked at the automatic, frantically fumbled, threw off the safety. She aimed. Hugh raised his foot, kicked. Glass tinkled. Hugh reached, seized Don's cold arm.

Jean fired. The bullet struck Hugh's shoulder; he flinched, but seemed to feel no pain. He tugged at Don. With a sliding rush the body slid out on the floor.

Jean took a step forward, aimed, fired. Hugh clutched his abdomen in surprise. Jean pulled the trigger, firing steadily. Hugh's knees sagged. Blood suddenly spouted from a hole in his neck. His knees buckled; he toppled like a stricken mantis. Jean aimed her gun at the faces in the doorway, the shapes behind Hugh. They scuttled and ducked like beetles.

"Jean," said Ivalee, "the house is on fire."

"Fire!" came a cry from the hall. Ivalee went to Cogswell, tried to pull him to his feet. He lay limp, his breath coming in stertorous gulps. There was a shuffle in the hall, a curious lull. Then a sudden terrified sounding of feet, a scream, not so much of pain as terror.

Ivalee ran out into the hall; Jean saw the flicker on her face. For an instant the silver of her hair and ice of her face were alloys of gold. She turned back to Jean. "We can't get out the front."

Jean ran to the body of Donald Berwick. She knelt beside it, rubbed the cheeks. They were cold and damp from condensed moisture.

"Jean," said Ivalee gently, "Don is past all that."

"But Iva — we can do something — we've got to do something… The doctors — they could revive him…"

The flames poured into the room, bringing clouds of smoke. "We've got to get out of here," said Ivalee.

Jean looked down aghast at Don's body. "Can't we — can't we —" she began in a tired voice.

Ivalee lifted her to her feet. "We can't help him now, Jean…"

"But — he's really alive, Iva…The doctors can bring him back to life! It's so horrible! I can't abandon him!"

"He's dead, Jean…The doctors could bring him back to life in the tank…With the right timing and their drugs…Don is dead, Jean. And so is poor little Cogswell."

"Dr. Cogswell — *dead*?"

"Yes, dear. Come, we can't stay any longer…"

By force she dragged Jean out into the hall. Sheets of flame blocked the way to the front door, and filled the rear hall.

"To the second floor," said Ivalee. "It's our only chance."

They ran up the stairs, pursued by hot smoke, stumbled into the front bedroom. Ivalee went to the window, while Jean leaned against the wall, numb with grief.

"The street is full of cars," said Ivalee. "The firemen are bringing hoses in from the corner. Listen, the mob is still singing. They don't know that Hugh is dead."

From one end of the street to the other the voices quavered, swelled in a chant of triumph. Jean tottered to the window. "Can we jump?"

"It's too far," said Ivalee.

Searchlights played on the house. Firemen hauled hoses down the sidewalk, running, shouting, pushing people aside. The nozzles were dry; no water came. The firemen turned, looked back along the line in rage, dropped the nozzles, ran back along the hoses.

"The service stairs," said Jean. "Maybe they're still open."

They ran to the rear of the house. Behind them a gust of flame roared up the main staircase. Jean opened a door on the service stairs, closed it quickly on the wave of flames and blast of smoke.

Ivalee went to the back window, a heavy old stained-glass piece, tried to open it, without success.

"We're worse here than we were up front." They turned, looked back down the hall. The main stair-well acted as a chimney; flames were consuming the upper bannisters.

Jean picked up a chair, threw it at the stained glass. It broke, but lead held the pieces together. The air was very hot, and rasped their throats. Smoke seemed to seep from her lungs into her blood, into her brain. Vision swam in Jean's eyes, her knees began to sag.

Behind her she heard a sound, felt a blast of cool air; she felt a strong arm. She looked up. "Donald!" She could not hold on to her senses. Slowly she fainted; and when she awoke, it was four hours later, and she lay in the emergency hospital with Ivalee Trembath in the next room.

The nurse had no information to give her.

Three o'clock the next day she and Ivalee Trembath were discharged. They took a taxi to the old Marsile home across town. Two reporters were waiting. Ivalee sent them away; they were alone.

Jean stood, hollow-cheeked, dry-eyed. She said, "Iva — just before I passed out — I saw him. Donald. Alive."

Ivalee nodded. "He carried us out."

"But how? He was — dead."

"I saw him too…" Ivalee sat down in a chair. "Let's see if we can find him — or get news…" She covered her eyes with a scarf.

Newspapers throughout the United States ran an account of the fire at 26 Madrone Place. The headlines read:

LUCKY BERWICK

RUNS OUT OF LUCK

ENDS CAREER IN RELIGIOUS RIOT

Sometimes in the same story, sometimes in a different column the death of Fighting Hugh Bronny was reported:

> Members of the Christian Crusade revel in an ecstasy of religious excitement. Only an hour before his death Hugh Bronny exhorted his followers: "Rally to the Crusade; I am the new Messiah!"
>
> According to the Reverend Walter Spedelius, Hugh Bronny's passing follows the Christ-pattern. "Christ died to show humanity its sins; Hugh Bronny died to lead us out of the mire to purity. He was a great spirit, a saint, a prophet, and we shall follow him in death as we did in life."

XVIII

Donald Berwick lay down in the tank. He felt the weight of the camera on his chest, the mass of the automatic at his side. Overhead were the faces of Clark, Aguilar and Foley. He turned his eyes, glimpsed Jean through the glass. Then he felt the sting of the hypodermics, the clamp of the gauges. The motors whined below him; the air suddenly grew cold. He closed his eyes. When he tried to open them, he could not — already his muscles were numb.

He felt life leaving him, like the tide receding from a shallow shore. He felt chilled, then suddenly warm and numb; then for a last transparent interval, freezing cold, through and through. Feeling left him and he died.

He had no feeling of leaving, no sensation of drawing away from his old frame. That was far away, and everything pertaining to it. Another phase of Donald Berwick existed, and it seemed always to have been. Now it came into its own.

From a new and strange perspective, Donald Berwick looked around the room. There were other shapes present; after a moment he recognized them. They were diaphanous, and stood swaying like seaweed, their feet anchored in small man-shaped pellets. One small cold pellet lay near his own feet, quiet and detached: the old Donald Berwick.

The new Donald Berwick felt a pang of pity, then took stock of himself. He had memory; he recalled the whole of his life, including fragments and details forgotten alive. Suddenly he realized there had been a great oversight in his preparations. Building the archetype "Lucky Don Berwick" in the collective unconscious, he had ignored a prime source of power. Who could know Donald Berwick with greater intensity than Donald Berwick himself? He examined his form: the uniform, the gun, the camera. All there. Wrist watch on his wrist. He examined it. His own watch the brand of which had never been publicized. Here was a measure of the difference between the strength conferred upon him by others and the strength derived from himself. He compared watch and camera. The camera was harder, brighter, solider. Twice as hard, thought Berwick. Such was the measure.

Jean — he picked out the supple waving shape that was Jean. Her eyes were on him. This was Jean: composite of her own unconscious and that of all who knew her. Different in small ways from the Jean he knew, but not greatly... Ivalee Trembath: her ice and silver composure was less noticeable; her mouth was soft and wistful. And the others — but later, later. First a picture to test the dream-camera. He set the aperture, aimed, snapped the shutter. Now — we'll quickly look over this after-life country — then back … How did time go? Fast or slow? He looked at his watch. The hands waggled, spun back and forth … Well, thought Don, evidently it's whatever time I think it is … Now, I'll step out into the street …

The walls went dim; he moved his feet, he stood in the street. It looked much as he recalled it; cars moved like phantoms, in and out of his vision unless he concentrated … The street was suddenly full of cars.

Don thought, now — up! If I am a thought, I travel like thought! And he passed through walls and floated in the dark sky. Below was the city; around him in all directions spread the carpet of lights … But this was not the city of reality; this was the composite of a myriad imaginations; the lights glowed softer, like crystal balls; the distance melted into nothingness.

If I'm a thought — then north! And mountains were below him, clad in dark pines, and ahead was a granite ridge, white and gray; and strangely it was early morning; Berwick stood on a peak and looked to all four directions.

China! He felt no movement; he was a thought; he was in China. This was not the China of reality, it was the composite China, the stereotype, or rather, the paradoxical set of stereotypes that made up the collective unconscious: the drabness of Communist China, the splendor of the old empire. He remembered his camera; he pulled the tab, looked at his first positive. Fair. Not bad. He tucked it into his pocket.

He set the aperture, photographed a pagoda, a comic-opera rickshaw. In the background were the hazy mountains and graceful willows of old Chinese paintings. Below he could see other faces and shapes.

He thought himself to the ground. This was the old Bund, in Shanghai. He willed himself to see it; suddenly it took form and full solidity. He stood on the street. A coolie in flapping blue denim trotting toward him, halted, stepped aside, looked back.

Hey, thought Don, I have materialized … It seems easy … I'll return to Orange City and materialize at Madrone Place.

He thought: up. Drift slowly. Over the Pacific … He spied the moon. Should he dare? But of course, it was now his nature; he was Lucky Donald Berwick, who dared anything!

He thought: moon. And he was on the moon. Faster than light, as fast as thought. He stood on a silver and black plain; a scene from an imaginative painting.

He pulled the China photograph from the camera, aimed his camera at the moonscape. It occurred to him to wonder about his organic processes…Was he breathing? He felt pressure in his chest; then suddenly he materialized; he stood on the stony reality of the moon's surface. His skin pulsed, his eyeballs bulged, cold struck up through the soles of his shoes. He had time for a brief thought: he was already dead; where would he go now when he died?

He let himself drift back into the unconscious. And the moon became the unconscious stereotype…Don scanned the sky. Mars!

Quick as thought, faster than light!

He stood on a dim red desert, the thin wind hissing past his ears. The sea-bottoms of ancient Barsoom? He turned his head; there in the distance was a ruined city — a tumble of white stone, a movement of the weird hordes of green warriors. He looked again; there seemed to be tall nodding vegetables behind, like dark dandelion fluffs… He took a picture, then thought of the canals…He stood beside a wide channel full of gray water. Ah! thought Don. It was proved! The canals of Mars did exist! He laughed at his own foolishness…All in the mind, all the collective unconscious. Was he on Mars at all, or was he merely a thought? He concentrated his attention; he stood on cold dry sands, under a black brilliant sky; and this was Mars indeed. How had he arrived? Were mind and universe one? Was the "real" world only another place of unreality, with mind and matter interacting and co-generating, like a man lifting himself by his boot-straps?

He glanced at his watch. What time was it? He had stepped into the tank at 9 o'clock. The hands read 9 o'clock. He had surely been dead ten minutes…The hands read 9:10. Or had it only been a single minute? And the time was 9:01. The time was whatever he chose it to be. Very well then. Back to Earth. At this rate there would be ample time for exploration.

He was in space, diving for Earth — a glorious sensation of freedom! Don sang in exultation. It was fun to be dead! Earth — lovely familiar old Earth. There it was, laden with its two billion souls!

Was it Earth, or was it a thought?…For the first time it occurred to him to wonder: where were all the other souls? The spirits of all the dead? The angels? Jesus Christ? Mohammed and his houris? And he vibrated up into a fantastic golden land, flowered with white clouds. There indeed walked radiant winged beings, and there indeed, off in the distance, was a shining city of glass and gold; and there indeed was an effulgence, a blinding bright figure with a merciful face... Only an instant. Then an instant of a great garden, with lawns and flowers and marble pavilions, rows of cool cypress and poplar, turbaned shapes sipping sherbets, sublimely beautiful maidens... Don thought, there is no false religion; whatever Man believed, that was; whatever stage of abstraction Man could conceive, he could attain... Religion was, God was. But they were functions of Man; the mind of Man was the Creator.

Where was Molly Toogood, Ivalee's control? And the wandering spirits of the dead?... He saw Molly, a pleasant-looking woman: perhaps not as bright or hard as he was. She nodded. He sensed other shapes, flimsier than Molly. Where was Art Marsile? He looked around him, and — wonder of wonders — he stood in front of the old Marsile home under the pepper trees. He walked up to the door. Art looked out. "Hello, Don. I been waiting for you. Got time for a chat?"

Don looked at the house, half-expecting to see Jean come running out, blonde and fresh and pretty. "No," said Art. "She's not here, Don. It's not her time yet. Maybe you'd better go check. There's trouble down there. Hugh as usual."

A flicker of thought. Don stood on the porch of 26 Madrone Place. In the street were numerous pellets of human beings, with their souls attached like frail balloons. All except one. Don recognized it: Hugh Bronny. Bronny's soul was tall, broad, and glowed with fiery intensity. The pellet of Hugh Bronny came up to the house; the soul — call it a soul, for lack of a better word — looked Don in the eye.

"Go away," said Don.

The soul opened its mouth, but the pellet squeezed shut the natural channel of its brain, ignored the message, knocked on the door.

Don thought himself into the laboratory. He watched while the Hugh Bronny pellet marched into the room; he tried to speak to the lovely wraith anchored in the Jean pellet, but she was too absorbed and upset.

The pellets moved, like shining quicksilver. He examined his body.

Dead — but with the potential for life. He tried to slip his feet back into the cold pellet, but there was no purchase; he slipped away.

The Hugh Bronny pellet destroyed the Don Berwick pellet. Jean's wraith shimmered and twisted. Her body pellet seized the gun.

Don heard the shots as dull clicks, stones tapped under water. Hugh's soul seemed to bulge, to sparkle, to take on mass. It was a monstrous ominous presence — it looked like Hugh, but it was strong and tough and muscular. The face was Hugh's face as Hugh must have conceived it: hard, fervent, unyielding.

The Hugh pellet was dead. The Hugh Bronny soul was free. It came toward Don. They looked eye to eye an instant.

Hugh reached out his powerful arms; Don knocked them aside. The contact was solid, but elastic, like two pieces of heavy rubber colliding.

Hugh moved off, and was gone. Don looked back to the house. It was in flames. The men who had worked with him — where were they? Cogswell — "Hello Doctor," said Don to the pale soul which stood beside him. "I see you're dead."

"Yes," said the soul of Dr. James Cogswell. "It's very easy, isn't it?" The soul looked Don over with a trace of surprise. "My word, you look hard and strong! It's amazing."

"We worked enough for it," said Don. "Lots of people believe in me."

"Not too many believe in me!" said Cogswell in wonder. "Yet here I am!"

"You believed in yourself, didn't you?"

"Yes, of course."

"That's the most important."

"Interesting," said Cogswell. "This is a most fascinating place. Well, I must be off to explore."

"See you around," said Don.

The house was in flames. The wraiths of Jean and Ivalee Trembath shifted, as Jean and Ivalee ran around the house.

Jean's wraith looked at Don beseechingly.

"Of course," said Don gently. He dropped low, stood inside the room. He concentrated, materialized.

The women were drooping like flowers at twilight. The fire crackled behind him.

Jean raised her head, looked into his face with vast surprise. He lifted her — how light she was! — went to the window.

A problem! He was now a material body, and subject to the material laws of gravity... He could no more descend the thirty feet to the ground than could Jean.

Don thought himself to the roof. He materialized, tore down the ancient radio aerial, lowered it past the window, let it hang.

He materialized again inside the room, and now the smoke was thick. He wrapped Jean and Ivalee with drapes from the windows, looped the aerial first around Jean's body, lowered her to the ground. He thought himself down, released her, repeated the process with Ivalee Trembath. Then he carried the two of them through the back entrance to the alley.

He motioned to a man driving past in a car. The man ignored him. Don materialized in the seat beside him. The man's jaw dropped, strangled words came from his throat.

"Stop the car," said Don. "There are people hurt back there."

The man gasped out his acquiescence. Don put the two women in the back seat.

"Take them to emergency hospital."

"Y-yes, sir."

Don relaxed his clutch on reality, expanded away into the after-life.

XIX

The police jailed as many Christian Crusaders as they could identify; the next day they were fined $100 apiece, lectured by the judge and released. Tramping out of the court house they defiantly broke into their hymn, *Onward Christian Soldiers*.

The Reverend Walter Spedelius attempted to rent Orange City Auditorium, but was turned down. He called a mass-meeting on the farm of one Thomas Hand, at the outskirts of the city. And there in a great square framed by eight bonfires, the Reverend Spedelius took up Hugh Bronny's torch.

"Verily, brothers," he cried in the brassy sing-song monotone of the evangelist, "our brother Hugh lived and died like a Christian saint — like a crusader of old! He gave all his earthly life to show us the way — just as many years ago Jesus Christ, yea, Jesus Christ, did the same — and brothers, I say unto you, Hugh Bronny, Fighting Hugh Bronny, is here with us tonight — and I say unto you, brothers, we won't let him down — we'll fight in the name of Jesus and Moses and the Prophet Elijah and the Prophet Hugh Bronny — and we'll fight till we bring the Kingdom of God to this wonderful land of ours …"

The Christian Crusaders were news; reporters and photographers were on hand, and the papers and news-magazines throughout the United States announced the new crusade. Segregationists, anti-Semites, America-Firsters thronged to ally themselves with the movement.

The opposition stirred. A dozen liberal organizations denounced the movement, editorials appeared in the great newspapers, bitterly critical of Fighting Hugh Bronny, Walter Spedelius and the Christian Crusade. In the tumult Lucky Don Berwick was almost forgotten. He was no longer news.

XX

In the region beyond time, Donald Berwick lived and moved. He became aware of a tug, a pull; and since he was no more than a thought, dwelling in the massive composite of all the thoughts that ever were, he responded.

Ivalee Trembath was calling him. She and Jean sat in the living room of the old Marsile house.

Don looked into the face of the swaying soul that stood with feet anchored in Ivalee's body-pellet. The soul spoke, "Release me, Donald, and take my place for a while, and I'll roam; and when you want to leave, I'll be back …"

It was strange speaking with Ivalee's mouth, hearing with her ears. Sight and muscle coordination, at the moment, seemed impossible.

"Hello, darling Jean," said Don.

"Hello, Don. How are you?"

"I'm very well. Things over here are just as we expected. I've got pictures for Kelso."

"Don — I miss you terribly."

"I miss you too, Jean …"

"You helped us out of the fire. You materialized."

"Yes."

"Is that hard?"

"It wasn't then. I was at the height of my intensity. I'm not so strong now."

"I don't understand, Donald."

"I don't either. The stronger I am, the easier it is for me to materialize."

"Are you weaker — because people aren't thinking about you so much?"

"Yes. I believe so. More or less."

Jean's voice quavered. "Then Hugh must be very strong."

"Yes," said Don. "I've seen him. He glows with strength. You'd never recognize him."

"Is he — as wretched as he was on Earth?"

"He's different. He's as evil. But the smallness, the petty detestable part of Hugh has dwindled. Hugh is now something magnificently evil."

"What happens when he sees you?"

Don paused, then said matter-of-factly. "He tries to kill me."

"Kill you!"

"Sounds odd, doesn't it? I'm already dead. But that's how it works."

"How can he kill you? You're immaterial — a thought!"

"A thought can drown another thought out; reduce it to oblivion, make it something furtive and despised."

"Hugh is trying to do that — to you?"

"Yes."

Jean was silent a moment. Then: "You know what's going on down here?"

"Not altogether. I've been — out, away."

Jean explained, and Don was silent for several minutes.

"Don," said Jean diffidently, "are you still there?"

"Yes. I'm thinking."

There was another minute of silence. Jean sat tense, watching the limp form of Ivalee, her hands twisting and knotting a ribbon.

"Jean."

"Yes, Don."

"The battle is between a pair of ideas. Hugh represents one, I represent another. I must fight Hugh. Kill him. Kill the idea of Hugh."

"But Don — are you strong enough?"

"I don't know."

"How can you fight?"

"Just as on Earth. Tooth and nail."

"If you lose — will I ever see you again?"

The voice was fading, indistinct. "I don't know, Jean. Wish me luck. I can see Hugh now... He's coming."

Ivalee Trembath twitched, mumbled, then lay quiescent.

There was a sudden roar in the room, like a train passing through. The roar subsided to a rumble, faded.

"Iva," said Jean gently. "Iva."

No response. Jean listened. The air was very still, but seemed to be stiff and it crackled like cellophane.

Jean slowly got to her feet, went to the telephone.

Hugh Bronny stood over Donald Berwick. They were on a featureless expanse, a plain without end; it might have been the Ukrainian Steppe, or the perspective of a surrealist painting.

Hugh was wearing his black double-breasted coat. His enormously muscular arms filled out the shoulders. His eyes blazed like electric arcs, his face was the size of a shield; his legs were knotted with strength.

"Donald Berwick," said Hugh, "I've hated you in life and I hate you here in the after-life."

"You could not help but hate me," said Don, "because you're the personification of hate — here as you were on Earth."

"No," said Hugh, "I was a great religious leader; now I am a saint."

"Words can't conceal facts."

Hugh took an ominous step forward. "I will expunge you, you miserable sick pap-mouthed chicken."

Jean telephoned Godfrey Head. "Godfrey — I must see you."

"Sorry, Jean, can't make it... I'm bound for a meeting of the Faculty Association. Two of the University Regents have become Crusaders; can you believe it?"

"Godfrey — I've just talked to Donald. He's fighting Hugh Bronny right now. We've got to help him."

The telephone line buzzed with silence. Then: "Help him? How?"

"Let me come with you to your meeting…I take it you're all anti-Bronny?"

Godfrey Head snorted. "Naturally. But what can you do?"

Jean laughed bitterly. "I'm several times a millionaire. There's a lot I can do."

Hugh snatched out, caught hold of Don's shoulder. Fingers dug into flesh like tongs into a bale of hay.

A sword, thought Don, and he held a sword. He swung, hacked; the blade clanged against Hugh's neck. Hugh reached out his other hand, seized the blade, snatched it from Don.

"I will chop you to small atoms," he chanted, "I'll smear you into smoke, I'll blow your memory out of time…" He lashed out with the sword. Don sprang back; the blade hissed past his chest, leaving a red groove.

He thought sword, and held in his hand another sword.

Hugh bellowed out a gust of mocking laughter. He took a stride forward, lashing with his sword.

Godfrey Head diffidently addressed assembled members of the University Faculty Association.

"A friend of mine wishes to speak to the meeting. I want to warn you in advance: be prepared for a surprise. What you will hear may strike you as unprecedented and unsettling. But, remember, we presume ourselves an intellectual elite, and we've got to shoulder the responsibilities which go with the status — or else admit ourselves to be fast-talking four-flushers." His mild face glowed; he glared at the surprised audience as if they had challenged him.

"This meeting was called to establish a position in regard to the Christian Crusade. What Jean Berwick will tell you bears on the subject." He motioned Jean up to his side. "This is Jean Berwick. Listen carefully to what she says, and think carefully, because I think a time has come for us, and all other intelligent people, to make a choice."

Jean stood up on the podium, frail and intent. "My name is Jean Berwick. My husband Don Berwick died recently, in what might be called the first armed aggression of the Christian Crusade. He is dead, but he is still fighting — in spirit." She smiled wanly. "In spirit, he needs our help.

"I have a proposal to put to you — one of far greater scope than any of you had expected to hear tonight. Why do I come to you? Because you are the first large group of influential and intelligent people I could reach, and because you understand the implications of the Christian Crusade. I want to crush the Christian Crusade, grind it into oblivion. It is not enough to jail one or two demagogues; the Christian Crusade is an idea. We must organize a counter-idea, stronger and more inspiring, to smother it.

"Exactly what is this so-called Christian Crusade? It is hate, enforced conformity, authoritarianism, race bigotry. Are the Crusaders Christian? They make a rite of submission to a malignant and vengeful God, who rewards his friends like a ward-boss and sentences his opponents to torture in Hell. Christ would turn away in disgust from this God. What is the counter-doctrine? A crusade for human dignity and the right — the obligation — to non-conformity, as passionate as Bronny's crusade for his orthodoxy! A declaration of independence from religiosity, the assertion that men are masters of their own destinies. These are the issues: human values against superstition; pride and confidence against humility at the feet of idols, real or imaginary; civilization against barbarism; faith in man against faith in theosophical dogma.

"What do I expect of you here tonight? I want you to rise to the challenge that our knowledge of right and wrong has set before us. I want you to endorse the manifesto I have outlined, to set it as a standard to which proud and intelligent men and women can rally.

"We are on the verge of space; already we can tap unlimited energy. There is the outer threat of Communism, less dangerous than this internal threat symbolized by the Christian Crusade. These are problems and opportunities. How shall we meet them? With the mill-weight of the past around our necks? Or as proud, indomitable, self-reliant men of the future?

"What is your answer? If you're with me, clap... If you're not —" she smiled. "Then you can hiss."

She waited. There was ten seconds silence, in which the churn of minds was palpable; honest enthusiasm tugging at conventional caution.

There was a sudden sound of clapping. It grew in volume. It filled the hall.

Jean relaxed against the podium. "I am not speaking to you. I'm not an orator. It's Donald Berwick speaking through me. If Hugh Bronny symbolizes the past, then Donald Berwick is the symbol of the future."

Hugh laughed at Don. "Strike. You cannot cut me. Your sword is dull."

Don looked. The sword had turned to dull gray pewter. He saw a glint, ducked. Hugh's blade whistled over his head.

Gun, thought Don, and he held his .45 automatic.

Hugh's sword became a monstrous revolver, shooting yellow projectiles the size of hand-grenades.

Don aimed, fired.

There was discussion. A brisk sharp-featured man said, "Do you propose that we issue a Manifesto of Atheism? We can't do that. There are many Christians among us, as well as Moslems, Jews, a few Buddhists, Orthodox Hindus — in addition to the free-thinkers, Unitarians, agnostics, and atheists."

"No," said Jean, "I don't ask you to endorse atheism, or any other belief. Because I don't know. There's an elemental mystery to the universe: the why of things. Everyone is free to speculate. I speak not for atheism, but against compulsory theism, or compulsory dogma of any kind."

"I see. In that case you have my whole-hearted support."

Godfrey Head addressed the chairman. "I move that we adjourn the meeting, that we immediately convene as the Society for Intellectual Freedom — with the purpose of drafting the Declaration Jean Berwick has proposed."

Don pulled the trigger of his gun. The bullet smashed into the barrel of Hugh's great weapon. The projectile buzzed past Don's ear, exploded somewhere behind.

Hugh sprang forward, they grappled. One enormous arm circled

Don's throat. Hugh pressed his weight against Don, trying to force him over backwards.

Don swung up a desperate fist, struck Hugh on the nose. He felt the cartilage crush; then Hugh's weight pushed him back. He landed with a bone-shaking jar. Hugh's hands went to Don's throat.

"I'll tear your head off," hissed Hugh. "I'll strip you arm from arm..."

The Society for Intellectual Freedom became known to the nation; to the world, on the following day. It was bitterly attacked by certain of the organized religions; by the Christian Crusade in particular, and hailed with joy by people uneasily aware that anxiety and uncertainty had driven them to accept doubtful dogma.

And who was Jean Berwick? The wife of Lucky Don Berwick — who had been killed resisting the Christian Crusade!

By a tremendous racking effort, Don threw Hugh off him. They rose to their feet, stood facing each other. Hugh had lost something of his over-powering confidence, but he was possibly more ferocious. Don grew larger, more solid.

They both glowed with a cool blue light. The background had shifted; they stood in a valley between two ranges of low black hills.

"Hugh," said Don, "I could kill you with my hands... But I prefer to demolish you with my mind."

Jeffrey Hannevelt, President of the Unitarian Association, executive chairman of the Society for Intellectual Freedom, told reporters, "We could take Walter Spedelius, Casper Johnson, Gerald Henrick to court — we might get them indicted for conspiracy. But that's not enough. We've got to discredit them. We're modern men, in charge of our own destiny. We're moving into a new era of civilization, setting up a whole new culture-pattern. It's up to us how it'll turn out. How do we want it? The kind of world men dream and hope for? Or a world of groveling subservience to authority — political, religious, or otherwise? You know what the answer is. We can advance to a state where humanity proudly accepts and asserts responsibility for its own actions, where each man is proud to be a free-willed individual."

"Would you say, sir, that it's a case of rational versus the irrational? Good versus bad?"

"It's too big to compress into words," said Jeffrey Hannevelt. "To call it science against superstition would be about as close as you could come."

Hugh thought a war-club into his hands, and leapt forward to smite. Don retreated, thinking a glass dome over Hugh.

The dome swiftly contracted, fitted around Hugh, then would go no more. There was a struggle, Don thinking another stronger glass skin around Hugh, Hugh thinking it away. The glass cracked, split. Hugh stepped out like a moth from the chrysalis.

Hugh thought a flame-thrower; in the split-second before the flame reached him, Don thought a metal wall. The flame spattered back.

Only Hugh's upward glance warned Don; he thought himself a mile back; a lump of iron, the size of a small asteroid, crashed into his footsteps.

On Hugh's right hand, Don conceived a mass of uranium shaped like a bucket; on Hugh's left hand he conceived a mass shaped like a plug. They darted together; Hugh saw them coming; they did not appear to be aimed at him. He stepped back with contempt.

The pieces joined. Don thought himself twenty miles away.

Thought is faster than radiation; thought is faster than any shock-wave. The great glow dazzled Don's eyes; otherwise he was unharmed. Where Hugh had stood was a glowing crater.

XXI

On the terrace of Godfrey Head's beach cottage ten miles south of Santa Barbara, Jean, Ivalee Trembath, Godfrey Head and his wife, Howard Rakowsky sat quietly. It was a warm evening. The Pacific lay flat and calm, glistening under a half-moon.

"Did you see that?" said Jean suddenly.

Godfrey Head looked around the sky. "What? Where?"

"A flash! A great light!"

"I didn't see anything," said Head.

Rakowsky shook his head; Ivalee said nothing.

"Might have been an atom-bomb explosion in Nevada."

The telephone rang; Godfrey Head answered. They heard his voice: "How many?...Really...That's wonderful. It looks as if we did some good after all..."

He returned to the terrace. "That was Claiborne in Los Angeles. The Christian Crusaders put on a monster rally out in Gardena."

"Really?"

"Three hundred and twelve people showed up. There's also a warrant out for Spedelius. Misappropriation of funds."

"I guess that does it," said Rakowsky. "Funny how these movements come up — and seem so important and critical. Then suddenly when they break like a balloon, when they're past, how weak and paltry they seem in retrospect."

Godfrey asked Jean, "What of the parapsychological research?"

"We'll get started up again. As soon as possible. We've barely scratched the surface. What is mind-stuff? That's the basic question. Did it exist before man, before life on Earth? Did intelligence adapt itself to a pre-existing ocean of mind-stuff, or did intelligence generate mind-stuff? If there is intelligent alien life on other planets, do they use the same mind-stuff as we do? How do the material processes of the brain engage the non-material processes of the mind-stuff? What is the mechanism? Where's the linkage?"

Rakowsky held up his hand. "Enough to keep us busy several months right there."

"Of course it won't be the same...I don't want to go back to Orange City...Maybe we can build a research center somewhere up here, along the ocean..."

She rose to her feet. "Excuse me, I'm going to take a walk down the beach."

"Like some company?" asked Head.

"No thanks."

They watched her go. "Poor kid," said Rakowsky. "She's been through a lot."

Ivalee smiled. "Something very wonderful is about to happen to Jean."

Jean sat on a half-buried length of timber. She looked up — a man stood before her. She jumped to her feet, stepped back.

"Don't be frightened, Jean."

The blood was pounding in Jean's ears. "I'm not frightened."

He took her hands, kissed her. His face felt warm; there was a stubble of beard on his cheeks.

"Donald," she sighed. "You feel real."

"I am real."

"I wish you were, Donald…"

The surf roared quietly; the stars fulfilled the ancient patterns. Her voice sounded thin and far away.

"Sit down. I'll explain. It won't take long."

She slowly sat on the log. "How — how long can you stay?"

"Till I die."

"But — you're already dead."

"And now I'm alive again."

"Don, don't tease me, if it's not true."

"It's true. I died. I was a thought — hard and intense and definite. I materialized. Remember? But I was not hard and definite enough — not true matter. I slipped back. Then as the thought lost intensity I became weaker. Until I fought Hugh Bronny. At first he was very strong — a giant."

Jean nodded. "At the same time we were fighting the Crusaders — and they were strong at first. But we won — just tonight."

"Tonight I killed Hugh Bronny."

Jean sighed, laughed wearily. "A dead man being killed."

"He's not utterly destroyed. Because the cycle goes on in the after-life. What's left of Hugh is the thought of his thought — a poor shambling wraith."

"I don't understand, Donald."

"I don't either… But suddenly I was strong — intense as I never had been before. More than anything I wanted to be with you. And here I am."

"Are you real? All of you? Not just your outside feel and look?"

"Look at me — touch me."

She did. "Mightn't it be — well, illusion?"

"I am real. Perhaps because it's the simplest way. A material body must move; what's more rational than muscles to move it? Material muscles. And what more rational than material blood to nourish the muscles? And what's more rational than functioning material lungs and a functioning material stomach to feed the blood? Is there an easier way to simulate a normal human being than to *be* a human being? There's nothing mystic or occult involved ... It's common sense. Carbon atoms crystallize into a diamond, not because a diamond is pretty or because a diamond has occult significance — but because that's the way carbon atoms fit together. The simplest way. The same way with me."

"Don — can you stay here — forever?"

"Until I die. I'm material now."

Jean looked up the beach, toward the lights of the beach-cottage. "Shall we go back — and tell the others?"

"Let's not ... Where's your car?"

"Up the road."

"Let's go."

"But Howard — Godfrey — Ivalee —"

"We'll telephone from Orange City."

Jean laughed softly, patted his cheek. "Shall I get my suitcase?"

"You'd better get your check-book," said Don. "I should have materialized a satchel-full of twenty-dollar bills."

"That's counterfeiting," said Jean. "How are we ever going to explain this?"

"My return? Lucky Don Berwick staggered out of the burning house, had an attack of amnesia, finally came to himself."

"It'll have to do." She turned away. "Can I trust you not to de-materialize?"

"Yes ... I'll wait in the car."

Five minutes later she returned to the car with her suitcase. "Donald?" She looked into the car. "Don! Where are you?" A sudden terrible fear loomed in her brain.

"Right behind you. What's the trouble?"

"Nothing." She got in, slammed the door. "I was just afraid."

"There's nothing to be afraid of." He started the motor, turned on the lights, and the car moved slowly along the driveway, out to the highway, and turned south toward Los Angeles. It accelerated; the tail-lights became a pair of red dots, a glimmer, and then were lost.

SAIL 25

I

HENRY BELT CAME LIMPING into the conference room, mounted the dais, settled himself at the desk. He looked once around the room: a swift bright glance which, focusing nowhere, treated the eight young men who faced him to an almost insulting disinterest. He reached in his pocket, brought forth a pencil and a flat red book, which he placed on the desk. The eight young men watched in absolute silence. They were much alike: healthy, clean, smart, their expressions identically alert and wary. Each had heard legends of Henry Belt, each had formed his private plans and private determinations.

Henry Belt seemed a man of a different species. His face was broad, flat, roped with cartilage and muscle, with skin the color and texture of bacon rind. Coarse white grizzle covered his scalp, his eyes were crafty slits, his nose a misshapen lump. His shoulders were massive, his legs short and gnarled: as he sat before the eight young men he seemed like a horned toad among a group of dapper young frogs.

"First of all," said Henry Belt, with a gap-toothed grin, "I'll make it clear that I don't expect you to like me. If you do I'll be surprised and displeased. It will mean that I haven't pushed you hard enough."

He leaned back in his chair, surveyed the silent group. "You've heard stories about me. Why haven't they kicked me out of the service? Incorrigible, arrogant, dangerous Henry Belt. Drunken Henry Belt. (This last of course is slander. Henry Belt has never been drunk in his life.) Why do they tolerate me? For one simple reason: out of necessity. No one wants to take on this kind of job. Only a man like Henry Belt can stand up to it: year after year in space, with nothing to look at but a half-dozen round-faced young scrubs. He takes them out, he brings them back. Not all of them, and not all of those who come back are space-men today. But they'll all cross the street when they see him coming. Henry Belt? you say. They'll turn pale or go red. None of them will smile. Some of them are high-placed now. They could kick me loose if they chose. Ask them why they don't. Henry Belt is a terror, they'll tell you. He's wicked, he's a tyrant. Cruel as an axe, fickle as a woman. But a voyage with Henry Belt blows the foam off the beer. He's ruined many a man, he's killed a few, but those that come out of it are proud to say, I trained with Henry Belt!

"Another thing you may hear: Henry Belt has luck. But don't pay any heed. Luck runs out. You'll be my thirteenth class, and that's unlucky. I've taken out seventy-two young sprats no different from yourselves; I've come back twelve times: which is partly Henry Belt and partly luck. The voyages average about two years long: how can a man stand it? There's only one who could: Henry Belt. I've got more space-time than any man alive, and now I'll tell you a secret: this is my last time out. I'm starting to wake up at night to strange visions. After this class I'll quit. I hope you lads aren't superstitious. A white-eyed woman told me that I'd die in space. She told me other things and they've all come true. Who knows? If I survive this last trip I figure to buy a cottage in the country and grow roses." Henry Belt pushed himself back in the chair and surveyed the group with sardonic placidity. The man sitting closest to him caught a whiff of alcohol; he peered more closely at Henry Belt. Was it possible that even now the man was drunk?

Henry Belt continued. "We'll get to know each other well. And you'll be wondering on what basis I make my recommendations. Am I objective and fair? Do I put aside personal animosity? Naturally there won't be any friendship. Well, here's my system. I keep a red book. Here it is. I'll put your names down right now. You, sir?"

"I'm Cadet Lewis Lynch, sir."

"You?"

"Edward Culpepper, sir."

"Marcus Verona, sir."

"Vidal Weske, sir."

"Marvin McGrath, sir."

"Barry Ostrander, sir."

"Clyde von Gluck, sir."

"Joseph Sutton, sir."

Henry Belt wrote the names in the red book. "This is the system. When you do something to annoy me, I mark you down demerits. At the end of the voyage I total these demerits, add a few here and there for luck, and am so guided. I'm sure nothing could be clearer than this. What annoys me? Ah, that's a question which is hard to answer. If you talk too much: demerits. If you're surly and taciturn: demerits. If you slouch and laze and dog the dirty work: demerits. If you're over-zealous and forever scuttling about: demerits. Obsequiousness: demerits. Truculence: demerits. If you sing and whistle: demerits. If you're a stolid bloody bore: demerits. You can see that the line is hard to draw. There's a hint which can save you many marks: no gossip. I've seen ships where the backbiting ran so thick it could have been jetted astern for thrust. I'm an eavesdropper. I hear everything. I don't like gossip, especially when it concerns myself. I'm a sensitive man, and I open my red book fast when I think I'm being insulted." Henry Belt once more leaned back in his chair. "Any questions?"

No one spoke.

Henry Belt nodded. "Wise. Best not to flaunt your ignorance so early in the game. Here's some miscellaneous information. First, wear what you like. Personally I dislike uniforms. I never wear a uniform. I never have worn a uniform. Secondly, if you have a religion, keep it to yourself. I dislike religions. I have always disliked religions. In response to the thought passing through each of your skulls, I do not think of myself as God. But you may do so, if you choose. And this—" he held up the red book "—you may regard as the Syncretic Compendium. Very well. Any questions?"

"Yes sir," said Culpepper.

"Speak, sir."

"Any objection to alcoholic beverages aboard ship, sir?"

"For the cadets, yes indeed. I concede that the water must be carried in any event, that the organic compounds present may be reconstituted, but unluckily the bottles weigh far too much."

"I understand, sir."

Henry Belt rose to his feet. "One last word. Have I mentioned that I run a tight ship? When I say jump, you must jump. When I say hop, you must hop. When I say stand on your head, I hope instantly to see twelve feet. Perhaps you will think me arbitrary — others have done so. After my tenth voyage several of the cadets urged that I had been unreasonable. I don't know where you'd go to question them; all were discharged from the hospital long ago. But now we understand each other. Rather, you understand me, because it is unnecessary that I understand you. This is dangerous work, of course. I don't guarantee your safety. Far from it, especially since we are assigned to old 25, which should have been broken up long ago. There are eight of you present. Only six cadets will make the voyage. Before the week is over I will make the appropriate notifications. Any more questions?...Very well, then. Cheerio." He stepped down from the dais, swaying just a trifle, and Culpepper once again caught the odor of alcohol. Limping on his thin legs as if his feet hurt Henry Belt departed into the back passage.

For a moment or two there was silence. Then von Gluck said in a soft voice, "My gracious."

"He's a tyrannical lunatic," grumbled Weske. "I've never heard anything like it! Megalomania!"

"Easy," said Culpepper. "Remember, no gossiping."

"Bah!" muttered McGrath. "This is a free country. I'll damn well say what I like."

"Mr. Belt admits it's a free country," said Culpepper. "He'll grade you as he likes, too."

Weske rose to his feet. "A wonder somebody hasn't killed him."

"I wouldn't want to try it," said Culpepper. "He looks tough." He made a gesture, stood up, brow furrowed in thought. Then he went to look along the passageway into which Henry Belt had made his departure. There, pressed to the wall, stood Henry Belt. "Yes, sir," said Culpepper suavely. "I forgot to inquire when you wanted us to convene again."

Henry Belt returned to the rostrum. "Now is as good a time as any." He took his seat, opened his red book. "You, Mr. von Gluck, made the remark, 'My gracious' in an offensive tone of voice. One demerit. You, Mr. Weske, employed the terms 'tyrannical lunatic' and 'megalomania', in reference to myself. Three demerits. Mr. McGrath, you observed that freedom of speech is the official doctrine of this country. It is a theory which presently we have no time to explore, but I believe that the statement in its present context carries an overtone of insubordination. One demerit. Mr. Culpepper, your imperturbable complacence irritates me. I prefer that you display more uncertainty, or even uneasiness."

"Sorry, sir."

"However, you took occasion to remind your colleagues of my rule, and so I will not mark you down."

"Thank you, sir."

Henry Belt leaned back in the chair, stared at the ceiling. "Listen closely, as I do not care to repeat myself. Take notes if you wish. Topic: Solar Sails, Theory and Practice thereof. Material with which you should already be familiar, but which I will repeat in order to avoid ambiguity.

"First, why bother with the sail, when nuclear jet-ships are faster, more dependable, more direct, safer and easier to navigate? The answer is three-fold. First, a sail is not a bad way to move heavy cargo slowly but cheaply through space. Secondly, the range of the sail is unlimited, since we employ the mechanical pressure of light for thrust, and therefore need carry neither propulsive machinery, material to be ejected, nor energy source. The solar sail is much lighter than its nuclear-powered counterpart, and may carry a larger complement of men in a larger hull. Thirdly, to train a man for space there is no better instrument than the handling of a sail. The computer naturally calculates sail cant and plots the course; in fact, without the computer we'd be dead ducks. Nevertheless the control of a sail provides working familiarity with the cosmic elementals: light, gravity, mass, space.

"There are two types of sail: pure and composite. The first relies on solar energy exclusively, the second carries a secondary power source. We have been assigned Number 25, which is the first sort. It consists of a hull, a large parabolic reflector which serves as radar and radio antenna as well as reflector for the power generator, and the sail itself. The pressure of radiation, of course, is extremely slight — on the order of an ounce per acre at this distance from the sun. Necessarily the sail must be extremely large and extremely light. We use a fluoro-siliconic film a tenth of a mil in gauge, fogged with lithium to the state of opacity. I believe the layer of lithium is about a thousand two hundred molecules thick. Such a foil weighs about four tons to the square mile. It is fitted to a hoop of thin-walled tubing, from which mono-crystalline iron cords lead to the hull.

"We try to achieve a weight factor of six tons to the square mile, which produces an acceleration of between g/100 and g/1000 depending on proximity to the sun, angle of cant, circumsolar orbital speed, reflectivity of surface. These accelerations seem minute, but calculation shows them to be cumulatively enormous. g/100 yields a velocity increment of 800 miles per hour every hour, 18,000 miles per hour each day, or five miles per second each day. At this rate interplanetary distances are readily negotiable — with proper manipulation of the sail, I need hardly say.

"The virtues of the sail I've mentioned. It is cheap to build and cheap to operate. It requires neither fuel nor ejectant. As it travels through space, the great area captures various ions, which may be expelled in the plasma jet powered by the parabolic reflector, which adds another increment to the acceleration.

"The disadvantages of the sail are those of the glider or sailing ship, in that we must use natural forces with great precision and delicacy.

"There is no particular limit to the size of the sail. On 25 we use about four square miles of sail. For the present voyage we will install a new sail, as the old is well-worn and eroded.

"That will be all for today." Once more Henry Belt limped down from the dais and out into the passage. On this occasion there were no comments after his departure.

II

The eight cadets shared a dormitory, attended classes together, ate at the same table in the mess-hall. "You think you know each other well," said Henry Belt. "Wait till we are alone in space. The similarities, the areas of agreement become invisible, only the distinctions and differences remain."

In various shops and laboratories the cadets assembled, disassembled and reassembled computers, pumps, generators, gyro-platforms, star-trackers, communication gear. "It's not enough to be clever with your hands," said Henry Belt. "Dexterity is not enough. Resourcefulness, creativity, the ability to make successful improvisations — these are more important. We'll test you out." And presently each of the cadets was introduced into a room on the floor of which lay a great heap of mingled housings, wires, flexes, gears, components of a dozen varieties of mechanism. "This is a twenty-six hour test," said Henry Belt. "Each of you has an identical set of components and supplies. There shall be no exchange of parts or information between you. Those whom I suspect of this fault will be dropped from the class, without recommendation. What I want you to build is, first, one standard Aminex Mark 9 Computer. Second, a servo-mechanism to orient a mass of ten kilograms toward Mu Hercules. Why do I specify Mu Hercules?"

"Because, sir, the solar system moves in the direction of Mu Hercules, and we thereby avoid parallax error. Negligible though it may be, sir."

"The final comment smacks of frivolity, Mr. McGrath, which serves only to distract the attention of those who are trying to take careful note of my instructions. One demerit."

"Sorry, sir. I merely intended to express my awareness that for many practical purposes such a degree of accuracy is unnecessary."

"That idea, cadet, is sufficiently elemental that it need not be labored. I appreciate brevity and precision."

"Yes, sir."

"Thirdly, from these materials, assemble a communication system, operating on one hundred watts, which will permit two-way conversation between Tycho Base and Phobos, at whatever frequency you deem suitable."

The cadets started in identical fashion, by sorting the material into various piles, then calibrating and checking the test instruments. Achievement thereafter was disparate. Culpepper and von Gluck, diagnosing the test as partly one of mechanical ingenuity and partly ordeal by frustration, failed to become excited when several indispensable components proved either to be missing or inoperative, and carried each project as far as immediately feasible. McGrath and

Weske, beginning with the computer, were reduced to rage and random action. Lynch and Sutton worked doggedly at the computer, Verona at the communication system.

Culpepper alone managed to complete one of the instruments, by the process of sawing, polishing and cementing together sections of two broken crystals into a crude, inefficient but operative maser unit.

The day after this test McGrath and Weske disappeared from the dormitory, whether by their own volition or notification from Henry Belt, no one ever knew.

The test was followed by weekend leave. Cadet Lynch, attending a cocktail party, found himself in conversation with a Lieutenant-Colonel Trenchard, who shook his head pityingly to hear that Lynch was training with Henry Belt.

"I was up with Old Horrors myself. I tell you it's a miracle we ever got back. Belt was drunk two-thirds of the voyage."

"How does he escape court-martial?" asked Lynch with an involuntary glance over his shoulder, for fear that Henry Belt might be standing near by with his red book.

"Very simple. All the top men seem to have trained under Henry Belt. Naturally they hate his guts but they all take a perverse pride in the fact. And maybe they hope that someday a cadet will take him apart."

"Have any ever tried?"

"Oh yes. I took a swing at Henry once. I was lucky to escape with a broken collarbone and two sprained ankles. And he wasn't even angry. Good old Henry, the son of a bitch. If you come back alive — and that's no idle remark — you'll stand a good chance of reaching the top."

Lynch winced. "Is it worth two years with Henry Belt?"

"I don't regret it. Not now," said Trenchard. "What's your ship?"

"Old 25."

Trenchard shook his head. "An antique. It's tied together with bits of string."

"So I've heard," said Lynch glumly. "If I didn't have so much vanity I'd quit tomorrow. Learn to sell insurance, or work in an office…"

✳

The next evening Henry Belt passed the word. "Next Tuesday morning we go up. Have your gear packed; take a last look at the scenes of your childhood. We'll be gone several months."

On Tuesday morning the cadets took their places in the angel-wagon. Henry Belt presently appeared. "Last chance to play it safe. Anyone decide they're really not space people after all?"

The pilot of the angel-wagon was disposed to be facetious. "Now, Henry, behave yourself. You're not scaring anybody but yourself."

Henry Belt swung his flat dark face around. "Is that the case, mister? I'll pay you ten thousand dollars to make the trip in the place of one of the cads."

The pilot shook his head. "Not for a hundred thousand, Henry. One of these days your luck is going to run out, and there'll be a sad quiet hulk drifting in orbit forever."

"I expect it, mister. If I wanted to die of fatbelly I'd take your job."

"If you'd stay sober, Henry, there might be an opening for you."

Henry Belt gave him his wolfish smile. "I'm a better man drunk than you are sober, except for mouth. Any way you can think of, from dancing the fandango to Calcutta roughhouse."

"I'd be ashamed to thrash an old man, Henry. You're safe."

"Thank you, mister. If you are quite ready, we are."

"Hold your hats. On the count…" The projectile thrust against the earth, strained, rose, went streaking up into the sky. An hour later the pilot pointed. "There's your boat. Old 25. And 39 right beside it, just in from space."

Henry Belt stared aghast from the port. "What's been done to the ship? The decoration? The red? the white? the yellow? The checkerboard."

"Thank some idiot of a landlubber," said the pilot. "The word came to pretty the old boats for a junket of congressmen. This is what transpired."

Henry Belt turned to the cadets. "Observe this foolishness. It is the result of vanity and ignorance. We will be occupied several days removing the paint."

They drifted close below the two sails: No. 39 just down from space, spare and polished beside the bedizened structure of No. 25.

In 39's exit port a group of men waited, their gear floating at the end of cords.

"Observe those men," said Henry Belt. "They are jaunty. They have been on a pleasant outing around the planet Mars. They are poorly trained. When you gentlemen return you will be haggard and desperate. You will be well trained."

"If you live," said the pilot.

"That is something which cannot be foretold," said Henry Belt. "Now, gentlemen, clamp your helmets, and we will proceed."

The helmets were secured. Henry Belt's voice came by radio. "Lynch, Ostrander, will remain here to discharge cargo. Verona, Culpepper, von Gluck, Sutton, leap with cords to the ship; ferry across the cargo, stow it in the proper hatches."

Henry Belt took charge of his personal cargo, which consisted of several large cases. He eased them out into space, clipped on lines, thrust them toward 25, leapt after. Pulling himself and the cases to the entrance port he disappeared within.

Discharge of cargo was effected. The crew from 39 transferred to the carrier, which thereupon swung down and away, thrust itself dwindling back toward earth.

When the cargo had been stowed, the cadets gathered in the wardroom. Henry Belt appeared from the master's cubicle. He wore a black T shirt which was ridged and lumped to the configuration of his chest, black shorts from which his thin legs extended, and sandals with magnetic filaments in the soles.

"Gentlemen," said Henry Belt in a soft voice. "At last we are alone. How do you like the surroundings? Eh, Mr. Culpepper?"

"The hull is commodious, sir. The view is superb."

Henry Belt nodded. "Mr. Lynch? Your impressions?"

"I'm afraid I haven't sorted them out yet, sir."

"I see. You, Mr. Sutton?"

"Space is larger than I imagined it, sir."

"True. Space is unimaginable. A good space-man must either be larger than space, or he must ignore it. Both difficult. Well, gentlemen, I will make a few comments, then I will retire and enjoy the voyage. Since this is my last time out, I intend to do nothing whatever. The operation of the ship will be completely in your hands. I will merely appear from time to time to beam benevolently about or alas! to make marks in my red book. Nominally I shall be in command, but you six will enjoy complete control over the ship. If you return us safely to Earth I will make an approving entry in my red book. If you wreck us or fling us into the sun, you will be more unhappy than I, since it is my destiny to die in space. Mr. von Gluck, do I perceive a smirk on your face?"

"No, sir, it is a thoughtful half-smile."

"What is humorous in the concept of my demise, may I ask?"

"It will be a great tragedy, sir. I merely was reflecting upon the contemporary persistence of, well, not exactly superstition, but, let us say, the conviction of a subjective cosmos."

Henry Belt made a notation in the red book. "Whatever is meant by this barbaric jargon I'm sure I don't know, Mr. von Gluck. It is clear that you fancy yourself a philosopher and dialectician. I will not fault this, so long as your remarks conceal no overtones of malice and insolence, to which I am extremely sensitive. Now as to the persistence of superstition, only an impoverished mind considers itself the repository of absolute knowledge. Hamlet spoke on this subject to Horatio, as I recall, in the well-known work by William Shakespeare. I myself have seen strange and terrifying sights. Were they hallucinations? Were they the manipulation of the cosmos by my mind or the mind of someone — or something — other than myself? I do not know. I therefore counsel a flexible attitude toward matters where the truth is still unknown. For this reason: the impact of an inexplicable experience may well destroy a mind which is too brittle. Do I make myself clear?"

"Perfectly, sir."

"Very good. To return, then. We shall set a system of watches whereby each man works in turn with each of the other five. I thereby hope to discourage the formation of special friendships, or cliques. Such arrangements irritate me, and I shall mark accordingly.

"You have inspected the ship. The hull is a sandwich of lithium–beryllium, insulating foam, fiber and an interior skin. Very light, held rigid by air pressure rather than by any innate strength of the material. We can therefore afford enough space to stretch our legs and provide all of us with privacy.

"The master's cubicle is to the left; under no circumstances is anyone permitted in my quarters. If you wish to speak to me, knock on my door. If I appear, good. If I do not appear, go away. To the right are six cubicles which you may now distribute among yourselves by lot. Each of you has the right to demand the same privacy I do myself. Keep your personal belongings in your cubicles. I have been known to cast into space articles which I persistently find strewn about the wardroom.

"Your schedule will be two hours study, four hours on watch, six hours off. I will require no specific rate of study progress, but I recommend that you make good use of your time.

"Our destination is Mars. We will presently construct a new sail, then while orbital velocity builds up, you will carefully test and check all equipment aboard. Each of you will compute sail cant and course and work out among yourselves any discrepancies which may appear. I shall take no hand in navigation. I prefer that you involve me in no disaster. If any such occur I shall severely mark down the persons responsible.

"Singing, whistling, humming, are forbidden, as are sniffing, nose-picking, smacking the lips, and cracking knuckles. I disapprove of fear and hysteria, and mark accordingly. No one dies more than once; we are well aware of the risks of this, our chosen occupation. There will be no practical jokes. You may fight, so long as you do not disturb me or break any instruments; however I counsel against it, as it leads to resentment, and I have known cadets to kill each other. I suggest coolness and detachment in your personal relations. Use of the micro-film projector is of course at your own option. You may not use the radio either to dispatch or receive messages. In fact I have put the radio out of commission, as is my practice. I do this to emphasize the fact that, sink or swim, we must make do with our own resources. Are there any questions?...Very good. You will find that if you all behave with scrupulous correctness and accuracy, we shall in due course return safe and sound, with a minimum of demerits and no casualties. I am bound to say, however, that in twelve previous voyages this has failed to occur."

"Perhaps this will be the time, sir," offered Culpepper suavely.

"We shall see. Now you may select your cubicles, stow your gear, generally make the place shipshape. The carrier will bring up the new sail tomorrow, and you will go to work."

III

The carrier discharged a great bundle of three-inch tubing: paper-thin lithium hardened with beryllium, reinforced with filaments of mono-crystalline iron — a total length of eight miles. The cadets fitted the tubes end to end, cementing the joints. When the tube extended a quarter-mile it was bent bow-shaped by a cord stretched between two ends, and further sections added. As the process continued the free end curved far out and around, and presently began to veer back in toward the hull. When the last tube was in place the loose end was hauled down, socketed home, to form a great hoop two miles and a half in diameter.

Henry Belt came out occasionally in his space-suit to look on, and occasionally spoke a few words of sardonic comment, to which the cadets paid little heed. Their mood had changed; this was exhilaration, to be weightlessly afloat above the bright cloud-marked globe, with continent and ocean wheeling massively below. Anything seemed possible, even the training voyage with Henry Belt! When he came out to inspect their work, they grinned at each other with indulgent amusement. Henry Belt suddenly seemed a rather pitiful creature, a poor vagabond suited only for drunken bluster. Fortunate indeed that they were less naïve than Henry Belt's previous classes! They had taken Belt seriously; he had cowed them, reduced them to nervous pulp. Not this crew, not by a long shot! They saw through Henry Belt! Just keep your nose clean, do your work, keep cheerful. The training voyage won't last but a few months, and then real life begins. Gut it out, ignore Henry Belt as much as possible.

Already the group had made a composite assessment of its members, arriving at a set of convenient labels. Culpepper: smooth, suave, easy-going. Lynch: excitable, argumentative, hot-tempered. Von Gluck: the artistic temperament, delicate with his hands and sensibilities. Ostrander: prissy, finicky, over-tidy. Sutton: moody, suspicious, competitive. Verona: the plugger, rough at the edges, but persistent and reliable.

✳

Around the hull swung the gleaming hoop, and now the carrier brought up the sail, a great roll of darkly shining stuff. When unfolded and unrolled, and unfolded many times more, it became a tough gleaming film, flimsy as gold leaf. Unfolded to its fullest extent it was a shimmering disk, already rippling and bulging to the light of the sun. The cadets fitted the film to the hoop, stretched it taut as a drum-head, cemented it in place. Now the sail must carefully be held edge on to the sun, or it would quickly move away, under a thrust of about a hundred pounds.

From the rim braided-iron threads were led to a ring at the back of the parabolic reflector, dwarfing this as the reflector dwarfed the hull, and now the sail was ready to move.

The carrier brought up a final cargo: water, food, spare parts, a new magazine for the microfilm viewer, mail. Then Henry Belt said, "Make sail."

This was the process of turning the sail to catch the sunlight while the hull moved around Earth away from the sun, canting it parallel to the sun-rays when the ship moved on the sunward leg of its orbit: in short, building up an orbital velocity which in due course would stretch loose the bonds of terrestrial gravity and send Sail 25 kiting out toward Mars.

During this period the cadets checked every item of equipment aboard the vessel. They grimaced with disgust and dismay at some of the instruments: 25 was an old ship, with antiquated gear. Henry Belt seemed to enjoy their grumbling. "This is a training voyage, not a pleasure cruise. If you wanted your noses wiped, you should have taken a post on the ground. I warn you, gentlemen, I have no sympathy for fault-finders. If you wish a model by which to form your own conduct, observe me. I accept every vicissitude placidly. You will never hear me curse or flap my arms in astonishment at the turns of fortune."

The moody introspective Sutton, usually the most diffident and laconic of individuals, ventured an ill-advised witticism. "If we modeled ourselves after you, sir, there'd be no room to move for the whiskey."

Out came the red book. "Extraordinary impudence, Mr. Sutton. How can you yield so easily to malice? You must control the razor edge of your wit; you will make yourself unpopular aboard this ship."

Sutton flushed pink; his eyes glistened, he opened his mouth to speak, then closed it firmly. Henry Belt, waiting politely expectant, turned away. "You gentlemen will perceive that I rigorously obey my own rules of conduct. I am regular as a clock. There is no better, more genial shipmate than Henry Belt. There is not a fairer man alive. Mr. Culpepper, you have a remark to make?"

"Nothing of consequence, sir. I am merely grateful not to be making a voyage with a man less regular, less genial, and less fair than yourself."

Henry Belt considered. "I suppose I can take no exception to the remark. There is indeed a hint of tartness and glancing obloquy — but, well, I will grant you the benefit of the doubt, and accept your statement at its face value."

"Thank you, sir."

"But I must warn you, Mr. Culpepper, that there is a certain ease to your behavior that gives me cause for distress. I counsel you to a greater show of earnest sincerity, which will minimize the risk of misunderstanding. A man less indulgent than myself might well have read impertinence into your remark and charged you one demerit."

"I understand, sir, and shall cultivate the qualities you mention."

Henry Belt found nothing more to say. He went to the port, glared out at the sail. He swung around instantly. "Who is on watch?"

"Sutton and Ostrander, sir."

"Gentlemen, have you noticed the sail? It has swung about and is canting to show its back to the sun. In another ten minutes we shall be tangled in a hundred miles of guy-wires."

Sutton and Ostrander sprang to repair the situation. Henry Belt shook his head disparagingly. "This is precisely what is meant by the words 'negligence' and 'inattentiveness'. You two have committed a serious error. This is poor spacemanship. The sail must always be in such a position as to hold the wires taut."

"There seems to be something wrong with the sensor, sir," Sutton blurted. "It should notify us when the sail swings behind us."

"I fear I must charge you an additional demerit for making excuses, Mr. Sutton. It is your duty to assure yourself that all the warning devices are functioning properly, at all times. Machinery must never be used as a substitute for vigilance."

Ostrander looked up from the control console. "Someone has turned off the switch, sir. I do not offer this as an excuse, but as an explanation."

"The line of distinction is often hard to define, Mr. Ostrander. Please bear in mind my remarks on the subject of vigilance."

"Yes, sir, but — who turned off the switch?"

"Both you and Mr. Sutton are theoretically hard at work watching for any such accident or occurrence. Did you not observe it?"

"No, sir."

"I might almost accuse you of further inattention and neglect, in this case."

Ostrander gave Henry Belt a long dubious side-glance. "The only person I recall going near the console is yourself, sir. I'm sure you wouldn't do such a thing."

Henry Belt shook his head sadly. "In space you must never rely on anyone for rational conduct. A few moments ago Mr. Sutton unfairly imputed to me an unusual thirst for whiskey. Suppose this were the case? Suppose, as an example of pure irony, that I had indeed been drinking whiskey, that I was in fact drunk?"

"I will agree, sir, that anything is possible."

Henry Belt shook his head again. "That is the type of remark, Mr. Ostrander, that I have come to associate with Mr. Culpepper. A better response would have been, 'In the future, I will try to be ready for any conceivable contingency.' Mr. Sutton, did you make a hissing sound between your teeth?"

"I was breathing, sir."

"Please breathe with less vehemence. A more suspicious man than myself might mark you for sulking and harboring black thoughts."

"Sorry, sir, I will breathe to myself."

"Very well, Mr. Sutton." Henry Belt turned away and wandered back and forth about the wardroom, scrutinizing cases, frowning at smudges on polished metal. Ostrander muttered something to Sutton, and both watched Henry Belt closely as he moved here and there. Presently Henry Belt lurched toward them. "You show great interest in my movements, gentlemen."

"We were on the watch for another unlikely contingency, sir."

"Very good, Mr. Ostrander. Stick with it. In space nothing is impossible. I'll vouch for this personally."

IV

Henry Belt sent all hands out to remove the paint from the surface of the parabolic reflector. When this had been accomplished, incident sunlight was now focused upon an expanse of photo-electric cells. The power so generated was used to operate plasma jets, expelling ions collected by the vast expanse of sail, further accelerating the ship, thrusting it ever out into an orbit of escape. And finally one day, at an exact instant dictated by the computer, the ship departed from Earth and floated tangentially out into space, off at an angle for the orbit of Mars. At an acceleration of g/100 velocity built up rapidly. Earth dwindled behind; the ship was isolated in space. The cadets' exhilaration vanished, to be replaced by an almost funereal solemnity. The vision of Earth dwindling and retreating is an awesome symbol, equivalent to eternal loss, to the act of dying itself. The more impressionable cadets — Sutton, von Gluck, Ostrander — could not look astern without finding their eyes swimming with tears. Even the suave Culpepper was awed by the magnificence of the spectacle, the sun an aching pit not to be tolerated, Earth a plump pearl rolling on black velvet among a myriad glittering diamonds. And away from Earth, away from the sun, opened an exalted magnificence of another order entirely. For the first time the cadets became dimly aware that Henry Belt had spoken truly of strange visions. Here was death, here was peace, solitude, star-blazing beauty which promised not oblivion in death, but eternity... Streams and spatters of stars... The familiar constellations, the stars with their prideful names presenting themselves like heroes: Achernar, Fomalhaut, Sadal Suud, Canopus...

Sutton could not bear to look into the sky. "It's not that I feel fear," he told von Gluck, "or yes, perhaps it is fear. It sucks at me, draws me out there... I suppose in due course I'll become accustomed to it."

"I'm not so sure," said von Gluck. "I wouldn't be surprised if space could become a psychological addiction, a need — so that whenever you walked on Earth you felt hot and breathless."

Life settled into a routine. Henry Belt no longer seemed a man, but a capricious aspect of nature, like storm or lightning; and like some natural cataclysm, Henry Belt showed no favoritism, nor forgave one jot or tittle of offense. Apart from the private cubicles no place on the ship escaped his attention. Always he reeked of whiskey, and it became a matter of covert speculation as to exactly how much whiskey he had brought aboard. But no matter how he reeked or how he swayed on his feet, his eyes remained clever and steady, and he spoke without slurring in his paradoxically clear sweet voice.

One day he seemed slightly drunker than usual, and ordered all hands into space-suits and out to inspect the sail for meteoric puncture. The order seemed sufficiently odd that the cadets stared at him in disbelief. "Gentlemen, you hesitate, you fail to exert yourselves, you luxuriate in sloth. Do you fancy yourselves at the Riviera? Into the space-suits, on the double, and a demerit to the last man dressed!"

The last man proved to be Culpepper. "Well, sir?" demanded Henry Belt. "You have earned yourself a mark. Is it below your dignity to compete?"

Culpepper considered. "Well, sir, that might be the case. Somebody had to get the demerit, and I figured it might as well be me."

"I deplore your attitude, Mr. Culpepper. I interpret it as an act of deliberate defiance."

"Sorry, sir. I don't mean it that way."

"You feel then that I am mistaken?" Henry Belt studied Culpepper carefully.

"Yes, sir," said Culpepper with engaging simplicity. "You are absolutely wrong. My attitude is not one of defiance. I think I would call it fatalism. I look at it this way. If it turns out that I accumulate so many demerits that you hold back my commission, then perhaps I wasn't cut out for the job in the first place."

For a moment Henry Belt had nothing to say. Then he grinned wolfishly. "We shall see, Mr. Culpepper. I assure you that at the present moment I am far from being confident of your abilities. Now, everybody into space. Check hoop, sail, reflector, struts and sensor. You will be adrift for two hours. When you return I want a comprehensive report. Mr. Lynch, I believe you are in charge of this watch. You will present the report."

"Yes, sir."

"One more matter. You will notice that the sail is slightly bellied by the continual radiation pressure. It therefore acts as a focusing device, the focal point presumably occurring behind the cab. But this is not a matter to be taken for granted. I have seen a man burnt to death in such a freak accident. Bear this in mind."

For two hours the cadets drifted through space, propelled by tanks of gas and thrust tubes. All enjoyed the experience except Sutton, who found himself appalled by the immensity of his emotions. Probably least affected was the practical Verona, who inspected the sail with a care exacting enough even to satisfy Henry Belt.

The next day the computer went wrong. Ostrander was in charge of the watch and knocked on Henry Belt's door to make the report.

Henry Belt appeared in the doorway. He apparently had been asleep. "What is the difficulty, Mr. Ostrander?"

"We're in trouble, sir. The computer has gone out."

Henry Belt rubbed his grizzled pate. "This is not an unusual circumstance. We prepare for this contingency by schooling all cadets thoroughly in computer design and repair. Have you identified the difficulty?"

"The bearings which suspend the data separation disks have broken. The shaft has several millimeters play and as a result there is total confusion in the data presented to the analyzer."

"An interesting problem. Why do you present it to me?"

"I thought you should be notified, sir. I don't believe we carry spares for this particular bearing."

Henry Belt shook his head sadly. "Mr. Ostrander, do you recall my statement at the beginning of this voyage, that you six gentlemen are totally responsible for the navigation of the ship?"

"Yes, sir. But —"

"This is an applicable situation. You must either repair the computer, or perform the calculations yourself."

"Very well, sir. I will do my best."

V

Lynch, Verona, Ostrander and Sutton disassembled the mechanism, removed the worn bearing. "Confounded antique!" said Lynch. "Why can't they give us decent equipment? Or if they want to kill us, why not shoot us and save us all trouble?"

"We're not dead yet," said Verona. "You've looked for a spare?"

"Naturally. There's nothing remotely like this."

Verona looked at the bearing dubiously. "I suppose we could cast a babbitt sleeve and machine it to fit. That's what we'll have to do — unless you fellows are awfully fast with your math."

Sutton glanced out the port, quickly turned away his eyes. "I wonder if we should cut sail."

"Why?" asked Ostrander.

"We don't want to build up too much velocity. We're already going 30 miles a second."

"Mars is a long way off."

"And if we miss, we go shooting past. Then where are we?"

"Sutton, you're a pessimist. A shame to find morbid tendencies in one so young." This from von Gluck, speaking from the console across the room.

"I'd rather be a live pessimist than a dead comedian."

The new sleeve was duly cast, machined and fitted. Anxiously the alignment of the data disks was checked. "Well," said Verona dubiously, "there's wobble. How much that affects the functioning remains to be seen. We can take some of it out by shimming the mount…"

Shims of tissue paper were inserted and the wobble seemed to be reduced. "Now — feed in the data," said Sutton. "Let's see how we stand."

Coordinates were fed into the system; the indicator swung. "Enlarge sail cant four degrees," said von Gluck, "we're making too much left concentric. Projected course…" he tapped buttons, watched the bright line extend across the screen, swing around a dot representing the center of gravity of Mars. "I make it an elliptical pass, about twenty thousand miles out. That's at present acceleration, and it should toss us right back at Earth."

"Great. Simply great. Let's go, 25!" This was Lynch. "I've heard of guys dropping flat on their faces and kissing Earth when they put down. Me, I'm going to live in a cave the rest of my life."

Sutton went to look at the data disks. The wobble was slight but perceptible. "Good Lord," he said huskily. "The other end of the shaft is loose too."

Lynch started to spit curses; Verona's shoulders slumped. "Let's get to work and fix it."

Another bearing was cast, machined, polished, mounted. The disks wobbled, scraped. Mars, an ocher disk, shouldered ever closer in from the side. With the computer unreliable the cadets calculated and plotted the course manually. The results were at slight but significant variance with those of the computer. The cadets looked dourly at each other. "Well," growled Ostrander, "there's error. Is it the instruments? The calculation? The plotting? Or the computer?"

Culpepper said in a subdued voice, "Well, we're not about to crash head-on, at any rate."

Verona went back to study the computer. "I can't imagine why the bearings don't work better...The mounting brackets — could they have shifted?" He removed the side housing, studied the frame, then went to the case for tools.

"What are you going to do?" demanded Sutton.

"Try to ease the mounting brackets around. I think that's our trouble."

"Leave them alone! You'll bugger the machine so it'll never work."

Verona paused, looked questioningly around the group. "Well? What's the verdict?"

"Maybe we'd better check with the old man," said Ostrander nervously.

"All well and good — but you know what he'll say."

"Let's deal cards. Ace of spades goes to ask him."

Culpepper received the ace. He knocked on Henry Belt's door. There was no response. He started to knock again, but restrained himself.

He returned to the group. "Wait till he shows himself. I'd rather crash into Mars than bring forth Henry Belt and his red book."

The ship crossed the orbit of Mars well ahead of the looming red planet. It came toppling at them with a peculiar clumsy grandeur, a mass obviously bulky and globular, but so fine and clear was the detail, so absent the perspective, that the distance and size might have been anything. Instead of swinging in a sharp elliptical curve back toward Earth, the ship swerved aside in a blunt hyperbola and proceeded outward, now at a velocity of close to fifty miles a second. Mars receded astern and to the side. A new part of space lay ahead. The sun was noticeably smaller. Earth could no longer be differentiated from the stars. Mars departed quickly and politely, and space seemed lonely and forlorn.

Henry Belt had not appeared for two days. At last Culpepper went to knock on the door — once, twice, three times: a strange face looked out. It was Henry Belt, face haggard, skin like pulled taffy. His eyes were red and glared, his hair seemed matted and more unkempt than hair a quarter-inch long should be.

But he spoke in his quiet clear voice. "Mr. Culpepper, your merciless din has disturbed me. I am quite put out with you."

"Sorry, sir. We feared that you were ill."

Henry Belt made no response. He looked past Culpepper, around the circle of faces. "You gentlemen are unwontedly serious. Has this presumptive illness of mine caused you all distress?"

Sutton spoke in a rush, "The computer is out of order."

"Why then, you must repair it."

"It's a matter of altering the housing. If we do it incorrectly —"

"Mr. Sutton, please do not harass me with the hour-by-hour minutiae of running the ship."

"But, sir, the matter has become serious; we need your advice. We missed the Mars turn-around —"

"Well, I suppose there's always Jupiter. Must I explain the basic elements of astrogation to you?"

"But the computer's out of order — definitely."

"Then, if you wish to return to Earth, you must perform the calculations with pencil and paper. Why is it necessary to explain the obvious?"

"Jupiter is a long way out," said Sutton in a shrill voice. "Why can't we just turn around and go home?" This last was almost a whisper.

"I see I've been too easy on you cads," said Henry Belt. "You stand around idly; you chatter nonsense while the machinery goes to pieces and the ship flies at random. Everybody into space-suits for sail inspection. Come now. Let's have some snap. What are you all? Walking corpses? You, Mr. Culpepper, why the delay?"

"It occurred to me, sir, that we are approaching the asteroid belt. As chief of the watch I consider it my duty to cant sail to swing us around the area."

"You may do this; then join the rest in hull and sail inspection."

"Yes, sir."

The cadets donned space-suits, Sutton with the utmost reluctance. Out into the dark void they went, and now here was loneliness indeed.

When they returned, Henry Belt had returned to his compartment.

"As Mr. Belt points out, we have no great choice," said Ostrander. "We missed Mars, so let's hit Jupiter. Luckily it's in good position — otherwise we'd have to swing out to Saturn or Uranus —"

"They're off behind the sun," said Lynch. "Jupiter's our last chance."

"Let's do it right then. I say, let's make one last attempt to set those confounded bearings..."

But now it seemed as if the wobble and twist had been eliminated. The disks tracked perfectly, the accuracy monitor glowed green.

"Great!" yelled Lynch. "Feed it the dope. Let's get going! All sail for Jupiter. Good Lord, but we're having a trip!"

"Wait till it's over," said Sutton. Since his return from sail inspection, he had stood to one side, cheeks pinched, eyes staring. "It's not over yet. And maybe it's not meant to be."

The other five pretended not to have heard him. The computer spat out figures and angles. There was a billion miles to travel. Acceleration was less, due to the diminution in the intensity of sunlight. At least a month must pass before Jupiter came close.

VI

The ship, great sail spread to the fading sunlight, fled like a ghost — out, always out. Each of the cadets had quietly performed the same calculation, and arrived at the same result. If the swing around Jupiter were not performed with exactitude, if the ship were not slung back like a stone on a string, there was nothing beyond. Saturn, Uranus, Neptune, Pluto were far around the sun; the ship, speeding at a hundred miles a second, could not be halted by the waning gravity of the sun, nor yet sufficiently accelerated in a concentric direction by sail and jet into a true orbit. The very nature of the sail made it useless as a brake, always the thrust was outward.

Within the hull seven men lived and thought, and the psychic relationship worked and stirred like yeast in a vat of decaying fruit. The fundamental similarity, the human identity of the seven men, was utterly canceled; apparent only were the disparities. Each cadet appeared to others only as a walking characteristic, and Henry Belt was an incomprehensible Thing, who appeared from his compartment at unpredictable times, to move quietly here and there with the blind blank grin of an archaic Attic hero.

Jupiter loomed and bulked. The ship, at last within reach of the Jovian gravity, sidled over to meet it. The cadets gave ever more careful attention to the computer, checking and counterchecking the instructions. Verona was the most assiduous at this, Sutton the most harassed and ineffectual. Lynch growled and cursed and sweated; Ostrander complained in a thin peevish voice. Von Gluck worked with the calm of pessimistic fatalism; Culpepper seemed unconcerned, almost debonair, a blandness which bewildered Ostrander, infuriated Lynch, awoke a malignant hate in Sutton. Verona and von Gluck on the other hand seemed to derive strength and refreshment from Culpepper's placid acceptance of the situation. Henry Belt said nothing. Occasionally he emerged from his compartment, to survey the wardroom and the cadets with the detached interest of a visitor to an asylum.

It was Lynch who made the discovery. He signaled it with an odd growl of sheer dismay, which brought a resonant questioning sound from Sutton. "My God, my God," muttered Lynch.

Verona was at his side. "What's the trouble?"

"Look. This gear. When we replaced the disks we de-phased the whole apparatus one notch. This white dot and this other white dot should synchronize. They're one sprocket apart. All the results would check and be consistent because they'd all be off by the same factor."

Verona sprang into action. Off came the housing, off came various components. Gently he lifted the gear, set it back into correct alignment. The other cadets leaned over him as he worked, except Culpepper who was chief of the watch.

Henry Belt appeared. "You gentlemen are certainly diligent in your navigation," he said presently. "Perfectionists, almost."

"We do our best," grated Lynch between set teeth. "It's a damn shame sending us out with a machine like this."

The red book appeared. "Mr. Lynch, I mark you down not for your private sentiments, which are of course yours to entertain, but for voicing them and thereby contributing to an unhealthy atmosphere of despairing and hysterical pessimism."

A tide of red crept up from Lynch's neck. He bent over the computer, made no comment. But Sutton suddenly cried out, "What else do you expect from us? Do you think we're fish or insects? We came out here to learn, not to suffer, or to fly on forever!" He gave a ghastly laugh. Henry Belt listened patiently. "Think of it!" cried Sutton. "The seven of us. In this capsule, forever!"

"All of us must die in due course, Mr. Sutton. I expect to die in space."

"I'm not afraid of death." But Sutton's voice trailed off as he glanced toward the port.

"I am afraid that I must charge you two demerits for your outburst, Mr. Sutton. A good space-man maintains his dignity at all costs, and values it more than his life."

Lynch looked up from the computer. "Well, now we've got a corrected reading. Do you know what it says?"

Henry Belt turned him a look of polite inquiry.

"We're going to miss," said Lynch. "We're going to pass by just as we passed Mars. Jupiter is pulling us around and sending us out toward Gemini."

The silence was thick in the room. Sutton seemed to whisper something, soundlessly. Henry Belt turned to look at Culpepper, who was standing by the porthole, photographing Jupiter with his personal camera.

"Mr. Culpepper?"

"Yes, sir."

"You seem unconcerned by the prospect which Mr. Sutton has set forth."

"I hope it's not imminent, sir."

"How do you propose to avoid it?"

"I imagine that we will radio for help, sir."

"You forget that I have destroyed the radio."

"I remember noting a crate marked 'Radio Parts' stored in the starboard jet-pod."

"I am sorry to disillusion you, Mr. Culpepper. That case is mislabeled."

Ostrander jumped to his feet, left the wardroom. There was the sound of moving crates. A moment of silence. Then he returned. He glared at Henry Belt. "Whiskey. Bottles of whiskey."

Henry Belt nodded. "I told you as much."

"But now we have no radio," said Lynch in an ugly voice.

"We never have had a radio, Mr. Lynch. You were warned that you would have to depend on your own resources to bring us home. You have failed, and in the process doomed me as well as yourself. Incidentally, I must mark you all down ten demerits for a faulty cargo check."

"Demerits," said Ostrander in a bleak voice.

"Now, Mr. Culpepper," said Henry Belt. "What is your next proposal?"

"I don't know, sir."

Verona spoke in a placatory voice. "What would you do, sir, if you were in our position?"

Henry Belt shook his head. "I am an imaginative man, Mr. Verona, but there are certain leaps of the mind which are beyond my powers." He returned to his compartment.

Von Gluck looked curiously at Culpepper. "It is a fact. You're not at all concerned."

"Oh, I'm concerned. But I believe that Mr. Belt wants to get home too. He's too good a space-man not to know exactly what he's doing."

The door from Henry Belt's compartment slid back. Henry Belt stood in the opening. "Mr. Culpepper, I chanced to overhear your remark, and I now note down ten demerits against you. This attitude expresses a complacence as dangerous as Mr. Sutton's utter funk. You rely on my capabilities; Mr. Sutton is afraid to rely on his own. This is not the first time I have cautioned you against this easy vice."

"Very sorry, sir."

Henry Belt looked about the room. "Pay no heed to Mr. Culpepper. He is wrong. Even if I could repair this disaster, I would not raise a hand. For I expect to die in space."

VII

The sail was canted vectorless, edgewise to the sun. Jupiter was a smudge astern. There were five cadets in the wardroom. Culpepper, Verona, and von Gluck sat talking in low voices. Ostrander and Lynch lay crouched, arms to knees, faces to the wall. Sutton had gone two days before. Quietly donning his space-suit, he had stepped into the exit chamber and thrust himself headlong into space. A propulsion unit gave him added speed, and before any of the cadets could intervene he was gone.

He had left a short note: "I fear the void because of the terrible attraction of its glory. I briefly felt the exaltation when we went out on sail inspection, and I fought it back. Now, since we must die, I will die this way, by embracing this black radiance, by giving myself wholly. Do not be sorry for me. I will die mad, but the madness will be ecstasy."

Henry Belt, when shown the note, merely shrugged. "Mr. Sutton was perhaps too imaginative and emotional to make a sound spaceman. He could not have been relied upon in any emergency." And his sardonic glance seemed to include the rest of them.

Shortly thereafter Lynch and Ostrander succumbed to inanition, a kind of despondent helplessness: manic-depression in its most stupefying phase. Culpepper the suave, Verona the pragmatic and von Gluck the sensitive remained.

They spoke quietly to themselves, out of earshot of Henry Belt's room. "I still believe," said Culpepper, "that somehow there is a means to get ourselves out of this mess, and that Henry Belt knows it."

Verona said, "I wish I could think so...We've been over it a hundred times. If we set sail for Saturn or Neptune or Uranus, the outward vector of thrust plus the outward vector of our momentum will take us far beyond Pluto before we're anywhere near. The plasma jets could stop us if we had enough energy, but the shield can't supply it and we don't have another power source..."

Von Gluck hit his fist into his hand. "Gentlemen," he said in a soft delighted voice.

Culpepper and Verona stared at him, absorbing warmth from the light in his face.

"Gentlemen," said von Gluck, "I believe we have sufficient energy at hand. We will use the sail. Remember? It is bellied. It can function as a mirror. It spreads five square miles of surface. Sunlight out here is thin — but so long as we collect enough of it —"

"I understand!" said Culpepper. "We back off the hull till the reactor is at the focus of the sail and turn on the jets!"

Verona said dubiously, "We'll still be receiving radiation pressure. And what's worse, the jets will impinge back on the sail. Effect — cancellation. We'll be nowhere."

"If we cut the center out of the sail — just enough to allow the plasma through — we'd beat that objection. And as for the radiation pressure — we'll surely do better with the plasma drive."

"What do we use to make plasma? We don't have the stock."

"Anything that can be ionized. The radio, the computer, your shoes, my shirt, Culpepper's camera, Henry Belt's whiskey..."

VIII

The angel-wagon came up to meet Sail 25, in orbit beside Sail 40, which was just making ready to take out a new crew.

Henry Belt said, "Gentlemen, I beg that you leave no trash, rubbish, old clothing aboard. There is nothing more troublesome than coming aboard an untidy ship. While we wait for the lighter to discharge, I suggest that you give the ship a final thorough policing."

The cargo carrier drifted near, eased into position. Three men sprang across space to Sail 40, a few hundred yards behind 25, tossed lines back to the carrier, pulled bales of cargo and equipment across the gap.

The five cadets and Henry Belt, clad in space-suits, stepped out into the sunlight. Earth spread below, green and blue, white and brown, the contours so precious and dear to bring tears to the eyes. The cadets transferring cargo to Sail 40 gazed at them curiously as they worked. At last they were finished, and the six men of Sail 25 boarded the carrier.

"Back safe and sound, eh, Henry?" said the pilot. "Well, I'm always surprised."

Henry Belt made no answer. The cadets stowed their cargo, and standing by the port, took a final look at Sail 25. The carrier retro-jetted; the two sails seemed to rise above them.

The lighter nosed in and out of the atmosphere, braking, extended its wings, glided to an easy landing on the Mojave Desert.

The cadets, their legs suddenly loose and weak to the unaccustomed gravity, limped after Henry Belt to the carry-all, seated themselves and were conveyed to the administration complex. They alighted from the carry-all, and now Henry Belt motioned the five to the side.

"Here, gentlemen, is where I leave you. I go my way, you go yours. Tonight I will check my red book, and after various adjustments I will prepare my official report. But I believe I can present you an unofficial resumé of my impressions.

"First of all, this is neither my best nor my worst class. Mr. Lynch and Mr. Ostrander, I feel that you are ill-suited either for command or for any situation which might inflict prolonged emotional pressure upon you. I cannot recommend you for space-duty.

"Mr. von Gluck, Mr. Culpepper and Mr. Verona, all of you meet my minimum requirements for a recommendation, although I shall write the words 'Especially Recommended' only beside the names 'Clyde von Gluck' and 'Marcus Verona'. You brought the sail back to Earth by essentially faultless navigation. It means that if I am to fulfill my destiny I must make at least one more voyage into space.

"So now our association ends. I trust you have profited by it." Henry Belt nodded briefly to each of the five and limped off around the building.

The cadets looked after him. Culpepper reached in his pocket and brought forth a pair of small metal objects which he displayed in his palm. "Recognize these?"

"Hmf," said Lynch in a flat voice. "Bearings for the computer disks. The original ones."

"I found them in the little spare-parts tray. They weren't there before."

Von Gluck nodded. "The machinery always seemed to fail immediately after sail check, as I recall."

Lynch drew in his breath with a sharp hiss. He turned, strode away. Ostrander followed him. Culpepper shrugged. To Verona he gave one of the bearings, to von Gluck the other. "For souvenirs — or medals. You fellows deserve them."

"Thanks, Ed," said von Gluck.

"Thanks," muttered Verona. "I'll make a stick-pin of this thing."

The three, not able to look at each other, glanced up into the sky where the first stars of twilight were appearing, then continued on into the building where family and friends and sweethearts awaited them.

JACK VANCE was born in 1916 to a well-off California family that, as his childhood ended, fell upon hard times. As a young man he worked at a series of unsatisfying jobs before studying mining engineering, physics, journalism and English at the University of California Berkeley. Leaving school as America was going to war, he found a place as an ordinary seaman in the merchant marine. Later he worked as a rigger, surveyor, ceramicist, and carpenter before his steady production of sf, mystery novels, and short stories established him as a full-time writer.

His output over more than sixty years was prodigious and won him three Hugo Awards, a Nebula Award, a World Fantasy Award for lifetime achievement, as well as an Edgar from the Mystery Writers of America. The Science Fiction and Fantasy Writers of America named him a grandmaster and he was inducted into the Science Fiction Hall of Fame.

His works crossed genre boundaries, from dark fantasies (including the highly influential *Dying Earth* cycle of novels) to interstellar space operas, from heroic fantasy (the *Lyonesse* trilogy) to murder mysteries featuring a sheriff (the Joe Bain novels) in a rural California county. A Vance story often centered on a competent male protagonist thrust into a dangerous, evolving situation on a planet where adventure was his daily fare, or featured a young person setting out on a perilous odyssey over difficult terrain populated by entrenched, scheming enemies.

Late in his life, a world-spanning assemblage of Vance aficionados came together to return his works to their original form, restoring material cut by editors whose chief preoccupation was the page count of a pulp magazine. The result was the complete and authoritative *Vance Integral Edition* in 44 hardcover volumes. Spatterlight Press is now publishing the VIE texts as ebooks, and as print-on-demand paperbacks.

Colophon

This book was printed using Adobe Arno Pro as the primary text font, with NeutraFace used on the cover.

This title was created from the digital archive of the Vance Integral Edition, a series of 44 books produced under the aegis of the author by a worldwide group of his readers. The VIE project gratefully acknowledges the editorial guidance of Norma Vance, as well as the cooperation of the Department of Special Collections at Boston University, whose John Holbrook Vance collection has been an important source of textual evidence.

Special thanks to R.C. Lacovara, Patrick Dusoulier, Koen Vyverman, Paul Rhoads, Chuck King, Gregory Hansen, Suan Yong, and Josh Geller for their invaluable assistance preparing final versions of the source files.

Source: Mike Berro, John Rick; Digitize: Donna Adams, Richard Chandler, John Councill, Mike Dennison, Joel Hedlund, Charles King, Kyle Scott McAbee, David Mortimore, John A. Schwab, Gan Uesli Starling, Per Sundfeldt, Dave Worden, Suan Hsi Yong; Format: Patrick Dusoulier, R.C. Lacovara, Koen Vyverman; Diff: Joel Hedlund, Damien G. Jones, David A. Kennedy, Charles King, Hans van der Veeke; Diff-Merge: Suan Hsi Yong; Tech Proof: Rob Friefeld, Ed Gooding, Joel Riedesel, Fred Zoetemeyer; Text Integrity: Patrick Dusoulier, Rob Friefeld, David A. Kennedy, Charles King, Paul Rhoads, John A. Schwab, Steve Sherman, Tim Stretton, Koen Vyverman; Implement: Donna Adams, Derek W. Benson, Mike Dennison, Joel Hedlund, Damien G. Jones, David Reitsema, Hans van der Veeke; Security: Paul Rhoads; Compose: Joel Anderson; Comp Review: Mark Adams, Christian J. Corley, Marcel van Genderen, Karl Kellar, Charles King, Bob Luckin, Robin L. Rouch; Update Verify: John A. D. Foley, Rob Friefeld, Marcel van Genderen, Charles King, Robert Melson, Bob Luckin, Paul Rhoads, Robin L. Rouch; RTF-Diff: Mark Bradford, Deborah Cohen, Patrick Dusoulier, Charles King, Bill Schaub; Textport: Patrick Dusoulier; Proofread: Neil Anderson, Nicola de Angeli, Erik Arendse, Michel Bazin, Brian Bieniowski, Malcolm Bowers, Mark Bradford, Ursula Brandt, Lisa Brown, Sean Butcher, Angus Campbell-Cann, Deborah Cohen, Christian J. Corley, Chris Dearmitt, Michael Duncan, Patrick Dusoulier, Harry Erwin, Fred Ford, Marcel van Genderen, Rob Gerrand, Carl Goldman, Ed Gooding, David Gorbet, Yannick Gour, Martin Green, Erec Grim, Jasper Groen, Evert Jan de Groot, Kurt Harriman, Gilbert Harrus, John Hawes, Linda Heaphy, Marc Herant, Ruth Hunter, Peter Ikin, Damien G. Jones, Lucie Jones, Jurriaan Kalkman, Karl Kellar, Ken Kellett, David A. Kennedy, R.C. Lacovara, Menno van der Leden, Stephane Leibovitsch, Lee Lewis, Bob Luckin, S.A. Manning, Robert Melson, Wiley Mittenberg, Bob Moody, Mike Myers, Eric Newsom,

Till Noever, Michael Nolan, Jim Pattison, Quentin Rakestraw, Glenn Raye, Simon Read, Chris Reid, Joel Riedesel, Axel Roschinski, Robin L. Rouch, Jeffrey Ruszczyk, Bill Sherman, Steve Sherman, Mark Shoulder, Gan Uesli Starling, Mark J. Straka, Andrew Thompson, Willem Timmer, Hans van der Veeke, Dirk Jan Verlinde, David White, Dave Worden

Artwork (maps based on original drawings by Jack and Norma Vance):

Paul Rhoads, Christopher Wood

Book Composition and Typesetting: Joel Anderson

Art Direction and Cover Design: Howard Kistler

Proofing: Christian J. Corley, Steve Sherman

Jacket Blurb: Steve Sherman, John Vance

Management: John Vance, Koen Vyverman

www.ingramcontent.com/pod-product-compliance
Lightning Source LLC
Chambersburg PA
CBHW051517250626
47156CB00001B/126